ATTILA
THE JUDGMENT

BY WILLIAM NAPIER

ATTILA

THE JUDGMENT

William Napier

ST. MARTIN'S GRIFFIN

NEW YORK

ATTILA: THE JUDGMENT. Copyright © 2008 by William Napier. All rights reserved. Printed in the United States of America. For information, address St. Martin's Press, 175 Fifth Avenue, New York, N.Y. 10010.

www.stmartins.com

ISBN 978-0-312-59900-3

First published in Great Britain by Orion Books Ltd.

First U.S. Edition: November 2010

10 9 8 7 6 5 4 3 2 1

LIST OF PRINCIPAL CHARACTERS

Characters marked with an asterisk were real historical figures. The rest might have been.

Aëtius*—Gaius Flavius Aëtius, born 398 in the frontier town of Silestria, in modern-day Bulgaria. The son of Gaudentius, Master General of Cavalry, and himself later Master General of the Roman Army in the West

Aladar—Hun warrior, son of Chanat, one of Attila's eight generals

Amalasuntha*—only daughter of King Theodoric of the Visigoths

Andronicus—captain of the Imperial Guard, Constantinople

Arapovian—Count Grigorius Khachadour Arapovian, an Armenian nobleman

Ariobarzanes—Lord of Azimuntium

Athenaïs*—married to the Eastern Emperor Theodosius II, and renamed Eudoxia

Attila*—born 398, King of the Huns

Bela—Hun general

Cadoc—a Briton, son of Lucius

Candac—Hun general

Chanat—Hun general, father of Aladar

Checa*—first wife of Attila

Chrysaphius*—a Byzantine courtier

Csaba—Hun general

Dengizek*—eldest son of Attila

Ellak*—son of Attila

Enkhtuya—a Hun witch

Galla Placidia*—born 388, daughter of Emperor Theodosius the Great, sister of Emperor Honorius, mother of Emperor Valentinian III

Gamaliel—an aged, well-traveled medical man

Genseric*—King of the Vandals

Geukchu—Hun general

Honoria*—daughter of Galla Placidia, sister of Valentinian

Idilico—a Burgundian girl

Jormunreik—Visigothic wolf lord

Juchi—Hun general

Knuckles—baptized Anastasius, a Rhineland legionary

Leo*—Bishop of Rome

Little Bird—a Hun shaman

Lucius—also Ciddwmtarth, a British leader of his people

Malchus—a captain of cavalry

Marcian*—Eastern Emperor, 450–457, married to Pulcheria

Nemesianus—a wealthy man of Aquileia

Nicias—a Cretan alchemist

Noyan—Hun general

Odoacer*—a Gothic warlord

Orestes*—a Greek by birth, Attila's lifelong companion

Priscus of Panium*—a humble scribe

Pulcheria*—sister of Theodosius II

Romulus Augustulus*—the last emperor

Sabinus—Legionary Legate of the VII at Viminacium

Sangiban*—King of the Alans

Tarasicodissa Rousoumbladeotes*—Isaurian chieftain, also known as Zeno

Tatullus—First Centurion of the VII at Viminacium

Themistius*—an orator

Theodoric*—King of the Visigoths, 419–451

Theodoric*—Visigothic prince, eldest son of King Theodoric

Theodosius*—Eastern Emperor, 408–450

Torismond*—Visigothic prince, son of King Theodoric

Valamir—Visigothic wolf lord

Valentinian*—Western Emperor, 425–455

Vigilas*—a Byzantine courtier

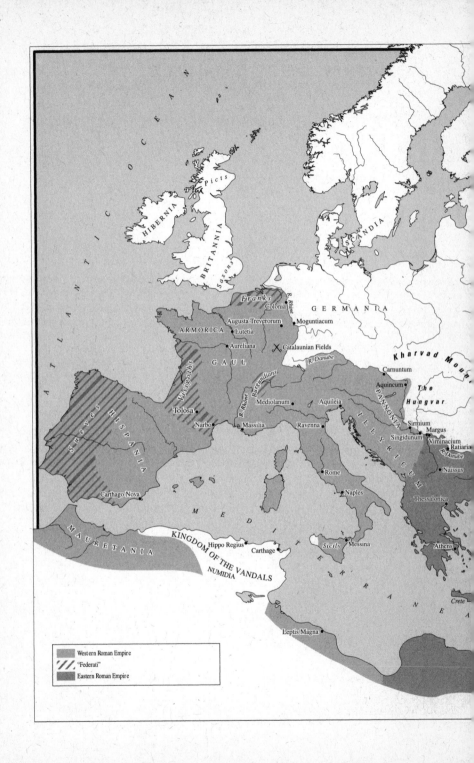

Western Roman Empire

/// "Federati"

Eastern Roman Empire

THE ROMAN EMPIRE AND THE BARBARIAN LANDS, AD 449

S C Y T H I A

R. Borysthenes

Hunnic homeland

Tanais

R. Tanais

Ophiusa

MAEOTIS PALUS

ARAL SEA

CHORASMIA

R. Oxus

SEA OF RAVENS

Chersonesus

Caucasus Mountains

EUXINE SEA

OESIA

Marcianopolis

ACE

Adrianople

stantinople

Nicomedia

PONTICA

Nicaea

ARMENIA

The Caspian Gates

SASSANID PERSIA

Ephesus

R. Tigris

Antioch

R. Euphrates

Cyprus

N

Jerusalem

Alexandria

E G Y P T

PART I

THE FURY

1

MARGUS FAIR

The southern banks of the Danube, AD 449

A morning in early summer. The great river meandering slowly through the rich Moesian plains and eastward to the Euxine Sea. A patchwork of plowland and meadow, and further away from the town, blossoming orchards and copses of ancient woodland. The smaller River Margus flowing down northward from the hills to join the majestic Danube.

Darting over the surface of the water, the bright green metallic flash of damselflies, and columns of tiny waterflies rising and falling in the warming summer air. Willows along the banks of the river and alders beside the damp streambeds. Black poplars releasing their fluffy white seeds in clouds, landing and revolving and floating on downstream. Minnows flashing and darting in shoals, trout in among the brown boulders, beautiful grayling. Nodding kingcups reflected in the water, and the meadows all around scattered with the yellow of marsh marigold and yellow flag. No sound but the wind rustling the reeds, or the single peep of a duckling as it raced over the water back to its mother, beating its stubby little wings to no effect.

Riverine nature so peaceful and serene on this morning in early May, that for a brief moment you might think yourself back in Adam's Eden, long before the Fall.

And then the shadow of a heron over the waters, cruising in silent and low, its cold and passionless yellow eyes swiveling downward in search of prey.

Come closer to the little town of Margus with its ancient walls and its cathedral tower with its solitary iron bell, and you hear the sound of human bustle and chatter. There are naked children laughing and splashing in the shallows, brown and shiny as pebbles, mischievously opening the sallow-wood fish traps and letting the fish swim free. There is laughter on the roads, and then in the meadows stretching up to the walls of the town itself, laid out in many colors and resounding with the languages of many different peoples—the great and celebrated Margus fair.

A vast, rowdy, polyglot encampment, teeming with energy, enterprise, and greed. Open-sided canvas tents and pied awnings and stalls of carved and painted wood. People buying and selling with clacking tongues and a whole grammar of gestures and winks and hand signals. Buyers slowly producing worn leather purses from inside their robes, and sellers biting coins to test their worth—plenty of bronze coins around that have been washed with arsenic to make them pass for silver. Fur merchants from the far north, from beyond the Roman Empire, selling bearskin and marten, beaver and sable. Bright-eyed songbirds whistling in their osier cages. Everywhere the savor of smoking fish and roasting meat, and girls selling slugs of wine straight from the barrel in wooden cups. More elaborate inns and taverns under canvas. Pickpockets, of course, preying on the drunk and unwary, and women looking for husbands or at least money, walking light stepped and lazy eyed, swaying their hips between the groups of men.

Further off, the warm ripe smell of livestock in wooden corrals. Cattle dealers and sheep sellers communicating in their secret language and occult numbers, with barely discernible nods and winks for deals. And the air everywhere filled with greetings and curses, jests and lewd remarks, the high piping cries of excited children, the cackle of geese, and a single screaming monkey in a cage. From the land of the Nubians, so the monkey seller said, without any great conviction. The monkey reached out its paw and pulled the hair of unwary bystanders. And all this ripe human chaos under the supposed regulation of a handful of frontier troops from the towering legionary fortress of Viminacium, ten miles east.

There was a girl there, a gentle, dreamy girl with a harelip, because a hare had walked across her mother's path when she was pregnant with her. So they said. She carried a yoke of wooden pails and sold goat's milk by the cupful, but she was not in truth a bold or assertive seller and she made little money. She too frequently gave cupfuls of milk away to hungry-eyed, plaintive children pestering her. When she returned at the day's end, her mother would scold her for not having sold enough, accusing her of daydreaming her days away. And scold her even more for not having found a husband to take her off her poor old mother's hands.

She disliked jostling crowds, and was drawn to the edge of the fair where the gaudy tents and stalls gave way to open meadows, and then the low line of the hills to the west, and the jut of Mons Aureus, the mountain of gold, with its fabulous mines. The vaults of Viminacium were full of gold, so they said. When it was transported down the great imperial trunk road to the emperor in Constantinople, it went with an escort of a thousand men. And the emperor . . . the girl always imagined him as made of gold himself, seated on his high throne covered in gold leaf, like a statue, immobile, unapproachable. A living god.

Now she lingered shyly before an old woman's canopy of grubby canvas supported on gnarled staves.

"Come you in, girl, come you in. It's a lover you'll be wanting at your age!"

The old woman grinned and bobbed about among her strange wares, performing almost a little dance, her white hair in a tight bun, her ringed fingers fluttering. The old woman was no witch, no purveyor of instruments for cruelty, malice, and revenge, but only a fortune-teller. A preacher had earlier that morning come out of the town to stand by her tent and preach on the text "Thou shalt not suffer a witch to live," but the people only scowled at him and passed on, leaving the preacher impotent and the old woman alone and unlynched.

The girl hesitantly set down her pails and the old woman took her hand and drew her in. Within the shadows of the tent there were animals' feet and tails, and strangely shaped stones like seashells, long dyed feathers of heron and bustard, tufts of multicolored rags tied round sticks topped with small brass bells, leather pouches of herbs, bottles of dubious liquor. Then something else caught the girl's eye, something very beautiful, which she took at first for a mirror. A little vanity such as rich ladies use to admire themselves when they are carried to dinner in their gilded litters, through the grand wide streets of great cities. Jeweled ladies with their white-chalked faces and forearms and little flattering mirrors.

The old fortune-teller knew at once what she wanted and bobbed over and retrieved it. It was a strange box made from hinged colored glass, held together with silver wires. It would be very costly and the girl had no money but for the few desultory coppers she had earned so far that morning. But the old woman brought the colored glass box out into the sunshine anyway and passed it to her without mockery.

"Look into it," she said. "Hold it up to the light. Some see the world as it is, though in many pretty colors. But some, who have the gift, see the world as it will be."

The girl hesitated. She didn't know that she believed in such things. Not really. Besides, who has the strength to see their own future? Especially a poor goat girl with a scold of a mother and a harelip?

The woman nodded encouragingly. "Look, child. The future may yet be sweet, and you have the gift."

Somewhere in the distance there was a boy crying out from the river, drawing up his boat. Yelling, screaming about something. Running toward the fair. It was all the excitement no doubt, nothing more.

So the girl held the little box of colored glass up before her face and opened one of the delicate little hinges. It was the deep red glass that she held up to her eyes, and she looked through and shuddered. Because she saw the world as if covered in blood. The mountain of gold to the west was a mountain of blood. The screaming of the boy running up from the river grew louder, closer. She saw the straggling meadows leading away along the river bank, groups of people carrying their baskets, pushing their handbarrows, coming through the long grass toward the fair on this gentle summer day. And beyond that, the low line of hills still catching the morning sun, but all red, all clouded red. The future.

She felt the old woman tugging at her sleeve, heard her saying something, and was about to tear her eyes away from this ghastly vision, this world of a blood-red future, when a movement in the far distance caught her eye, and instead of lowering the evil box she continued to stare through its red haze.

Rising up over the crest of the low hills to the west, she saw a line of horsemen. Banners in the breeze and spears against the sky.

2

MARGUS FALLS

Never would the people—those few who survived, stumbling away through the blood-soaked grass to cry their story into horror-stricken ears—never would they forget that day, nor their first sight of the horsemen from the east.

They rode muscular little ponies with big, ungainly heads, brutish and monstrous, like the heads of bulls. Shaggy even at the fetlock, with deep chests and haunches betraying their massive strength and stamina. Hooves and manes were dyed blood red with crushed insects or dried berries from last autumn, boiled up again in water and fat. The riders had long arms and barrel chests, short legs and narrow, slanting eyes of cunning and glittering cruelty. Some of them, disdaining to wear helmets as they rode down upon the near defenseless fair, seemed to have skulls deformed and domed by some evil practice in infancy. Others wore pointed Scythian caps of leather, *kalpaks*, fringed with gray wolf's fur. Wolves falling on the stricken townspeople not in lean winter but in fat high summer, driven not by the stark necessity of hunger but by the love of destruction for its own sake.

Some had the sides of their heads scarred with burns to kill the hair there, others were crudely shaven, and almost all had their cheeks and the sides of their heads cut and deep dyed with tattoos. The thin, sparse beards on their chins were further garlanded and beribboned, or twisted into little plaits, and in their ears they wore heavy hoops of gold. Some rode barefoot and some wore leather leggings, gripping the sides of their mounts so surely that they seemed one with their horses. They wore barbarian breeches but most rode naked to the waist but for jangling bone jerkins, their dark chests and backs tattooed with snakes and grotesque faces. Their wrists and sinewy arms were wrapped with iron bands, gold bracelets, cloths and strips of leather, and they wore beaded silver torcs and the teeth of wolves and jackals on thongs around their dirty muscular throats. They rode with their reins hung with the flensed skulls of slaughtered enemies, with human scalps or hanks of blood-dried hair.

Each warrior bristled with the tips and points of a multitude of weapons. Short stabbing spears, long steel knives, curved swords slung across squat, powerful backs, curved spiked hatchets, and, clutched in the right fist, the deadly recurved bow of the steppes, with a bunch of arrows clutched along-side. Arrows strung and shot and falling interminably onto the stricken fair.

The people turned and ran among the falling tents and the already blazing stalls, but there was no escape. Already a column of the murderous horde had ridden round and taken the hills to the south, and cut the people off from flight that way. To the north there was only the river. Some fugitives threw themselves in and tried to swim for it, and of these a few survived, carried downstream and crawling back onto the southern shore miles away like half-drowned animals to tell their tale.

Singled out from among the wailing masses was the half century of bewildered soldiers from Viminacium. The first were cut down where they stood, whirling on the spot in a spray of blood, unable to believe that this little light guard duty at a summer fair had suddenly turned into massacre, and this bright sunshine day to nightmare.

The captain of the guard, a centurion named Pamphilus, registered the numbers of the barbarian horde and immediately bellowed orders to a couple of his riders to head east, straight to Viminacium to call the full legion to arms. As an added precaution he despatched another squadron, an eight-man *contubernium,* to requisition a boat and make for Viminacium by river, just in case his riders were cut down on the road. Though he doubted very much that barbarians would have the foresight for such things.

But how had they got across the river? What had happened to the Danube lookouts? And the signaling stations that stretched all the way along the imperial frontier from the Euxine to the mouth of the Rhine? How could this have happened without warning? Where was the intelligence? Why hadn't the *exploratores* reported back in advance? Raiding parties like this didn't erupt out of nowhere.

None of it made any sense. All he could do now was drag his men back to the town bridge and form ranks. It was a hard decision.

His *optio* stared at him.

Pamphilus shook his head. "It's not a general massacre. Most of them will be taken as slaves."

"A nice fate."

"Button your lip, Optio. We fall back to the town if we can. Otherwise we hold this damn bridge till the legion arrives."

Whoever this horde might be, however many in number, he still had full confidence in the VII Legion, Claudia Pia Fidelis. "Six times brave, six times faithful" was the legion's motto. Stationed here for four long centuries on this far northern border, looking out over the Danube and into the wastes of Scythia. Waiting for the barbarians. And meanwhile building the imposing fortress of Viminacium, with wide roads south, east, and west, and six miles of fine aqueduct. Good builders like all Roman soldiers, shovel in hand more than sword. The VII wasn't the force it had been, true enough. None of the legions was. Numbers were down, the best drawn back to the field army based at Marcianopolis, the remainder derided nowadays as no more than an "hereditary peasant militia." Some militia. Holding some fortress.

Still fifteen hundred of them, all told, though half of them would be out at their farms or in their workshops at any one time. Who could blame them? There wasn't much to do back in the fort but drill and wait, under the stern eyes of the legionary legate. Otherwise they drank, they diced, gambling with the meager pay too rarely received on time. But a legion was still a legion, or a rump of it, with a legion's proud memories. And the legate of the VIIth, that big-bellied Gallus Sabinus, was no fool.

Pamphilus set up his men in ranks across the narrow bridge.

"Barbarians out of the wilderness like these, opportunist raiders, they may be fast but they've got no staying power, and no siege craft." Pamphilus was talking to his *optio* again, knowing he was only trying to reassure himself. "And no horse will ever charge a line of pikemen four ranks deep.

"We hold them here for as long as possible. Fall back on the town if and when we can. They can't outflank us on this bridge. And we wait for the legion and the cataphracts. We want as many heavy cavalry as possible. See how those naked devils take to being cut up by a line of charging lancers in full armor. Plus mounted archers. And then the good old mincing machine of the infantry. I don't care how many of them there are, numbers are nothing. Till then, we hold out. It's no great problem."

You could see the milling, murderous horde for what they were: common criminals, taking easy pickings from a thinly defended frontier town, before their flight back over the river and into the wastes of Scythia. Terrifying they might look at first sight, but that was all this was: a terror raid. The odd killing, more slave taking. But they would melt away soon enough when the VIIth came marching down the road.

Pamphilus wondered briefly who this latest horde might be. Gepids? Sarmatians? Alans? All plains curs in breeches. *Ex Scythia semper aliquid novi.* He smiled grimly to himself. Some tatterdemalion column of looters and plunderers, eaters of raw meat, some vainglorious gang of slavers, rapists, and arsonists who fancied themselves great warriors. Rome had encountered such before. Filling the vacuum left by the retreating Huns, he presumed, after the Western Emperor sent out that order to the VIIth for a punitive expedition over the river. Not in His Divine Majesty's jurisdiction, of course, but the prefect of Pannonia agreed to his request. Ill-advisedly, in Pamphilus's humble opinion; but it wasn't for a junior centurion like him to decide on foreign policy, thank the Crucified Christ.

So a couple of cavalry *alae* from Viminacium had been ferried over by the Danube Fleet and descended on some outlying Hun encampment. Orders were to take prisoners for ingenious execution later, in a vivid and educational tableau or playlet staged back in the arena in Constantinople or Ravenna, featuring stern-eyed and remorseless legionaries slaughtering chained and submissive barbarians, their necks obediently bowed to the Roman blades. A playlet complete with real deaths. People liked that sort of thing: it reassured them in these edgy days.

But the half-naked savages in the encampment had erupted from their tents and attacked the cavalrymen. On foot, barely armed, and taken by surprise, they had still put up quite a fight. Clearly not the force they had once been back in old Uldin's day, when they'd fought as auxiliaries for the great Stilicho. But a fierce remnant of a people all the same. They'd dragged a couple of cavalrymen from their horses and broken their necks with their bare hands, stabbed a couple more. After that the cavalry commander had given the general order of execution. And two days later the rest of the Hun people, so imperial spies reported, upped sticks, folded tents, burned the newly built wooden palace of their king to the ground, and slouched away north and east into the unknown wastes of Scythia, suitably chastened and humiliated.

A messy business, but the price of freedom.

The two troopers from Margus reined in their furious gallop on the hot and dusty road.

The dust slowly cleared, and there ahead of them were the barbarians. Sitting their squat horses in a neat column, six abreast, as orderly as a legion. Arrows strung lightly to their bows. At their head sat a round-faced man on a grubby little pony.

"Viminacium?" he asked. And shook his head, smiling, his gold earrings dancing. "Alas. Not today."

The arrow-strings hummed.

The eight-man squadron found the lightest boat they could, a skiff with a tattered sail. They dragged it down to the foreshore, waded out and then set to rowing furiously with the current. They hadn't gone more than half a mile when their coxwain stopped his bellowing and fell silent. The rowers looked up, saw his expression and stopped rowing. The boat drifted a little and they looked round, blinking the sweat from their eyes.

Being towed into the far bank by a small rowing-boat was one of the hefty barges of the Danube Fleet. From Viminacium. Hanging over the sides where they had been slain were the bodies of the marines, stuck with arrows.

Beyond that, almost incomprehensible at first sight, were countless more barges and flat-bottomed horse transporters, captured from God knew where, crossing and recrossing, bringing innumerable men and horses across from the north. A little further down on the southern bank, the black and smoking remains of a wooden observation tower.

The horde of a thousand or two at Margus: that was just a bridgehead. This was no hit-and-run terror raid. This was a full-scale invasion.

In terror the eight men tried to turn the skiff round, still being carried forward on the strong current of the Danube. But in their scrabbling panic they were deaf to their coxwain's orders to coordinate their strokes, portside forward, starboard back. From downriver, rowing strongly upstream, another boat was coming toward them, long and lean, and dimly they were aware of more of the tattooed warriors appearing on the bank to their right, looming up through the reeds, startling little waterfowl into flight. The soldiers thrashed and beat the bright sunlit water so violently that they never heard the bow-strings hum, and their terror ceased only when the fine iron arrowheads hit home.

In the meadows to the west, Margus fair was collapsing into burning chaos, the people harried and driven before the yowling, tattooed horse warriors. On the single town bridge, little wider than a haywain, stood Pamphilus and his thirty men. Like Horatius of old, as the schoolboy ballad told it: three of them, then two, then just Horatius himself, keeping the bridge single-handed against the entire army of Lars Porsena. As if. War stories for schoolboys.

Behind them, the trembling town of Margus. The frontier had already been redrawn.

Slowly the barbarians started pressing the people back up against the bridge. Now and again they jabbed with their spears, treating the trapped and terrified populace like cattle.

Pamphilus watched grimly.

"Sir," said his *optio*.

He tightened his grip on his spear.

"*Sir*," repeated the *optio*. "Behind us, sir."

Pamphilus glanced back and cried out.

The barbarians had already broken down the gates and were in the town. Margus was ablaze. Behind its walls, the red-tiled rooftops were smoking, and flames licked up round the narrow tower of St. Peter and St. Paul. The iron bell would already be glowing red. Pamphilus thought he could hear distant screams.

They must have moved like lightning. How had they crossed the river? Apart from the town bridge, there was no crossing until miles upstream. Was it possible that this howling horde of barbarians was in fact highly organized?

That behind this film of blood and chaos, there was some keen, all-commanding mind at work?

Idiot barbarians, though. The keen-eyed watchmen on the walls of Viminacium would have seen the smoke, and already be sending out riders to ascertain the cause. An idle Margus housewife not minding her hearthfire, a street of wooden houses going up in flames? Or something worse? Then one of his riders or one of the refugees would get through, and the legion would be called to arms.

It was good to know that reinforcements were on their way. Meanwhile, they must try to hold their position and survive. Surrounded.

"Two rear ranks—about-face!"

Then on the far ridge of the hills, a mile distant or more, he thought he saw him: the barbarian leader. A group of men gathered closely around him, but that was the king. He held a sword above his head and moved it in precise strokes downward, left and right and before him. And on the plain before him, his horse-warriors wheeled to order, as disciplined as columns of imperial cavalry. More so. More agile. They wheeled as a flock of starlings wheels in the sky, as one body.

Now gradually they were closing in, herding rather than killing, crushing the people back against the bridge.

Pamphilus cursed.

He would have fought like Horatius on this bridge, along with his men, against these contemptible horsemen. His blood was up now. Too many of those he had been sent to guard had fallen already. They had watched the savages riding through the fair, whipping and lassoing, destroying and burning, picking off selected victims for sport and target practice. Usually men of fighting age, fools who came at them with pitchfork or stake. But sometimes they had cut down anyone in their path, fleeing girls, infants, and those nursing infants. Those broad-cheeked faces expressionless, those yellow eyes unmoved.

But how could Pamphilus and his men fight back, with this human tide around them? That of course was the plan of this warlord, this king.

He looked again and the warlord had galloped down from the ridge and in among the press of his warriors. Soon the trapped legionaries could see him approaching with his little band of captains, and then reining in. Pamphilus observed him across the heads of the trapped and huddled people, through the haze of drifting smoke. The stony face of the barbarian warlord. Iron-gray hair bound up in a topknot, blue weals on his face, a gold torc round his strong, grimy neck. Dusty leather breeches, deerskin boots. Nothing fancy. Naked to the waist but for spiraling tattoos, quiver and bow and scabbard across his back. No great king, then. Still fighting in the line with his fellow warriors. Beside him, a man with lighter skin, very close shaven or bald, blue eyed. Very still, assured, and silent.

A hush fell over the people.

Glittering yellow eyes fixed on him.

"Your name?" called the warlord.

He gave it.

"From Viminacium?"

Pamphilus nodded.

The warlord stroked his wispy beard. "It was forces from Viminacium that executed my people. You would call it a punitive expedition." He spoke faultless Latin, with perfect, rather aristocratic pronunciation.

Pamphilus's head whirled and he glanced sideways at his *optio*. These were the Huns. Not vanished after that bloody foray at all, as the intelligence had said, but making only a feigned, a Parthian retreat. The cunning devils. For the first time Pamphilus sensed that they were here not for a bit of light raiding and enslaving after all, but for some more memorable act of vengeance. He steeled himself against fear, stemmed his rising panic, gripped the spearshaft tighter in his sweating hand, and put from his mind as best he could all rumors of barbarian tortures. Crucifixion, excoriation, impalement . . .

Beside him his *optio* was shaking. His men were backing into each other. Behind them, the burning town was beginning to roar under the noonday sun. Where was the VIIth, O Jupiter, Mithras, Christ? They must have seen the fires by now. If they could just hold out for a while longer, the first of the cavalry might yet arrive. He prayed for them to come soon.

The warlord was speaking again, his voice low and harsh and grating as old steel. Pamphilus shook his head at what he heard, so the warlord repeated it. "Either we kill all these people before you," he said, "or we kill you."

He shouted back, "The price your people pay then will be terrible."

The warlord grinned, a horrible, wolfish grin, and his men raised their swords.

"They will make good slaves!" blurted out his *optio*.

"And you will make good corpses."

One of the savages struck down his first victim, an old man stumbling before him, penned in by the people around him, eyes staring in blank terror.

"Let them go!" bellowed Pamphilus.

Their discipline was instant. Their leader gave the nod, and the encircling horsemen pulled up their bristling weapons. Every ugly little pony took several neat steps backward on command.

The huddled people remained frozen like prey for a moment. Then the warlord said something more in his low voice, and the people, dazed and stumbling, turned and fled away south into the waiting hills.

The warlord looked back at Pamphilus.

The centurion lowered his spear, couched it under his right arm and set the butt against one of bridge planks. Leaned his weight against it.

"Well, men," he said. "Sell yourselves dear."

The town burned on all through the late summer afternoon and on into evening. No help came. Through the blood-red sunset, the slaughter went on. This was the beginning of vengeance, the beginning of sorrows.

Here a Kutrigur warrior rides down another victim, using a trident for a spear, jabbing it into the back of a fleeing girl.

She stumbles and falls, sinks to her knees, finally dropping the yoke of wooden pails she has carried all the long day, even in the midst of the slaughter. She reaches back to her wound before she slumps and dies. The goat's milk runs across the hard ground, mingling with her blood. The warrior wrenches his cantering mount round almost on its hind hooves and whacks its rump with the flat of his crude and bloodied trident and grins through the orange firelight and yowls and rides on.

His fellow warriors yowl and grin, too, milling murderously among their last sacrificial victims. Men like wolves, but wolves who love chaos and firelight. Wolves in winter come in from the cold and the snow-bound steppes and from the edges of the great northern forests when the dewdrops harden into glassy unforgiving ice on the resinous needles of the firs. They come hungrily eyeing the well-fed towns and the comfortable firesides with their fathomless yellow eyes, creeping westward across the wind-frozen plains toward the warm evening glow in the west. They slink down darkened streets, past lamplit taverns and houses where the plump merchants and bankers and well-paid bureaucrats of the empire sit at their ample dinners, joking and feasting and sipping their good Moselle wines shipped down to the Danube to these Eastern provinces of Moesia and Thrace. None knowing that the wolves are coming—indeed, are already come, a tide of gray fur sweeping across the steppes. Yellow eyes gleaming, white teeth ready for the kill.

These wolf men have come in high summer, but their white teeth gleam in the darkness just the same. They throw back their shaggy heads and laugh to the sky, giving thanks, their copper-banded arms raised to their gods of wind and storm and sky: to Astur the Eagle, and Savash the Lord of War, and the Lady Itugen, each of them a different face of the Maker of the Universe, who loves battle and rides with them and shall remain with them always. They grin in the firelight and their yellow eyes flash with delight as the town goes up in flames, and the helpless people flee before them and fall like mown feather grass on the steppes, and the loot piles up in one corner of the stricken and burning town as fast as the corpses pile up in another. The church bells still clang in unholy panic, but it is the alien warriors who are ringing them now, in jest and victory. The priests have long since been stripped and slain, amid wailing people and howling dogs and the screams of abandoned children.

So Margus falls.

Afterward, drunk on wine, they rode out, still rejoicing, past the black charcoal remnants of the once colorful Margus fair and back to the grasslands. They are no townsmen, and the ruins of booths and buildings are already haunted by the ghosts of those they have slain. They retreat to their tents and wagons in the meadows.

Among the many bodies lie an old woman and a girl. The girl with the harelip, lying still among her pails. She had seen the future truly, as the old woman had said. Truly she had the gift.

3

THE VII

Viminacium: at the confluence of the Danube and the Mlava, headquarters of the VII Claudia Pia Fidelis, raised by Julius Caesar himself back in 58 BC to knock hell out of the Gauls and then do the same to their cousins over in Britain as well. An ancient legion with more than five hundred years of memories, stationed here on the Moesian Danube since Trajan's day. Four long centuries since the crucifixion of Christ.

Gallus Sabinus, legionary legate, veteran of frontier battles and frontier boredom, with a bald bull head, rolls of fat at the back of his neck and an impressive, solid mound of a belly, but muscles in his arms still strong enough to lift a hundred-pound sandbag above his head without noticeable effort. At his rickety ink-stained wooden desk, going through the quartermaster's monthly returns by the light of a sputtering oil lamp. Only three times more he'd be doing this bureaucratic donkey work. Only three more months, and then he'd be off to his Thracian vineyard, complete with neat little villa and courtyard, a fountain and everything, even a bit of mosaic floor, albeit a fairly crappy one by some local shyster, featuring a dolphin which looked to him more like an overweight eel. But his Domitilla was very proud of it, out there sweeping it clean every morning at the crack of dawn. The woman he hardly knew, his wife, Domitilla: sharp of tongue, broad of behind, frosty of expression, but serviceable enough, all things considered.

He leaned forward and his desk wobbled. One day they'd get round to giving it four equal legs.

He'd miss his men. They weren't so bad, for a motley scrag end of *limitanei*: frontier wolves. Dalmatians, Illyrians, Thracians, Teutons, a proper gaggle of mongrel geese. But Sabinus looked after his own. No political appointee from a senatorial family, who disdained such Spartan frontier postings anyway nowadays, Sabinus was a soldier to the backbone and proud of the traditions of the VII. The mobile field army might be the glory boys nowadays, the generals' gilded darlings, an elite force ready to march and fight wherever barbarian incursion threatened. But the frontier wolves were quartered out here permanently, doggedly training and arming and waiting for the day. Reduced in numbers, both rations and armor thinner than before, but still proud to call themselves a legion, with their eagle standard, plus the bull ensign common to all the Caesarian legions. Waiting for the barbarians to come.

In his years here Sabinus had done his best. He couldn't do squat about their pay, but he'd drilled and trained them and instituted field exercises they'd grumblingly enjoyed. Both weapons and wall artillery were well up to scratch. As for the walls themselves, he just hoped they'd hold. Especially the Porta Praetoria, with its ominous ground-to-battlements crack in the left tower. One day, the prefect would stir himself off his fat arse enough to do a complete rebuild, or maybe far-off Constantinople would realize that the old fort was in need of a lick of paint or two.

Till then, three more months . . .

He looked up. "Well?"

The *optio* stood hesitantly in the gloom. "Margus is still burning, sir."

Sabinus laid down his pen, sat back, and pointed at his own eyes. "What are these, Optio?"

"Eyes, sir."

"Correct. And with them I can see that Margus is still burning, in the same way I can see that you are still a useless idiot. By 'Well' I meant 'What news?' *Why* is it still burning?"

"We don't . . . that is, the riders haven't returned, sir."

"When did they ride out?"

"About the ninth hour."

"What traffic on the road?"

The *optio* glanced nervously toward the open door.

"Reports—unconfirmed reports—of incursion, sir. Over the river. Barbarian horsemen, so an old fellow says who crawled out of the river covered in duckweed. Said he'd floated down on driftwood from Margus itself. Babbling and half mad."

Sabinus kept his expressionless gaze on the hapless *optio*. "So . . . you've ordered the full legion to arms, for safety's sake?"

"I will, sir."

"Forget it. I will." His chair crashed backward as he stood up. "And put yourself on fucking latrine duty."

The legionary fortress of Viminacium stood square behind thick stone walls thirty feet high, battlemented and bastioned, with twin towers at each gate, north, south, east, and west. From the flanks of the fortress ran a much lesser wall, flung out wide and embracing the many acres of the proud town with its churches and chapels, wide streets, richly decorated villas, splendid basilica and porticoed marketplaces and, beyond the walls, its own ten-thousand-seat hippodrome. People came from miles around to see the spectacles there. But now, thought Sabinus with a grim smile, another altogether more real kind of spectacle would drive them many more miles away.

He found a tall young decurion.

"What's happening in the town?"

"People moving out already, heading for the hills."

As he'd thought. "Any asking for refuge here?"

The decurion shook his head.

They both knew what that meant. The people had already judged. They were finished. He smiled again to himself. Like hell they were.

The legate's bull roar sounded across the darkening fort from where he stood on the tower of the west gate, followed by a distant sound of stirring and then a steady crescendo of slamming doors, footsteps, the slap of leather soles on worn stone stairs, clanging weaponry, voices, heavy weights dragging, winches creaking.

His orders ricocheted around the fortress walls like missiles.

"Tubernator, sound the recall! Every last soldier still working out in the fields, get him in. Ditto from the farmhouses. Families to the barracks. Muster rolls to be counted. Every other century on the walls! Cavalry *alae* armed and ready at the south gate. Artillery units on the towers. Four machines to each bastion, two for frontal bombardment, two for enfilading fire, standard set-up, do I have to tell you? All gates double rammed! And I hope you got those holding braces repaired on the Praetorian Gate like I ordered, Decurion!

"Yes, sir!"

"We're expecting a night attack?"

"We're expecting the devil himself, like good soldiers should. I want wall artillery fully supplied. Pedites, move your arses! This isn't a visit from your dear old granny we'll be getting. Back-up supplies of all missiles up to the walls. First, fourth, and seventh centuries at the south gate with the cavalry. Ditch the dice and move it, you lard-assed layabouts! No sleep till dawn, if then. You've got work to do at last! Smiths, get those furnaces fired up if they're not already. Medics, confirm your supplies to me. Quartermasters, every man on the walls supplied with water and hardtack. And see to it all roof thatch is thoroughly doused. All water butts full to the brim, though I assume for your sake they already are. Primus Pilus, report to me on the west gate. No walking, no talking."

"Concentrate wall troops to the west, sir?"

"If they've already taken Margus they won't be so stupid. Space troops all round."

Sabinus marched off down the stone steps to the lower guardroom, where he found everything in a state of wordless, impressive bustle. Except for one poor greenhorn of a recruit who'd stacked up a pile of sling balls in such a poor pyramid that they collapsed the moment Sabinus walked past them. So he gave him a good belting and told him to do it again.

"Even the Egyptians can build pyramids, boy!" he roared in the quaking novice's ear. "And they fuck their own sisters and worship *cats*!"

The legate took his place again on the left tower of the west gate along with his useless *optio* and they gazed out into the setting sun. It was too bright, too red. Just over the horizon, a mere two hours by quick march, Margus was still burning. The leaping flames mingling with the sun's holocaust.

"Some incursion, sir," said his *optio*.

The south gate stood open below and families of the farmer-frontiersmen streamed in: women, infants in arms, elderly parents, children running about, wide eyed, looking more excited than scared. Into the safe brawny arms of the mighty legionary fort. God protect them.

Tatullus appeared silently on the tower. Legionary *primus pilus*—first spear—his senior centurion. Thank Christ for him at least. Well into his fifth decade but not an ounce of fat on him, his legs taut with sinew and muscle, his arms folded tight across his broad chest. His hard, weather-beaten face and bony nose accentuated by the plain, close-fitting helmet he wore ready for battle, the long, sinister noseguard protecting his deep-set, unblinking eyes, a chainmail aventail to save his neck. A soldier of quality to find in a neglected frontier fort in these ignominious days.

Behind Tatullus stood two more soldiers, one of them dripping copiously.

"Who the hell are you?" growled Sabinus, rounding on him.

"He's a deserter," said Tatullus coldly.

"I wasn't asking you, Centurion."

Damp though this one was—sodden through, in fact—he didn't tremble.

"Anastasius, sir," said the soldier, his voice so deep and hoarse it sounded like he gargled with gravel. "But it's never suited me, so I been told. Caestus, most people call me. Knuckles."

Knuckles. Sabinus turned and inspected him more closely. The name suited him better than Anastasius, that was for sure. He still had his *caestus,* his studded bullhide strap round his meaty forearm. His knuckles were black with hairs, and not that far off the ground. Mind you, had he stood up straight he would have been six feet tall or more. A good recruit for the Legio I Italica in that respect, at least. Though Sabinus doubted Knuckles had quite the right family connections to get into that socially exclusive legion. And he'd frighten the cavalry horses, for another thing. Cause a bloody stampede.

His huge rounded shoulders, one slightly lower than the other, made him look almost like a hunchback but still as powerful as a dray horse. Hands as big as spades. A human mole, Sabinus thought, he could dig a tunnel into the bare earth with those hands. Huge splayed feet, knock knees, a sagging belly, a fifty-four-gallon barrel chest, a muscular tree stump of a neck as broad as his head, a great bony nose, multiply broken, mouth battered about and askew as well, a heavy brow sprouting bushy black eyebrows, but his eyes oddly wide and sincere, although one eyelid sagged over the eye from an old swordcut. Coarse black hair in an inelegant pudding-basin style, and no single square inch of his bare skin free of a scar.

Sabinus liked what he saw. This was what he called a proper soldier. Ugly as hell and almost as long enduring.

"And you deserted? From Margus?"

"No, sir. Not deserted. Just on business. But I got caught up at Margus. On unforeseen secondment, you might say."

Sabinus scowled. "You're wasting my time, soldier. Give it me straight."

Knuckles straightened a little. "Sir. Legionary of the XIVth at Carnuntum. Coming downriver with shipment of wine. A private enterprise."

"Customs dodging. Profiteering."

Knuckles hurried on. "Boat sank at night. Got ashore at Margus. Centurion there, Pamphilus, promptly co-opted me into his guard."

"So what happened?"

"We got wiped out two days later is what happened. Which is to say, this morning. All of 'em except me. They're Huns, the centurion said."

Sabinus brooded. What a mess. If you're going to drive off a barbarian tribe, make sure you do it with a good hard sword thrust, not a pinprick. Else they'll be back. Gadfly to a horse's ass. He blew out air. What a bloody mess.

"Go on, soldier."

"Well, the centurion, he sent out riders back here for reinforcements but . . . the Huns got to them before they got to you."

"Evidently. And then?"

"Total bloody slaughter."

"Numbers?"

"Couldn't say. Not that many, it didn't look like, but organized."

"Organized?"

"Organized," repeated Knuckles doggedly.

Sabinus rasped his stubble. He turned and bellowed a fresh couple of orders to his men. Then he asked, "And you?"

"Well, sir, we was on the bridge, trapped and about to get wiped out frontways and backways, if you take my meaning, and we'd already lost formation and the arrows was piling in so to be honest I thought, Stuff this, and decided to take my chances overboard, but then I thought I might as well try and take one of those blue buggers with me."

"Blue?"

"Tattoos. Black and blue all over. They do it with a needle and soot, apparently. Horrible. No self-respect sir, those fuckin' barbarians. So, anyhow, I figured I could drown him and I might even get his horse up and off the other bank and away. So up I jumped and got the bugger in a neck lock and pushed and hung on and we crashed off the side of the bridge and down into the river, the savage still sittin' on his horse and me sittin' on him. And by happy chance, and with the blessings of Jupiter, Lord of all Creation and whatnot, I managed to get a hold of his reins floating around in the mucky water and wrap 'em round his neck. What a rumpus, him still fighting and struggling—a real wild one he was, and no spring chicken, neither. But then there was this great pier of the bridge loomin' at me out of the water. We was still down there with the fish and I was longin' to get a good lungful, but business had yet to be concluded, so to speak. I had a good grip on his head with his own reins, throttlin' 'im—the horse was long gone by this time, upped and swum for it, the brute. So I started a good swing with his head—he was in need of a lungful by this time, too, I reckoned, and not at his finest as a fighting man, it's safe to say, so I swung 'im and yet . . . I don't know if you've ever tried to swing a man's head round under water, sir?"

Sabinus had not.

"But it moves awfully slow, 'cos of all the water, so I banged and banged and banged him into that bloody great oak pier I don't know how many times until finally after many a hefty bang he stopped hangin' onto me and I let him go and he sank back very gentle like, and I presume went on down to the bottom to be a dinnertime treat for the fishes. I didn't hang around to see, to be honest, as I was very nearly drowned myself by this time, so I made for the sunlight and got my lungful after all. Back on the bridge it was a massacre so I let myself be carried downriver and on down here, and if that counts as desertion, well . . ."

"It does," said Tatullus.

"The rest of the guard were all killed?" said Sabinus.

"All of 'em. The officer's head, sir, Pamphilus, stuck on the bridgepost at the end as I swam off. And he wasn't a bad sort."

"Then you came downriver?"

"Yes, sir, by way of a horse."

"Don't bullshit me, man."

"Which is to say a dead horse, sir. Dead some three days or more, I reckon, and givin' off a perfectly horrible smell, though to be honest with you, sir, I've known worse in an eight-man mess tent on campaign. Or there was that tavern we used to frequent in Carnuntum, sir, with a lady upstairs, getting on in years though very accommodating in her way—"

"Less detail, soldier, more pace."

"Well, so I hung on to this dead horse, its back legs all slimy and bits slidin' off in me hands, and its belly all bloated and givin' off gas like you wouldn't believe, must have been dead a few days, as I say, and not just killed in the scrap, but it made a good enough float, like an army-issue bladder, and so I came floating on downriver to the fort, sir. Because I thought it was time I got myself behind some decent walls. You know those Huns."

Sabinus brooded for a moment. Then he told his *optio* to get the man a cup of wine.

Tatullus started. "Sir . . ."

The legate turned on him. "Have a care, Centurion. I'm no spoiled young puppy from some rich senatorial family in Ravenna or Rome. And I don't need you to question my orders."

Tatullus's thin lips were clenched almost to invisibility. After a moment's pause he said again, very low and soft, "Sir."

Knuckles held up a huge paw.

"No, sir, anyway, thanking you kindly. No wine for me. Never since that incident in Carnuntum with the fishmonger's daughter, and my unfortunate accident."

Sabinus raised his eyebrows. "Frontier intelligence never reported that particular incident."

"I'm relieved to hear it, sir. An unedifying business altogether. But I'm sworn right off the wine now until the joyous hereafter."

"Very well." Sabinus looked away and rested his hand on the low walls of the tower. "You may be a better storyteller than a soldier, I don't know. But from now on, you're in my close guard."

"How much is that worth a month, then?"

"Enough for a water drinker." Then Sabinus turned his attention to the other man, keeping silent at the back, and summoned him forward.

A magnificent fellow, olive skinned, tall and lean, his erect bearing emphasizing his height. An easterner, surely. A long sword in a damascene scabbard at his side, his fine black mustache immaculately oiled and combed around his mouth, his face smooth, his nose hawklike, his whole bearing supremely aristocratic.

"And you are?"

"Count Grigorius Khachadour Arapovian," replied the newcomer.

Behind him, Knuckles snorted.

"Shut it, soldier," growled Sabinus. He regarded the newcomer again. "Armenian?"

"Armenia was the land of my birth and sixty generations of my forefathers since the days of Adam. But now I have no country. She has auctioned off her soul to the highest bidder. Now I fight only for Christ, my Lord."

"Jesus," breathed Sabinus.

"The same," said the Armenian gravely.

"Right," said Sabinus, "you're on the roll. We need every man we can get. For now you're paired with him on supply, on the south wall. Get to it."

Arapovian did not glance back at Knuckles, but said simply, "I will not keep company with that belching ox. He sickens my senses."

"You know each other?" Sabinus guffawed. "Let me guess, you smuggled wine together? You were business partners?"

"The sons of Arapovian have not soiled their hands with trade in sixty generations," said the Armenian crisply. "This oaf was merely giving me transport. I had known him for but half a night before we separated again. Yet long enough to wish we might never meet further."

"What's the problem?"

The Armenian curled his thin lips. "He is an ape."

Sabinus glanced at Knuckles. "You flatter him."

Arapovian did not smile. He looked genuinely pained.

But Sabinus was grinning broadly now. "That's it. You're a pair. Now get to it."

Slowly, with injured dignity, Arapovian turned and made his way back down the steps. Knuckles lumbered after him.

"That was no deserter," Sabinus said over his shoulder to Tatullus. "You know what real desertion looks like. That was retreat."

The centurion remained steely. "No order of retreat was given."

"Because there was nowhere to retreat to. Just like now."

4

TENS OF THOUSANDS

Knuckles and the Armenian lugged hundred-pound rocks up the narrow steps to the top of the south gate tower. The latter stopped at the top when they set down their load and wiped the sweat from his long arched eyebrows. He gazed out toward the hills, ghostly under the rising summer moon.

"That I, Grigorius Khachadour Arapovian, the son of Grigorius Nubar Arapovian, the son of Grigorius Ardzruni Arapovian, should be found carrying rocks like a convict. Teamed with a boor who does not even know who his father was."

But insulting Knuckles was like insulting a stone statue. "True enough," he rumbled, wiping his face dry in his own armpit. "But I know that my mother was a whore. The daughter of a whore, descended from a long line of the most highly regarded Rhenish whores for sixty generations." He belched and grinned.

Arapovian did not smile.

Sabinus paced the twilit battlements of the fort, staring out uneasily into the thickening dusk. Just over the horizon Margus burned on, flames rising and smoke spiraling, the molten orange firelight in a murderous melding with the last glow of the setting sun. In that orange light, the severed heads of his own men, of that good centurion Pamphilus, decorating the wooden posts on the old town bridge.

Damn them.

Different reports, and he'd have despatched his two heavily-armored cavalry *alae,* his fearsome cataphracts, to slice through the enemy, save the town and hang the barbarians' corpses from its walls. But he sensed otherwise this time. It had been a nasty business, the trans-Danube expedition by that self-same cavalry, though orders were orders, and peace might have come of it. But it hadn't. That clumsy, ill-advised needling of a once-powerful, still-troublesome tribe had only brought the Huns back on the crimson path of vengeance.

It wasn't the numbers that unsettled him, it was the planning. "Organized," that hulking Rhineland brute Knuckles had reported, and Sabinus trusted his judgment. Margus had been assaulted and sacked with great stealth, with judgment and control. Now the enemy held back, not riding on, howling, toward the next town full of vainglory. They were awaiting the right moment, planning. But planning was supposed to be for Romans, not barbarians.

"So," he resumed. "Nothing from the hill stations? Nothing from the signal posts upriver? Nothing from *intelligence?*"

Tatullus stood with his legs set apart on the platform roof like a bronze statue, gazing out over the darkening plain. "Nothing, sir."

From Margus itself, still nothing. From the imperial trunk road south to Naissus, nothing. From the east by river, pushing up through the dark gorge of the Iron Gates from Ratiaria, headquarters of the Danube Fleet, nothing. And now not even the watch on the hill stations responding. With Margus burning like a village bonfire at Saturnalia.

To have skirted south unseen and taken each and every station and watch tower in advance, without setting off a single alarm signal—that would have taken intelligence. Organization.

"Tell you what, Centurion. I get the unpleasant feeling we're cut off."

Tatullus nodded expressionlessly.

Sabinus wished he could stop talking. But something blackly ominous in the air tonight made him talk, even with so unsympathetic a confidant as his iron centurion.

"Of course, no barbarian horde is ever going to take a legionary fortress. But if we're going to go down fighting and not come up again—*if*—it would be good to know that someone would exact a decent revenge in our name. What do you reckon?"

"I wish I knew, sir."

Both knew what that meant. Some chance.

The Eastern generals corrupt and squabbling, the field army at Marcianopolis, under that impetuous easterner Aspar, too little tried and tested— certainly never against an enemy like the Huns. Emperor Theodosius in his gilded chambers at Constantinople, practicing his calligraphy.

Tatullus said, "It'd be good to have some reinforcements from the west."

Both knew what that meant, too.

Master General Aëtius. Mistrusted by both emperors equally. The empire's last best hope.

Another refugee arrived, a rat-faced little man with his hair plastered across his narrow skull, and water still squelching from his sodden leather sandals. He wore the dull brown uniform of the *exploratores.* A scout.

"Why is everyone so bloody *wet* around here?" demanded Sabinus.

"Sir," gasped the half-drowned man, "river was the only refuge from the barbarians. Scythians."

"Huns."

The little man stared up at the legate. "Is it?" He didn't look much consoled. "Well, their horses don't take kindly to water. Not used to it off the plains, I reckon."

Sabinus made a mental note. "Anything else?"

"Numbers, sir."

"I've heard a thousand. At Margus."

The man looked pained. "No, sir, afraid not. That was only a detachment." He wiped the water still dripping from his nose. "Maybe even a distraction. More were coming across downriver all the time."

"Without being seen?"

"All observation posts knocked out, sir. Rest of my watch all put to the sword. They know what they're doing."

He was beginning to realize that. "So: numbers?"

"In total?" The man took a deep breath. "In a valley up in the hills to the south, saw them myself . . . ten thousand?"

Sabinus felt Tatullus beside him stir.

"But other reports say that they're only one grouping, as it were, sir. One legion, you might say. As many again in . . . other valleys."

"Tens of thousands?"

"It could be, sir."

"But only a third, a quarter of them fighting men." Sabinus mused. "Always a damn-fool way to move around, with your women and children along for the spectacle." He looked at Tatullus. "We could try and get through to Singidunum, to—"

The scout dared to interrupt. "No, sir. Not this time, not this lot. They're all males. No families, no women and children, just warriors."

Sabinus stared at him as the worsening news sank in. "Shit." He held the back of his hand up to his mouth, then dropped it again. An unseemly gesture.

So their flight north was a feint, after the punitive expedition. It was only to hide their women and children away, somewhere north or east, out in that endless wilderness.

"We could try tracking them, use special forces, the *superventores*. Bring them in, hold them for ransom, exchange, treaty."

But Tatullus was already shaking his head.

No, Sabinus couldn't see any such trans-Danube operations going ahead, either. Not now. And did he have the men, anyway? No. He did not have the bloody men.

"Cunning bastards," breathed Tatullus. "They've learned a lot."

There was a long silence, then Sabinus said to the scout, "Go and get some dry clothes on."

Tatullus called after him, "And a weapon."

Sabinus set his clenched fists on the wall. "Trying to drive them off the Trans-Pannonian plain with a pinprick. With *my cavalry*. Damn that fool in Ravenna. Him and his magic."

"Sir?"

"The Emperor Valentinian. And right now I'd tell him so to his sickly face, and damn the consequences. Sacrificing cockerels under the full moon. Punitive expeditions. He thinks we're still living back in Trajan's reign. Today's barbarians are . . ."

"Organized."

Sabinus stared out grimly and said nothing.

"So now we have to face some tens of thousands of Huns. But they know nothing of siege craft."

"True. Though they're smart enough to use only enough warriors for each job. Any more than a thousand at Margus and they'd have been trampling on each other. But I still don't rate them against a legion plus heavy cavalry in open battle." He leaned his weight forward on his fists. "We need to clear them out. The Huns have been a force to be reckoned with before. I don't want any more losses like Margus in this province."

"Still," said Tatullus quietly. "Tens of thousands . . ."

And his centurion was no coward.

They both knew their only option.

Eventually Sabinus leaned back again and said, "Very well. We sit here. We keep 'em at bay. We wait for news to get through, they'll get word soon enough, and the field army will arrive hotfoot from Marcianopolis. Then . . . we put an end to them."

"Easy," said Tatullus.

Sabinus glanced sideways at his centurion, but it was impossible to read him.

The legate ate a light supper on the tower roof, standing. Bread, lentils, a few slices of pigeon breast. No booze. Not tonight.

He racked his brains, trying to remember the name. Rumors abounded. Emperor Valentinian's fearsome old mother, Galla Placidia—the Eastern Emperor's cousin, come to that—had always had a special thing about the Huns, so they said.

And her master general—sorry, the *emperor's* master general—Aëtius, he spoke Hunnish himself, among other tongues. He'd lived with the Huns for a time as a boy. They should be allies, but some said that was all in the past. The Huns were Rome's sworn enemies now, and Rome had better get used to it.

What was that leader's name?

He sent a junior officer back to his office to find the communication.

That was it. He smacked the piece of paper. The new warlord of the Hun tribe.

His uncle, Ruga, had been a sot and a willing client. There was every reason to think Ruga's eldest nephew, Bleda, would succeed to the same drunken, obedient position. Then a younger brother suddenly appeared out of the wilderness. Vanished for three long decades, but still not forgotten in Rome or Ravenna, apparently. He'd been a captive—hostage, rather—in the capital, in the Imperial Palace itself, back in Honorius's day. Made repeated escape attempts, and eventually succeeded in fleeing north through Italy at the height of the Gothic invasion. Evaded every attempt at capture, the little tyke, and got back to his homeland. Sabinus remembered the story vaguely. The boy had been all of ten or twelve when he did it. It was said that the emperor's mother still remembered him bitterly, still wanted him gone. And somehow or other, that old winebag Ruga had helpfully got rid of him, for a few more hogsheads of cheap wine.

But not forever, it seemed.

Now he was back, and not a bit mellowed by age, apparently. Frontier intelligence said he'd promptly slaughtered his uncle, then his brother, set the crown on his own head, pulled together a whole horde of disparate tribes out of the godforsaken wilderness, and then led the lot of them back over the Carpathians to the Huns' old pasturelands north of the Danube. A deliberate provocation. That was when Valentinian had ordered a punitive attack. Theodosius agreed. Idiots, both of them, Valentinian stupid and corrupt, Theodosius just stupid. Their most idiotic failing, to underestimate this thorn in Rome's side since his boyhood. Now the VIIth itself would have to settle the matter.

As always, it was kings and emperors who ran up the bill and the soldiers who paid it.

Sabinus swallowed a last chunk of bread.

Deep night fell.

Attila. That was his name.

The western sky burned on.

5

MERCY AND TERROR

In a bowl in the hills, a few dozen stragglers huddled. Six or seven families, children and toddlers, dogs, a goat kid, a single handbarrow laden with household goods, kitchen utensils ill chosen in panic for saving. They lit no fire. They had heard of the terror visited on Margus, and had fled from Viminacium at dusk. Fled from the wrath to come. At Margus, the rumors said, the savages had slaughtered everyone. Every living thing. Dogs and cats, priests and sheep, babes in arms and ancients in their beds. Blood flowed in the gutters. The earthen backstreets were churned to rust-colored mud.

One refugee from a farm, his bloody arm wrapped in filthy bandages, had come to Viminacium and spread the news. Some had counseled retreat within the walls of the fortress, but the refugee laughed, a horrible, weak laugh. "Not with these ones," he said. "We'd be no more than live bait to a wolf."

"With a whole legion to protect us?"

The refugee shook his head. "That legion is finished. History. Poor bastards."

They fled into the hills.

Now it was a chill summer night, but they lit no fire. The fire of Margus away to the west still burned. It would be their own beloved town of Viminacium next, their houses and homes. Now they had nothing but their own families and a few pots and pans. The people could not even look at each other for sorrow. Above them the pure white stars wheeled. All was silent. They prayed and waited for nothing to happen. Only silence and the night. Please God.

In answer there came a distant rumbling. Horsemen. The pagan horsemen.

Mothers clutched their hands over infant mouths. A man pushed the goat kid roughly to the ground and hauled a bag over its head. The rumbling came closer. Many horsemen. They were ascending into the hills all around. The people looked up at the dark rim of the bowl where they lay hidden, eyes wide with terror. Above them the stars shone down. The moon was behind clouds but the vagabond people were brightly lit by starlight.

And then against the starlit nightsky, dark shapes arose. Horses tramped their forefeet and their nostrils steamed. Their riders pulled up their reins and looked down.

The rim of the bowl filled with the silhouettes of the pagan horsemen, spiky with bows and spears. The people below them, trapped and unarmed, groaned low. Mothers clutched infants to their breasts as if that might save them. Some buried their faces in their cloaks. Very young children began to cry, sensing their parents' terror.

After an agonizing time, the line of horsemen parted and a single figure came riding down the slope toward them. The people's groans died away and they waited. The horseman stopped beside them. He was naked to the waist even in the cold night. His cheeks were deeply grooved and blue with ritual tattoos. He looked over them. Then he spoke, his voice deep and hoarse.

"See how your army protects you. See how your emperor loves you." He shook his head.

One or two of the refugees dared to look up.

"The army that did not protect you will be destroyed. Your emperor, too, and his empire, will be destroyed. All that you love, will be—must be— destroyed. It is written. But you." He shook his head again, and those who dared to look thought they saw him smile. "You I will not destroy. Now go your ways. Flee away south. Or east, west, north, it matters not. But remember: I am coming."

He pulled his horse round and galloped away up over the rim of the bowl, and in seconds every one of his warriors had vanished after him.

The people stared at each other.

The stars shone down.

In a tent of the Huns, a captive from Margus stood blindfolded with his hands roped behind his back. He wore the close-fitting white gown of a priest of the Church and a wooden Chi-Rho on his chest.

He felt strong hands seize his blindfold and tear it off.

He blinked.

By firelight and the single torch in the tent he saw several barbarian chieftains. Before him, a half-naked savage wearing his hair in a topknot. Big gold earrings danced against his cheeks. The man's arms and chest were scarred and tattooed and very strong.

The man smiled and, to the priest's astonishment, spoke in perfect Latin.

"You are a Christian priest, yes?"

He nodded.

"You drink the blood of your God and eat his flesh," said a strange little man at the back of the tent.

It was Little Bird the shaman. He shook his head and his beribboned topknot danced. "What a barbarian you must be."

The warlord signaled and another of his warriors raised the tent flap. Seated outside by a low campfire were a woman in a grimy red dress and three children, two girls and a boy.

"And this is your family? The boy's name is Theophilus, as is yours."

The priest swallowed. "I do not know them."

"And three times Peter denied Christ."

The priest was even more astonished. A savage who spoke Latin and alluded to Holy Scripture.

"Even the devils in Hell believe in God, and tremble." The warlord smiled. It was not a smile to comfort anyone. "You are not only a priest, you are a bishop. The Bishop of Margus."

He shook his head. "I, I . . ."

The warlord reached out and put his big right hand round the priest's throat. He rested it gently there.

"Do not lie to me again, or I will squeeze your soul out of your gullet."

"He will, you know," put in Little Bird helpfully. "I've seen him do it."

"You are the Bishop of Margus, and this is your family. She is your wife, or perhaps your concubine. The children are your seed."

The priest wept. "Mine is the family of Christ. I do not have a family. Leave them be."

The warlord squeezed, briefly.

After the priest had sucked in air and staggered to his feet again, mopping the tears from his eyes, the warlord recommenced.

"You know her." He raised his voice. "She is your concubine, your whore. You disdained to marry her."

Hearing those words the woman looked up. The warlord glanced back, caught her expression of fury, and smiled.

The priest's shoulders sagged and he hung his head.

The warlord released him.

"Now listen to me," he said. "As your god redeemed you, so you can redeem your family. You will go to your emperor in Constantinople, the Calligrapher. I will give you a horse."

The bishop was looking out at his family again. The warlord signaled and his warrior dropped the tentflap.

"You must attend," he said.

The bishop raised his eyes and looked at him.

"It is no great task, but you will remember my words. This is a job for a bishop, smooth-tongued and proficient in diplomacy as you are."

The bishop shivered at his tone.

"You will ride south down the imperial trunk road for Naissus."

"My lord," he stammered, "do not send me, I implore you. The hills are full of savages." The warlord showed his teeth. "Of . . . of bandits, of brigands. I might be killed by Roman detachments, even, reinforcements, uncertain, bewildered—"

"There are no reinforcements coming."

"Or by common cutpurses, bears, wolves—"

"Life is uncertain," admitted the warlord genially.

"Then why me? Why not send your own?"

"Because life is uncertain." His yellowish eyes glittered with amusement. "They might be killed by common cutpurses, bears, wolves." More harshly he added, "Besides, my warriors are fit for better things than running mere errands.

"Now, this is your task. You will wear a cloak I give you. My men in the hills about will not molest you: the word has gone out. You will have a good horse—good enough for a Christian bishop, anyway. In Naissus you will report directly to the city prefect. His name is Eustachius. Of course you know him well; he is your cousin." The warlord enjoyed his captive's amazement. "You will tell him that Margus is laid waste, but nothing more, and demand immediate escort to Constantinople. There you will demand audience with the emperor.

"You will speak to him directly, and none other.

"You will tell him that he has insulted the Hun people. You will tell him that his armies have assaulted and slaughtered our innocents. They have trampled on the grave mounds of our ancient kings, they have looted our burial grounds." The warlord's voice grated with cold anger. "And you will say to the emperor these words from me:

"'If you ignore me, oppose me, or attempt to deceive me, I will destroy you. If you do not admit your guilt in regard to the descration of our burial mounds and the massacre of our people, I will destroy you.'"

"My lord," stammered the messenger, "I cannot say these words in person to His Divine Majesty. His anger will be terrible."

"His anger will be nothing to mine. Say them. Say them just as I said them to you, word for word. The emperor in his perfumed palace will hear you. He will not destroy you, but if you fail me I will destroy you and your seed forever. Just as I will destroy him and his empire: every wall, every stone, every man, woman, and child left within. Understand me. Look into my eyes. Do I look to you like a liar?"

The priest could not speak.

"Say to the emperor that if he does not render to me half his empire by way of recompense, I will destroy him."

"Half . . . the empire?"

"Your ears work well. Of course, I will destroy him anyway, but he need not know that yet. And you can add for him the old Roman motto '*Nemo me impune lacessit*—no man insults me with impunity.' Suitable, no?"

The bishop said nothing.

"I will know if and when you have delivered this message in full, and correctly. If you do, you may return here and be reunited with your family. And then, if you have any sense, you will flee far from this empire doomed to fall. If you do not return—in twenty days—your family will be crucified, the whore and the children both."

The bishop groaned.

The warlord struck him. He reeled backward. With his hands tied behind his back he could not wipe his mouth so he licked and leaned aside and spat the blood that welled from his split lip.

The warlord's voice grew fiercer. "How often in your life have you had a chance to redeem your entire family from death by a single act of great bravery? Never. Am I right? Of course I am. You are a provincial priest of a mean frontier diocese. Your family were mere yeoman farmers, slow sons of the soil with clay for blood."

He looked away.

"You should go now. Naissus is two days distant, and the capital another ten. So you will need to hurry to be back here in twenty days and collect your prize." He laid his hand on the man's shaking shoulder, almost gentle again. "You will need to ride fast. Understand?"

The bishop controlled himself and nodded.

The warlord turned to his warriors. "Find him a horse."

As he departed, the priest looked back. "My lord, I still do not know what name I should give."

"Attila. My name is Attila."

Orestes watched him at the doorway to the tent. Great Tanjou. He remembered the day when the two of them had come back to the camp of the Huns, a small and humbled people, before Attila took them in his fists and remade them. And when Attila dug into the grave mound, grubbing into the very bones of his father, Mundzuk, with a common spade. Now he preached the desecration of the Hun grave mounds as a pretext for war. Yet Attila was no hypocrite. That was not the word.

One law for the lion and the ox is oppression. That was Attila's creed, or something like it.

Attila said, "Let them use their own to pass on messages of disaster, to issue threats to their emperor." He took his place cross-legged at the fireside. "Let them use their own *cursus* to pass on my words."

Orestes murmured, "Like the time we let those Turcoman bandits steal our gold. Heavy wagons of Chinese gold."

An old warrior with long, graying hair regarded him. It was Chanat. "Tell the tale."

Orestes smiled thinly. "We let them drag it over mountain passes, across fast-flowing rivers on rafts, across parched gravel deserts. A terrible journey back to their steppeland home. We trailed them all the way. They never knew. And when they had kindly transported all that Chinese gold for us, safely back to the northern steppes, we fell on them by night and slew them all."

"And took back your gold?"

Orestes nodded. "And took back our gold."

Chanat munched happily on his leg of mutton. He liked this story. "Will this emperor indeed render up to us half his empire? Is he such a woman? They say he wears perfume, and boots studded with pearls."

"I don't doubt he does," said Attila. "But as for handing over half his empire, if he does not, I will destroy him. And if he does," he smiled, "well, I will destroy him anyway. And then . . . Rome."

"And then . . . ?"

"Ah. Then."

They fell silent. Chanat drank. Memories of China.

"Whatever else he does, Theodosius will call on the West for aid," said Attila. "But no aid will come."

Orestes frowned. "The Roman boy, this master general, Aëtius . . ."

"I remember him. He would ride to the rescue of any fallen damsel, even Theodosius. But he will not come. I have other plans. Constantinople has strong walls, but the strongest legions remain in the West. Aëtius's own legions are the finest. We could take on both empires at once, but it is easier to divide and rule, as the Romans used to say when they colonized new lands. Divide and destroy, I say.

"We concentrate first on the East. Soon enough, Theodosius will send out a message by sea to Ravenna. Also to his field army at Marcianopolis, and perhaps to the legionary forts at Sirmium and Singidunum to attack our flank. Such messages will be . . . disrupted."

"At sea?"

"The Vandals are masters of much of the Mediterranean now. King Genseric."

Orestes stared. "One of the brothers also held hostage in Rome in your boyhood."

"With his sleek ships in that fine harbor of captured Carthage. What irony there."

"He is your ally now? I did not know this."

"He is not my ally, he is my servant." Attila grinned. "But he does not know this." He took a deep draft of kumiss.

"You should sleep," said Orestes. He had been awake all night, talking, the bloodlust of Margus still coursing in his veins.

Attila ignored him. Orestes laid his hand on his shoulder. No other man could have done this. Attila shrugged him off.

Finally he said, "Such dreams I have nowadays. You have no idea. Such dreams . . ."

"Such dreams," echoed Little Bird from the back of the tent, shaking his head sorrowfully.

Orestes did not know if they were good dreams or bad, if his friend awoke in the cold midnight raging with dreams of world conquest or trembling from other visions altogether.

"I do not sleep," said Attila. "I cannot sleep."

Two more warriors stepped into the tent, Aladar, son of Chanat, and one of the Kutrigur Huns.

"Another of the Chosen Men is dead," said Aladar.

The Kutrigur warrior nodded. "You seek the Lord Bela. I saw him go down into the water. One of the Romans, a brute of a man, fell on him and dragged him off the bridge, drowned him."

Attila gazed at the messenger. First eager Yesukai, doomed to die young. Now Bela, one of the four steadfast brothers.

The king said not a word, made not a sound, but in a single, explosive movement smashed his wooden cup to the ground. Little Bird whimpered. No one else moved.

"His body?"

"Never found."

Attila's eyes searched the ground splashed with koumiss, muttering. "Drowned. What an end for my warrior Bela."

Bela of the bull neck and the bull torso. The strong and silent, slow-witted, immovable Bela. Loyal unto death, like all his Chosen Men.

Chanat said, "The brothers will have their revenge, my lord."

"I don't doubt it," growled Attila.

Aladar took a deep breath. "And Candac is also gone."

Clever, cautious, round-faced Candac.

"Then find him. Find his body. He will be given full and honorable—"

"No, Great Tanjou. He is gone. I saw him go."

Attila's scowl was ferocious. Two deep vertical grooves between his brows, his forehead furrowed deep and dark. Three ancient parallel scars just visible, fine and white. His traitor's mark. His voice was soft and low, always the worst.

"Not deserted," he said. "Not my Candac, not my Chosen Man. He would not desert me."

"I saw him ride, too, my master," said Little Bird, nodding furiously. "He rode away north and gone, all wordless into the wilderness."

Attila's bewilderment erupted into violence.

Little Bird yelped and scuttled to the darkest side of the tent, where he squatted down and wrapped his arms over his head like a monkey.

Orestes ducked under the wooden stool that the king was flailing wildly, smashing to splinters against the shuddering tentpost. He seized his arm. It was not seemly for a great man to show such passion. Attila froze and looked at Orestes as if unable to recognize him. His blazing eyes were filled with madness. Orestes returned his gaze steadily. Attila gradually grew calm again, dropped the remains of the stool at his feet and turned away.

"Explain," he said eventually. His shoulders seemed to sag. "Explain to me the desertion of my Chosen Man, my beloved Candac."

"My lord," said Aladar gravely, "I cannot. Except that . . ."

"I heard him speak," said Chanat.

Attila looked back.

The old warrior regarded his king gravely. "I saw him surveying the killing field of Margus, and the mounds of dead bodies, and the deeds of the Kutrigur Huns, our brothers in arms: taking scalps, debauching the slain, having their usual enjoyments."

The Kutrigur warrior, messenger of Bela's death, remained impassive at the tent door.

"Terror is a fine weapon," said Attila. "And very cheap."

Chanat did not argue. "Our brothers in arms," he repeated boldly and bitterly. "Our comrades riding with us in the great and glorious conquest of this mighty Empire of Rome. I saw Candac standing among the flames, and I saw him drop his bow to the ground and not retrieve it. He watched them, the Kutrigurs, about their business, their exotic deeds and their violations, with the chieftain of the Kutrigurs, Sky-in-Tatters himself, among them. And I heard the Lord Candac say—I thought to me, though he did not turn his head—I heard him say, 'This is not the treasure I fought for.' "

There was a moment of silence. Then, "Why did you not tell me this earlier?"

"You would not have heard this earlier."

Old Chanat.

"Ach," murmured Attila. One soft, sad syllable. There was no more to be said.

After a while his warriors rose and retired from his tent. Even Orestes stepped after them, leaving him to his dreams.

Proud tempers breed sad sorrows for themselves.

Orestes searched for Little Bird but he was nowhere to be found. Like Candac, he had gone into the wilderness, though not forever, only for a little while. He would never desert his master, come what may. He would always go with him through the storm and to the very gates of Hell, joking as he went.

In the hills to the south, looking out over the smoldering ashes of Margus, seated cross-legged upon an outcrop of pale moonlit limestone among the yellow rockroses, was an outlandish, beribboned creature. He wore a string decorated with tiny bird and animal skulls around his neck, and a torn goatskin shirt decorated with little black stick men.

A solitary girl fleeing south, a shepherdess, stumbled on him and gave a cry of terror but he never stirred, never even noticed. She fled onward.

For all his years he still had the face of a child, the color high and hectic in his broad cheeks. A small fire of sticks burned at his feet and he threw strange seeds into it and leaned forward to inhale the smoke.

His attention was fixed far beyond the ruined town. He saw turning stars and balefire and black night, and he felt afraid. He rocked back and forth and stirred his hands in the air. He saw his noble master, Lord Widow-Maker, Great Tanjou, Khan of Khans, drawing black night down over the world like a tent to cover and smother all. Not only the hated empire of Rome but the Hun people, too, would be caught in it, would suffocate and die under that dark sky heavy with hatred. He whimpered. The tent of the world twisted and became a monster made up of blood-red flame and black night, which would turn and devour them all.

6

THE TORTURE SHIP

Sabinus took a cup of wine after all. It wouldn't make him slow on a night like this, only steady his nerves.

His palms sweated. He calmed his breathing.

Around the battlements he could see the white, strained faces of his men. Down below, the restless cavalry horses were tethered. The cavalrymen resting again, seated in the dust, helmets cradled in their laps. Little campfires burning. No one spoke.

They prayed that it would come soon.

Some already harbored fantasies of hearing the sound of distant hooves and drums, and the cry going up from the south towers overlooking the road east to Ratiaria and Marcianopolis, "They're coming! The field army's coming!"

But no such cry came.

From the walls they could see fires in the hills: villages aflame. They could hear the high calls of nightbirds, the bark of a dog fox. But a terrible feeling of aloneness. As if they were the only living men left on earth, surrounded by darkness and by the forces of darkness.

No one else even knew. The rest of the empire slept peaceful and oblivious tonight. Not one shepherd, not one wandering tinker refugee, had got through to Naissus of the Five Roads or to Ratiaria, with its vast weapons factories, to report the incursion, it seemed. No help was coming for this fight they faced against tens of thousands of savages, streaming down again from the valleys where they had lain hidden. Under Sabinus's command, no more than two thousand at best, many of them rustic auxiliaries. Properly armored, equipped and trained, he had all of five hundred men.

Wisps of cloud across the moon, a thickening mist on the river, a terrible unease. Only a few hours ago he'd been sitting doing the legionary accounts. That seemed a long time ago now.

A cry in the night. The legate started, strained his ears. Sounds were getting muffled by the rising mist. Screams still coming from Margus? No, that was impossible. Margus was ten miles distant. Only the cry of a bird, a night-heron over the darkening river.

He turned to speak to Tatullus by his side and then froze.

There came the sound of drums.

There was a stir among the men on the northwest tower. They were pushing forward to see something. Sabinus strode over.

The crossbowmen and artillerymen parted for him. Tatullus trod close behind. There was that hulking brute Knuckles again, both his great bear-like arms and huge fists tightly wrapped round with bull-hide strips studded with lethal bronze studs, and dragging a crude club, like some troglodyte Hercules.

"Where's your pike, man?" demanded Sabinus.

"Down below, sir. I got an eye on it, don't you worry. But I lost me last club back on the bridge at Margus, so I been makin' meself a new one. I like a club, sir, when it gets up close and personal, like. It don't rust and get caught in your scabbard, it don't break or get stuck in somebody's guts, it never gives up on you. You keep a firm grip on it and it won't let you down. I always swear by a club, sir, when the fightin' gets messy."

Knuckles's club had a special adaptation. Stuck on the end was a great lump of lead solder which one of the smiths had done for him earlier. Most men would have had difficulty even lifting the thing.

"Once, sir, I had to put a mare out of her misery and me good old club did a clean job of it in one go."

Sabinus didn't doubt it.

A flicker of something caught his eye. He looked out over the river and something was wrong. It was on fire.

Out of the darkness still came the sound of drums. Deep, booming barbarian drums.

The night glowed, a flame-red mouth opening up in the darkness, long streaks of reflected flame licking along the surface of the slow-moving river. Then a ship came gliding out of the thin mist.

A galley, wreathed in flames. One of the galleys of the Danube Fleet, captured from God knows where. Gliding downstream like some infernal ghost ship, sailing into dark eternity unmanned. Silent but for the crackling of the flames and the collapsing spars and showering sparks. Yet there were humans still aboard. Hanging from the masts and yardarms, strangled, dangling, obscene, as if still dancing amid the flames that licked at the soles of their feet, hung the naked bodies of massacred soldiers. They festooned the ship like hellish decorations. Fire danced from their crucified limbs. Their hair flamed. The ship came gliding past, close enough to the north wall of the fort for them to see the victims' blistering skin, their melting faces.

Sabinus gripped the wall.

"God's teeth," muttered Knuckles, "that's worthy of a show in the arena, that is."

Tatullus had his vinestick in his hand in a flash, and struck Knuckles such a blow across the back of his head as would have cracked the skull of a lesser man. Knuckles gasped and reeled and staggered, more bow-legged than ever, his eyes rolling up to the whites before collapsing against the low battlements of the wall. Shaking, in a cold sweat, he sucked in deep lungfuls, gradually letting the pain recede and his vision return.

Tatullus never raised his voice. There was something in this iron-cold centurion that chilled even Sabinus. "Those were your comrades you see tortured and crucified below you, soldier. Talk of them with respect."

Knuckles, still hanging onto the battlement as if it were a rock in rapids and he were a drowning man, pale and nearly sick with the blow, managed a slow nod. "Sir."

Other soldiers gathered from along the walls to stare aghast. Some had their arms round each other's shoulders as the torture ship passed by. Four of them stood in a line, silent witnesses to the spectacle, like gladiators sum-moning esprit de corps before the coming doom. Two brothers, their father and their uncle. Local boys, part-time farmers, the VIIth in all its glory. Soon they would be fighting for their lives.

Another spar on the ship came crashing down to the deck in a flurry of sparks, another piece fell free and sizzled out in the black water. But even that sound was muffled by the mist and the night.

Now they would at last be tested, perhaps beyond endurance. They would fight for themselves and each other, for their families and their farmsteads. They had never even seen Rome or Constantinople. The emperor was far away, the empire a thing of the mind. Today they would fight merely for survival. No reinforcements.

The torture ship passed on eastward, its ghastly light dimming into the darkness. They imagined it finally drifting down through the shadowy gorge of the Iron Gates, reduced by then to a smoking, blackened wreck, to be dashed to pieces there in the whitewater narrows. Bits of peat-black timber and spar washing up on the strand at Ratiaria. Blackened bones.

Away to the west, the drums ceased.

The oldest of the four men turned to Sabinus as he passed by. "Are we finished?"

The legate paused, then laid a hand on the man's shoulder—an unheard-of familiarity.

"No, man," he said gently, "not by a long way. No barbarian force has ever taken a Roman legionary fort. Not in seven long centuries."

"To your stations again now, lads," said Tatullus behind him. "Storm coming."

Another soldier came running, sweating in the torchlight.

"Sir! Man below the west gate. I think he comes to parley."

They hurried down to the first level and along the battlements to the west gate. Sabinus gazed out from the tower.

Under the louring walls of Viminacium sat a single man on a dusty skew-bald pony. He was naked to the waist but for a purely decorative breastplate of thin bones, and wore no armor but for a close-fitting helmet that shone in the moonlight.

He must be insane.

The man looked up and fixed his glittering eyes on Sabinus, never doubting he was in command. He looked like he needed sleep. His face was deeply grooved and ashen gray, with a wisp of an old man's chinbeard, yet his yellowish eyes still burned. He did not seem to raise his voice, yet on the tower they heard each word distinctly.

"I do not come to parley," he said. "I do not come for your words. I come for your lives."

Sweat beaded down Sabinus's spine. He felt cold. How had the Hun heard them talk of parleying? How had he known? There was something about their visitor not of this earth. Was this Attila himself?

Close behind him, Sabinus became aware, the Armenian, the one who called himself Count Arapovian, was swiftly and silently nocking an arrow to his bow. A short, powerful eastern bow, a compound bow, like the Scythians themselves used. The legate did not stop him.

It all happened in the blink of an eye. The warlord on his pony remained quite still. Arapovian stepped forward with practiced swiftness took aim and loosed his bowstring. In the same instant, another arrow came out of the darkness, a single arrow. It arced through the night and struck home. The Armenian gasped and stepped back, dropping his bow clattering to the floor and clutching his forearm. The arrowhead had punched straight between the two bones of his arm and out the other side, so neatly that he barely bled—not until the arrow-shaft was drawn, at any rate.

It had struck him just a moment before he let fly his own. A hair's breadth of movement, compounded by distance, and Arapovian's arrow had hit the ground beside the hooves of that motionless skewbald pony.

Arapovian fell back against the wall.

"Get him to the medics," growled Tatullus.

He was helped down the steps.

"Then get him back here," called Tatullus after them.

"I will return," came the Armenian's voice. "Don't doubt it."

"And no one else try anything."

As if in commentary on what had just occurred, having seen or foreseen everything, the unmoving man down below said, "Fools. The blood of my people is on your heads. I come to destroy you."

From behind his back he drew a spear, bare but for a single black feather, and drove it into the hard ground before the fort. Then he pulled his workaday mount round and walked it away into the darkness.

Sabinus and his *primus pilus* exchanged looks. Tatullus rested his hand on his sword hilt. Now they knew what manner of man their enemy was.

Until they had seen the fire ship, and the man whose mind had dreamed up such an atrocity, Sabinus had still held out hope of imminent rescue. He had thought of ordering out the boats if all the land routes were taken. They could have rowed downriver to Ratiaria, to Marcianopolis, have the whole thirty-thousand-strong Eastern Field Army here in a few days. . . . But the fire ship told them—among other things—"We have control of the river, too. You will never get through."

The Huns and their Attila: mastermind of panic, conjuror of hysteria. This barbarian warlord with the mind of a fox. Piling on the pressure, drawing out their deepest fears, destroying their reason and their resolve with monsters and threats both real and imaginary.

The abandoned town of Viminacium within its paltry curtain walls began to burn. No citizens fled from the flames. They had all gone already. The remnant VII Legion in their fortress were utterly alone.

Except for their sworn enemies round about. They could hear faint yowls and shrieks of triumph. In the town the savages were looting anything not yet on fire, and outside the town they were ransacking the chapel in the cemetery. They smashed apart an elaborate grave and prised open the lead sarcophagus within, to steal from the dead a gorgeous cloth threaded with gold. The corpse, the crumbling body of a young man, they left hanging grotesquely half out of the battered sarcophagus. Other corpses were strewn more widely about, so that it looked as if the dead had come back to life. As if they had awoken in the night and danced themselves to death again by moonlight, to collapse again half putrid where they danced.

Emerging as if from the very heart of destruction, there came again the low, monotonous beat of war. The witch Enkhtuya sitting cross-legged somewhere in the outer darkness, hammering a drumskin with a bone, murmuring low.

Weave the crimson web of war,
Raise the bloody banners high,
Make it as it was before,
All men must fight, all men must die.

Horror covers all the heath,
Clouds of carnage blot the sun,
Sisters, weave the web of death,
Sisters cease, the work is done.

Sabinus nodded to his *optio,* gave orders for the standard-bearers to report, and returned to his *principia* to put on his armor, and to take one last look around.

One last look. The phrase echoed in his thoughts, but he preferred not to analyze it.

They marched swiftly through the small but elegantly colonnaded court-yard, into the atrium, past the triclinium. Strange to glimpse the comfortable couches still ranged about in there, as if waiting for the next modest banquet with local dignitaries. But the legate's accommodation was no longer in the best repair. Starlings had made their nests under the eaves, and frogs had colo-nized the cellars. Soldierly duty kept the place clean and tidy, but its neglect could not be concealed. No fashionably attired dinner guests visited now, few inhabited the frontier towns. All had migrated south toward Constantinople to make themselves and their families rich with courtly patronage. Senatorial families dreamed of imperial donatives and sinecures, ignorantly at ease in their plush villas in Naissus, Marcianopolis, Adrianople, or the gleaming golden capital itself. The old provincial dutifulness was gone. Only the poor paid taxes, they joked. And how it showed. But the rich would pay for their selfishness in time. In a currency red as blood.

As Tatullus had said: "Storm coming."

7

THE TOWERS

After his *optio* had strapped on his armor, Sabinus took his splendid helmet with its nodding plumes, then led his standard-bearers into the chapel. There stood the central shrine, the eagle, the bull ensign and the lesser centurial banners. Beneath the shrine, beneath the altar itself, lay the fort's strong room, packed with stamped gold ingots from the mines of Mons Aurea.

One of centurial banner bearers shook so badly that he nearly dropped the staff as Sabinus handed it to him. A mere lad, sixteen or seventeen, a once-weekly shaver, scarce dry from the egg. His name was Julianus. Sabinus spoke to him gravely but not unkindly. "Hold it steady, lad," he said evenly. "Yes, we are cut off. Yes, there are a lot of them. But this is a still a legionary fort. It's stood for four centuries now, against barbarians just as vile as these." He told the lad—he told all of them—to hate their enemies. "Think of your families. Think of what will become of them . . . and swear hatred of the barbarians," he said. "Your hatred will drive out fear, and then you will fight like lions."

As the legionary bull standard was lowered and passed out of the door of the chapel into the night, he gave it a brief, idolatrous bow.

Alone he visited the hospital and saw that all was in good order. The medics stood to attention. Only four patients in there now, one clearly dying. Another with leg sores, being cleaned up nicely by hard-working maggots collected fresh from horse dung. Poultices, bandages and dressings, copper pots steaming on the stoves, jars of gray-green willow-leaf infusion for wounds.

He resumed his place on the west tower beside Tatullus. The centurion did not stir. A fortress of a man.

The waiting was always the worst. Oh, let it begin soon.

But they were kept waiting. They waited all night until the dawnlight came up behind them.

A low morning mist, thickest over the silent river to the north. Smoke sitting heavily over the lost town, where it had once stood proud on the green summer plain. Smoke slowly drifting eastward toward the fort, mingling with wraiths of mist in the cold shadows of the north wall.

All night long the stars had burned, and, out on the plain around, myriad campfires like a starry floor. Their enemy, of course, but a strange feeling of company. Then toward dawn, with the temperature still dropping sharply from the warm day, the mist had risen from the river and the marshy meadows round about and thickened toward sunrise. Now it lay dense and milk white around them, Sabinus on the tower like the captain on the deck of some ghost ship abandoned in remote uncharted seas.

"This visibility is bad," he said.

"Bad for us," said Tatullus pointedly. "Not for our attackers."

The attack must come soon. The soldiers on the walls stamped their feet, blew into cupped hands. How their tensed bones ached in their chill coats of mail. The mist clung to them, beaded dewdrops on cold metal.

All wore their heavy helmets through the long night so that their necks ached. Leather straps cut into throats. Feet were white cold. The wall artillery was primed and loaded. The swords were ground sharp. The world was silent around them. No birds sang.

On the northwest tower, a legionary gazed out toward the river, trying to judge whether the mist was thinning in the rising sun, and how fast. Still no sight of the opposite bank. Then he frowned. Something was wrong. The mist was darkening, close to. Shadows moving within it. Over the tributary channel, just along the wall. Something was happening. Coming nearer.

The chain was across the entrance back by the river watchtowers, wasn't it?

They'd talked about the waterways last night. Apparently, the refugees had reported the invaders using horse transporters of some sort: rafts. But if any bone-headed barbarians seriously tried attacking downriver they'd get in a right bloody mess. The emperor chain would be across the Iron Gorge, with auxiliaries stationed on the cliffs above, and the marines of the Danube Fleet ready to row out of Ratiaria if necessary and finish them off. There was no chance there.

But presumably their plan, assuming they had a plan, was to take Viminacium and then head on south down the imperial trunk road to Naissus and the rich pickings of Sardica. Like they'd ever get that far. Not with a legionary fortress in the way, and their knowledge of missile technology extending as far as an arrow dipped in flaming tar. The walls of Viminacium should be able to withstand a few of those.

But now . . .

"Sir?" he said to his decurion.

"Hm?" The junior officer had his helmet off, resting it on the top of the battlements, polishing it with his woolen neckerchief, so that the first arrow punched straight into his head. His helmet rolled over the wall and fell silently and he slumped forward across the wall.

The soldier opened his mouth to shout in terror but instead gargled blood as another arrow passed up through his throat and into his skull. Still scrabbling at his throat, he stumbled and rolled down the stone steps to the battlements.

The artillerymen stared around, bewildered.

Then one of them saw what was happening. Out of the mist were coming high-sided boats, drifting slowly down the tributary channel. No, not the Danube Fleet from Ratiaria, come to the rescue. These were other boats entirely, captured from God knows where, moving slow and serene as great swans in the white summer mist. Each one was filled with archers, ready to rain down arrows on the fortress walls.

"Enemy at the north wall!"

But along the west wall they already had their own concerns.

Sabinus heard his centurion grunt. He himself took a step forward in fascinated horror, his whole body trembling. He saw but did not immediately understand. He reached out to steady himself.

The barbarians had no siege craft. He said it to himself again. The barbarians had no siege craft.

Tatullus spoke for him. "What the hell is this, civil war?" Then ducked and took cover as a single arrow clattered into the stone beside him. Covering fire for the—

Sabinus did not duck. He stamped his heavy sandals, the hobnails thudding on the thick wooden planks. This was no dream.

This was real. And this was the day he would die.

The mist cleared a little more. There was the lone horseman's spear from last night, decorated with the single black feather, still stuck in the ground before the west gate. A cool, light wind blew, a very light wind, and the mist drifted away off the wet meadows toward the river. Except they could not see the wet meadows. They were covered in horsemen.

At their head sat a group of long-haired, half-naked, tattooed Hun noblemen, generals, perhaps, gold gleaming around their arms and necks; and another man of different race, fair with close cropped or thinning hair. At the head of them in turn, gazing up at the walls of Viminacium, smiling cheerfully, sword dangling loosely in his right hand as if ready to ride up and attack the fortress with bare steel, was their leader. The one from the night before. Attila.

"Sir, boats passing along the north wall. Men taking fire."

Sabinus ignored him. What was emerging before their horror-stricken eyes out of the mist to the west was everything now. For it was not the vast horde of savagely armed and decorated horse warriors standing before them that chilled the blood, so much as the weaponry they brought with them. Against all intelligence and expectation. Among the horde, still half veiled in thin mist, stood two huge wooden siege towers on great solid wheels, two mighty torsion-spring onagers with boulders already set back in their basins, a bronze-headed battering ram expertly protected under a moveable steep-sided tortoise of strong wooden planks and iron plates, and, scattered among the horsemen, a number of other smaller artillery pieces, sling machines and ballistas. Things that barbarians should not have.

Around the onagers was a busy commerce of men and oxen and wagons, and the distant creaking of ropes and winches and leather slings. Soon would come the nerve-shredding, ascending screech of twisted torsion springs tuned to screaming pitch, and then the snap and thud of release, the loosed beam flying up and hitting the padded crossbeam, and the boulder hurtling through the air toward the walls of Viminacium.

"Now we've got a fight on our hands," murmured Tatullus.

Sabinus shook off his trance of horror. "Turn the catapults!" he roared. "Wall artillery! Every unit on the towers. Do it *now*!"

Suddenly the U-shaped bastions were alive with panic and the noise of the light wall artillery, the ballistas and the crossbow machines, being scraped round on their solid iron frames and ranged for the initial shots. Windlasses winding up a ferocious amount of energy in the thick reels of sinew, cranked back with mighty force on a long wooden lever and ratchet, men's arms bulging, the sinew stretching tighter and tighter still, the high-pitched creak as it was wound back and back more, the bowstring drawn back and a heavy iron-headed bolt laid in the groove before it. When the trigger was released, all that pent-up energy discharged the bolt with lethal force. One bolt was good, but a whole bank of such machines discharging their bolts in a volley could bring down an entire line of cavalry, dragging down those in the rear in a bewildered jumble. The Huns would not have encountered such a thing before.

"Long fire bolts loaded! Buckets of tar on every bastion. Light 'em up!"

The *pedites,* the military runners, ran.

"And bales, rocks, overturned wagons, *anything,* stacked up inside the west gate. We won't be using it for a while."

There weren't enough men.

"The question is," said Sabinus, looking out again, "those onagers: do they know how to use them?"

And then out of the mist, unrangeable, unreachable, the onagers started firing. They heard the muffled shock of massive beam clunking up into padded crossbeam, and the eerie, almost inaudibly low hum of the great missiles gliding in low, expertly aimed for the foundation stones of the fort. Each of the two machines required precisely one ranging shot. A big boulder fell short and slewed to a halt in the dust, its weight and force such that the ground creased up in wavelets before it. Sabinus waited, barely breathing. The second boulder hit the southwest tower a minute later. The sound seemed to come out of the bowels of the earth, like subterranean thunder. Men staggered atop, clutching their spears.

"Question answered," said Tatullus stonily. "Yes, they know how to use them."

The onagers halted. Out on the plain the vast Hun war machine was beginning to roll forward again. And the Huns, ignorant and unlettered barbarians though they were, their very language no more than a series of unwriteable growls and grunts, knew better than to try and use onagers at the same time as their own lines were advancing in front of them. Yes, they knew exactly what they were doing. They must have formed an alliance with some power skilled in siege craft. Who? Could it be treachery? Master General Aëtius had been close to the Huns as a boy. Could he have allied with his old friends, to conquer the Eastern Empire for himself?

But no. Not Aëtius. Then who?

Huge solid wooden wheels creaked and groaned under the inertia of their giant loads. Oxen were lashed beneath their wooden canopies. Squeals and rumbles of animal, man, and machine horribly commingled. And coming to the fore the two siege towers. The braying of war trumpets, thunderous mounted kettledrums, each blow with a bone drumstick like a punch in the guts, the crashing of Hunnish *zils* or cymbals, the earth itself trembling.

Sabinus bellowed another order: "All noncombatants to the dungeons, all current prisoners to the execution dungeon."

A soldier blanched. "Families, sir? Children?"

Sabinus looked at him. "You have family?"

"A sister, sir, in VI Barrack, and her two young ones."

"Then believe me, man, you'll thank me soon enough." He looked back over the plain. "The dungeons are the best place for them."

On the battlements just below, an archer drew back his bowstring, though the oncoming horde were still far out of range. It was Arapovian again, the impossible, indefatigable Armenian, his self-possession absolute amid the noise and panic of the artillery. His left arm, his bow arm, had been tightly bandaged by the medics, but there still showed through on his forearm a small circle of deep dark blood. The man's olive-skinned aquiline face was beaded with droplets of sweat but expressionless. No order had been given to fire, but Arapovian was clearly a kind of freelance in his own estimation, and not subject to the orders of ordinary mortals. Sabinus watched, intrigued despite himself. Even as Arapovian pulled back his bowstring, Sabinus thought he could see that small circle of blood spreading. What it must have cost him. His biceps bunched as he drew back the sinew string of that lethal eastern bow, sinuously curved and then recurved at each end. The arrowhead was ablaze with a blob of pitch. He sighted along the arrow and fired.

Other soldiers turned in surprise to watch its arc.

The arrow struck the ground at the foot of the Hunnish spear, which still stood like an insult and a judgment before the west gate, its black feather bobbing in the light breeze. Then it went out. There was wisp of smoke, then nothing. He had fired too hard, the burning arrowhead had buried itself in the dusty ground and been snuffed out. An unfortunate omen. But there came another wisp of smoke and the pitch blazed again. A lean tongue of flame licked up the Hun spearshaft and it began to burn.

On the towers, the relentless activity of the ballistas and sling machines faltered as men paused to watch. Let 'em, thought Sabinus. Moments like this were worth an extra cohort.

It was an astonishing shot, first time.

Now arrow shaft and spear shaft burned together. After only a few seconds the tar-fueled flames reached the long black feather dancing on top and reduced it to a few motes of ash. What had seemed like so powerful a symbol of intimidation had vanished in a lick of flame, a puff of wind.

He was an impossible one, this Armenian. But not altogether stupid. A great cheer went up from the ramparts. Arapovian neither turned, acknowledged it nor reacted in any way.

"Stuck-up son of a bitch," growled Knuckles nearby.

He deserved a decoration for that flamboyant act. Sabinus called over to him, "When this is over, you'll walk away with a *corona obsidionalis*."

"When this is over," said Arapovian, never shifting his gaze from the approaching horde, "I'll be glad to walk away with my life."

He nocked another arrow to his bow and rested his injured arm on the battlements and waited.

The enemy rolled nearer.

They could see now that the Hun siege towers were serious constructions, frontages padded with huge sewn bolsters of rawhide, stuffed with riverweed and horsehair and thoroughly soaked against fire arrows. They rolled in unison toward the west wall, one to the left and one to the right. Good dispositon. The supporting lines of horse warriors slowed and stopped, still out of effective range.

Sabinus bellowed to his artillery, "Concentrate on the towers!"

To the north, report came of the drifting boats on the slow-moving tributary laying down a deadly rain of arrows. Anchoring themselves there with

supreme confidence for the long stay. So Sabinus gave the order to clear the
north walls and abandon them. The water would save them there.

From the eastern gate, the Porta Praetoria, leading down the Via Lederatea
to Ratiaria, only the empty road. No dust cloud. Shadows of buzzards in the
morning sky. No help coming.

The two men on the west gate tower, the legate and his *primus pilus*, regarded the approaching towers steadily. Then, "You see what I see?" said Tatullus softly.

"I do," said Sabinus, and he gave a faint smile. "Amateurs."

Though the massive towers looked impressive enough, the Huns, or their
enslaved builders and carpenters, perhaps deliberately, had failed to give them
a low enough skirt. The four big wooden wheels on which each tower rolled
forward were hopelessly exposed.

"Let's get 'em in close first," said the legate. "False shooting to start."

He quit the west gate tower and made for the southwest. "Unit III, get
your slingshots down! Decurion, lower the trajectory. I want flat slings hitting the head of the tower. Slingshots on the level. I want the towers under
bombardment at two hundred yards. What angle's that?"

"Around twelve degrees from the horizontal, sir."

"Then give the order."

"I could do you five degrees, sir, hit 'em at only a hundred yards, but harder
still."

Sabinus shook his head. "Too damn near. Give it ten degrees, then."

The machines were ratcheted.

"And never mind the whole tower, just take out the head. We'll fire up the
rest."

He ordered the same for the northwest tower, giving the unit there a rapid
inspection. They had two big crossbow machines and two iron-frame slings.
He gave calm words of advice to the young unit commander, then returned to
take his stand in the western gate tower. Face on to the enemy.

At two hundred yards the first slingshots and bolts were loosed against the
towers. There was a satisfyingly curt brutality to the flight. Long-distance shots
might look impressive as they arced up high and fell over half a mile away, but
most of the impulsive power was lost by then, and the missile traveled so
slowly—as much as ten seconds from shot to landfall—that there was ample
time for the enemy to see it coming and dodge it. But under Sabinus's orders

there was the low, vibrating twang of horsehair rope, the snap of torsion springs, the smack of sling beam, and only a second or two later the weighty lead and stone slingshots flew out almost horizontal from the machines and thumped violently into the flanks of the approaching towers. The well-trained artillerymen bent down and adjusted the ratchets a fraction more. The nerve-shredding creak of torsion springs, further shots. Satisfyingly loud claps of impact, the cracking report as balls and bolts hit their target. Not much damage to the great towers yet, though, until a lucky strike passed straight through one of the narrow slits in the tower and a scream from within suggested a direct hit.

The towers weren't going to be brought down, nor even knocked headless. Already the great wickerwork drawbridges were being lowered, like dark and hungry jaws opening upon the battlements of the fort.

Sabinus waited a little longer, judging the moment, hands clenched on the wall. Then, finally, "Now! Lower units, hit the wheels!"

With instant discipline, the artillery units on the first level of the towers set up a punishing crossfire, hitting the wheels of the siege engines at the widest angle they could. Medium-weight sling balls and heavy iron-tipped ballista bolts cut across each other's trajectories from the corner towers before slamming in low. Almost immediately one good shot chipped off the edge of a front wheel.

Tatullus nodded and murmured, "It's deliberate, a bad build. Cunning. But pity the poor sods when their Hun masters realize it."

Sabinus said nothing. There would be too many dead to pity by today's end.

He ordered a single eight-man unit of his heavy cavalry to stand ready inside the south gate with all but one of the braces drawn back ready. Tatullus glanced at him.

More careful adjustments to the arc. The pounding was relentless. Within the towers the slave-driven captives moaned, sweating and heaving at the drive posts. And there came a deeper moaning, too. A bellowing . . .

"*Amateurs!*" said Sabinus again, smacking a fist into his palm. "Listen to that!"

He was right. Against all the rules, the Huns had roped up oxen inside the siege towers to provide the drive power. It might have seemed a good idea in the cool, rational calm before the battle started, but battles didn't stay that way. And roped-up oxen could start causing no end of trouble to their own side once the missiles started piling in, men started screaming, noxious tar fires started burning out of control. . . .

Sabinus gave the order at once. "Fire and tar, get some flames around them! That'll soon have the brutes breaking free."

The tower coming in on the right stubbornly refused to burn, but curls of smoke soon told a different story from the other. And as soon as they smelled the smoke, sure enough, the oxen within began to bellow and panic and heave themselves sideways in their yokes. Terrible studded flails fell across the creatures' bony backs, but the maddened pair, one already feeling the heat of the flames on its tawny flank, only wrenched away the harder, their fear of fire far greater than any whip. Both of them giving a simultaneous lurch in chance harmony was enough to break one of the yoke straps so that they staggered awkwardly and one tripped to its knees where it could no longer move. The entire tower was wrenched round to one side, the captives inside heaving desperately at the drive poles, naked and blinded with their own sweat, their backs beribboned by the long whips wielded by the small team of Hun warriors walking their horses close behind them in the shelter of the tower. But to no avail. The unbalanced tower, one wheel rim already chipped and dragging down in the earth, was pulled further out of kilter by the miscreant oxen and suddenly the unprotected flank of the great tower and the two huge, uncurtained wooden wheels were exposed to direct Roman attack.

"Okay!" roared Sabinus, the infectious note of victory in his voice. "Artillery units: both towers—take 'em out and fire 'em up! I want the wheels in splinters and the towers in cinders! *Go!*"

Pedites communicated the order to the corner towers. A further flurry of resolute activity and soon all eight machines on the bastions were venting their missiles in low, short flights against the unprotected wheels. A sling ball or a bolt was hitting the nearest every five seconds in a ruthless rhythm. Splinters flew from the rim, one of the centreboards split, the axle boss itself gave off a fine spray of sparks as an iron-tipped bolt clanged off it.

"Bull's-eye!" yelled the artillerymen, guffawing.

"Waste of time!" roared Sabinus. "Split the boards!"

In came more shots. In the shelter of the faltering tower, the Hun horsemen in their fury had just whipped one captive to death, hanging still shackled from the drive pole shiny with his own blood.

But still more ruthlessness was called for. If they were going to beat off this horde, no quarter could be given. Not for a second.

Sabinus brought a crossbow squadron up close. *Pedites* dragged up more chests of bolts behind.

"There's a gang of 'em behind, driving it forward. Draw a line on the back of the tower. Any glimpse of one of those naked bastards and you take him out. But not until you see him. I want a dead shot off every bolt you fire."

The crossbowmen crouched at the battlements, squat bows of chestnut and ash cranked back and tight with explosive power. One Hun pony stepped back from the shelter of the siege tower a little too far and promptly lost the use of a rear leg. It fell back and tilted, the rider rolled in the dust. Three more bolts from the battlements hit him instantly. The other Hun horsemen now crammed together for shelter in the lea of the creaking and damaged tower.

All the while Sabinus kept one eye long-range on the Hunnish cavalry. They were approaching again, slow and orderly but still a long way off. For some reason that stone-faced warlord—he could pick him out clearly enough still amid the dust clouds of twenty thousand tramping hooves—was letting the towers do what they could alone. Maybe he had no great faith in them. Not yet. He was prepared to let them be destroyed, so that he could watch from a distance, and learn.

The towers might be done for, but the battle was far from won. Those ten thousand horsemen with their murderous rain of arrows would come soon enough.

Finally a slingshot, or possibly a lucky double shot striking simultaneously, hit the already splintered wheel and one of the central planks was knocked out completely, hanging free. The entire tower seemed to hesitate for a moment, gave a slow, creaking lurch, the axletree craning and trembling. Then the damaged wheel collapsed abruptly into its constituent planks, shattered back to the boss, and the clumsy structure shuddered, leaned at a precipitous angle, and came to uncertain rest on the corner where the wheel had been. Within, one of the tormented oxen was almost strangled in its yoke as it was lifted off the ground by the counterpull. It roared and kicked out, and the rest of the broad leather yoke straps finally tore asunder. The terrified beast managed to squeeze itself round in its narrow stall and erupted, bellowing, out of the back of the tower into the melee of livid and bewildered Hun horsemen. The ox charged through them, oblivious of a last few whiplashes, and stumbled away. The men milled back and broke, and immediately a further ruthless volley of crossbow bolts from the battlements drove into them. At least half were hit. The tattered remainder turned and fled back to their own ranks in disgrace. Slow flames licked up the side of the broken tower, and, up above, the light wickerwork drawbridge roared. Within, the shackled captives were too exhausted to scream.

"Now the other one!" roared Sabinus, banging his fists victoriously on the wall. "No slacking. Get those ballistas loaded up afresh. Pedites, keep running. I want to see you sweat blood!"

He gave it a short while, then halted the artillery again with a downward slice of his hand. "Crossbowmen, stay trained. Anyone comes down from the tower, take 'em. Guards, open the gate! Cavalry"—he grinned and swung his big, meaty arm forward through the air—"it's all yours."

The last brace was drawn, the heavy twin gates swung back easily on their huge greased hinges and the eight heavy cavalrymen drove their big mounts forward furiously, from stationary into canter and then flat gallop in the blink of an eye.

The rear pair of lancers split off and disappeared behind the back of the burning siege tower. Now they really would be *clibanarii,* "boiler boys," their long mailcoats and solid bronze helms as hot as ovens. But they did their stuff, hacking and levering at the shackles in the gloom, gagging on the dense smoke, fighting off the clawing and blinded captives even as they worked so hard for their release.

At last the wretched, beaten, slave-driven creatures staggered free and stumbled, still half blinded, back toward the open gate.

All the while Sabinus kept up his double vision. At any moment that stone-faced warlord might release a company of his lethal archers to gallop across the plain and descend on the little pack of heavy cavalry. But he still stayed his hand. In fact, the Hun lines seemed to have halted altogether, still a good half a mile off, maybe more. Not necessarily good news, in the long term. They were watching. Learning.

The second tower to their right, barely scathed yet, lightly smoldering, was still rolling forward when the Hun horsemen behind it suddenly realized what was happening. Eight of them, armed with flails and lassos, bows still across their backs, heard the approaching thunder and looked around to see six, then eight, iron-mailed, bronze-helmeted lancers at full gallop almost upon them, long ashen lances couched low. It was the first time these Hun warriors had ever encountered anything like a Roman heavy cavalry charge, and they were powerless. They pulled their mounts round, heeled them into a rearing gallop, spurted forward—and the iron wave slammed into their flank. The light Hun ponies were punched sideways and thrown clear of the ground, their hooves scrabbling in the air, before crashing back winded and half broken. Riders were flung free, one in a spectacular arc through the dusty air, back concave, until he fell to earth again and was immediately despatched by single thrust of a long cavalry sword.

Not one Hun arrow was fired, not one curved yataghan was drawn, not a single battle cry was given. The shock and force of the charge flattened them like a stormwind. The iron soldiers wielded their swords in silence, and eight warriors soon lay dead. The commander, a captain called Malchus, reined in and pushed back his helmet and scanned the middle distance, sweat coursing, raven hair plastered to his brow, his vision blurred. He blinked hard. At any moment, the savages would ride down in vengeance . . . but no, the Hun lines hadn't moved. So they roped up the surviving ponies, freed the shackled captives, slew the two ungovernable oxen where they roared in their yokes and then tethered the cadavers behind them, and smashed the rear axle tree of the tower. Malchus kicked his horse back and sliced his arm down toward the ruined tower. Let the fire come down.

They rode back at a strong trot, dragging the dead beasts, leaving the flames to finish the work of destruction.

Riotous cheers went up from the battlements.

"Roast ox tonight!"

"Let's hear it for the Boiler Boys!"

The south gate was safely slammed shut and bolted, and Malchus bounded up the steps to the legate's platform, helmet couched beneath his arm.

"Second tower out of action, sir!"

The Hun line did not stir. A gentle breeze, black banners, no movement. Stone-faced thousands. A terrifying enemy, so silent and disciplined.

But Sabinus felt good. A stir of hope. Now the enemy had seen how Romans could still fight.

They waited.

On the tower to Sabinus's right, one of the tar barrels used to set fire to the siege tower started burning out of control, puffing up big clouds of black, oily smoke and then, without warning; roaring into flame. Men fell back from the intense heat, shielding their eyes.

"Damp that fucking thing down *now*!" roared Tatullus, striding over. "Pedites, get buckets of water up here!"

It blazed furiously. The water arrived too slowly. Tatullus sent more men, including Knuckles, to bring up two massive iron-bound pails on a wooden yoke. But it got worse. Flames licked up, flourished, shook off any buckets of water thrown at them, spat them back in clouds of burning steam, and then suddenly engulfed the open-sided wooden roof, the only protection the men there had from falling arrows.

Sabinus roared further orders. And then, with his double vision still working, he saw a stir. On the plain below, the warlord with the eyes of a hawk, and the heart of a hawk, too, turned his head. If Sabinus had been any closer, he'd have seen his yellow eyes gleam. But he saw his signal well enough. His copper-banded arm stretched out, and a little band of horse warriors began to gallop in.

"What in the name of Light. . . ?"

There was another surprise. Two of them dragged a little piece of field artillery. The rest broke into their lethal circling gallop and began to fire arrows onto the burning tower, through the flames. The men up there, choking on smoke and blinded by the rebellious flames, starting taking hits as well. The protective wooden roof began to sag and collapse.

A second group of warriors reined in some hundred yards off, set up their field machine with unbelievable speed and efficiency, and started sending in hard, fist-sized rocks at the wall of the burning tower. They re-angled the beam and the next shot came curving in leanly over the wall and smacked straight into the side of the flaming tar barrel. They were trying to demolish it. Molten tar would run all over the place, the wooden boards burn, and that tower, that essential corner bastion, would be as good as finished.

The crossbow units started taking them out one by one, but every time they scored a hit, another tattooed warrior came galloping in and took his place.

Damn that warlord and his ruthless cunning. Every stumble, every weakness or misfortune, would be exploited.

Two, three more auxiliaries trying to damp out the flames were shot through. One fell forward into the burning tar itself. He was dragged out by the legs, dead. Two more still tried to damp it. One fell back choking on foul smoke, lungs scorched. The situation was getting desperate. Even Tatullus seemed momentarily lost.

"Fuck this," rumbled Knuckles, shoving his way through. "I'm gettin' a headache. That barrel's gotta go."

He squatted down and put his shoulder to the edge of the blazing barrel, tipped it so it leaned against the low stone wall, slid his meaty hands beneath the rim and then, slowly, unbelievably, began to stand straight again. The barrel scraped up the wall. He peered blearily through the pitchy smoke to the ground below.

"Right, which one of you bloody hooligans wants this on his head?"

He gave one final, terrific heave, and the barrel, blazing more furiously than ever, the very spars beginning to darken into charcoal from within and disintegrate, was sent over the side. No direct hit—that would have been too lucky—but it crashed to the earth with the force of an explosion, spitting burning splinters and flecks of blazing tar into the rumps of two or three ter-rified horses, which reared and then rolled to the ground, screaming, to extin-guish their burning hides. The stench of singed horsehair filled the air. The Hun riders slipped free, staggered to their feet in a daze, looked around—and one, then two were struck through with arrows. They pitched forward and died. The third had begun to run, a fellow warrior galloping in close to scoop him up onto the back of his own sturdy little mount. But another arrow hit him square in the back and he dropped down dead. His would-be rescuer wheeled dismissively and galloped out of range again.

It was Arapovian, shooting without mercy from the battlements. He ducked as a riposte of Hun arrows clattered around him. Then the horsemen below galloped into a full retreat. The little field machine was dragged away behind.

"Now douse the roof, what's left of it!" shouted Sabinus. "Clean up that tower and get it back in order. Jump to it!"

Auxiliaries ran.

Knuckles shambled over to the Armenian and hit him on the back.

"Not bad, that," he growled.

Arapovian turned to look at him, saying nothing. His eyes widened a little. Knuckles's complexion was charcoal. Half an eyebrow was burned away. His shaggy fringe was noticeably shorter than before, and his hair appeared to be smoldering. The Armenian glanced down and saw worse: those giant, spade-like hands were badly blistered and seeping blood. He silently produced a little bottle from within his robes and passed it to him.

"One mouthful," he said. "Armenian brandy. The finest."

Knuckles grunted and obediently took the delicate little bottle, looking like a giant holding a lady's thimble. Sipped delicately. It was good.

"That's it, is it?"

Arapovian took the bottle back. "That's it." He pushed the cork in and stowed the bottle back in his robes. "We're going to need more later."

" 'We,' is it now?"

Arapovian looked back over the plains of war. Perhaps the shadow of a smile passed over his aquiline features. He cranked his injured left arm up and down, blood oozing through the bandages again, but his face betraying no hint of pain. Then he nocked another arrow to the bow and waited.

Knuckles made his way back along the battlements, until Tatullus stood in his way.

The centurion regarded him. "Not bad," he said, "for a deserter."

"Thank you kindly, Your Honor."

"Show me your hands."

Knuckles showed him, with commentary. "I don't need medical attention, sir, really I don't. I got a bit of a problem with doctors, the truth be told, ever since that time back in Colonia, when I caught a nasty dose off of a certain young lady of nevertheless very obligin' disposition, and the doctor there made me—"

"To the hospital," said Tatullus. "That's an order."

Looking anxious for the first time that day, Knuckles made his slow and reluctant way down to the hospital.

He needn't have worried. The legionary doctor, a young and apparently diffident fellow from Thessaly, knew his stuff. He larded Knuckles's hands with goose fat infused with garlic to prevent the blisters becoming putrid. Stung like hell at first, but then, he had to admit, felt not so bad. Less like his palms were about to split open to the bone at any moment. Altogether very different from that unfortunate experience back in Colonia.

There was little time for self-congratulation.

Sabinus called Tatullus over and they watched as the Hun lines began to move forward again. The front ranks broke out into two huge loops, revolving circles of galloping archers spiraling in closer.

"Very pretty," muttered Tatullus.

Light cavalry? Arrows? Sabinus was puzzled. "What are they up to? You don't take a Roman fort with horsemen."

The Huns came wheeling in, and then as one body loosed a volley of arrows. They flew in high arcs, none of them aimed for anything in particular, just the fort in general. But there were thousands of them, darkening the sky like strange birds. The air was filled with iron sleet.

"Take cover!"

They came arcing down onto the wooden roofs of the towers, the exposed battlements, the scrambling men. Cries rang out. An unlucky crossbowman rolled down the narrow stone steps.

"Medics!"

"Another volley coming in!"

Some dashed for the towers, others huddled tight in against the low wall, shields pulled over heads and shoulders. Safe enough, for now, but rendered useless: pinned down, unable to return fire or lob so much as a rock. The artillery were ineffectual, too. The southwest unit tried to fire heavy bolts into the whirlwind of horse warriors, but were immediately picked off over the low battlements. Hun archers were able to take careful aim, even at full gallop, and fire flat shots straight through the narrow niches of the towers. There were distant screams. Christ, they were good. Sabinus had heard that a Hun warrior loosed his arrow only in the moment all four hooves of his horse were off the ground, to fly smooth and straight. Absurd, of course. But now he saw them in action. . . .

Another soldier, an artilleryman, fell forward over the wall. A Hun horseman immediately rode in and lassoed him, and dragged him away across the plain, yowling, the body swerving and flayed in the dust. Hector before the walls of Troy. Sabinus saw even the brute Knuckles cross himself at the sight, and prayed the soldier was dead already. He gave the order for the artillery to cease firing.

The iron sleet did not cease, and those who sent it into the air and over the walls did not cease moving. They made an impossible target. It was an appalling revelation. Two vast, galloping circles, well spaced, gracefully avoiding the twin obstacles of the ruined, still-smoldering siege towers. The Roman crossbow units crouched below in the guard towers, protected better at their narrow niches, did their professional best, but too few of their bolts struck anything but whirling dust. And there was a limit to how many bolts they had in store. Sabinus gave them the ceasefire, too, and pondered. No, you don't take a Roman fort with cavalry. But you clear its walls and neuter its defenders with arrow fire this intense.

Then the next stage of the battle became clear. The galloping horde below the walls had them immobilized, unlike previously with the towers. They stopped firing and galloped three or four hundred yards off again, out of effective range. They could be back in a flash once they'd reloaded their quivers from the wagons. If any of the defenders stood, tried to fire back, he would be stuck with a dozen arrows. With only five hundred good men to lose, that was bad arithmetic. Meanwhile, there was still another machine to come. And it was coming now.

They had a ram.

Sabinus thanked the stars the west gate was well bagged up. He ordered the *pedites* to bag up the south gate, too, in case they switched direction. The east gate they must keep free for their own cavalry.

As the *pedites* ran across to the gate, a detachment of horsemen came galloping in fast by the wall, and another slew of arrows went up and came down almost vertically. How did they know? The very ground of the fortress was studded with feathered barbarian arrows. So, too, were several *pedites*, struck down or screaming. Too many. Sabinus winced. The poor runners dragged bags and lumber into the shadow of the south gate as best they could, but still the arrows fell. Finally he gave the order for them to run for cover again. Of the twenty who had gone out, eight came back. He ground his teeth in anger.

The horsemen turned and wheeled away as one, like a flock of starlings, before they could take any damage. They vanished into the last of the morning mist, shot through with eastern sunlight.

8

THE RAM

The legate took a quick tour of the north wall. Out there on the river, not far from the shore, lay the stolen ships manned by Hun archers. He kept low. His north wall was secure. No need to man it. They couldn't get out that way, and flee downriver to Ratiaria. Nor could the Huns get in. He'd done the right thing to neglect it. The battle would take place at the south and west walls, and out on the flat plain. They didn't like water. And, he reflected, they wouldn't like mountain warfare, either.

Now here came the ram—an altogether more threatening proposition than the tall, unwieldy towers. It was a low-slung beam shaped from a single fir, with a brutish bronze head, and sheltered under what looked, from this distance, like an expertly shaped and crafted iron-plated tortoise. Already, Sabinus could see that this time the big wheels were entirely sheltered. Then he could see that they weren't wheels at all this time, but solid rollers made from single trunks of fir. Unbreakable.

No one came in support. He guessed that the Hun way was to force a breach in the gate, and then the cavalry, having waited safely out of range until then, would come zigzagging in like lightning.

The great engine turned and the monstrous ram under its armored shelter began to trundle toward them. The west gate was strong but not that strong, even with its double oak bars. Bagged up though it was, it needed more. Sabinus looked around in desperation.

"Every auxiliary off the walls. Stack up the west gate as much as you can, low angled. Find column drums, barrels of sand, anything. I want that gate rock solid. Move it!"

Without the auxiliaries, the legionaries ranged around the walls looked sparse indeed.

Tatullus grimaced. "We can't afford to lose any more."

On the tower roofs, one scorched and blackened but the other still intact for now, the artillery units worked tirelessly. Fat hanks of twisted skein were cranked back on mighty torsion springs. Barrels of tar burned low—carefully supervised. The long bow arms of the arrow-firing machines were taut in readiness. An iron-tipped bolt from one of those sleek machines could go through armor plate, if it struck at a right angle.

Then, to Sabinus's surprise, came the distant, dull clunk as the two Hun onagers kicked back and spewed forth their titanic loads again. The long, low hum of their missiles. And twin thunks into the dust. Activity out there, as they ranged again, shooting as their own men advanced. They must be damnably confident of their accuracy.

"Skilled?" he muttered. "Or stupid?"

Arapovian nearby interrupted. "The Huns have never been stupid. Ask King Chorsabian."

"Never heard of him."

"Quite," said Arapovian, tight lipped. "He had a kingdom once, in the Zagros Mountains. And then the Huns came."

Yet Sabinus had hope now. The ratio of his men to the enemy was ridiculous, but what did that matter? Rome had always been outnumbered by her enemies, and never dismayed by it. They were winning so far. No barbarian had ever taken a legionary fortress, and he was damned if his was going to be the first.

As for their siege craft, it was there, but wanting. Tatullus suggested they had formed an alliance with a bunch of Alan mercenaries, some wandering Iranian or Sarmatian people. Or perhaps renegade Vandals, a motley crowd of deserters. There had even been talk of the Huns forming a dark confederacy with King Genseric and his people in North Africa, who had learned so quickly the arts of both sailing and siege craft from their own enemies.

Perhaps. Well, let 'em come. The VII Legion was ready for the next wave, all five hundred of them—perhaps down to four eighty or four sixty now. The army of an entire people was besieging the fort—an entire nomad empire. And fate, or the gods, or whoever, had appointed the VIIth to fight them off on its own.

He called for another glass of wine, well watered.

Tatullus drank nothing.

The great shorn trunk of fir with its crude but doubtless brutally effective bronze head—no more than a lump of dully shining metal—reminded Sabinus of Knuckles's club. No elaborate carving of real rams' heads for this army on the move.

He ordered a first volley. The Roman arrows clattered uselessly off the iron plates of the tortoise—what else, at this angle?—and Sabinus raised a thick forearm to hold fire again. The ram came on.

The Hun onagers thunked again. This time the southwest tower took a huge hit near the base. The entire west wall shivered at the shock. Hell.

"Decurion! Gimme damage and bag it up!"

The second onager wasn't far off target, either, now.

Time to reply.

He ordered a couple of the sling machines to lob a few missiles in a high trajectory and drop them on the waiting Hun cavalry quarter of a mile off, just to keep them on their toes. The sling balls flew up and over in rainbow arcs, and the horsemen watched them coming and skittered aside. Some of the sling balls were painted pale blue so they wouldn't be so easily seen against the sky as they came, but the keen-eyed steppe warriors still followed them all. The sling balls fell to earth. He told the men to fire again.

What would a heavy cavalry charge do to those light, unarmored horsemen, though? An iron wedge punching into them at full gallop? Seeing what it did to the drivers behind the siege towers . . .

Here was the gang of Hun horsemen driving forward the ram tortoise. Their leader was a snake-haired, wild-eyed young fellow on a white gelding. He encouraged the captives with song, and a whip. Those dragging the ram against the fortress that had once been their greatest protection were, once again, the enslaved and expendable captives of Viminacium town, panting at the drive poles, bloody under the flail.

Arapovian stepped near. "You need to take that out."

"I know it." Sabinus eyed him. "You fit, man?"

"I breathe."

"Still draw a bow?"

"Never better. Pain concentrates the mind wonderfully."

Sabinus grimaced.

"I take their leader?"

Sabinus shook his head. "Wait. Bring 'em in close. We will have them at the gates. They've got no chance there."

And for the enslaved captives, alas, it would be another bad day.

But the tortoise was changing tack again, pulled round from the inside. Away from the massively balked west gate. The cunning swine. Sabinus was momentarily nonplussed.

"Crossbow unit III only," he roared. "Pick off what you can. Whichever way they go, keep at 'em."

He had few men, but plenty of arrows. Storehouses full of 'em.

"And pedites, I want to see you sweat!"

Poor buggers looked exhausted already. But they'd look a whole lot worse if that ram came though the gates, followed by ten thousand tattooed horsemen.

The tortoise shifted slowly and clumsily to the right, toward the trajectory of one of the Hun's own onagers, smacking boulders into the southwest tower. Idiot barbarians. They'd smash their own ram at this rate.

But no. As Arapovian had cautioned, they weren't fools.

The tortoise straightened up again and the ram was aimed dead center at the bottom of the fortress wall, only twenty yards or so from where the onager was hitting. They were indeed damnably confident in the accuracy of their own artillery, and they knew about rams and stone walls.

During the Persian wars against that hard nut Shapur, the Eastern Army had quickly discovered, to their surprise, that the walls of fortresses on the Euphrates, like Nisibis, held well against rams. Built of no more than cheap bricks of mud and straw, baked hard in the Mesopotamian sun, they gave off clouds of red dust, but they absorbed the shock. Whereas beautifully laid walls of finely dressed stone shivered and shattered: far more expensive, a lot better looking—and vulnerable.

Like the walls of Viminacium. Finest dressed Illyrian limestone facing a rubble hardcore. As soon as the facing was gone, the core would collapse, leaking out of the ruptured stonework like gray gore. But how did they know? That scarred and tattooed leader. He knew too damn much.

So they were concentrating their attack on the corner. Not bad strategy. The onager missiles were coming into the southwest tower at a steady rate, fifty or sixty pounds of missile every minute or two, from maybe four hundred yards. As the ram came closer, Sabinus could see how well built it was. Even the brutish great lump of ram's head was protected by a projecting roof. A common mistake to forget that feature. The Goths always used to get it wrong. Bring a ram up to the enemies' walls, all beautifully shaped and slung, beneath a steep, sloping roof—and with the ram's head sticking out the front. It comes in close, ready for the first swing, and your men roll a big rock over the wall. It smashes down onto the protruding ram's-head, the head drops down, the rest of the beam flips up, probably kills a couple of the team with it, slams upward into its own protecting roof, often half demolishes it. Or snaps its own ropes, or gets tangled coming down again—all sorts of trouble. But not this time. The ram was perfectly protected. They were already swinging her back on good long suspension ropes, all very expert. Sabinus could almost have cursed the grandstand view he had from this damn west gate tower.

A sharp thud, distant trembling, cries from down below. The stones held for now. But not for long. He sent what *pedites* he could spare. The wall needed balking up behind—rubble, sandbags, anything. They were running out of materials, so he told them to take sledgehammers to the nearest barrack blocks and use what materials they could get from the ruins. He reckoned his men would sleep well enough under the open stars after this was over.

Soon, another thud. A lot of dust. The stones were going.

An onager missile sliced over the top of the southwest tower. There was a terrible crash and unearthly screams. Not one of the crossbowmen so much as glanced to the left. With the ram still hitting and that concentrated onager assault, that whole corner of the fort was going to go soon. And then they would be in.

Time to reply.

If only he had a squad of *superventores*—special forces, "over comers"—but they were all with the field army nowadays. Or a few cohorts of Aëtius's superb, reformed Palatine Legion from the West. The frontier legions were expected to look after themselves. And so they would.

But it was looking bad. The arrow machines on the southwest tower had both been smashed by that onager strike. The planking sagged. Most of the men had been smashed, too. It was carnage up there. He looked away. The northwest tower was charcoal. What fire arrows the archers could get in were too few, and the tortoise well protected with iron plates.

Below galloped the commander of the ram, flailing his whip, oblivious of stray arrows. Still ordering his captives to draw back the ram and slam into the walls again, even as they were under attack.

Sabinus would have to send men down.

Tatullus read his mind. "The bear with the club will be no good. You need fast movers."

Sabinus nodded.

"I will go," said a voice behind. "I have experience."

It was the Armenian again.

"You have?"

Arapovian did not deign to repeat himself.

Malchus was desperate to volunteer, too. It seemed mad to send his best cavalry officer, but Sabinus had seen the man's joyful ruthlessness in a fight. He loved fighting, that one. The more men he slew, the more of his own blood he shed, the more he loved it. He was a pure, grinning predator.

One more.

Tatullus stepped forward.

Sabinus nodded. "Coronas and medals for all of you, whether you come back or not." He glared at them. "But you better fucking had. I'm short of men."

Small gangs of Hun horsemen were darting in toward the walls in lethal forays, letting off light, unpredictable little showers of arrows over the exposed battlements, covering fire for the ram. The three defenders bowed their heads low and ran. They didn't need to speak. It was obvious what they had to do, and that was keep low, move fast, and do as much damage as they could. The last thing Arapovian did was unsling his beloved eastern bow and shove it into Knuckles's bandaged hands. Then they were in close behind the low battlements, just above the tortoise, the narrow wall shivering beneath their hobnailed boots at the shocks of the ram, yells from below, and rising clouds of powdery dust. Another titanic thud as an onager bowled another long-range rock into the tower to their left, and another spray of feathered arrows clattered around them. They'd been spotted. There was the briefest pause in the iron-tipped shower, a single breath, and then they were up and rolling over the battlements and gone. The distant Hun horsemen were already galloping toward them. They would have to move at blinding speed.

"Crossbow units, hit the horsemen!" roared Sabinus. "Forget the ram! Take out any horsemen coming!"

The finely trained crossbowmen, bows already primed, knelt swiftly at their niches and let fly. The bolts cut through the air and hit the approaching horsemen hard. Several tumbled. The others pulled up in dismay. One or two trained their arrows on the battlements but it was useless. They were already learning. No one shot that well, not from that distance. They began backing off. Another volley of bolts plowed into them. A rider's head lolled, half severed, and his horse fled.

"Keep at it," said Sabinus. "Don't let 'em get close."

Malchus, Tatullus, and Arapovian had dropped down onto the ridge of the tortoise on their hands and feet, knives between their teeth. The Hun commander spotted them immediately and came galloping round, flailing his whip. Malchus and Tatullus managed to prize off a couple of the big iron plates from the crest of the tortoise and send them slithering to the ground. Then they followed, rolling down the steep side away from the oncoming Hun horsemen, protected from incoming fire by the tortoise itself. They hit the earth oblivious of bruises and came up again like cats. The Hun commander promptly lashed out with his whip and caught Tatullus round the neck. The centurion simply gripped the rawhide, slashed it through with his sword, unwrapped it from his throat and tossed it back. The Hun warrior gave a strange howl.

Arapovian was at the end of the ridge, crouched down, gripping the edge of the planking and rolling over. He landed on the rump of a Hun driver's horse. The Hun felt his horse buckle, wondered what had hit him. Then someone grasped his hair from behind and pulled his head back, and he felt the warm gush of blood down his bare chest as his throat gaped open. Arapovian rolled off the horse, ducked under a wild blow from another warrior, and brought his dagger up hard into the Hun horse's belly. The agonized creature reared up, screaming. Tatullus appeared at the back of the tortoise, then Malchus, too, swords slashing, and all hell broke loose.

Out on the plain, the stone-faced leader himself was coming, with a couple of hundred warriors bristling with lances and swords. The three defenders had about half a minute to finish the job before they were as good as dead. And that was impossible.

"Crossbow volley at the main body coming in, on my command," said Sabinus, his eye steady on the approaching horsemen. "And any man who takes out the warlord with the fancy sword gets an extra biscuit for his dinner."

He waited. Sweat beaded on furrowed brows, dripped down noses. Clenched knuckles whitened. They were almost at the ram. Sabinus stood immobile. Sweat dripped onto oiled bowstocks, gleamed there like dew.

"Steady your aim," said Sabinus. "And . . . *fire*!"

Eight bolts raked into the close-packed horsemen and each one found a target. Sabinus kept his eyes so closely fixed on the gray-haired warlord that he thought he saw him bare his teeth like a wolf. Then the warlord raised a brazen arm and hazed his men back out of range again. He even seemed momentarily nonplussed. Behind their retreating hooves they left eight of their comrades stone dead in the dust.

Sabinus grunted with satisfaction.

The savages were indeed learning.

Then screaming started inside the tortoise.

Sabinus saw with approval that the three had managed to loosen some of the iron plates, and so gave the order, "Fire it up." The *pedites* began rolling small flaming tar barrels over the battlements onto the ridge of the tortoise, trying to hit it where the iron plates had gone. A barrel smashed down onto the ridge and broke open. Spars scattered, and flaming tar spattered down the sides.

It was a start.

Sabinus turned his crossbow unit back to the drivers behind the ram. "Take 'em when you can."

In the melee, two Hun warriors broke cover, then arched back, crying out, their backs stuck with bolts. Their horses reared and panicked.

"Reload and aim."

"Sir," nodded his *optio*.

They had dropped a net over the wall above the ram so that the three comrades could scramble back to safety once they had done their work. If they were still alive. Now a Hun warrior came galloping in between the tortoise and the wall, ducking down low and flat along his pony's back, and with a circus rider's skill vaulted from his horse onto the net. He scrambled toward the top, a knife in his teeth.

Sabinus nodded. "Take him."

The fancy rider dropped back, dead.

Across the plain, the formation of riders had gone very wide, and there were a lot more of them. A thousand were coming in now. Open spaced, galloping, circling, determined not to let their ram fail in its task.

"Tubernator, call our three back."

The bugle went to his lips.

"Sir," said the *optio*, "the rope's still not cut."

"Shit."

Inside the tent-shaped tortoise, which was beginning to fill with smoke, Arapovian was astraddle the beam itself, hacking alternately at a big Hun horseman coming at him from below and at the thick suspension ropes of the ram. The point of the Hun's lance pierced the Armenian's thigh and he cried out. He slipped his leg back and took cover behind the ram, hanging by one arm, still hacking wildly at the rope. The thing was fraying slightly but no more. In the distance, the faltering note of a bugle, and the thundering of hooves. A lot of hooves.

"Fire the fucking thing!" bellowed Sabinus at his *pedites* in frustration. He was going to lose three good men for nothing. Three very good men. Those thousand horsemen would be here in seconds. Already the first, wild arrows were clattering against the walls. Sabinus ran from the guardroom to the battlements. One of his men offered him his shield but he brushed it aside. Another arrow clattered nearby. Absent-mindedly he picked it up and snapped it across a burly thigh. "Fire it now!

"Pedites, get more tar barrels up here. I don't give a fuck if there's arrows, man! Of course there's arrows, we're in the middle of a fucking siege. Now get 'em up here! Crossbow squadron, to me." He ducked down, the low battlements barely sufficient to shield his bulk.

The eight men crouched likewise.

"I want everything that moves in and around that tortoise, except our three men, stretched out in the dirt. You hear me?"

Bows were cranked. They stood, aimed, fired, and crouched again in one clean, swift movement.

"Now you, pedites! Get those tar barrels fired up and over the side."

The arrows thickened to an iron rain. One of his crossbowmen lost a cheek. Another started to help him down the steps.

"He hasn't lost his eyes, and you're needed here on the wall, soldier! Let go of his hand!" He said to the wounded man, more gently, "Good work, soldier. Now get to the hospital and have that stitched. The whores will go crazy for the scar."

The deserted southwest tower shivered again.

"Load up."

He was like a rock, this legionary legate who swore like a common trooper. Nothing seemed to make him afraid. The men cranked back their bows.

A good thing they thought him a rock. Sabinus knew well enough he was as scared as any of them. But a better actor. That's why he kept his hands gripped into fists: to stop them shaking. He grinned and punched a man on the shoulder. "Kill 'em all."

He stood up again, hitching back the straps of his bronze cuirass on his bullish shoulders, impervious to arrows.

"Loose the rest of the tar barrels! There's got to be more than that!"

The *pedites* sweated blood. Fire arrows ignited more tar. The offside of the shell was burning steadily.

He turned and watched the wild long-haired rider down below, screaming barbaric verses.

"I want him dead. That one, the poet." He hawked and spat. "No fucking poet besieges *my* fortress."

Again in a swift and perfect rank they stood, stepped forward, clocked their target through the lethal oncoming arrow shower, fired, and dropped back. None of them was hit.

Sabinus squinnied through the embrasure. "Biscuits all round," he grunted.

Three bolts missed. One hit the Hun's horse. Three hit the warrior in the thigh, one in the side, one in his shoulder. He and his horse screamed in unison, a hellish duet, horse rearing, forelegs paddling in the air. The warrior wrenched it savagely down, blood running in a thin trickle from the bolt tail in its muscular haunch. He pulled round and shouted, flailing his whip left handed, his right arm across his chest, hand clamped over his shoulder, fingers reddening. But the bolt had already broken in and leaked blood into his lungs, and his voice was wild and weak and desperate.

"Kill them! Draw back the ram! Astur will utterly destroy all the earth in the day of his fierce anger! Work, slaves!"

But he was mad. There were no slaves left to obey him.

"Second volley," said Sabinus. "Take him this time."

The deranged rider was stuck by two more bolts, his horse likewise. He was a madman. One bolt glanced off his round iron helmet. He shook his head. His long black hair flew and scattered drops of bright red blood— Sabinus thought of Medusa. Then he flung down his whip and drew his long curved saber. To the horror of the watchers on the wall, in his blood madness he rode in and began to slaughter the captives tethered beneath the now-blazing tortoise. They fell apart, crying, hands held over their sliced heads. Arapovian found himself trapped between the captives roped to the ram and the insane Hun, trying to protect them as the rider tried to kill them. Arapovian cut free what captives he could who were still alive, only for the warrior to wheel round and scythe through them as they fled, riding them down. Arapovian gritted his teeth in a white fury and launched himself at another Hun driver, driving his blade straight through him. Then he was up on the beam again, slashing at the suspension ropes. At last one of the great ropes frayed and twisted and snapped, and the ram thumped down into the dust, the heavy rams head half buried where it hit. Arapovian was thrown off the end as from an unbroken horse. He rolled smoothly, picked himself up and grimaced.

"It's done!" roared Sabinus. "Tubernator, get the men back! Blow your guts out, man!"

He turned the other way. "Every tar barrel over the wall. I want to see that tortoise melt down!"

The Hun warrior was maddened still further by the defeat, dying, flailing his saber. He rode into the walls, spurring his bloody horse. The creature turned alongside, the warrior slashed at the stonework, rode through his own shower of sparks. Someone dropped a stone on him. He reeled and stared upward sightlessly through a mask of blood, eyes rolling back to the whites. He tottered forward again, still in the high-fronted wooden saddle, and spurred and pulled away. An adolescent boy emerged, blackened, from under the tortoise: the last of the enslaved captives, hoping to make his escape. The warrior cut him down as he passed by without a second thought, and galloped away across the plain back to his army, still alive somehow, his body lolling, his head to one side, saber hanging down from his left hand.

The men on the walls fell silent.

"God's teeth," growled Sabinus.

"By St. Peter's holy Jewish foreskin," agreed Knuckles.

Tatullus and Arapovian were back on the walls by the time the tortoise, smoldering and half wrecked, tottered and sank down useless into the dust. The ram beneath it blazed. Then they realized to their horror that Malchus had not followed them. Tatullus roared an order to the young cavalry officer, who stood dazed and bloodied near the smoking wreckage, but he appeared not to hear.

The horsemen came galloping in. Malchus had left it too late. He could barely walk. He grinned. He had lost too much blood to climb past the savaged remnants of the tortoise and vault back over the battlements.

Arapovian reached down a futile arm, crying out to him, his face angry and already sorrowful. "Move yourself, man!"

Malchus turned his head and smiled dimly up at him through a mist of blood. He raised a red forearm, and touched the flat of his sword to his bare forehead. He turned away from them and looked out across the plain.

A barked order sounded in Arapovian's ears, the voice of the legate, but he did not hear or understand. He was up over the wall and down the net like a cat. Malchus was oblivious. He stood alone before the fortress. No, he walked away from it. Tottering, he walked toward the oncoming horde of thousands, barely able to lift his sword.

Arapovian dodged round the ruined tortoise and ran to him, but the horsemen were coming in faster. It was impossible.

Malchus settled his helmet more firmly on his head and waited. He would have liked to end by running toward them. Even walking purposefully would be something. But he was too tired, so he simply stood his ground. At least he was still on his feet. He took a deep breath and raised his sword above his head one last time. Then the horde came down upon him and he was gone.

Arapovian skidded to a halt. Another few breaths and they would be on him, too, but incredibly, he seemed to pause and consider for a moment or two. He hefted his sword in his right hand, and with his left drew his fine dagger with its jeweled handle. Eyed the horde. Then he resheathed both, turned and dashed for the wall. The instant he did so, some of the horsemen sheathed their swords and swept their bows from their shoulders, nocked arrows and fired, faster than the eye could see. Arrows clattered into the stonework. Arapovian crawled up the net as best he could with his lanced leg. The crossbowmen above stepped forward and hit the nearest horsemen. Men howled with rage and pain, horses tumbled.

Arapovian, clinging to the top of the net with one arm, stopped and looked back. He was as crazed as that Hun poet, this Armenian. More orders roared in his ears. He drew his dagger from its sheath again, and hazed the bright little blade out over the army of horseman until he found his target. He pointed the point of the dagger straight at the stone-faced warlord and smiled a rare smile. Then he clamped his teeth on the blade again and was up and over the battlements, pulling the weighty hemp net up behind him. Knuckles seized the other end, then more men came to help. One acrobatic Hun vaulted and clung to it, so they hauled him up to the top, where Knuckles leaned over and cuffed him off again with a massive blow to the head, as you might swipe away a fly. The warrior cartwheeled back to the ground. The net came safely up over the battlements, and the rest of the horsemen faced blank fortress walls again.

In a surge of victorious energy, arrows, ballista bolts, sling balls, even rocks hurled by hand, struck the Hun horsemen in a single, brutal volley. From the unit again operating at full capacity on the half-burned northwest tower, there came a pummeling onslaught from the well-drilled artillerymen. Two big ballista bolts and two medium-weight slingshots were fired hard and almost horizontal, arcing down fast into the fleeing horsemen. The four missiles took out four riders, sending them tumbling to the earth at breakneck speed. You could hear the vertebrae snap. The riders behind tumbled into them, and more fell. Some lay stunned beneath their whinnying horses or entangled in their reins. Arrows sang from the battlements, and each arrow told. The rest of the horsemen fled.

Arapovian sank down behind the low wall and sheathed his dagger. He removed his helmet, swept back the long black hair plastered to his brow and bowed his head in grief for a brave lost comrade.

Knuckles handed him back his bow. "Madman," he said.

"Hero, surely?" said Arapovian bitterly.

"Same thing," said Knuckles.

Below them, the great structure of the burning tortoise gave one last groan, like some primeval animal in its last throes, then leaned, tottered, and collapsed in a huge eruption of soot and sparks. Hot iron plates clanged down on each other, and amid the smoke and flame, and the acrid stench of burning rope, was the worse stench of bodies roasting. The bronze head of the great ram, half buried, shone dimly up through the flames. One last wounded warrior crawled out of the chaos, arms flailing as if he was trying to swim through sand. He got to his knees and made a grab for a riderless horse which milled around and snorted with surprise.

"Finish it," said Tatullus irritably.

A bolt stilled him. The dust settled. The men breathed again.

It was not yet noon. The *pedites* brought round water.

Sabinus was coming along the battlements. Arapovian got to his feet.

Tatullus saluted. "Sir. Ram out of action."

Sabinus would have smiled, but Malchus was gone, and he couldn't afford to lose men like that. He nodded and went back to the west tower.

There was a brief respite in the Hun onslaught. The horsemen were pulled way back against the crest of hills to the west. Their onagers fell silent. A feeling of temporary hesitation. This undermanned and isolated fortress wouldn't be so easy a nut to crack after all. But Sabinus and his officers remembered well enough the demeanor of that grim-faced, tattooed warlord on his grubby little skewbald pony. He would be back. Any respite would be short.

He ordered Tatullus to make a discreet head count, and the answer was a shock. They were down to fewer than four hundred front-rank soldiers: already a fifth of his men were casualties, wounded or slain. The *pedites* and medical orderlies had taken it even worse. There was no shelter from those bitter arrow storms, and the Huns would soon come again. Many thousands of them.

If the gods were just, and rewarded ordinary men who fought like heroes, then surely reinforcements must come soon. Or perhaps some goddess, the gray-eyed Pallas Athena, as she came down from Olympus to the windy plains of Troy to protect her beloved Odysseus. Sabinus's lip curled sardonically. Fat chance. The old gods were dead. The emperor and his bishops had declared it so, and the Altar of Victory no longer stood in the Senate House. From now on, men must fight on their own, with only a symbolic fish or a wooden cross for succor.

There were six thousand men under arms at Ratiaria. Another thirty or forty thousand, at Marcianopolis: the Eastern Field Army in all its glory. But the horizon all around was empty and still.

The summer sun burned down. In the blue sky overhead, swifts and martins wheeled and hawked through the mild air as if this was a day like any other. From the river the men on the walls could hear the distant cry of a heron. Here they died, while life went dumbly on.

The Romans drank water with a dash of vinegary wine, gnawed barley-flour biscuits and salt pork, rested in the shade of the towers or barrack blocks. Tatullus paced around tirelessly, inspecting weapons and wounds, giving quiet orders. He made sure his men's shields were properly stowed with a full complement of *mattiobarbuli*, lead-weighted darts which were the perfect weapon for defending heights against attackers below. He paused to watch one young slinger carefully carving insults onto his sling balls, one by one, sitting cross-legged, tongue out between his teeth, concentrating like the finest goldsmith on his craft.

Tatullus peered over his shoulder. *"Hoc ede, equifutuor,"* read the lyrical inscription. *"Eat this, horse fucker."*

"Very witty, soldier," growled the centurion. The slinger jumped to his feet and saluted. "And if you come out of this in one piece, I'm sure you could get a nice job as a stonemason inscribing fancy headstones with lies for rich dead people. But until then, *do some useful fucking work!*"

"Sir!"

The next soldier to arouse his centurion's wrath owned a shield that was all wrong. Tatullus plucked it out of the man's hand and twirled it round to stare at the back.

"A Roman shield has a sturdy central handgrip behind the boss," he said. "So what's this? An armstrap, with a handgrip near the edge. What use is that, shit-for-brains?"

The soldier stared dumbly.

"Is your shield offensive or defensive?"

"Defensive, sir."

"Balls! It's both. Take incoming arrow fire, sure, and then close in and knock your man off the battlements with a good blow from the boss. But what are you going to do to a man with a feeble sideswipe? Tickle him? Strip that arm strap off right now, soldier. Refix the handgrip alone, right behind the boss. Decurion! See to it that none of the other men have shields with arm straps. They're for pansies. You get tired holding it, you rest the rim on the ground and squat. Look to it."

He reported back to Sabinus, showing a sympathy for his men he'd never dream of showing to their faces.

"They're dog tired. Only mortal. No man can fight forever. They've fought for five, six hours already now, after a night without sleep."

Sabinus knew what he was suggesting, his iron-hearted centurion: rest for half, duty for half. But the walls could not be manned with just two hundred men. Even four hundred was ludicrously inadequate. And in truth, his *primus pilus* knew it as well as he. All four hundred must rise to fight again. The legate's anger and weariness made him brutal.

"They can sleep on Charon's ferry."

Some of them were almost asleep with exhaustion, when there came a distant thunk and, two or three seconds later, another terrific shudder from the southwest tower. Bang on target yet again.

"To your stations, on the double!"

Dry, sleepless, dust-filled eyes once more flared wide. Men once more dragged grimy, exhausted limbs up stone steps and along battlemented walls to their places of thankless duty.

9

THE BOILER BOYS

This time, the Hun warlord was in cold control. He held his numberless horsemen back out of range and did not use them. For half an hour or more, there was merely the screech and ratchet of the gigantic torsion springs, the shuddering release of beam against padded crossbeam, and the southwest tower and its surrounding walls, weakened if not brought down by the ram, continued their slow-motion fall.

Thus began the long afternoon of attrition.

The VII Legion had triumphed over the siege towers and the ram, yes. Helped by the fact that the Huns had started wrong, attacking piecemeal instead of along a single, concerted front. Had they brought up the siege towers and ram together, against different walls, while giving the machines full, coordinated covering fire from horseback, Viminacium might have already fallen, and the legionaries would all be on Charon's ferry across the Styx by now. But over the onagers the VIIth could not triumph. They were hopelessly out of range. Even the Romans' best ballistas and sling machines were nothing like the size and power of the besiegers."

The tension of waiting could drive a man mad.

"Pennants!" a young voice screamed. "I see pennants! Wind socks and dragon banners!"

It was a *signifer,* the young boy Sabinus had tried to steady in the legionary chapel. He sat astride the battlements like a sunstruck fool, gesticulating wildly. "I think it might be the Ioviani Seniores. Or the Cornuti. Look, to the east! From Ratiaria!"

The boy had imagination, certainly.

Tatullus strode over, dragged him back from the battlements, looked into his eyes and saw the frantic, burning light in them. The boy continued to gibber, so he cuffed him senseless and ordered him lugged down to the hospital.

The centurion scanned the eastern horizon.

There were no pennants.

Whumpff. Another hundred-pound ball hit the southwest tower. Plumes of dust rose high into the still summer air.

And then out of the west, the tide of horse warriors came surging in.

Knuckles came slouching by, a stubby little crossbow clutched in his huge paw.

"You look like a bear trying to peel a grape," said Sabinus.

Knuckles stopped and wiped his brow. "If only I could get at 'em with me club, sir, I could do a power of good for Rome and the Lord Jesus Christ, sir."

"You'll have your chance for a bit of face-to-face yet, soldier. Don't doubt it."

There came a blizzard of arrows arcing in high.

"Take cover!"

"You need to get off the wall, sir, under the canopy."

Sabinus moved. Around him, cries of stricken men. The clatter of arrows, sometimes the soft thock as they hit flesh. Outlandish screams. They couldn't afford to lose any. But they were. The walls had to be manned.

They couldn't just wait and be picked off by those lethal arrow storms. Somehow they would have to attack.

He gave the order to pull the men back off the east wall, manning only the south and west. The attack remained concentrated there, and Sabinus reckoned it would stay that way.

They must counterattack soon. They must do something.

Down in the yard, the heavy cavalry stirred.

From the artillery units still working on the southern gate towers, ballista bolts cut through Hunnish warriors and their horses alike. A perpendicular hit could go through three men in a line, it was said. Sabinus called up every last crossbow unit to the battlements. Densely packed volleys proved murderous to the ranks of the unarmored horse warriors, however loosely spaced and fast. They died by the dozen. Eventually they pulled back out range again.

"They're not invincible," said Tatullus quietly.

"I never thought they were," said Sabinus.

"Mad as fuckin' badgers, though," said Knuckles.

Arapovian sat and rebandaged his arm, then took up his bow again.

Centurion and legate departed.

"Tell me about Armenia, then," said Knuckles. "I could do with a laugh."

"Armenia?" The look in Arapovian's eyes gave even Knuckles pause. "One day I will tell you about Armenia. For now, I kill Huns."

The onagers started up once more. And with them, looping round wide, came the horse archers. You could almost hear the collective sigh of exhausted men stumbling to their feet again, cranking back their bows, hefting their shields, stowing a new row of lead darts.

The onslaught recommenced.

Soon a decurion came running. "First-floor guardroom, sir. Stone came straight through the wall. Tower still holding but roof's beginning to pitch badly."

"Bag it up. Give 'em covering fire."

"No archers, sir."

"What do you mean, 'No archers?' They're your unit; where are they?"

"My unit's gone, sir. In heaven or hell, wouldn't like to say. Enemy arrows are coming in like rain." He gasped for breath, waving his empty hands. "Their cavalry below the walls. Continuous stream of them. Every man on the open roof was caught out. Lying up there like sticklebacks, sir."

"Jesus."

Tatullus reviewed the situation for his commanding officer. "The siege towers weren't a problem. Light cavalry, obviously not, however many arrows they drop on us. The ram's finished. It's the onagers that we have to take out, and fast. The southwest tower won't take a lot more, then we're fighting hand to hand over the rubble." He grimaced. "Outnumbered a hundred to one."

He was right, and Sabinus knew it. The big onagers back there, half a mile off, bucking in the dust, spewing out their massive loads, kicking back like the wild asses they were named after, they were the enemy. And they were going to break in. It was only a matter of time. Another shuddering thunk, the whole west wall trembling, bruised, and battered, a fresh crack running to the foundation stones, men reeling back from the battlements choking on dust. The onagers relentless, kicking up again, and again. No, they could not just sit here and let it all fall. Not now. Not after so many years of patient endurance . . .

Once a single gap was breached, once the barbarians were inside the fort, the hand-to-hand fighting would be brief indeed. His auxiliaries would flee. His runners would do what they did best, and run. And his last three hundred would fight like Leonidas's Spartans to the bitter, bloody end. So he truly believed. Perhaps take twice as many of the enemy with them as they went, screaming blue murder, down to hell. Six hundred of the enemy slain would make no difference. Life was cheap to them. Tens of thousands more would ride straight on down the imperial trunk road to Naissus. Then Sardica? Adrianople? And then the capital itself? It would be like a monstrous wave, a bristling, shaggy wave of savages armed to the teeth, sweeping across Europe without end.

At last the onagers paused in their onslaught. The galloping horsemen below pulled back again to regroup, and replenish their quivers from the Hun supply wagons back on the crest.

Now.

"Tubernator! Sound the cavalry charge!"

Down at the south gate there was a disciplined frenzy of activity. The cavalrymen, already armored up by assistants, hauled themselves onto their huge, shaggy-hooved mounts, settled themselves into their high-fronted saddles with a bronze brace at each corner, rock solid, massy, inhuman. Their leader was Andronicus. No fool: but, alas, no Malchus either. They checked their long cavalry swords, hefted their emblazoned shields, couched their long ashen lances, and formed up at the gate in a long Teutonic column, four abreast. It was they who had carried out the original punitive attack on the Hun people north of the Danube, which had brought down this terrible vengeance. Inexorable orders from the Highest Authority, it was true; a grim but necessary task. Now they rode out against the enemy with real anger in their blood.

Sabinus raised his hand, glanced out once more across the plain. The Hun horsemen were vanishing away, ghostly figures glimpsed through clouds of ochre dust. His hand dropped. The gatekeepers hauled back the mighty oak timbers, the two iron-bound gates groaned open, and the column moved out at a steely trot. A great glittering serpent gliding out from its lair into the waiting world beyond.

The men on the battlements gave a cheer to see them. The majesty and power of the Schola Scutariorum Clibanariorum. Less majestically, the Boiler Boys, since they would bake inside their weighty armor on days like this. But they deliberately trained in the hottest weather, sometimes wearing extra clothing beneath the armor. They were used to it.

They pulled their horses' heads in low and continued to trot steadily to maintain formation till the last. Their mounts wore shining silver chamfrons, masks of armor, of little practical use against arrows but highly effective in scaring the enemy horse. Horses were scared by everything: camels, elephants, other horses in masks. Sabinus had even heard that horses would turn back from attack at the merest scent of lion dung. Sadly he had no sacks of lion dung available just now.

The retreating Hun horsemen were still barely aware of the impending attack on their rear. Andronicus rose up in his saddle and gave the nod, and the column moved into an easy canter. A Hun glanced back and cried out a warning. Immediately Andronicus drove his spurs into his horse and it gave a low whinny as it moved into a full charging gallop. The column drove forward.

The massed ranks of retreating Huns broke loose and separated before the juggernaut of iron and bronze could slam into them, and Sabinus saw immediately, from his accursed grandstand view on the western guard tower, that his last, desperate attempt at counterattack would fail. What a heavy cavalry column did best was hit a hard target, but here there would be no hard target to hit. The nomad horsemen galloped away into empty space before the Roman heavy cavalry, the Pannonian plains to them much like the limitless steppes of their native Scythia. The great armored column punched into empty air, into taunting nothingness. And then some of the Huns, those with a few arrows left in their quivers, wheeled round and came back at them from the side, deft and fast, bows already slipping from muscular, copper-skinned shoulders.

Sabinus felt like the emperor himself in Constantinople, high up in his *kathisma,* his private box in the Hippodrome, watching an afternoon's harmless entertainment. He tightened up with self-loathing. He had been to the capital, had seen the Obelisk of Theodosius the Great in the Hippodrome, triumphally erected back in 390. He had stood and surveyed the bas-reliefs of scruffy barbarians in animal skins, bowing low to the emperor and his family on high in their royal box. What arrogance. What hubris. What a hostage to fortune that haughty, self-laudatory monument would prove to be. The Emperor of the Eastern Romans, God's Vice-Regent on Earth, perpetually victorious over the pagan hordes . . . To watch his men about to be slaughtered like this was almost more than Sabinus could bear.

"Hunting the Huns on the open plain is like hunting a tiger in a dark forest," said a soft voice nearby. It was Arapovian. "At night. With a stick."

"Stow it, soldier."

Sabinus was ready to sound the recall already, but then Andronicus gave a seeming yell of triumph, and Sabinus hesitated. It seemed the cavalry officer believed there was still a chance they might get through to the onagers and destroy them, before they themselves were destroyed.

Keeping his men in a tight and perfect column, essential when so vastly outnumbered, Andronicus turned them as tightly as he could and plowed in left across the files of fleeing Hun horsemen. No, there was no satisfying hard target to splinter and demolish, but these light horsemen, out of arrows, barely armored, indeed some barely clothed, could be cut down ruthlessly in smaller groups. And getting in among them like this, there was no chance their Hun comrades could reply with arrow fire. They would only kill their own. It was a good move.

Sabinus nodded with satisfaction. One thing that stone-faced warlord had not expected, he guessed, was any such counterattack. Well, let him feel it now. Now those light-horse warriors would feel what it was like to have the Boiler Boys crashing into their flank.

When a lancer drove into the flank of a Hunnish horse, the massive weight of the armored knight tended to carry him right into and over the flailing and tumbling steppe pony. Either the rider was trapped or trampled beneath, or else, if he tried to come up, again, the next lancer would be ready immediately behind to finish him off. Andronicus himself drove his lance in low, straight into a squat pony's belly. The pony squealed and keeled over, dragging his lance from his hand as it went. Andronicus promptly pulled up and drew his *spatha*, his long-sword. The Hun horseman rolled and came up standing, covered in dust, half blinded, whipping round, drawing his curved saber. The lancer behind Andronicus came past the Hun on the other side, galloping in close enough to touch him. He lowered his shield, aimed the heavy bronze boss straight for the Hun's spinning head, and let his horse do the rest. The effect at that speed was to club the warrior headless where he stood, leaving nothing but the stump of a cadaver gouting blood from the neck hole.

It became a rout of the arrowless, fleeing steppe warriors, torn asunder by the heavyweight lancers, who were getting closer to the onagers all the time. Once there, a few well-aimed sword strokes could do a lot of damage and buy them useful time. But in the whirling, blinding dust, the cavalrymen took too little notice of fresh Hun horsemen coming down from the ridge, quivers packed and bristling.

Suddenly the Roman column found itself falling behind, unable to pursue at such speed, and with some way still to go to reach the onagers. And then the Huns came back, deft and fast, lightweight gallopers as fast as swooping falcons, curling in on either side of the column, loosing off arrows on lethal flat trajectories—no elegant high arcs through the morning sky now—and angled to the column so as not to fly on and hit their own. The warriors held their small, deadly bows almost horizontal, shooting from the side, arrows barely visible as they spat from the bow from a mere hundred yards, fifty. They thocked into heavy wooden shields, each shield on each lancer's left arm soon stuck with eight or ten arrows, weighing the rider down, tiring him. Soon even those strong arms began to drop, necks and shoulders became more exposed. The lancers were drenched in sweat within their coats of mail, eyes blinking furiously, straining to see.

The Hunnish horses didn't seem afraid of the big Roman mounts masked in their unearthly silver chamfrons. Perhaps their riders didn't allow them to be afraid. More arrows skidded off shoulder guards or steep-sided *Spangenhelms*, sometimes ricocheting into softer flesh—the power behind each missile was awesome. Others hit direct and passed on, barely slowed by plate or chain mail, to bore into meat and bone. Blood gleamed on polished armor, as thin as oil on water, or trickled beneath, runnels of blood and sweat commingled.

A pair of buzzards, male and female, with two scrawny chicks to feed, circled overhead.

Andronicus pushed back his visor and left it up, raging and oblivious of pain in the chaos of the fight. He was hit in the thigh, but time enough for it to hurt later. He bellowed another order and then tightened up again, roaring round to the right, holding his long sword thrust straight out before him like a lance. He had realized what was happening. Although they had done good damage to the arrowless riders in retreat, they were now surrounded, like hornets in a beehive. All he could see around them, their only horizon, was one vast, extended circle of galloping riders. The Huns loosed their arrows when passing through only one quadrant of the circle, so they wouldn't hit their own men the other side. Smart. They reloaded around the rest of the gallop.

Andronicus's men were going down everywhere, reeling in the bright sunshine, crying out, heads thrown back, lances trailing. He drove his wheeled spurs into his charger's broad flanks and led his men to break out of the circle again. No Hun line could withstand that shock. But instead of withstanding it, the enemy simply melted away before it. The circle ebbed around them and reformed and they were still surrounded. The Huns' tactical agility was extraordinary. But how did they know when to reform, when to hold fire, when to move? Who gave the order? It was uncanny. Even now, Andronicus could admire it. He had heard of the Huns. Now he saw them, and understood. No demons out of the wilderness, after all. Just awesome warriors. Perhaps the hardest that Rome had fought in all her long history.

Across the plain, on the low rise, the Hun warlord sat unmoving, like some primitive votive statue cut from basalt in the desert. He gave no orders to his whirling thousands.

Another flight of arrows came in and Andronicus crouched low in his saddle, his face buried in his horse's coarse mane. Sometimes that rough, sweet horse smell comforted him, in the stables at the end of a hard day's training or, better still, a hunt. But not now. All comfort was far from him now. An arrow clanged on his shoulder and cut his neck open. His sweat stung in the wound. His linen soutane was sticky with blood.

Too many of his men were fallen, and the column's coherence was lost. The day, too, was lost. The sun was well past noon, and sinking, its light beginning to shine from behind the stone warlord on the crest and his innumerable ranks of warriors, to burn cruelly in the eyes of the Roman lancers and their comrades on the doomed walls of Viminacium. The judgment of the sun was plain.

From those walls came the desperate, far-away sound of the recall. Andronicus could have laughed. Some hope. "Come and get us, friends," he muttered, finding his mouth was full of blood.

Now mere isolated individuals, some cavalrymen tried to pull their mounts round and head back to the fort, but they were picked off one by one. Others milled vacantly. Andronicus twisted in his saddle and looked around, and another arrow cut across his back. Had he been sitting straight it would have killed him. There was only one thing left to try. There would be no return to the fort for them. He gave one last, desperate order, spraying blood. "Free charge for the onagers!" He gritted his teeth. Think of it as a suicide mission. Never give up hope. Die in the attack.

The onagers stood impassively, a hundred yards off still, thickly surrounded by Hun horsemen, arrows nocked. He spurred his horse forward with a last fury. Crazy. To take out those onagers and do any lasting damage, many men would be needed, with leisure time to spare. Not like this. One blood-boltered fool flailing his sword in the air. It seemed to him now, out on his own, with his men trailing wounded or dead behind him, that the Huns were waiting for him, with a true warrior curiosity as to how profound his courage might be. How would he die? Like a man, after all?

Andronicus galloped on, sword stretched out before him, arm shaking, the sun in his eyes. If it is with all dying men as they say, he saw his own family before him when he died, arms outstretched to embrace him, and not the searing sun.

The Huns said among themselves that he died bravely, that leader of the iron horsemen. Later that night, stripped of his armor, they would lay him on a pyre with their own dead, and send him to the otherworld in the care of his gods whose names they did not even know.

A long way back, a single Roman lancer had obeyed the recall and broken free of the Hun circle uninjured. Sabinus ordered the south gates open. But the Huns' murderous impudence knew no bounds. A single copper-skinned warrior, clad in nothing but fur and feathers, came galloping in fast and low on a filthy little piebald, slewed in hard virtually under the heavy charger's thundering hooves, drew his bowstring back into his chest and loosed an arrow. Traveling all of five yards, it smacked into the lancer's face, punched through and came out the back of his helmet. The heavy horse continued to canter forward, its dead rider lolling. The little horse warrior of the steppes pulled up to inspect his handiwork, and from his fellows an admiring cheer went up at this deed of battlefield daring. As if it was mere sport to them, even as many of their own tribe lay dead around the walls of the fort. All men must die. Why not die gloriously, in battle? War was much like a hunt over the steppes, and the best hunters always make the finest soldiers.

Tatullus bestrode the battlements, ordering his crossbowmen to take the Hun rider out, but they couldn't hit him. They were few now, and very tired. Their crossbows trembled in sweaty hands, their arm muscles ached atrociously, their tired eyes blurred. The rider kept galloping, turning. He even punched his fist at them. Obscenely the dead rider, the arrow stuck through his head, still lolled in his wooden saddle when his horse trotted in through the gates.

"Get him down," said Tatullus, "and close up."

"Sir?"

Tatullus glared at him. No, there would be no more coming back.

The gates began to close.

"Another man coming in!" came a call from the walls.

Hell.

But not one should be lost out of fear. The gates would stand open for any who came. Tatullus sent a runner to the guard tower.

Sabinus was hit, but he would not have anyone know it. His side was heavily padded with linen bandages, which he hoped would soak up the blood. But every time he shouted an order, he bled more. He could feel his face whiten and sweat. His ears rang as his blood pressure dropped. Let me not faint, he prayed. He pleaded. Not for himself but for his men and the honor of Rome. Let those of us who still live and breathe, heroes every one—after this much battle, this much loss—let us not die now. Let rescue come soon. Let justice be done.

A loose Roman horse was ambling back from the scene of the cavalry's carnage, nodding its big head sleepily, as if returning from no more than a day in the hay meadows. As it passed a tangle of slain Hun warriors lying close to the fort, one of the dead rose up from among them, black with old blood, seized hold of the horse's reins and saddle, and hauled himself up onto the peaceable beast. Together they rode on serenely toward the south gate.

It was Malchus! The man was indestructible. Multiply wounded, ridden down by a horde of a thousand, taking refuge out there among the middens of the slain. Through the mask of black blood gleamed the white teeth of his smile.

Behind him rolled a dust cloud of numberless horsemen.

"Every other unit off the walls and to the south gate!" bellowed Sabinus.

Men scrambled, some nearly laughing with tiredness.

The legate clutched his side. He sent one of the few *pedites* still standing down to Tatullus.

The centurion understood. For their own sake, Malchus must be saved. Such small miracles were everything now; now everything else was lost.

"Take your pikes! Holding pattern at the gate—and I mean hold them!"

Tatullus himself had taken up his beloved billhook, a fearsome weapon which combined a broad curved pike blade and a long, thin side spike. He would never ask his men to do what he would not. He stood out before the gate unshielded. An experimental arrow flew close by. He appeared not to notice it, settling his close-fitting helmet more firmly on his head, his deep-set eyes looking out unblinking and unafraid.

Malchus was still a hundred yards off, trotting calmly, though a little un-steady in the saddle. And then the thundering hooves.

"I want him in! Do not close the gate."

The exhausted and the walking wounded men formed a semicircular pike line about the south gate, thick ashwood pike butts jammed in the hard ground, blades ranged outward at chest level. On their left arms, propped forward, their big oval infantry shields. No horse would charge a line of standing pikes. Only mortal men indulged in the heroics of suicide.

The black and bloody chimera that was Malchus brushed between two parted pikes, saying never a word. But he was indeed grinning. He vanished into the courtyard and the pikes closed up. They managed to take a couple of steps backward for the safety of the gate. Then the Huns were on them.

Curved sabers flashed in the air. One or two horsemen, vainglorious and young, tried to hurl themselves from their saddles over the line of pikes, knives clutched in their fists, only to be battered down by embossed shields, or impaled in the air as they leaped. A pike sank down to the earth with the dead weight, and another horseman rode in close and lashed out with his bull-hide whip, pulling the pikeman after him. The wretched man fell forward, stumbling over his own shield, and a third Hun lopped his head off.

"Pull back in formation! Gatekeepers, stand ready."

It was desperate.

Other Huns were dismounting, comprehending quickly that horses were an encumbrance now, and instead running at the line of lowered pikes, aiming to slip between them and knife the defenders. The shields tilted further forward, the only gap between them for the pike staffs. A billhook slashed sideways. It was Tatullus, standing at the very front of his men, as implacable as a bronze statue. A Hun warrior's stomach opened and he sprawled in his own guts. Two of his comrades leaped back, hissing, one of them only just in time to avoid another lethal sideswipe from that billhook.

In the very shadow of the gate tower, a big fellow swung a club. It was Knuckles. The club was already dove gray with spilled brains.

"Hold them!" yelled Tatullus again, stepping slowly backward, the circle of pikemen shrinking behind him. He prayed there were crossbowmen left on the wall above. They were finished without a good volley.

Suddenly the Huns fell back again and in another instant, from behind them, arrows came arcing down on the isolated pikemen in short, high trajectories. Shields were hauled up but often too late, the arrows whistling down cruelly on exposed heads and sagging shoulders. Angry shouts, screams, men clutching and staggering and falling back, losing formation.

Yet even as those still standing stepped backward over their fallen comrades, they lowered their pikes again and locked shields, and took another stand, now in the very arch of the gateway. Their discipline was magnificent. A Hun horseman who had blindfolded his horse rode at them screaming in fury and crashed into the immoveable shield wall. Pikes finished him.

More Huns milled frustratedly, dismounting and remounting aimlessly, seeing the gates standing open just before them, some even screaming insults at each other as if unable to believe that, after all the day's punishment, this handful of dusty, dogged men were still able to hold them back, thousands of them. Truly, these Romans were no women.

Sabinus stood unsteadily on the south wall above, marshalling what remaining crossbowmen he could. So much for their limitless supplies. The store of crossbow bolts was at last running low. They had never reckoned on an assault of this magnitude. In the distance he could hear a harsh, grating, goading voice above the melee, and guessed that it was the implacable Hun warlord ordering his men on, telling them to finish it. Sabinus grunted. Let 'em try.

He raised his hand. His last crossbowmen stepped up to the battlements. His hand dropped, and a last, terrific volley of iron-tipped bolts sliced mercilessly into the front rank of the milling and frustrated Huns. Instantly, Tatullus turned and drove his men back inside the fort, and the gates were slammed together. Even as the gatekeepers set the first oak crossbar in the huge holding braces, a great weight slammed into the other side. The soldiers dropped their pikes and shields in the chaos and threw themselves against the gate.

"Get the second bar in *now*!" ordered Tatullus. Not loudly, but they heard him.

From the wall came a second Roman volley. The gate was now almost blocked by the heaps of the Hun dead. Yet another slamming assault on the other side, though, until the second, higher crossbar was in, and then the gate settled together, rock solid. The Huns broke against it like waves at the foot of a cliff.

Up on the walls the crossbowmen cranked their bows for one last volley, set the bolts in the grooves, held the stocks to their eyes and took aim into the clouds of dust below. But as the dust slowly settled they saw that the enemy had gone.

Arm muscles shaking and burning, they lowered their weapons and bowed their heads. Sweat ran down their filthy faces. Not one had the strength to wipe it away.

Sabinus turned from them so as to control his voice. "Well done, men," he said quietly.

But they could not go on.

He ordered a head count.

Tatullus came up the stairs and saluted. He glanced briefly at Sabinus's wadded side, then looked him straight in the eye. A momentary pause.

"Sir."

Sabinus nodded. "Centurion."

"Fit: twenty-four. Wounded: as many as two hundred. Walking wounded: perhaps fifty."

And slain? Sabinus could do the sums. Half the legion. More.

"How many auxiliaries still with us?"

Tatullus looked out over the fort. The auxiliaries were busy helping the limping wounded, hauling the dead, taking round water, bringing up the last of any missiles they could find. He looked back. "All of them, sir. None has abandoned us. Not one."

At those words, it seemed to Sabinus that even his centurion's hard eyes shone bright with emotion.

Wiping his bespattered club clean beside a water butt, Knuckles came upon the cavalry captain, Malchus.

He had refused medical aid, and was sewing, swabbing, and bandaging himself from a little wooden box by his side. Knuckles watched in fascination. Malchus smeared a whitish paste over his stitched wounds. Knuckles could smell it was garlic, and maybe oxide of zinc. The captain threw back his head and closed his eyes and clenched his teeth awhile. Must have stung a bit. Then he bandaged his shallower cuts. There were a lot of them: on his arms, his legs, a nasty one on his thigh, and a nastier one still across his chest. One of his ears didn't look much like an ear any more, either. Then he took out a squat bottle of watery red liquid and poured it in a thin trickle over his bandages, letting the linen soak it up.

"Red meat, wine, garlic," muttered Knuckles. "What you doin," makin' a fuckin' casserole of yourself?"

Malchus looked up and grinned painfully. "Very tasty dish I'd be, too."

Knuckles grunted. "Ladies first."

Across the plain, if any cared to watch, the slain cavalrymen were being stripped of their armor. And a more mysterious figure was moving against the sinking sun. A vulture seemed to keep watch over her, circling high above. She wore long dark robes, an elaborate headdress, and seemed to hold a twisting snake in her hands. Occasionally she knelt down beside one of the fallen Roman cavalrymen like a ministering angel. Arapovian watched from the walls with his deep-set hawk eyes, and thought he saw one of the cavalrymen stir and try to scrabble desperately out of her long shadow. The Armenian gripped his bow more tightly as he watched, but he was helpless. They were all helpless. The woman knelt beside the cavalryman, and when she rose again he moved no more.

She would be ministering to them all soon enough, if no help came.

10

LAST STAND

Sabinus visited the wounded and exhausted men seated around the white-washed walls of the little hospital. The pallets within had all long since been filled. The air echoed with soft groans. The men, their bare skin, their clothing, their armor, all seemed only a coat of dark dust and shining redness. About them the stench of sweat and blood. A few auxiliaries tried their best to keep away the tormenting flies. Oh God for reinforcements. There would be none left to reinforce soon. Abject rescue, then. But still from the east and Ratiaria . . . nothing. They were as alone as ever.

"Sir," said his last standing decurion. "Hun deputation at the west gate again."

It took him time to walk back up to the gate tower, treading very carefully, hand on his side.

Below the tower sat the stone-faced warlord, ringed by his finest, freshest warriors, a hundred of them, arrows nocked to the bow.

The warlord raised his face to him. "You have fought well," he said. "Almost like Huns. So much for the decadence of the West." He smiled a brief smile, as if at some private joke. "Nevertheless, your cowards of cavalrymen who rode against my innocent people are all destroyed. As are you. Now I will grant you amnesty. Those of you who still live may walk free from this fort and leave us to raze it flat. You may walk to the next frontier fort eastward. It is called Ratiaria—you know it well enough. The Legio III Pannonia is stationed there, a full six thousand men. The legate's name is Posthumus. He shares his bed with a whore called Statina." Another smile. "Do not think we are entirely ignorant savages, Roman. Do not underestimate us."

"I do not underestimate you," said Sabinus.

"Very well, then," said the warlord. "Lead your survivors east to Ratiaria, and tell them there of your destruction."

Sabinus looked around. A single exhausted legionary sat nearby in the deepening shadow of the battlements, bow resting on his knees. They exchanged looks. The legionary was too tired even to speak, but he shook his head.

Further along, one of his comrades growled, "Tell him to go fuck himself. Pardoning my language."

Sabinus's grim smile did not reflect the tangle and stir of his emotions. He looked back down at the warlord. "What is the name of your god?"

The Hun scowled ferociously. He had not come to bandy words, but to give orders. "No Roman dog speaks that holy name."

"Their god is called Astur," said another voice nearby. It was Arapovian. "Astur, the All Father, Great Eagle of the Eternal Blue Sky."

Sabinus gazed down very steadily at the warlord and said, "May Astur curse you. May you and all your tribe vanish from the earth."

At those words, a shadow of preternatural darkness passed over the warlord's face. Sabinus kept steady. A hundred arrowheads were aimed at him. Then the warlord wrenched his pony round and tore away across the plain, his men following.

The legate took a careful breath. He ordered all fit and walking to the walls once more. "The day is not yet done."

And the men rose to their feet once more, the last few dozen of them. About sixty or seventy men, bearing twice as many wounds between them. Some helped others stumble forward, some used their own pikes for crutches. Some went up the narrow stone steps to the battlements on their hands and knees.

The sun was going down in the west. For a while the Huns appeared to pause in their attack.

"Perhaps they will allow us a good night's sleep," growled Tatullus. It was a joke, of sorts. Night was when they would come again to finish it.

For now, there was an eerie peace. Swallows hawked low over the evening river, feeding on clouds of water flies. A moorhen called her chicks. A muted splash among the nodding reeds—otter or water vole. The warm summer sun going down in the west. Burning orange against the great white flanks of the Alps. Setting the Rhine and the Po on fire. Casting long, cool shadows over the vineyards of Provence and Aquitania, over the ancient, lion-colored castles and hill towns of Spain where Hannibal once marched, and over the Immortal City itself on its seven hills. The evening shadow of the Column of Marcus Aurelius, and the Colossus of Nero . . . Sabinus's heart heaved with sorrow. This beloved empire. He had seen the future, in the implacable face of that mighty barbarian warlord who rode out of nowhere, at head of an army of horsemen that no man could number. The empire was sinking in the west, as surely as the silent sun.

Lone horsemen galloped back and forth across the plains below, stripping armor from the dead, burning them like refuse. Occasionally, through the sun-reddened dust, the watchers on the wall glimpsed a yowling figure in tribal wear but now sporting some additional decoration. A triumphal Kutrigur Hun, naked except for a tattered deerskin loincloth, bristling with bow and quiver, shaven headed but for a single plume of limed hair, his skin half blue with tattoos, and proudly riding with a curtal red cavalry cloak fluttering round his coppery shoulders, and, slung from his saddle, a freshly severed head. He waved his sword beneath the walls of the fort and howled like a wolf in winter.

Knuckles threw a rock at him and missed. Overhead, the buzzards circled in the last of the sun. More had joined them, red kites. "Fuckin' carrion birds," growled the hulking Rhinelander. Then he raised his head to the sky and shouted to them, "Plenty of carrion tonight, friends! Guzzle your cropful! Hun and Roman flesh together, it all tastes the same under the skin!"

Just after the first stars appeared in the darkening sky, Lyra and Altair high and Regulus falling, there came wearisomely familiar sounds: distant thump, then shuddering quake. They were hitting the southwest tower once more. They would be in very soon.

"Start bagging again!" ordered Sabinus.

And the men, who had not slept for thirty-six hours, forty, began to bag up the broken defenses by torchlight. One collapsed under a sandbag. Tatullus kicked him to his feet again. "You can sleep when you get to Hades," he growled. "Which won't be long now. Until then, soldier, you get on your feet and work."

Sabinus himself reascended to his post on the west tower and slumped.

I had hope when violence was ceas't . . .

The line echoed in his head. An old poet. Virgil, perhaps. His schooldays seemed an age ago. Merely lifting his head was an effort, his very neck bones aching with weariness. But he gazed heavenward anyway and surveyed the fixed stars pinned to the canopy of night. Some said they were alchemical furnaces where new souls were forged; the pristine, superlunary abode of the gods, of mercy and justice eternal. They looked very far away. The night was so silent. Help would not come. They could not go on. They were finished.

Tatullus stood beside him.

It was unjust. The gods were unjust. They had fought all day and half the night like lions, and by the next dawn they would all lie dead. Yet how should you complain to the gods? You might as well try to reason with Mount Etna. The world was as it was.

Tatullus glanced at him. And for some reason, at that moment, unutterably weary and foredefeated as they were, the two men smiled. As if to say, in concord with each other, Well, all men must die. We did our best—and our best was good.

The Armenian appeared. He did not wait for permission to speak. "I said you would not defeat them in open country."

Tatullus turned a menacing eye on him. "He's 'sir' to you, soldier."

Arapovian was apparently unaware of the glowering centurion's presence. And he addressed no man as "sir."

"You know your only chance now: to fight them hand-to-hand and damage them. To hold them, to bloody them, to buy time until reinforcements come." He adjusted his sword belt. "Of course, if they wish to overrun you here no matter what the cost, and no reinforcements come to your aid, we shall all die anyway."

Another seismic onager strike.

"A Roman legionary legate does not customarily take counsel from a common soldier," said Sabinus, aware even as he said it that Arapovian was no common soldier.

The Armenian continued, unabashed, "My ancestors fought the Huns before. Hepthalite Huns. On the high plains of Ararat, where the Euphrates rises from snowmelt off the mountains, flowing down to water the broad corn lands of Erzinjan and Erzerum, and the sweet orchards of—"

"Forgive the interruption," said Sabinus, "but now is really not the time for poetry."

Arapovian heard him with dignity. "My grandfather died fighting the Huns. They will always gallop faster than you, shoot further than you. You need to draw them in, separate them from their horses, as you did with the line of pikemen. That hurt them."

"Thank you for your sage military advice, my lord," growled the legate, one hand holding his side, one fist clenched on the wall. "And how do you suggest we do that, in your mysterious eastern wisdom? Send them a fucking dinner invitation?"

Another massive shock. The sound of collapsing masonry.

Arapovian inclined his head in that calamitous direction. "Let them into the fort. Stop reinforcing the wall and the tower, and let them fall. Meet them in the rubble, hand-to-hand, where their arrows and horsemanship are useless. That fellow Caestus, the boor, he will fight well enough face to face with them. Now he is wasted. Soon he will be shot."

Sabinus reflected a moment. Then, "Get back below, soldier."

He reflected some more. It insulted his pride to hear advice from a common soldier, Armenian *naxarar* of ancient lineage or no. It insulted his pride even more to put that advice into action. But . . .

The rumble of galloping hooves, a sudden shower of arrows out of the gathering gloom. Another cry from the battlements. Another fall.

The tower would collapse soon enough, anyway. They could ready themselves for it.

Along the wall, one young soldier had lost it. The boy Julianus, the one he'd tried to nerve with fine talk. But what could have prepared him for this? The boy was crawling around on his hands and knees, sobbing, howling like a dog. Another soldier dragged him off down below. He would not be back this time.

Sabinus held his breath a moment, slugged back a last mouthful of wine to kill the pain. Then he gave his runner the order.

"Stop bagging up the southwest tower! Evacuate! Let it fall."

The man hesitated. "Sir?"

He did not repeat himself. The soldier went.

Perhaps the Armenian was right. Over the chaos of rubble where the tower lay in ruins, they'd make their stand. The barbarian horsemen would find that a harder line to break. The Spartans used to boast that their walls were made of men, not stones.

It was as Sabinus had reckoned. The Hun artillerymen—the very phrase seemed an idiotic contradiction in terms for these know-nothing horse warriors, but whoever they were, Huns or Vandals or other unknown easterners, they continued their steady onslaught into the night.

Sabinus ranged his last men with their pikes, Tatullus with his billhook, Knuckles with his club, facing the battered southwest tower and wall. It was dark. Behind them he had his auxiliaries light a row of big braziers.

Another massive hit. The walls trembled and stilled. Then as if in a dream, very slowly, reluctantly, the tower began to subside into itself, the neighboring walls began to fold and fall. Sabinus hazed his men back. But the tower was so damaged below that it simply collapsed in on itself with a muffled subterranean music. It seemed to take forever for the stones to reach the earth, or pile up one another at broken angles. The noise of collapse ebbed, and from far away they could hear rising cheers and ululations. The dust gradually diminished and they saw what faced them. A rupture in the walls about fifty feet wide, blocked by a mound of stones, rubble and projecting wooden beams, about half the height of the old walls: fifteen, twenty feet.

"To the top!" roared Sabinus. "Watch for incoming fire!"

The last of the legion climbed arduously toward the top of the rubble ridge and peered over.

An army of horsemen was galloping toward them. The Romans were seen, silhouetted against the light of the braziers, and the horsemen loosed their arrows. The defenders ducked down and the arrows clattered uselessly over them.

"Come on, you pigeon-livered savages!" roared Knuckles, the veins like cords in his neck. He smacked his club into his hand. "Come and get cozy!"

The savages barely reined in as they approached, seemingly intent on galloping up the rubble mound and straight on into the fort. But no one's horsemanship was that good. One young hothead tried it. Arapovian stepped from the shadows and shot him.

"Lose your bow, soldier!" bellowed Tatullus angrily. "Draw your sword! This one's hand-to-hand!"

For once, Arapovian obeyed.

The dead Hun's horse twisted and fell, a foreleg caught between two broken stones, and rolled back screaming. Huns milled again at the foot of the mound, bewildered.

"Yeah, horse fuckers!" roared Knuckles. "You'll have to leave your girlfriends behind this time!"

But not yet. The Huns wheeled away again into the night, accustomed only to their warrior arts of archery and horsemanship. They loosed more volleys of arrows in retreat. The arrows came over the barricade and clattered uselessly into the yard beyond. They did the same again and again, feeling not a single arrow in returning fire. But their attack was useless. They struck nothing. Even the Huns couldn't keep up this wastage.

"They've got to engage soon," murmured Arapovian. "It's a matter of pride."

One last try. A fast gallop before them, a column of horse archers firing directly into the defensive line.

"Heads!"

Step back, duck, shields up. The arrows thumped into the big oval shields or slid over the top, again to no avail. Not a Roman was hit. They galloped away.

Tired but jubilant legionaries set their shields down in the rubble again, lopped off the jutting arrow shafts. Took deep breaths, wiped away the sweat.

"We're still here, you yellow-bellied horse fuckers!"

Now the Hun generals understood. It would have to be hand to hand to finish this. Their warriors rode near in the darkness, slipped from their mounts, hooked their bows onto their saddlepoints, drew their swords, and came scrambling up the rubble.

The defenders took to the top of the ridge.

"Okay, boys!" roared Sabinus. "Face to face at last! No quarter!"

The Huns came up in a mass surge, without discipline now, desperate to finish it, to squeeze into the fort and have the victory—they, too, had taken plenty of casualties today. But a thousand, two thousand, were trying to squeeze through a gap held by fifty men, and their greater numbers told against them. They barely left each other room to swing their swords. And now the burning amber light of the big braziers behind the defenders showed itself of use. The defenders fought dark and silhouetted, but the attackers had to face into it. Their eyes dazzled, coppery skin shiny with sweat, arms and shoulders rippling with muscles and tattoos and elaborate hennaed runes of protection, which did nothing to protect them from those severe, pragmatical Roman pikes. Up close, the legionaries saw the barbarous magnificence of their enemies at last, magnified in the flaming darkness. Like warriors out of Homer or an even deeper past: the deep, unwritten Scythian past. The untamed warriors looked almost beautiful to them as they cut them down.

Knuckles clapped his bronze-studded forearms together round a warrior's shaven head and split it open like a raw egg. He turned and kicked a heavy boot into another Hun. The Hun staggered and swiped at him with his dagger. Knuckles twisted, more agile than he looked. The desperate struggle was too tight-packed for him to swing his club, so he drove it into the Hun's face like a ram. The big easterner fell back and knocked his comrade behind him flying. Arapovian leaped forward and with two sharp thrusts skewered them both where they lay stunned amid the tumbled masonry, then fell back into line.

Huns howled with fury, came on relentlessly. Tatullus worked like Knuckles, thusting his billhook in long, low stabs. Arapovian's swordsmanship was as good as his bowmanship. Another wiry little Hun nearly had him with a swipe of his yataghan but Arapovian squatted down just in time and drove his sword into the man's naked belly. He immediately stood again, kicked the corpse off the end of his blade, and drew back ready for the next one, who came on at once.

The Hun warriors hated this fight. Too fetid and enclosed, without space to maneuver, with no room for the sudden spurting gallop, the extravagant caracole, the graceful arc of lethal, streamlined arrow. This was furious and filthy stuff, bloody pummeling in the shadows of ruined and alien walls, the clean air of the steppes a thousand miles away. Their horses milled behind them, uncertain. If their father Astur should cry to them out of the night sky, they would not hear him.

Their loss of confidence showed in their expressions, their movements, and the defenders punished it without pity. Knuckles's mastery of the blunt arts of bludgeon and punch, those straps of bull's hide wound round his apelike forearms, took a terrible toll. So, too, did his quick, surprising agility, like a big cat, the way a lion can be nimble for brief bursts when hunting. He gave himself a moment of space, his huge club slewed sideways, men's brains shot from their ruptured skulls as if spat out, gray roe slithering down their comrades' shoulders. Stumbling in the blood and slime, the Huns were filled with enfeebling disgust, panic, even claustrophobia. Where now was the glorious Parthian flight upon the open plains, wind in your hair?

Tatullus killed two attackers with two hard thrusts, only moments apart. Knuckles cracked open another skull. A smaller Hun tried to dive in sideways and thrust his yataghan into his flank, but again Knuckles swiveled, dodged the thrust, swept his arm back and with a mighty swashing blow caught the warrior across the side of his head. The dull bronze studs thunked, the fellow saw red and dropped senseless. Knuckles moved his foot and broke his neck.

The steep and jagged outward slope of the rubble ridge was slippery with blood, and worse. Sabinus moved carefully along behind and below his men, shouting words of encouragement. Not one of the line was down yet. My God, it's like old times, thought Sabinus: Roman soldiers doing what they do best, standing shoulder to shoulder, pitiless, immoveable, the steel mincing machine. Meanwhile, down at the bottom of the ridge, the Hun bodies were piling up like swine in an abattoir.

Arapovian's plan had been a good one; or the best they could come up with as things stood. Stab, thrust, slash. The defenders were beyond exhaustion, but drawing some infernal gallows energy from the terrible attrition suffered by their bewildered enemy. The Huns could not make headway, and their fury made them foolish. Wave after wave came up against the line of pikes ranged against them, cold as moonlight. And wave after wave fell back again, ruptured or slain. Even for these adamantine steppe warriors, this night was turning into nightmare.

Sabinus saw Arapovian pause and look away.

The Armenian turned back to the line, defended himself against another attack, lopped off an arm, planted his foot in the man's chest and kicked him back down the slope. Turned his head and listened again.

Sabinus's heart leaped. The Armenian's sharp ears had heard . . . trumpets! The legate turned to listen to that sweet sound. A pause. And then . . .

He closed his eyes. It was not trumpets. It was a massive weight hitting the south gates.

One last time he struggled up the steps to the battlements.

They had brought one of the onagers up. It was fifty yards off, loosing boulders into the oaken south gates on a low, flat, brutal trajectory.

He went down again, tightening his bronze cuirass about his big belly as tight as he could bear. Like dying in harness. He went steadily over to the south gates. *Whumpff.* The gates rocked back, the big crossbeams rattled in their braces, splinters flew. The Armenian's idea had been a good one, for a desperate last stand. But it, too, had failed.

But they, the VIIth Legion, how well they had failed! Could any legion have failed as gloriously as they had? Oh that one or two should survive, to tell their story to posterity. Such a story would live for generations. A night and a day they had stood firm against a whole army. And still they fought. That wasn't bad. That must count as a kind of heroes' death.

The gates beside him reeled again under impact, and unmanly tears came to his eyes as he watched the last of his men fighting and dying there upon the dark, discolored rubble of the ruptured tower. They had still not heard the onager. Part-timers, farmers, married with wives and children. He knew what they were fighting for, with ferocity born of desperation. Not for Rome, either old or new, nor for the emperor on his gilded throne. They were fighting for the wives and children left on their farmsteads and smallholdings, or trembling down in the dungeons. The gates beside him splintered further. God have mercy on those trapped wretches down below. Only two fates possible for them now, the better of which was a life in chains amid barbarian tents.

For him, there would be no Thracian vineyard, nor sharp-tongued, ardent-hearted Domitilla. Three months to go. The luck of Cassandra. For these barbarians, who had destroyed his life and his peaceful old age, he let his hatred well up. Felt its coursing power burn in his veins. Hefted his sword, a short, old-style *gladius.* The fury and the mire of human veins. The distant fury of battle. But coming close now, in this last act, last scene of his battered old life. His own death was already in the past, written in the old book of the gods. He tightened his belt another notch around his bleeding belly. It wasn't true that you felt no fear. Even old soldiers felt fear. But all men must die. The gates were nearly done. He looked up one last time. Make it glorious, my brave legionaries. Make it cost them dear.

He leaned down painfully to take the shield from one of his own dead, gently unloosing the man's stiffened fingers from the wooden grip. Stood again. When those gates finally gave way, the Huns would find one still in their path.

The attack in the corner had slowed briefly, leaving his men standing down, stoop shouldered with exhaustion. Ungainly stick figures lit from below by the orange brazier light. Heroes all. Beyond, the enemy had pulled back yet again, heavily bloodied, sullen, furious. And now in the stillness, the last legionaries heard what Arapovian had heard. The sound of the accursed onager hurling its rocks, and the south gates going. Soon, very soon now, they would be surrounded. Attacked from before and behind, the fort overrun through the south gate, however hard they fought here. They looked at each other, barely able to raise their heads on their shoulders. Their eyes shone. They nodded. Heroes all.

They looked back to their commander below by the wall. He could not climb up to them any more. They knew it. He leaned close to the south wall, shield on his shoulder, short sword drawn, face plastered with cold sweat, looking up at them.

Only one of his men still had the spirit to speak. "It has been an honor serving with you, sir!"

Sabinus raised his hand to him. To all of them. A salute to equals. The rest of the men saluted him in reply. Some of them almost smiled.

And then the gates flew in.

11

THE DUNGEONS

The last of the defenders instantly lost all formation, and broke and ran. Within moments the neat grid-pattern streets and alleyways of the fortress were overrun with screaming horsemen. They galloped in triumph, racing each other to set each barrack building alight. Cutting down any last stragglers of the destroyed legion, or lassoing them as they fled, and dragging them along behind in the dust as tortured trophies. Fires blazed up in the night, sparks and stars. The appetite for destruction seemed inexhaustible. Soon they clustered around the legionary *principia*. They ransacked the elegant rooms, smashed vases and glassware, dragged out tables and couches, made a huge bonfire in the center of the colonnaded courtyard. Others roped together teams of horses to drag down the pillars and roofbeams and crash the whole building. Word had gone out from the Great Tanjou. Not a stone should be left standing. The very name of Viminacium would denote eloquent desolation for an entire empire.

Warriors still on horseback, inseparable from their mounts, some wearing embroidered Roman curtains for cloaks around their naked shoulders, rode into the chapel and collected the last of the legionary standards to add to the fire. Then word came from the leader that there was gold beneath the altar.

Behind VII Barrack stood the long, low punishment block, comprising a row of dank, evil-smelling cells without windows, and a narrow corridor with one doorway at the end. The building was heavily tiled, not thatched, for greater security. As if by instinct, Knuckles and Arapovian found themselves backing into it side by side, peering out for oncoming Huns.

"Christ. No getting away from some people," said Knuckles.

"The families," said Arapovian, jerking his head back.

Knuckles glanced round. Aside from four or five corpses already strewn across the stoneflagged floor behind him, in the gloom at the other end of the corridor he saw a heavy iron-bound trapdoor set into the flagstones. It must lead down to the dungeons. They could still—

"Jesus!" Arapovian rarely swore, but suddenly the doorway was shadowed by a Hun horseman. He brought him down with single arrow and Knuckles finished him with his club. They stepped back into the shadows.

"Brilliant," said Knuckles. "That'll bring 'em in like flies."

"Bag up the trapdoor at the end," gasped Arapovian. "With those bodies."

Knuckles scowled. "I don't take orders from you, you Parsee bastard."

Arapovian ignored him. There was a group of plumed and feathered warriors coming down the alley, stained bloody in the torchlight. They had seen the riderless horse, the dark shape on the ground.

"Do it *now*. Hide the trapdoor. When they come stampeding in over our corpses, they might not find it—the families might yet survive. The dead and the living both walk free in their own way from these unbelieving savages."

"Christ in a crib," growled Knuckles. But, grumbling about being no slaughterhouse slave, he began to haul the bodies down the passageway, the flagstones slathered in gore, and stacked them over the iron door like fish. Thump, thump of meat. He wondered about the families, women and children and toothless ancients, down in the pitch darkness of those foul dungeons. The airless terror, the unknowing. Yet they might survive.

He surveyed the stack of bodies. "Can't we hide under 'em?" he suggested.

"No time," said Arapovian, and slashed out with his sword.

The building was surrounded. The two men fought again side by side like demons in the protection of the narrow doorway. Copper faces, bodies, torchlight, bared teeth, a muscular neck before them decorated with severed ears on a thong. Arapovian beheaded him. Nearby they could hear the battering of someone trying to break through the walls, but the building was strongly

built: men held for execution often try to escape. Likewise on the roof, warriors tearing off the heavy baked tiles found only more thick crossbeams beneath. The confusion was atrocious, the Huns' desperation to be in and finish
this job making them careless. Knuckles swiped one aside with his studded
forearm, caved another face in with his club. Behind the milling crowd, another Hun still mounted loosed an arrow at them and succeeded only in killing one of his own in the crush. It was absurd, but they could not get at these
last two. One waved a squat pickaxe, howling and almost dancing with frustration. Arapovian slashed at him, and Knuckles continued to use his club
like a fist to defend the narrow doorway, punching out, smashing heads, caving in chests. Warriors howled execrations, tore at each other in their frenzy
to kill these two trapped men, these standing insults to their victory.

"Collapse the roof!" called a Hun commander calmly from behind. He sat
back on his horse, indicating his meaning with a wave of his hand. "Then fire
it. Bring up that handcart there. The rest of you, fall back."

Frenzied or not, the painted savages obeyed in an instant. Then they ran
the flaming handcart across the doorway and tipped it inward. Knuckles and
Arapovian leaped back as blazing bales tumbled into the blocked corridor
amid roiling clouds of smoke, and their lungs began to constrict, their eyes to
redden and water and go blind.

Geukchu nodded with grim approval. "Let the fire take them. A fine cre-
mation for two such mighty heroes of the empire. A warrior pyre."

Arapovian squatted back, his arms held out as poor shields before his face.
They were piling more blazing bales onto the roof. The timbers began to
burn.

"You know something?" roared Knuckles. "Rome's city firefighters, they
never eat roast pork. Can't stand the smell. Exactly the same as roast human."

Arapovian shuffled in the dense smoke. "We need to clear the dungeon
door again."

Knuckles didn't move.

"Fine. Stay here and roast."

Knuckles made a noise like frustrated bear and lumbered after the impossible Armenian.

Choking on smoke, hair singed, coursing with sweat and deafened with the
roar of the flames, they recommenced the foul work. Dragging corpses from
the pile was worse when you pulled an arm or a leg and the body didn't come

with it. By the time they had cleared the trapdoor the smoke was impenetrable.

"Can't see a fuckin' thing," rasped Knuckles. "But I bet you need a bath."

Silence.

"Parsee?"

Still silence. Then the creak of the heavy iron trapdoor.

"You did it!" Knuckles flailed around for a moment to give the easterner a thump on the back, but Arapovian was already down the steps. Knuckles's hair was smoldering and he couldn't breathe, so he groped his way down— just ahead of the crash of the collapsing roof, and a ferocious through draft which cleared the smoke from the building and set the fires roaring up like furnaces. The two men were suddenly and hellishly illuminated as they descended the narrow stone steps to the dungeons, backlit by a curtain of flame. The people below, the mothers and maidens and wide-eyed infants, gazing up in terror, saw two figures descending toward them out of the jaws of the fire, blood red and blackened from head to toe.

They must be in hell.

Knuckles turned awkwardly on the narrow steps, slippery with algae, pulled one of the cadavers over the raised trapdoor as best he could, and then let it slam shut over his head. They were in darkness. He groped for bolts, then stopped. No bolts on the inside of a dungeon door. He grinned in the blackness. Idiot.

A small oil lamp was lit, and the abject people viewed the two demons. One a huge brute with a club locked under his simian arm, the other tall and lean, cruel and clever. A woman about to wail had her mouth immediately stopped up by this one. His hand was sticky with fresh blood. She nearly vomited. He held a ringed finger to his thin, cruel lips.

Aside from her, there were five or six more women, young mothers, one old. Half a dozen children, blubbing and snotty, and an infant fast asleep and oblivious. One old fellow, who clutched his knobbly stick as if ready to fight them.

"Calm down, grandad. We're on your side."

They huddled together in the airless cell, and not a word was spoken as the punishment block burned to cinders above them.

Above the dungeon, onager missiles were still hitting the walls of the fort. For sheer joy, a kind of victory celebration, and for practice, as the Hun warlord said laughing. He rode round the ruins of the blazing fort on his little skewbald pony, Chagëlghan—he always called his horses Chagëlghan, no one knew why. His gold earrings danced, his yellow eyes shone with delight in the darkness.

"I want these walls flat," he said.

Later, as the first gray light of dawn was coming up, he sat his horse out on a mound to the south of the city with Orestes and Chanat beside him, stroking his gray mustaches thoughtfully. Standing before them was a captive bound in thick ropes, his hands just free enough to hold a testament.

Attila grinned. "Read to me," he said, "out of that fine old book of the Christians. The words of the prophet Nahum."

He surveyed the devastated city as a different man might view some lovely fresco of Venus, or Atalanta in Corydon, while his trembling captive read.

> Woe to the bloody city! The horseman lifteth up the bright sword and the glittering spear: and there is a multitude of the slain, and they stumble upon the corpses. Behold, I am against thee, saith the Lord of Hosts: the gates of thy land shall be set wide open unto thine enemies: the fire shall devour thee. Thy shepherds shall slumber, and thy nobles dwell in the dust; thy people is scattered among the mountains, and no man gathereth thee. Thy wound is grievous, and all who hear of it shall clap their hands: for upon whom hath not thy wickedness been visited continually?

Attila nodded and smiled. "Even the God of the Christians has spoken."

He retrieved the precious testament from the captive and handed it to Orestes. Then he sliced his sword across the captive's neck and the three rode on down the mound for the city. His men were already having victory horse races in the half-ruined hippodrome. They were dressing horses in the robes of butchered priests, and carrying the crucifix itself about the circuit, Christ himself topped with a *kalpak,* a pointed Scythian cap. Later they would set the crucifix in the sand and make it their own totem, hanging from it severed heads, the skin peeled off and stuffed with straw. There would be feasting on slain livestock by firelight, and toasts in looted silver chalices decorated with Christian symbols, or Silenus chasing his nymphs.

In the gloom of the single sputtering clay lamp, the two soldiers discerned another iron-bound door.

"No way out there," said Knuckles. "The execution dungeon. And I don't think we're ever going to find the key now, do you?"

Arapovian stepped between the women and children and knocked on the door, absurdly polite. A moment later there came an answering knock.

"Eh, well," said Knuckles. "He was going to get chopped anyhow. This way, he'll just starve to death instead. Comes to the same end, like all of us."

Arapovian stood before the iron door and rattled his stiletto dagger in the big lock-hole for a moment. Then he drew his brooch-pin from his cloak and knelt down and probed. Moments later, something clicked. He dragged at the doorhandle and it grated slowly open.

Knuckles looked faintly disgusted at this showmanship. Blew a soft raspberry.

A figure slowly emerged, blinking in the lamplight, shackled hand and foot. But for the heavy black beard, he might have been Knuckles's younger brother.

"Water," he rasped.

"You'll get some," said Arapovian. "You are?"

"Barabbas," said the prisoner in a voice suggesting he hadn't drunk water for a week. Arapovian stood back. The man's breath was foul.

Knuckles stepped up. "Don't take the piss."

"S'true," said the prisoner.

"So what are you, the original Wandering Jew or something?"

The prisoner shrugged. "My father's son."

"What you in for?"

"Theft from the granary."

"Tut tut. You haven't got a clue what's been going on, have you?"

The prisoner shook his shaggy head miserably. "I thought I could smell smoke. Fire?"

"Some." Knuckles turned to Arapovian. "You got to laugh. Everyone else gets the chop. The one prisoner due for the chop walks out just fine."

"As wiser men than we have previously observed," said Arapovian, "the humor of heaven is more often ironical than benevolent."

"You took the words right out my mouth."

Arapovian rested the tip of his dagger against the prisoner's neck. "I do not understand why, but it seems that, like your gospel namesake, you are destined live in others' stead. You go with us. But one moment of foolishness and I will kill you. You think you are hard, but I am harder."

"He is, too," confirmed Knuckles, jerking his head. "He looks like some Persian Royal who's spent his life in baths of asses' milk. But he's not."

"Armenian," said Arapovian.

"Whatever," said Knuckles. "East is east."

Something thumped onto the trapdoor above their heads. A burning beam.

"Shit," said Knuckles.

"You have more oil?" asked Arapovian.

A woman shook her head.

"Then snuff the lamp for now. We must wait a long time."

The people tried to sleep. Arapovian recited softly to himself the litanies of his religion in the ancient tongue. Knuckles snored, clutching his beloved club to his chest like a child clutching its doll. The fire roared dimly above them.

After what he thought must be many hours, Arapovian crawled through the darkness and up the narrow steps to the trapdoor. There was a pause and then he gasped.

Knuckles was awake and heard him. "Don't tell me. It's hot."

Arapovian returned.

"Never touch an iron-bound trapdoor that's been in the floor of a blazing building all day," Knuckles said helpfully, "even if you are Parsee fire-worshipper. You'll give yourself a nasty burn. Even my granny could have told you that, bless her whorish old heart."

"Hold your tongue, you ape," hissed Arapovian.

"Don't call me an ape."

"Don't call me a Parsee and I'll think about it."

Knuckles sighed.

Arapovian squatted, nursing his burned fingertips, feeling like a fool. An unaccustomed feeling for him, and one he did not appreciate. He looked upward in the pitch blackness. If those bands got any hotter they'd start to glow in the dark. The wood on the upside must surely be charring down. Then the door would fall in, and they'd be done for.

The terrified families stared around sightlessly in the darkness. The old man said, "Have the invaders gone?"

"No," said Arapovian. "The legion has gone. We are all that is left."

Shock, then slow sobs as the terrible news sank in. The cell was full of widows and orphans.

The old man reached out in the dark and clutched the Armenian's arm. "Will we live? Our children?"

Arapovian gently loosed his grip. There was a long silence. "I don't know," he said at last. "If the trapdoor holds, then . . . maybe."

The fire roared louder.

Soon, in the gloom there was a dull red glow. The iron bands of the trapdoor were growing red hot. Oozing through the gaps round the edge of the trapdoor, sizzling, came runnels of melted fat. The odor of roast pork. Arapovian hoped the women and the children would not understand what it was.

"Pray," he said. "All of you."

12

FLIGHT

Silence, broken only by the occasional, low bludgeoning thunderclap. The Huns were still marauding, still about their work of destruction. And they themselves were still trapped. When would it be better to surrender themselves than die here? Perhaps not much longer.

No sense of time. They slept fitfully. The families remained for the most part speechless with terror and grief. Cramped, stained, exhausted by their own trembling. Tongues sore and swelling with thirst, nostrils sickened by the stench of their own bodies. The children's throats painful and dry as sharkskin. They sucked the damp walls, the bitter green taste of algae on their lips, until Arapovian forbade it. "That will kill you sooner," he said.

The only consolation was that the fire had not sucked the air out of the dungeon. It was foul down here, but it was enough for them still to breathe.

His heart was heavy for them. These children now fatherless, these women husbandless, this old couple with their son perhaps lying slain just outside. This noisome, putrid latrine their whole world now.

Time passed. Above, all was silence again.

"We got to get out," said Knuckles.

"Another twelve hours."

"How will we know?"

"Thirty more full litanies or so."

"You're joking."

Arapovian did not reply.

"Tell you what. Tell us about Armenia instead."

After a long silence, Arapovian began to tell them about his homeland. He told them about his friends Jahukunian, Arutyunian, and Khorenatsian, dead and buried in the earth of a land no longer theirs. He told them about the heroine Queen Paranjem, who fought the Persians under Shapur the Great when he devastated the land, and King Arshak, who was captured and blinded and imprisoned in the Castle of Oblivion for thirty years. He told them about the pagan fire temples of the Zoroastrians erected over Christian shrines, and the broad plains of Erzinjan and Erzerum, and the egrets and the francolin in the marshes, and the great monastery of Echmiadzin, the oldest in the world, they said. At last the people slept.

Thirty muttered litanies later, he and Knuckles shook the people awake, and moved toward the steps in the inky darkness.

Knuckles held his club ready while Arapovian reached up and set his sword hilt against the trapdoor overhead. He gave a gentle push. The door sighed and fell down around his shoulders in fluttering leaves of ash. The wood was no more than a blackened parchment, a tissue-thin veil of charcoal between them and the inferno. Only the iron bands remained. He levered them back and stepped up, sword ready. Immediately outside were some charred bones. He pushed them aside with his foot, concealed them beneath smoking timbers as best he could before the families emerged.

They came up shakily into the light of day. For it was dawn. Even Arapovian was unsure how long they had been down there. Perhaps three whole days. A very Christlike resurrection, he thought grimly.

They stood and surveyed the still-smoking desolation, like some ragged band of beggars after the apocalypse. There was nothing left.

"Sweet Mother of God," whispered the old man.

The fort had gone. There were only acres of ash, and a few low stretches of broken wall like rotten teeth. Nothing else. The people moved like silent wraiths through this landscape of rubble and dust and the last thin plumes of smoke, forgetting for a moment even their abominable thirst. Where the great bastions and outer walls had stood, there was only more rubble, crooked forms, cascades of hard material. Beyond where the west gate tower had stood, they glimpsed the remains of the town, and farther off, scattered over the fertile plains, the smoldering ruins of their homes and farmsteads.

One woman gave a cry and stumbled. Knuckles steadied her and rested his huge paw on her thin shoulder and surveyed the scene. "Truth to tell," he said to her, by way of unorthodox comfort, "I'm beginning to get a bit pissed off with these Huns myself."

"Come on, you ape," said Arapovian. "Move out."

"Stop calling me an ape."

"When you stop calling me a Parsee."

Knuckles sighed. "This is going to be fun."

"No," said Arapovian, sheathing his sword again, tightening his belt, surveying the ravaged landscape. "It's not."

He led them through the ruins, trying to steer a course free of atrocities. For amid the burned timbers and stones, there were shapes of what had once been bodies. Tar blackened and twisted, scorched and fire maimed, as if formed out of pitch and then abandoned by some clumsy and heartless god, tossed aside still lifeless.

In desperation a mother flew to the lip of a smashed well, tearing the cloak from her back and lowering it down to see if she could reach water, to wring it out into the mouth of her child.

Arapovian stopped her. "It's poisoned."

She turned on him, eyes blazing with fury and anguish. Her child was already sick with thirst, his face a pallid mask. "How do you know?"

"Even the great river is unclean, the shore choked with bodies. But I will find you water." He pointed south to the hills. "Clean water. Do not be afraid. You will live now, you and your child. The Huns have gone."

He took the child gently from her and laid it over his shoulder and walked on through the wasteland.

They passed where the *principia* itself had stood, and the legionary chapel. A hole gaped in the ground.

Knuckles hawked and spat. "So they found the gold, then. How did they know it was there?"

Arapovian looked around. "The Hun warlord knows far more than that."

"And what'll they do with it? They don't look the kind for fine wines and silk undies."

"They'll hire more mercenaries. Alans, Gepids, Sarmatians." Arapovian walked on again. "They'll buy more power."

A thrill of uncanny horror ran through them as they approached the rubble mound of the west gate. There was still a platform standing, the bare wooden floor of what had been the first-floor guard tower. And there was a figure still up there, legs apart, gazing out over the plain. It must be a Roman corpse, skewered on a long spear and propped there by the Huns in their whimsical humor.

Arapovian passed the thirst-stricken child into Knuckles's arms.

"I don't do children," Knuckles mumbled in protest.

"Stay here."

The Armenian scrambled over the rubble and hauled himself up, his injured thigh throbbing. He could at least take the impaled corpse down. Cover it with rocks, say some appropriate words. He swung himself up onto the wooden platform and approached it.

The corpse turned.

Arapovian froze.

It was Tatullus.

Alive, yes. His eyes as flat and lightless as the dead, his forearms cut across, blood crusted over one side of his scalp. But alive. The iron-hearted centurion. He stared back at Arapovian, not seeing. Down his sunken, deep-grooved cheeks, smoke gray, filthy, were two clear white tracks.

Gradually the centurion's eyes seemed to focus.

"You!" he whispered. "You survived."

Arapovian nodded and saluted. "Sir. Two of us, and the families from the dungeons. And the prisoner, Barabbas. Down there—look."

Tatullus emerged with painful slowness out of his waking nightmare. He seized the Armenian's right hand in his own. His eyes shone brightly again, though he could not speak a word. Then he let his hand drop and turned away and with an abrupt movement wiped his cheeks.

Finally he spoke, his voice slow and careful. "See what water you can find."

"The wells are poisoned, sir. But in the hills . . ."

Tatullus nodded, still struggling to return to the world as it was. "Very well, then. Have them fall in." He drew breath. "We march south."

When they were assembled in order, two abreast, Tatullus came down. He looked at each of them in turn. Finally he came to Barabbas in his shackles.

"The granary thief."

Barabbas shuffled and looked at the ground.

"Fall out." Tatullus drew his sword. "Now kneel."

Before the eyes of the horrified women and children, he raised his sword. But he could not bring it down. A stronger arm than his restrained him. It was Knuckles. They looked each other in the eye a long time. Finally the centurion's arm relaxed. Knuckles let it go.

The Rhinelander picked up a heavy rock and shoved the prisoner's feet apart. Barabbas closed his eyes. Knuckles smashed the rock down and broke the chain. Then he pulled him up and stretched his hand shackles over a stump of wall. Smashed that smaller chain likewise. Barabbas pushed the iron bracelets back up his arms and rubbed his sores.

"Now go and sin no more," said Knuckles sardonically.

The granary thief stumbled away into the wasteland, cradling his broken chains to his chest.

They traversed the scorched farmlands and passed through the desolate orchards, scanning the horizon for horsemen all the while. But they saw none. The firestorm had moved on south. They went up into the hills, where they found a clear stream in a shallow valley. The soldiers filled and refilled their leather flasks, passing them round, making the people drink slowly. The effect, especially on the children, was miraculous. Like hunted harts in the mountains, thought Arapovian. One moment exhausted, tongue lolling, foaming with sweat. He had seen them thus, watched and waited, holding his horse back in the thickets, cradling his spear. The exhausted hart would bend, drink, look up, drink more. And then, as if reborn, would leap forward, cantering uphill, and the hunt would be on again.

One small boy wiped his mouth and passed the flask on and looked up at him. "I'm Stephanos," he said. "I'm hungry."

They rested all day in the green valley, hidden beneath a stand of gray alder trees, rebandaging their wounds. Later the three soldiers went hunting and brought back game birds and some early wild plums, not very ripe but edible in small quantities, and at last the people ate. They also set horsehair snares and in the morning took fresh rabbit with them.

They crossed the hills.

Two days later they came down through woods and saw below them the road south to Naissus. Either side of it rose higher and higher hills, and beyond them were bare mountains. This was the Succi Pass: a long, narrow, five-mile way through the Haemus range.

Tatullus shook his head. "We can't risk it."

"Nor can we travel over the mountains," objected Arapovian. "We three could, but not with the families, and without supplies."

It was true. The children were weak and fractious with hunger. Twice they had come to isolated hamlets in the hills and found nothing: no people, no food, no livestock, nothing. They ate stewed nettles, yarrow, the skinny white roots of wild parsnip, and caught occasional game. But it was never enough, not for twenty of them, on the move all day.

"The barbarians will have gone south," rumbled Knuckles. "Why should they turn back again?"

"They probably won't," said Tatullus. "But if they do . . ." They all knew what fate awaited them if they met the Huns on the road. "We could leave the families here and go on over the mountains ourselves."

They glanced over the hollow-eyed people, waiting for their decision as patiently as cattle.

Tatullus sighed. "Very well. Through the Succi Pass we go. Let's make it fast."

Each of the three took an infant on his shoulders and trotted. The rest of the people kept up as best they could, but still the soldiers frequently had to pause and wait for them to catch up. The sun rose high in the sky, yet the pass felt dark and cold and ominous. The further they progressed, the more threatening and precipitous the dark slate cliff faces rising on either side. There was no escape except forward or back. High overhead, a raven left its perch and circled cawing.

The families straggled behind them, the old ones the slowest of all.

"Faster!" rasped Tatullus. He'd hoped to be through the pass in an hour, but it would take them two.

There was a widening in the pass, tumbled rocks to left and right, and a small stand of trees up a scree slope, before the gap closed up again and ahead of them was an even darker and narrower stretch of the road. Arapovian scrambled up into the trees to find the water source and refill a couple of flasks. He reemerged almost at once, flasks unfilled, standing on a rock, looking back over them blankly.

"What is it, man?" hissed Tatullus. "Move it!"

Arapovian's expression remained blank, but he held his right hand out for stillness.

They stilled.

Then he said, "Into the trees, all of you. *Now.*"

The children scrambled up quickly enough and ran on into the green shadows, but the old ones needed hauling.

Knuckles crouched behind a clump of undergrowth and told the children to do the same. "Not a sound, now," he growled.

They crouched close around him, eyes wide with fear.

The last up over the rocks was the old man. Even as Tatullus pulled him up by his bony, shaking arms, he could hear what the Armenian had heard. The scuffle and clop of many, many hooves approaching.

Above them the raven cawed again. Arapovian pictured its black eyes bright with malice. The old man cried out softly and turned. The hoofbeats were very near now. The riders were only walking their horses, but they were mere seconds away round the corner. Tatullus lifted the old man bodily by his wrists, his scrawny arms straining in their sockets, and his knobbly vine wood walking-stick fell from his hand and clattered over the rock to the road below. Tatullus threw the quailing old man over his left shoulder and glanced back in despair. The stick lay at the edge of the track, brightly varnished, its grip still warm. But already he could smell the horses' sweet aroma on the cool air . . .

"No time!" whispered the Armenian from the trees.

Tatullus strode up the rock and into the darkness of the covert. He dumped the old man behind the thicket and crouched.

Immediately below them appeared the riders. They were Huns.

They reined in and looked around with a puzzled air. Some were already unslinging their bows. Hunters like these did not miss many signs.

Under the trees, the little party were as still as statues.

At the head of the Huns, a war party of a couple of hundred, rode their leader, an old man with long slate-gray hair and long mustaches, finely combed and oiled. He might have been in his sixth or even seventh decade, yet his chest and arms were still very strong. He sat his horse and bunched his reins in his fists on his saddle as his deep-set eyes roved around, and his nostrils seemed to quiver.

His gaze fell on the vine stick. He walked his horse over and gazed down. Then he slipped from his saddle, retrieved it and touched the knobbly grip to his cool cheek. Still warm.

He nimbly stepped halfway back up the rock, swiveled and leaped back on his horse, the vine stick still in his hand. He rested it over his shoulder like a spear and sat his horse again and waited.

The two hundred horsemen were utterly still and silent. The only sound was the caw of the raven overhead. Under the trees they barely breathed.

And then one of the hungry children hiccupped.

It was the boy Stephanos. Knuckles's huge hand shot out and clamped over the boy's mouth. The boy's eyes flared wide but he didn't struggle.

Down below, the Hun leader remained still. Perhaps he had not heard. Perhaps . . .

Then very slowly he turned his head toward them. And smiled.

Moving as silently as a cat, Arapovian stepped back and searched behind them. But it was as he thought. The little wood backed into a dark, damp cliff, which rose, uninterrupted, for three or four hundred feet. They were trapped. "Well," he whispered, and drew his sword. "So be it. Here we die. For the sake of a child's hiccup."

He heard the Hun warlord speak.

"Come forth! All of you. Young, old, the ancient who lately lost his vine staff. And do not show me your weapons. My men will cut you down before you appear."

After a moment's hesitation, Arapovian sheathed his sword.

The people came slowly out of the woods and stood upon the rocks, abject, with heads hung low. Trained on them were two hundred arrows.

Stephanos hiccupped again.

The warlord looked them over, singling out the three soldiers for special scrutiny. At last he said gravely, "I am the Lord Chanat. You Romans slew many of my men."

Tatullus nodded, his hand on the pommel of his sword. "We did. And we will slay many more in the next battle."

Chanat pondered deeply, in no hurry. At last he declared, "You Romans are not all women. You are a Khan?"

"I'm a centurion."

"A leader of men? Or a herder of women and children?"

"Leader of men, usually," growled Tatullus. "Leader of eighty."

"That is good." He nodded. "You will join us. You will be a commander of Huns."

Tatullus looked taken aback. Then he set his face again. "I am a Roman. I fight only for Rome."

"Your empire is destroyed."

Tatullus smiled very slightly, his teeth clenched. "Not yet it isn't."

"Then I will kill you."

"You can try."

Chanat made a strange noise, shucking his teeth. It would be wrong, by every tenet of the warrior code, to slay a man this heedlessly and magnificently brave.

He turned his attention to Arapovian, standing a little further back on the rocks, his hand not far from the hilt of his sword. "You. You are an easterner."

Arapovian did not reply.

"Answer me, fool."

But it was clear that Arapovian would not deign to speak to a Hun, though his life depended on it. He picked a burr fastidiously from his cloak.

"Stiff-necked easterner," growled Chanat. "You must be a Persian traitor fighting for the Romans."

At that, Arapovian could not keep silent. He drew himself to his full height and looked angrily down on Chanat. "I am an Armenian *naxarar* of the noblest birth. My name is Count Grigorius Khachadour Arapovian, the son of Count Grigorius Nubar Arapovian, the son—"

Knuckles intervened, jerking his head. "He is, too."

"And you," said Chanat, turning on him. Knuckles wished he'd kept quiet. "It is my belief that you are the brute who killed the Lord Bela on the bridge."

"I can't say I ever found out the sav—the gentleman's name, your mercifulness. But frankly, at the time, he wasn't behaving too favorably toward me, neither."

Chanat tugged his reins and half-turned his horse. "It is well," he snapped.

"It is war. Now be silent." He looked them over one last time, trotted back, surveyed the women and children, and then made a typically abrupt decision. "This time, you may live. Next time, we will kill you."

As he walked his horse away, he tossed the vine stick over his shoulder to clatter again upon the road.

"And you can have that back!" he called, laughing. "I am not so old as to need it yet!"

It was a fine story that night at the Hun campfire.

"Magnanimous," said Attila.

"Indeed," acknowledged Chanat solemnly. "I did not even demand one of the women for my tent."

"Old Chanat, your heart is as tender as a young lamb's."

"Alas, but I fear my loins will not easily forgive my tender heart. Some of those Roman women weren't so ugly."

Still dazed at their escape and the terrifying randomness of Hun clemency, the refugees camped that night well up in scattered pinewoods. It was good that it was summer. In these hills, winter would have killed them by now. Still, Arapovian allowed them a small fire. The women and children, though hungry, all slept.

They were draining the last of the Armenian brandy, heavily watered, which Arapovian had managed to conserve through everything, when he heard a footfall nearby. The faintest padding footfall in the dry needles. He raised his forefinger.

Knuckles frowned and shook his head.

Arapovian drew his dagger.

And nonchalantly into the firelight stepped Captain Malchus.

Knuckles growled, "How in the name of Cloacina, goddess of Rome's sacred shit pipes, did you . . . ?"

Malchus grinned. His face and arms were a terrible mess. He had sewn up his own wounds again with horsehair and a bone needle. They could see the holes, clotted with dried blood.

"Take more than that to finish me," he said. He sat cross-legged by the fire. "I've been tracking you. Good show when you met the Huns. I saw it all from the clifftop. It was me who set the raven off its ledge. Sorry about that."

They stared at him a while longer, as if to ensure he was no ghost.

At last Arapovian said, "I don't understand how you survived outside the fort, when the Hun charge ran you down."

Malchus reflected. "Imagine," he said. "You're one of two hundred horsemen galloping at a single man. How are you ever going to know which one of you killed him in the rush? If any of you?"

They shook their heads. Tatullus was stirring and awakening again.

"What you do is, you drop just before they hit you. It's all in the timing."

"And then two hundred horses gallop over you."

"That bit is playing with dice, I admit. You do like you're back in your mother's womb." He mimed a curled fetal position, wincing at his cuts. "Plus arms round your head. You know no horse likes to trample a living creature, not even those bullock-headed Hun brutes." He grinned again. "Well, maybe I was lucky. My legs got a bit bruised, but otherwise—here I am. And look." From a leather saddlebag he pulled a decent-sized flagon of looted wine, some very stale but edible bread, and some goat's cheese wrapped in lime leaves.

"Christ be thanked," growled Knuckles, grabbing for the wine.

Arapovian was faster. He set the flagon by his side. "Medical usage first. Those cuts need dousing and resewing." He began to strop his dagger blade, eyeing Malchus's gruesome wounds.

Malchus looked indignant. "What do you mean? They're fine."

"They're rubbish," said Arapovian.

Later Malchus took a long drag on the bottle and passed it to Knuckles, wincing again at his fresh stitches.

"I thought you took a vow," said Tatullus from the shadows where he lay on his side.

"It got canceled," said Knuckles. "By unforeseen circumstances." He took a huge glug.

Arapovian guarded the bread and cheese for the children's breakfast tomorrow. He eyed Knuckles's considerable belly. "You won't starve without it."

They drank more from the welcome flagon.

Knuckles yawned and belched. "Name of Light. That wine's gone straight to my lord and master. Wonder where the nearest whorehouse is?"

"You'd have to pay a month's wages for it, you would," said Malchus. "State of you."

"Look at you," said Knuckles. "While I, on the contrary, left many a broken-hearted lady behind me in Carnuntum, so fond had they grown of me and my hugely proportioned charms."

Malchus snorted with incredulity. Even Tatullus managed a faint smile.

"I was, to be honest, a most cock-witted lad in my youth," reflected the hulking Rhinelander, taking another huge glug of wine. "Give my own granny for a piece of skirt, I would. But with age comes wisdom. Perhaps I will endure tonight with neither fuck nor suck."

Arapovian looked scornful, banking up the wood fire. "Well, you'd better not sleep too near me."

Knuckles raised his eyebrows. "Don't flatter yourself. My lord and master has some dimscrim . . . dimscrin . . .'"

"Discrimination."

"Exactly."

Malchus lay back and stared up at the crescent moon winking fitfully through the dark canopy of the pines. The air smelled beautiful and fresh. His wounds were clean, no infection. The wine warmed his stomach. And they had survived. Life was sweet. Nearby, Tatullus could still barely speak for grief of his legion but, for Malchus, to be alive was victory. There was a tattered veil of cloud drifting across the night sky, luminous in the moonlight. The call of an owl.

"Isn't it magnificent?" he said.

Knuckles belched. "Not bad."

"Not the wine, you oaf. This." He spread his scarred hands wide. "The moon, the dark heavens, the summer stars."

Knuckles turned to Arapovian. "The boy waxes lyrical. Is it a fever?"

"Of sorts. Beyond my cure."

Malchus continued regardless, his voice a rapturous whisper. "This great Hunnic war that has only just begun. The sight of furious, perishing armies. A galloping black horse on a lonely plain. The sunlight glinting on spears. All of it. I love it. '*Sequor omina tanta, quisquis in arma vocas.*'" He sighed. "There is nothing as beautiful as war."

He was like a crazed Trojan hero out of Homer, this one. He'd die fighting, a big smile on his handsome face, his raven hair dripping sweat and blood. Then straight to the Elysian Fields.

"You're a fucking poet," growled Knuckles. "You better have some more wine. All poets are drunks."

"Don't you think," said Malchus, sitting up again, "sometimes, that everything is beautiful just the way it is? With all the beauty and pity and horror mingled, the way the unknown gods have made it? And that really there is no evil—how could it be otherwise? And that even death is beautiful?"

"You're pissed," said Knuckles.

"You're how old?" That was Arapovian.

"Twenty-four," said Malchus. "The youngest cavalry commander on the Danube frontier."

"Well," said the Armenian, settling down to sleep, "there's still time for you to believe in evil."

They slept with their crooked arms for pillows and awoke with their cheeks wet with dew. Arapovian bathed in a nearby stream, to Knuckles's fascination, and cleaned his teeth with a green hazel wand. Then he shared out the bread and cheese among the people.

Stephanos ate too fast and got hiccups again. "Sorry," he said, shame faced.

Arapovian touched him on the head. "You can hiccup all you like, boy. The Huns have gone now."

Some days later, well hidden from the road, they saw passing in the opposite direction a motley family: two girls, a boy, a woman in a grimy red dress, and a man attired in a close-fitting white robe like a priest of the Church, on his chest a wooden Chi-Rho. All their wordly goods were packed onto a mulish-looking pony, bull headed, deep chested, like those the Scythians rode.

The refugees came down from the woods and confronted them. The priest had been the Bishop of Margus himself. "But Margus is destroyed."

Arapovian took a deep breath. "Viminacium, too, is destroyed. We are the only survivors."

The man's wife repeated, faltering, "The legionary fortress . . . destroyed?"

They nodded. She crossed herself. The bishop muttered of the Devil.

"Where do you go now?" asked Arapovian.

"West. To Sirmium, perhaps further."

"You must report to the legate there. Your intelligence will be invaluable."

The priest did not commit himself. He looked over the ragged women and children, the aged couple propping each other up. "We will take the people."

The soldiers considered. It would be safer in the west, for now. The families, dazed and indifferent with tiredness, had no preference. They departed west, with the priest preaching to passersby on the road of the wrath to come.

The four soldiers went south.

Within a few miles they found themselves some acceptable horses, requisitioned from a party of Illyrian merchants. The merchants didn't argue. They rode on down the road at a canter. There would be more fighting to be done.

PART II

THE CITY OF GOLD

1

INTELLIGENCE

Attila was talking with his generals when Orestes stepped forward and passed him something. A fine kidskin parchment, rolled up and sealed with an impressive wax seal.

Geukchu peered at it. "And this is the Western Emperor's own seal?"

Attila nodded. "Identical."

The wily old general was full of baffled admiration. "How?"

"Information is precious." For their amusement, he recited what the sealed roll said from memory.

To my Beloved Brother in Christ, Emperor of the Eastern Romans, Theodosius, Greetings

It is with heavy heart that We must refuse your request for aid at this unhappy time, and make fast our own borders against the hordes of Scythia. All our forces are required for our own defense. We have trust in the Lord that you will repel this barbarous incursion alone. To do so is indeed your bounden duty, since it was your own forces from Viminacium which first stung Attila and his fearsome warriors into attack.

Your faithful Valentinian.

"Commander of the Arian Faithful?"

Attila stroked his thin gray beard. "I like it. Put that in, too."

He resumed. "How fondly I remember our happy boyhood together in Rome, my dearest friend. How we cared for each other in our youthful loneliness, in exile in those sullen courts of empire, so far from our respective homes. And how saddened I was to hear of the death of your noble-hearted brother Beric in that cruel hunting accident."

Even Orestes' eyes glittered with amusement at this. Attila had to wait a few seconds before he could speak again. "I should have been a court jester," he said.

"But to happier matters. The invasion has started. The Hun army, your loyal allies in the north, have conquered half the way to Constantinople already. The vainglorious Roman legions fall before us like grass before the scythe. Their degenerate cities are but fuel for the fire. None stands in our way. And consequently, there will be no Roman attempt upon your own empire of Africa, that rich territory that is rightfully yours by the judgment of Almighty God. May your people bless the wisdom, justice, and mercy of your rule. May the glorious dynasty of Genseric prosper. May the fine sense of your sons prevail."

"Too much," said Orestes. "His sons are renowned idiots. One resides in a dungeon in the palace, chained up and gibbering like an ape."

"Ah. Yes. Change the last two lines. May the martial valor and Christian righteousness of your dynasty prevail forever. And may Genseric come to reign preeminent in the West, as his most loyal ally Attila shall reign in the East, in a conjoined harmony of Emperors and Brothers."

"Hm," said Orestes. "Just about."

"Until such time as we decide to eliminate you and take your empire for our own."

The corners of Orestes' mouth twitched. He laid his pen aside.

"Oh," said Attila, wiping the tears from his eyes. "I should have been a jester."

2

POLITICS AND WITCHCRAFT

The moment Aëtius stepped from the ship, the worst was confirmed.

"Sir, the Huns have crossed the Danube. They have fallen on Margus fair."

"Very well." He nodded and turned away.

All was ready. It was time to begin.

It was time for the end to begin.

He turned back, looked the man in the eye. "And Viminacium? Can that be true?"

"As far as we can tell, yes, sir. Flattened."

"So they have siege craft?"

"They or their auxiliaries, yes, sir. They took down the walls of the fortress in a day and a night, if reports are correct."

Christ. "And the VIIth Legion?"

The *optio* shrugged. "Gone."

He winced. "That was a good legion." He straightened up. "To the palace."

Emperor Valentinian received him coldly. "My good and faithful servant. How precipitate your return."

"Those were my orders, Majesty."

"There was no need." Valentinian took his time, cradling his hands in his lap, gazing fondly down at them, stroking an open palm. He hummed a little tune. Aëtius waited patiently.

Eventually Valentinian said, "It is true about this Hun nuisance. But lines of communication have been reestablished, by sea and river, with Ratiaria, and by land with the Eastern Field Army at Marcianopolis. They are marching out to engage the savages even as we speak. They may have destroyed them already."

"Under General Aspar?"

Valentinian's eyes flared wide with anger.

"Forgive my interruption, Majesty. But their commander—"

"The Field Army, all five or six legions, will engage or has engaged these savages, this ridiculous, puffed-up little man *Attila,* somewhere on the River Utus. Yes, *under Aspar.* News is expected at any time. And so you see"—he smiled—"there is really nothing useful for you to do here, Master General. As ever. You may as well go back to Sicily and play with your boats."

"Your Majesty." He bowed. "If I may, I should like to wait and hear the happy news from the East along with you."

Valentinian waved his hand. "As you please."

Only a day later, the emperor was white with fury. "Our Brother in Constantinople accuses us of cowardice! Curses rain on him. Foulest curses!"

He mumbled of Lilith and Seth, ancient Hebrew demons.

Aëtius tried to steady him.

He pulled away. "He says we refused him help. How dare he! If he had asked we might have gone to his aid. We are no cowards! Those horsemen do not frighten *us!*" He seized a cushion and looked as if he were about to tear it apart in his thin white hands.

Aëtius looked away. He could not bear to watch these puerile rages. But he knew who was at the root of this discord. Neither Theodosius nor Valentinian, being played like puppets against each other, but another ruler altogether. A ruler of a very different stamp.

Everything moved at a terrible pace in those days, in that summer. Each new piece of intelligence came like *fama pinnata,* winged rumor, but at the pace of catastrophe.

Another letter arrived in Constantinople from Aëtius a few days later. (I know because I, Priscus, took the letter and read it myself.) It contained a genuine offer of help from the Western legions. They would not be starting on the Africa Campaign now. Six of the finest, twenty thousand men, both infantry and cavalry, could sail from Sicily direct for Constantinople. Seven days' sailing at most. Or they could come ashore at Thessalonica, cut across the flat plains of Thrace and attack the Huns' flank as they marched south. But my lord the emperor Theodosius would not even look at the letter. He ordered it to be burned, saying how he now knew who his true and loyal friends were.

There was a chamberlain in the employ of the Byzantine court in those days, a man called Pytheas. A man I had never felt at ease with. Theodosius admired and trusted him, but, alas, he was a poor judge of character, for all his lucubrations over the *Characters* of Theophrastus. Books, not life, had taught our emperor; and I am sorry to say, bibliophile and library dweller as I am myself, that thus far they had proved poor teachers. This Pytheas had grown very rich from corruption and manipulation of the funds of the Public Largesse. He held numerous offices, this state-salaried parasite: sinecures such as Overseer of Marble Procurement, Secretary of the Imperial Customs-Houses, Chief Clerk of the Records of Imperial Liberality, Accounts Archivist for the Province of Syria, Chancellor of the Domestic Wardrobe, and so forth. And in every department he was corrupt. But he had grown richest from another source altogether, from beyond the bounds of the empire, though none of us knew it then. He worked for Attila.

I remember a private audience he had with the emperor. I silently took notes, in my role as chief clerk in consistory.

Pytheas hesitated and then said, "My Lord, it is my heavy duty to bring you further distressing, but surely untrue, reports from the Danube frontier."

"Go on," said the emperor, poring over a manuscript on his wooden lectern.

Pytheas sighed theatrically. "At Viminacium . . . My Lord, I fain would not believe it is true"

"*Go on*," said Theodosius.

Pytheas glanced aside at me but he did not register me.

"At Viminacium," he said, speaking with exaggerated care, "it appears that alongside the Huns were fighting—were *seen* fighting—men with covered shields. But shields were evidently lost in the battle. And when the Hunnish hordes passed on southward, some of our own men managed to retrieve them."

I found this doubtful in the extreme. "There were none of our own men left *alive*," I objected.

Pytheas's look could have turned a Gorgon to stone. "Remember you are but a scribe, Priscus of far-famed Panium," he said sarcastically, "however elevated a scribe. So scribble, and be silent."

The emperor hardly registered this argument.

Pytheas continued, with a sigh and a leaden heart on his sleeve. "The recovered shields were painted red, with a gold rim, and a large black eagle in the center."

Now at last Theodosius raised his small, short-sighted eyes from his manuscript and looked around, puzzled.

Pytheas nodded. "Yes, my Lord. The insignia of the Legio Herculiani."

The Herculian Legion. One of the very finest. A Western legion, under the direct command of Master General Aëtius.

Theodosius still looked baffled. And then Pytheas, the consummate actor, produced his theatrical masterstroke. He called out, and a slave entered the room, walking backward so that he might not gaze upon the countenance of the Divine Majesty. He laid two objects at the chamberlain's feet, and then hurried away. Pytheas picked them up. One was a big round wooden shield with a bronze boss and gold-painted rim, decorated just as he had said with the black eagle insignia of the Herculians. The other was a long spear, with dyed feathers twined in behind the spearhead, and the shaft crudely decorated with shamanic runes of power. A Hun spear. He raised them up and held them side by side. Fighting together, thus.

The visual impact was tremendous.

The emperor staggered forward, his wooden lectern crashing to the floor. "No!"

"My Lord," said Pytheas, "it is my sincerest hope that this is a terrible misunderstanding."

But the image of Western legionary and Hun spearman fighting side by side was indelibly imprinted upon the vivid, vulnerable imagination of the emperor.

"Indeed," said Pytheas, "it may even be that this is some malign plan of Attila's, to drive a wedge between east and west."

Oh cunning chamberlain! Not the first to realize that, by stating the truth so candidly, you can drive it away.

"No!" cried the emperor. "I have heard enough. First I was refused aid, then General Aëtius wished to bring his army direct to our capital, without alarming us. Now I see why! My cousin Valentinian has said before that he always suspected Aëtius's ultimate aim was to make himself emperor, with help from the Hunnish hordes if necessary. Now I see that it is true. This will not be the first time the West has turned against the East. Remember Mursa, one hundred years ago. That was a calamitous battle."

It pained me, Priscus, to hear that name. The list of military catastrophes in the last century was long: against the Goths at Adrianople; against the Persians, and Shapur, King of Kings, at the Night Battle of Singara. Yet Mursa was the greatest wound of all, and self-inflicted, the ruinous feat of Constantine the Great's squabbling sons, and the usurper Magnentius; an empire rending itself to pieces, at the cost of sixty thousand casualties in a single day.

But now my beloved pupil Aëtius was master general in the West. Rome would live to fight again, and better. I prayed for it. Yet day by day, through the brilliant machinations and insinuations of Attila and his network of spies and accomplices, information continued to trickle through to baffle the scholarly, naïve, gullible, well-meaning Emperor Theodosius, too unskilled by far in the ways of men. So far from doing evil himself that he suspected none, or he suspected the wrong men—unerringly erring in every judgment he made.

After Pytheas's departure, I made so bold as offer advice to my lord the emperor. He had appointed no good advisers: the greatest failing of all for a ruler of men.

The first casualty in war is truth, I told him sententiously. He did not appear to listen, but he did not silence me, either.

"It is not in Aëtius's nature to deceive," I said. "Remember, my lord, I was his tutor for a brief while."

Theodosius looked up, brow furrowed. "That's right," he said softly. "So you were. I had forgotten."

"He was not the best of students," I murmured, with a fond smile of remembrance. Then, with more attack, "But Attila is the Great Deceiver. He will try every trick."

He seemed in an agony of indecision. I saw the man beneath the stiff golden robes, his very spirit writhing. How he hated to be emperor. It was nothing but a burden to him. Not for the first time, I was grateful I was not a ruler or a politician, whose lives are a long, thankless, much-scorned series of choices between lesser and greater evils. Politicians, unlike poets, do not live in the world of the Good and the Beautiful.

Then he waved me wearily away.

I slept poorly that night. Sometime toward dawn I stood out on my little balcony overlooking the still waters of the Golden Horn. Moonlight coming toward me in a silvered pathway; wisteria and judas trees, night-scented jasmine, nightingales in the pines; two night fishermen out on the water, drawing fish into their nets with lanterns on hooped sticks. By the moonlight I could see the ancient symbol of the stylized eye painted on the prow, white and blue, to ward off evil. Behind me, the city's golden domes and cupolas would be shining beneath the round-faced moon, unimaginably beautiful. The great statue of Constantine aloft on its pillar, only a little lower than God. Would all this fall? All the strange wonders of this magical city, caught between east and west (wonders which I, Priscus of Panium, had written up with modest scholarship, in a little guidebook regarded with no small admiration among certain literary circles in the city)? The strange triple-headed brass serpent on its pillar in the forum, taken by Constantine the Great himself from the temple of Apollo at Delphi, made to celebrate Greek victory over the Persians at Plataea, 479 years before the birth of Christ. Or the towering column of Pharaoh Thutmose III, unimaginably ancient, the polished hieroglyphs in the polished granite, as clear as when they were cut there by slaves in ancient Egypt millennia ago, in a kingdom long since vanished. So even the greatest empires fall into night. The iron law of change applies to everything. All is *metamorphosis*. Yes, one day, sooner or later, even all this would change and fall.

The Ancients said hope was merely a sign of foolishness. We Christians now do not have their pessimistic strength.

There is chaos and ruin. And so there is grace and light.

In the marsh-girdled palace of Ravenna, there was an atrocious mix of pride and panic in those days. There was mistrust, plots, and delusions of plots, wars and rumors of wars. Aëtius, despite his best efforts, could not persuade the emperor to release any legions to go east. Were the finest then simply to sit in Sicily, while the Huns ravaged all Moesia and Thrace? Yes, apparently.

Meanwhile, Valentinian harped on endlessly about what he called "my punitive expedition," which had apparently stung the Huns into invasion.

"We would not have heard from them again, had I led it in person," he explained to the assembled courtiers listening sycophantically, and to Aëtius. Unusually for Valentinian, he was out of doors, taking the air in the palace gardens. The group passed beneath fine mulberry trees, between rows of box hedges, among statues of interestingly deformed children and little cupids strangling geese. "I would have shown those Hunnish hairy men."

He called on one of his favorite court scholars, an orator named Quintilianus, to tell again what was known of the Huns.

Quintilianus bowed low as they walked. "Your Eternal Majesty. Like unreasoning beasts, these Huns are entirely at the mercy of the maddest impulses. They have no understanding of right and wrong, their speech is shifty and obscure, they know nothing of true religion or piety. Their greed for gold is limitless, they are fickle, prone to fury, serpentine of tongue. Their physical appearance is the outward sign of their inner animality. They have flat faces, yellowed skin like old parchment, high cheekbones which leave no room but slits for eyes. They stink of meat, milk, and mutton fat, which they lard upon their coarse bodies as protection against the savage Scythian winters that they love so well. They ride brutish mounts, often quite naked, or dressed in the most tattered, ill-cured animal skins, which add to their foul odor."

Valentinian nodded with pleasure at this eloquent description.

"And now this dreadful people is against us," murmured another courtier. "People say that we live in desperate times, and surely the End is coming."

"How dare they say that!" cried the emperor, turning and flailing his purple skirts, revealing his pearl-studded kidskin boots. "Those who breathe such treason, I will have them racked and scourged, I will have them crucified in the Colosseum. Let them be an example, let their screams be heard, let the sands run red with their watery blood!" He was dribbling slightly. "Let them—"

The wooden door to the enclosed garden opened and a tired old woman, tall once but now bowed and bent, shuffled in. Valentinian's gaze rested on her a moment, and then he turned away and continued.

"I was surprised to hear that my punitive expedition has not worked, but it was done inadequately, you see. They had no military understanding; they held back too much, my men."

That it was an Eastern legion meant nothing to him. The world was his and everything therein. No one really existed for Valentinian but himself. The rest were but figures in his own fevered dreams.

Returning to the palace alone, Aëtius found the old woman in the porphyry-pillared entrance hall.

"Your Majesty," he said, bowing.

"Aëtius," said Galla Placidia, her tired green eyes betraying a momentary pleasure. "I am glad you have returned."

Aëtius regarded her steadily, his expression too perhaps showing the faintest pleasure on seeing her. "One can only play King Theodoric at *latrunculi* so many times."

"And lose?"

"Deliberately, I assure you."

There were those in the court of Ravenna, and in senior positions in the Western Army, who were said to have talked to Aëtius in utmost secrecy, to have joined together in urging him to seize the imperial throne for himself, to set the diadem on his head and the purple about his shoulders. They said that Valentinian was a babbling fool leading the empire to destruction. But Aëtius said that it was as the Church taught: the emperor was God's annointed, for some purpose hidden from the eyes of men.

"Then we should have killed him before he became emperor," said Germanus, a stocky redhead with a round, rubicund face, one of Aëtius's best, most forthright generals.

"You cannot kill a boy."

"Would you not have killed Hannibal in boyhood, had you been able? Think how many lives you would have saved at Cannae."

Aëtius shook his head.

"Or Judas Iscariot himself?"

Aëtius murmured, "'In the lost boyhood of Judas, Christ was betrayed.'"

Germanus regarded him blankly. He wasn't a great one for poetry.

Aëtius sighed. "Had Christ not been betrayed to crucifixion, how would our sins have been forgiven? Judas, too, was an instrument of God."

"But the emperor's a gibbering fool!" sputtered Germanus.

Aëtius counseled him to lower his voice. "I know that," he added. "Many emperors are. But it is not for us to rescind the appointments of heaven. They are St. Paul's 'powers that be.'"

"Even if those powers are betraying the empire to disaster?"

Aëtius said nothing.

"You owe it to the senate and the people," persisted Germanus, "the good old 'Senatus populusque romanus,' to defend the weak and undefended, the widowed and orphaned, the Christian peoples of Europe."

"And so I shall defend that Christian peoples of Europe!" retorted Aëtius, beginning to anger. He quelled his undignified passion, and was silent for a time. Eventually he added, "But not that way."

He said they must live the life that God had allotted to them. He was a general of men, a commander of soldiers, not an assassin. He would do his duty. So must they all.

Valentinian continued to insist that, though the Western legions languished, the Eastern Field Army would soon deal with Attila.

"Besides," he said with a peculiar smile, "there are other operations afoot."

For the Vice Regent of God in the West, Defender of the Church, Shield of the Faithful, had given himelf up to degrading superstitions and the practices of witchcraft, which appeal only to those who are simultaneously corrupt and stupid.

Galla Placidia herself came to Aëtius one evening, shaking and white. He insisted she sit. She refused wine.

"My son," she gasped, and buried her face in her hands. Her shoulders trembled, and Aëtius realized that he was seeing her cry for the first time in his life. Men dying he could cope with. But women crying . . . At last he summoned the resolve to reach out and lay his broad right hand on her shoulder. Immediately she came round, like someone waking abruptly from a dream. She wiped her eyes with a small white cloth, then stood and walked slowly round the room.

"My son . . . is mad," she said.

Aëtius waited.

As conscious as Aëtius that time was running out, and perturbed by what secrets lay in Valentinian's private chambers beneath the palace, Galla's patience—and perhaps, she admitted now, her willful self-delusion—had at last evaporated. She had demanded entrance. A eunuch had been so insolently adamant that she was not permitted entry that she had grown enraged, given him a mighty cuff for a woman of her years, and entered the chambers in a fine rage.

She was met by a horrible sight, but one she had known in her heart she would find—she bit her lip almost to bleeding. There stood her son, clutching a ridiculous willow wand, naked but for a purple silk cape around his upper body, and wearing a primitive animal mask. The small chamber was in gloom except for flickering candles in grubby candelabra. In the impenetrable dark, a slave sat in a corner beating a drum. Foul concoctions steamed in pots, necromantic brews of curdled milk and bitter herbs. There were skulls around the floor, and in the center, around the emperor, a chalk circle inscribed with the names of JHWH and Hermes Trismegistus.

The great magician turned.

"Have you brought her?" he mumbled behind the mask. His eyes flared wide in the chiseled holes, and he snatched the mask off. "Mother!"

He wore kohl round his eyes like a harlot. She went closer. His naked belly was a sagging little white pouch like an old man's, though he was only in his early twenties, and, shame upon shame, his lower parts were smeared with fat, probably mixed with opium and henbane, wolfsbane and hemp. She prayed it was only animal fat. His pupils were black and dilated.

She could not speak. Almost unconsciously she held her arms out to him, her eyes blurring. Her son . . .

He regained composure of a sort; even smiled. "Who is this coming to the sacrifice?" he slurred. "For Abraham, it was his son. For me, apparently it is my mother."

She stood trembling, still speechless.

"But you are no virgin, are you, mother?"

Finally she regained control of herself, and called to the eunuch at the door. "Bring more light!" To the unseen slave in the darkness, she snapped, "And stop beating that wretched drum if you want to sleep tonight with the skin on your back."

At that Valentinian went berserk.

"I am God's anointed, not her! Drum, slave! No light, no light, this act of darkness shall transpire in darkness! Snuff the candles, senators! 'Render unto Caesar,' did not Christ say? Then render unto me, Mother! Down on your knees!" He tore off the flimsy silk cape. His nipples, too, were rimmed with kohl. "Render unto me, to me!" His voice was a bestial shriek. He arched his skinny white chest toward her. Suddenly he was staring intently at her breasts, his lips curled back like a rabid dog's, teeth bared, his gaze darting to her stricken face and back again, without embarrassment, his eyes glittering with maniac light. He leaned closer, almost touching her, teeth showing in a silent snarl, and Galla knew in that terrible moment what he wanted. His sick desire was to bite off the breasts that fed him, to lunge at the mother who still overshadowed him, and mutilate her into powerlessness.

She stepped back. She called him by the nickname he had as a little boy.

Slowly he came out of the nightmare, though his eyes still glittered and stared.

Then he twirled naked on the spot, apparently oblivious of his nakedness before her, and waved his willow thyrsus.

"I do but jest, mother," he said gaily. He tossed his wand away and rubbed his hands together briskly, as if to free them from dirt. He looked down. "Call me Adam, for I am naked, yet not ashamed."

Galla felt differently. "Bring his Majesty a robe," she snapped to the eunuch as she swept from the room.

The eunuch obeyed and went.

Galla lingered unseen in the shadows of the antechamber.

The eunuch returned with a clean linen robe. Following the emperor's orders, he also brought a platter bearing a fieldmouse drowned in spring water, two moon beetles, fat from a virgin nanny goat, two ibis eggs, two drams of myrrh, four drams of Italian galingale and an onion. The slave recommenced drumming. Valentinian masturbated into a clay dish, pounded his semen together with these ingredients, poured in oil, and then sculpted a raw figurine with quivering fingers. Then he placed the figurine, a foul anthropic caricature stuck with eggshell and mouse fur, before one of the grimy candelabra and raised his eyes ceilingward.

"I come announcing the blasphemy before heaven of Galla Placidia, that defiled and unholy woman. Take away her sleep, put a frenzied passion in her thoughts, and a burning heat in her soul. Make her mad before you destroy her, O gods."

"Having heard that," said Galla, "I departed."

Aëtius poured a small goblet of wine. Still she refused.

"A general is not accustomed to having his orders refused," he murmured.

A risky strategy. She looked up. But then she smiled the faintest smile and took the goblet.

"And no moon beetles drowned in it, either, I assure you."

She drank and set the goblet down again. "My son is mad," she repeated. "He is emperor and he is mad. I do not understand the will of God."

How tragic it had been, this flinty, green-eyed woman's life. At least one, perhaps both, of her husbands murdered. Her daughter a slut, pregnant by her own chamberlain when still a girl, and even now still in confinement in the Palace of Hormisdas in the East. Galla never saw her. Instead she saw, daily, her son, who was an idiot, and a malevolent idiot at that.

Aëtius said nothing. He would not lie, so there was nothing to say. The murder of any ruler was wrong. But there was this thin, world-weary care-worn woman sitting before him, whom in a way he did love. He had to remind himself that she was only a few years older than he was. They had grown old together, but she far faster than he. Life on the battlefield might be hard, but it was nothing like so hard as life at court. That friendless and airless world into which she had been born, a fetid world of backstabbings and plots, at whose heart she had remained out of sheer duty. No, he could not rebel against his emperor. And he could not kill this woman's only son.

They drank more wine, toasting each other.

"To wine!"

"The peasant's solution to all ills!"

They stepped outside.

Galla said, "I still do not understand why Theodosius is angry with us."

"It was Valentinian's decision to attack the Huns, remember. The VIIth Legion carried it out. Attila attacked the VIIth Legion in return, and has destroyed it, if reports are correct. So of course Theodosius feels he is paying a terrible price for carrying out his cousin's wishes. It was a brilliant stroke. The Huns have people working among us. As you have noted, Attila has attacked right at the border between the two empires. He is also playing havoc with communications—I do not yet understand how. I fear his grasp of intelligence is phenomenal."

They stood in companionable silence and anxiety. The stars glimmered over the palace roofs. There was the sound of the trickling dolphin fountain in the courtyard, and the mesmeric hum of mosquitoes coming in from the marshes for the evening feed. Aëtius slapped his forearm.

There were many things they could have said but sometimes it is better to say nothing. They stood together, looking out into the darkness with their thoughts: thoughts of decline and fall, of empires' collapse; of how the manifest destiny of Rome seemed to have grown obscured almost to vanishing point in these latter days and years. Behind them they felt centuries of history, a weight both pleasant and unpleasant, comforting and burdensome; the gaze of many steadfast emperors upon them, Augustus, and Trajan, and Marcus Aurelius; Constantine the Great, of the House of the Flavians, direct forefather of Flavius Aëtius; and Vespasian, too, that old soldier, who had his bust sculpted to show his laughter lines and his bald pate, and who liked to joke, "If you want to know whether the emperor is truly divine, ask the man who empties his chamber pot." He had even joked on his deathbed, saying sarcastically, "Good grief, I think I'm turning into a god!" Not all Rome's emperors had been mad with power.

Further off still, through distant mists of time, the stern, unflinching gray eyes of the old republic, which looked on the world and saw it clear, as it was, and were not dismayed. No Scipio or Cato had ever sought refuge in spells and charms. Now he and Galla and Theodosius were the last heirs of Rome. How would they be judged? What would their legacy be?

Down below, in his occult chamber, was the latest ruler of Rome, mad as the mist and snow. What swamps the Imperial Palace of Ravenna stood on, or was sinking into; swamps which no mere engineer could drain. What empire could find firm foundation in such base ooze, the sewage of dark centuries? In troubled times, end times, people turn to strange cults and practices. Conscious of their ebbing power in the real world, they turn to fantasy power, and to beliefs and false enchantments that would shame a stronger man. Normality itself falls victim, and everywhere there is the triumph of pained uncertainty and panicked delusion.

And we sit and fester, brooded Aëtius: Africa uncaptured, the empire slowly starving to death, and our offer of aid turned down by Theodosius, the scholar-emperor. Perhaps he was riding to war against the Huns even now, his head full of Homer's hexameters. O Christ, our Savior . . . Aëtius thought of the Hun horses, their heads like bullock heads, battering down men and walls in a ceaseless charge, men flying apart, lines of lightly armed Greek peltasts fleeing before their furious onslaught. In his dreams sometimes he saw those horses of the Asiatic steppes galloping down on him, screaming, their faceless riders lashing them forward without mercy, their mouths curled back against the cruel bit, tongues lolling, the very teeth of those brute-headed horses smeared with blood . . . but one rider was not faceless. One rider's face he knew of old.

3

TO THE HOLY CITY
OF BYZANTIUM

A ëtius could wait no longer for news of the great confrontation between Attila and the Eastern Field Army. It might be days yet, even weeks, and the thought of it made him horribly uneasy, with a prophetic unease.

"I am very displeased," said Valentinian. His eyes were narrow and darting and dull with broken sleep and haunted dreams.

"Neverthless, Majesty, I beg you will release me to sail east."

"And I am very mistrustful."

Aëtius said nothing.

"You will take no legions, nor ships from Sicily."

Aëtius bowed.

"And what of those oafish Visigoth friends of yours? I said I would not have them on the soil of Italy."

Aëtius could have reminded Valentinian that his mother, Galla Placidia, had once been married to a certain Athaulf the Goth. But he thought better of it.

He said, "The Princes Theodoric and Torismond and their one thousand wolf lords are stationed at Massilia, with their father's blessing. They would not have sailed with me against their Germanic kinsmen the Vandals, of course. But they would willingly sail with me east to fight their ancient enemy the Huns."

"You're welcome to them. Perhaps they will not return."

"I still believe, Majesty, that the Visigoths might yet prove our greatest allies."

Valentinian took a sudden, close interest in a loose thread in the hem of his robe.

Eventually, Aëtius said, "Majesty?"

He looked up testily. "Yes, yes, go, then. But I may not want you back."

Aëtius almost smiled. Oh yes you will, he thought.

"Take this," said Galla. She pressed a small, leather-bound book into his hands. It was a rich psaltery, most delicately illustrated.

He refused it. "Salt water," he said, "would ruin it."

"Then keep it well protected."

"And if we go to the bottom?"

There was a lost look in her eyes. Then she leaned up and kissed him. "Take it," she said.

He rode fast westward to Mediolanum and on to Massilia, cursing Valentinian at every milepost. He took only his boy *optio,* Rufus, who chattered excitedly much of the way. How large is Constantinople? What is the food like? Do they still have gladiatorial combats there? Aëtius told him Constantinople was much like Rome, except it didn't smell so bad.

On the edge of the great port of Massilia he found the Visigothic princes in a fine villa, their wolf lords' tents spread across parklands, vineyards, half a hillside. The villa was half wrecked, the adolescents disheveled, red faced, and hung over from last night's debauch. He gave them a talking-to. They hung their heads. He said he would be sailing on the evening tide and if they weren't ready, prepared, and sober, he would sail without them.

"Sailing?" said Torismond, looking anxious.

These steppe horsemen. "Don't tell me you've never been on a ship before?"

They hadn't. They thought they would be riding east, a thousand of them in gorgeous panoply, to fight the Huns on the Pannonian plain.

"Nope. You're sailing east to Constantinople, under my command. Just fifty of you and your horses. The rest of your wolf lords can head back to To-losa. There'll be no more room aboard. Ship's only small."

Torismond swallowed.

"Be ready."

Aëtius commandeered two naval ships, a fast Liburnian, the *Cygnus,* and a round-bellied cargo ship which would do for a horse transporter.

The two princes, the sons of Thunder, were there with their fifty as ordered.

"Some in Massilia said we'll never get through. They said the Vandals were the masters of your Mare Nostrum now," said Torismond.

Aëtius eyed him. "By 'some in Massilia,' I assume you mean a bunch of Cretan sailors, drunk in a whorehouse?"

Torismond said nothing.

"We'll get through," said Aëtius.

The wind was steady but not strong enough to whip up too big a swell. Torismond and Theodoric both looked sea green at times on that first day, but managed not to vomit. The horses were calm in the following transport ship.

How good it was to sail. To be moving toward some appointed destination at last. Aëtius stood at the prow of the *Cygnus,* heart racing, thinking of all the glorious works and days of man. The lethal underwater ram surged forward through the low swell, the sea arching back over it in slow curls. Slaves strained at the oars down below the fly deck, great firwood oars kept white and smooth with pumice and the scouring salt waves. Aëtius could hear their leathery creak in the thole pins, between the beats of the *hortator*'s hammer on the drum. Just below him hung the iron anchor, dripping, still trailing weed from Massilia. The immense red-and-white-striped sail hung from the top spar, catching a strong northwesterly and bellying out in the wind. Salt spray dashed in his face, dried and crusted on his cheek. He inhaled deeply. Now that he had decided upon a course of action, there was no stopping him.

The princes came to him.

"Sir," said the quietly spoken Theodoric respectfully, "we are only fifty. The Huns number many thousands."

Aëtius nodded. "Half a million, rumors say. When rumors give you numbers, always divide by ten."

"So they still outnumber us a thousand to one."

"You're a Visigothic Pythagoras." Aëtius grinned. "I'm not expecting you to defeat Attila on your own, boy." He cursed himself inwardly for calling the prince a boy, and vowed not to do it again. Theodoric was no boy. "Our first task is to . . . liaise with Emperor Theodosius, make our peace, offer him our services. We'll wait for news of the Eastern Field Army, and be ready to move fast."

"You mean you expect their field army to be destroyed?"

Aëtius said nothing.

"And their generals with it? So you're going to have to take command?"

"What, no fighting?" cried Torismond.

Now *he* was still a boy. For him, fighting meant fun.

"Oh, there'll be fighting," said Aëtius. "Never you worry."

At twilight, the rowers stood down to eat and sleep, curled up like dogs beneath the benches, and the second batch took their place on the blistering oars. The *hortator's* relentless beat continued, his hourglass running. Master General Aëtius himself had given the order to make all speed for the east.

The second day the wind came on stronger, the light ship bucking and rearing. Cat's claws raked over the surface of the sea, and spray flew back from bow waves half the length of the ship. The huge sail, much repaired, snapped back and forth as the wind grew unsteady and they altered course to meet it. Behind them the sky was darkening over Gaul.

Aëtius knelt down beside Torismond, who was sprawled on the deck beside the mainmast, clutching it in both arms, vomit staining a shirt front finely embroidered by his beloved mother.

"Storm coming," said Aëtius cheerfully. "Summer storms are always the worst."

A little cruel, but the plain truth. The lad would get inured to the sea either fast or not at all. His elder brother, meanwhile, Prince Theodoric, had donned his royal gold fillet, despite the sailors' looks and muffled jeers, wearing it as if to remind the insolent sea of his royal blood and his direct descent from the divine Odin and Nerthus, the Earth Mother. He paced the length of the ship ceaselessly, jaw clenched, hands behind his back, a rigid regal bearing, saying nothing. As terrifed as his younger brother, clearly, but determined to master it. He was quite a fellow. One day he would be a great king.

Torismond looked ghastly.

Aëtius said, "You really would rather face a whole army of screaming Huns, wouldn't you?"

The prince nodded, still embracing the mainmast like his first love. "Christ, yes."

The ship lurched sideways. He bowed his head.

"Head up. Watch the horizon. Slow, deep breaths."

Torismond struggled to comply.

"You'll have to let go of that, too. Sail coming in—look."

"Oh, Christ."

"Whoever. But I never saw any god come to rescue drowning sailors yet."

They reefed the mainsail into the standing yard and tightened it. The wind still gusted hard into the reduced sail, the long, lean dromond lightening in the water, raised up, the rowers' efforts almost superfluous, the ship doing eight, ten knots, a breathtaking speed. Aëtius prayed for still more speed. Attila would not be slacking; that barbarian tide sweeping down across the East, to break upon the walls of the New Rome.

The big rudder swung across its breach, the master steadied it, the ship surged forward again, almost planing up the smooth obisidian back of one driven wave before crashing into the next, trying to outrace the approaching storm—hopeless, of course. The timbers creaked, and two rowers below were released for emergency caulking. The horse transporter lagged behind them, almost out of sight. Broader beamed and heavier, she wallowed through the swell, making slower, steadier progress. The horses would survive.

A lonely black-backed gull passed overhead, heading inland for Italy, shelter from the storm. Aëtius grimaced and threw his red woolen cloak about his shoulders. The wind began to whistle in the halyards and clew lines, and a fine rain slanted in from the west.

The ship's master approached. "We could take shelter soon enough at Olbia. Going through the straits of Bonifacium in this wind will be dangerous."

"We go on through the straits, and never mind Olbia. We keep going. No shelter till we reach Syracuse."

Attila would not be seeking shelter from any storms, nor slowing in his advance on Constantinople. Nor could they.

The master gave orders for the sail to be reefed in further, the rowers to row their hardest. The bosun bellowed, "Blister your butts and bust your guts if you want to escape a whipping and eat salt meat tonight!"

Visibility was declining all the time. It was no more than two hundred yards when the lookout in his tiny crow's nest swaying from the mainmast said he could see land ahead to port. It was the dark and jagged outline of Corsica. Somewhere through the mist and mizzle to starboard, lay the gentler shape of Sardinia. Between them were the straits of Bonifacium.

The *hortator* doubled his beat and they rowed through the straits at the double, swift as an arrow cutting through the water. It was the only way to avoid being swept off course and onto the lethal submerged rocks around the islands. Eventually they came through, pulled round to the southeast, and felt the storm blowing up over the islands behind them. It wasn't getting any better. The master looked once more inquiringly at Aëtius, to see if he would allow them to take shelter. But he did not respond. He had given his last word. They would push on, through storm and surge, whatever.

The lookout was called down from the fighting top: any worse and he'd be thrown clear into the sea and lost. He scrambled gratefully down. The sails were reefed right up into double swags from the yard, the bull's-hide storm shields were shipped over the oarports, and the slaves down there, already soaked and salted like herrings in brine, rowed like furies before the storm. It was going to be a bad business, this one. The heavy pewter clouds seemed to suck in the sunlight. "Mare Nostrum" indeed, thought Aëtius sourly. Everything is against us now: the Huns, the Vandals, the sea . . .

Even Rufus, a good sailor, looked sea green, hanging on the taffrail like a rag. From back in the mist there came a muffled crack. The boy stared in that direction, rolling on the balls of his feet with the ship, drool still hanging from his lips. Theodoric and Torismond were collapsed on their pallets below, filling buckets.

"What is it, lad?" said Aëtius. He could see nothing.

The boy stared a while longer. "I thought I saw white horses," he said softly. "I don't mean breaking waves, I mean . . . real white horses, swimming. Drowning."

Aëtius looked grim. Had they lost the horse transporter? It was possible.

He sent an order to the master to kill the oars. The *Cygnus* slowed, then wallowed terribly in the heavy sea, groans arising from below. Aëtius himself held onto a rail post. The deck was rolling through ninety degrees, water sluicing back and forth across the boards. He strained to see or hear: nothing. They had to go back. Not for the horses—they could not save the horses even if they found them—but for the men.

They plowed back a weary league against the sea, but found nothing. No sighting of the broad transporter, not a horse, not a single waving man.

They pulled round and went on. Rufus returned to hanging sickly from the taffrail.

"Don't tell the princes," Aëtius instructed.

He himself returned to his station in the bucking prow, right arm tight round the jib mast. Standing face into the rain, praying to his god, gaunt on the poop deck: sleepless, grimfaced, hatless, windblown, Rome's last believer.

At last the storm died away and visibility returned. No sign of the horse transporter.

The princes came shakily up on deck and understood it was lost.

"We'll get more horses," Aëtius promised, "fine Cappadocian horses."

"I hate the sea," murmured Torismond.

"You might as well hate the Power that made it," said Aëtius. "It is ignoble to hate a thing as great and implacable as nature."

Torismond looked away.

They anchored at Syracuse, took on fresh water, sluiced out the lower decks, sold a couple of slaves who were as good as done for and bought a couple more. The princes tottered unsteadily down the gangplank for a walk round the harbor. Aëtius forbade them to drink, saying they were under his command now. They didn't look like they wanted a drink anyway.

The master brought him a squat, bearded fellow who was asking for passage east.

Aëtius eyed him. "What for?"

"I make for Alexandria, but I need to visit Constantinople first. I have two chests of . . . materials which I need to bring with me. With them, I will protect you against attacks by pirates."

Aëtius grinned broadly. "I have a retinue of fifty Gothic spearmen. I think we can look after ourselves."

"You do not know the Vandals."

"On the contrary, I know them well." He looked him up and down. "Name?"

"Nicias."

"Greek?"

"Cretan."

"Even worse. All Cretans are liars, beasts, and gluttons, as Saint Paul himself has told us."

Nicias snorted. "We Cretans have been living with that calumny for four centuries now."

"You'll be living with it for centuries to come, too. Is it not the word of God?"

Nicias kept a stubborn silence. This general was too clever by half.

"Very well. And what is in your magical chests?"

"Materials—alchemical materials."

"God help us." Aëtius saw the two princes returning. "You may take passage with us, but we neither want nor need your protection against pirates. Understood?"

The princes joined them, looking a little improved.

"You will not get through, I tell you," said Nicias. "Vandal pirates infest the eastern seas."

Prince Theodoric interrupted. "We Visigoths are no enemies of the Vandals. Our father is to marry our sister Amalasuntha to Genseric's son himself."

Nicias looked sardonic. "Pirates are no great respecters of treaties, son."

"We're finished talking," Aëtius snapped. "Now, leave me alone."

Nicias stumped away.

Aëtius looked at Theodoric sharply. "Your sister? That pretty slip of a girl? To marry Genseric's son?"

Theodoric nodded.

"Then your father is a fool."

The young man's eyes blazed. "How dare you speak of my father like that!"

Prince Torismond took a step nearer Aëtius. The general held his hands up. He had indeed overstepped the bounds of politeness. He apologized profusely. They relaxed.

"But I will have to beg of your father—"

"That is his policy. An alliance between the Visigoths and the Vandals, a Germanic empire in the West, neither friend nor enemy to Rome."

Aëtius shook his head. "The Vandals are already in alliance with the Huns. I know it in my bones. I will bring your father proof. That embittered, half-lame Genseric is playing him false."

"So you want to believe."

"So I do believe."

"The Vandals are your fellow Christians."

"Even the Devil himself believes in God," muttered Aëtius.

They sailed on the small evening tide again. The storm had blown out, the sea was subsiding. It was peaceful. And too damn slow.

Aëtius sent for Nicias. "Bring up your chest," he said. "Entertain us."

The Cretan needed no second bidding. In a trice he scuttled down to the hold and got one of the sailors to help him up with his chest. He raised the lid and knelt down reverently, like a holy man before an altar.

The princes and the Gothic wolf lords crowded along the rail to watch the show. The master and bosun craned from the wheelhouse to watch this great wonder worker about his miracles, and the sun-bronzed sailors sat along the yard above, swinging bare feet, grinning, gold earrings winking in the sunset. Only the slaves below worked on unregarded.

Nicias rummaged, giving a running commentary. "My recipe combines essence of nitre, phosphorus, and refined black oil from Mesopotamia."

"Must make a right stench," grunted the master.

"The odor is distinctive."

"And you better not set fire to my fuckin' ship."

The alchemist ignored this uncouth remark.

He drew out of his chest some wooden spars and an iron frame, and quickly assembled them into something like a miniature ballista. He set the machine on the deck beside the chest, and rapidly wound back a little brass winch. His audience was interested now, despite themselves. Even Aëtius kept his gray eyes fixed steadily on the proceedings.

Nicias produced a small ball from his chest, holding it between forefinger and thumb, and showed it around like a huckster in the marketplace trying to sell off a rare egg. It was a perfect iron sphere, studded all round with sharp spikes, rather like a caltrop thrown out to stop cavalry. Nicias set the sphere down at the end of his little ballista, turned a brass knob at the side one half turn, and was ready to fire.

"Hold," said Aëtius. "There are dolphins out there. Look."

Breaking the surface of the burnished sea, between them and the falling sun, there were dark, glossy shapes arcing and curvetting through the water in the wake of the ship, some fifty yards off.

"All the better!" said the little alchemist excitedly, turning his machine aft. The onlookers stepped back warily. "I will use them as my targets. I will show you what becomes of mortal flesh when one of my devices . . ."

Aëtius turned his head very slowly and regarded him. Nicias quailed and his voice trailed away.

"Dolphins were sacred to Apollo once," said Aëtius, "in the old days, under the old religion."

"But good to eat?"

"Indeed they are. But not for us to slaughter for mere amusement, like foxes in a hen coop."

There was a moment of awkward silence, and then Nicias said, speaking very quickly, "Very well, then, let us assume . . . let us imagine that out there is a ship, straight to port, an imaginary ship, a boat, upon the sea, an enemy vessel, which we needs must destroy, we must—"

"Enough talking," said Aëtius. "Just show us."

Nicias aimed his machine out across the water and loosed a lever. The tiny machine gave a crack of astonishing power, and the spiked ball whirred out on a flat trajectory straight over the waves, bouncing and cutting into the water as it went. It traveled for over two hundred yards.

Nicias looked around excitedly. "Do you see? This whirling caltrop of my own device, even in miniature, skims across the surface of the sea like a stone thown by a boy. But imagine what it would do in a bigger machine, built to scale, cutting across the canvas of an enemy sail. Tear it to shreds! Or to the deckboards over the heads of enemy rowers. It could tear up the planks, if it were big enough. Imagine the rowers below, thinking themselves safe from missiles beneath their awnings of hardened leather, suddenly blinking and terrified, exposed like helpless animals in their burrows. What power! We could destroy them utterly, from afar, without ever having even to engage. We could slaughter them at will."

Prince Torismond glanced round at Aëtius. He said nothing.

"Now," continued Nicias, "this is not all." Taking another iron sphere he grasped it carefully and unscrewed it into two perfect halves. He took a thick glass flask from the chest and poured some grayish powder into one half. He laid a thin circular wafer of leather over the powder, and then poured over it a dark treacle. "The ingenuity of the chemists of Alexandria and Antioch truly knows no bounds," he commented excitedly. "Prepare to be amazed. For I give you a fire that continues to burn in water, a sticky fire which can gum itself to a boat's wooden hull and burn perpetually, and which no number of water buckets can extinguish." Near the wheelhouse, the master stirred uneasily. "Imagine if such a fire stuck to your arm. You cannot imagine the screams if you have not heard them. Men leap into the water, burning alive."

Some wondered how Nicias knew this, and feared for the fate of any condemned prisoners in Alexandria who might have been passed his way for experimentation. He quickly screwed the iron ball back together again and set it into the shoot on his ballista. They noticed that his expression had grown markedly more nervous, and stepped back.

"Now," he said, eyes gleaming, mouth working, "consider this!"

It was unclear quite what happened next, but there was a tremendous explosion of flame and noise, a sparking cloud of smoke, and bellowing from Nicias in the heart of it. When the smoke cleared, the alchemist was still kneeling beside his charred chest, the skin on his face and one arm burned hairless and red, and the little ballista had vanished.

The deck was on fire, but, miraculously, no one else was hurt.

"Hm," said Aëtius, coming forward. "Needs working on, I think."

The master was roaring for buckets to be lowered and the fire to be put out, but the sailors were already letting out ropes.

Aëtius helped the dazed alchemist to his feet.

"Now," he said, "take your box of tricks back below, and don't let me ever see it on deck again. If I do, it goes into the water—and you follow it." He kicked the chest lid shut. "And get some vinegar on those burns."

The fire on deck sizzled out. Mercifully, Nicias's incendiary invention had not yet been perfected. Many there prayed that it never would.

4

THE SWAN, THE SHARK,
AND THE DRAGON

Three days on, they had passed several cargo ships plying the busy sea
routes between Syracuse, Nicopolis, Alexandria, Antioch, Rhodes, Thessalonica. They hailed them and asked for news of pirates, and the cargomen
shook their heads and said they had encountered nothing.

"Alexander the Great once captured a pirate," said Prince Torismond. "The
King demanded, 'How dare you molest the seas?' 'In the same way that you
dare molest the earth,' said the pirate. 'I molest the seas in one small ship and
I'm called a pirate. If I did so with a great navy, I'd be called an emperor.'"
The prince grinned broadly. "That's philosophy, that is. For what are king-
doms but great bands of brigands?"

"Very good," said Aëtius dryly. "Now define 'sophistry.'"

On the fourth morning, serenely sailing a calm sea in a gentle northwesterly, coming gradually round to north into the Aegean and losing sail power,
inshore of the isle of Melos, they saw a lone ship near the northern horizon;
she was coming their way. After maybe half an hour she had come much
closer, though set on a course astern of theirs. She had a big, faded sail which
might once have been black but was now a light, streaked gray. One of those
battered, barnacled ships that show their sailors are poor and harmless. Then
she turned and came toward them with surprising swiftness, and they realized
that these sailors were not of the poor and harmless variety, but contemptuous

of such menial chores of maintenance as scouring a ship's decks or keeping a trim sail. Such tasks are for slaves. These were the kind of sailors who, if their ship began to split at the seams, would simply scuttle her and take another. Meanwhile, this one was of that variety which is scruffy, grimy, and very, very fast.

Rufus stood nearby. "Sir, you see the other ship, too? There on the horizon?"

Aëtius squinted. Damn the boy. He could see nothing. "Describe."

"Another dromond. Seems to be turning bow-on toward us . . . sail bellying out."

And the wind was with them. The nearer ship was now a mile off, less. She would close on them in a few minutes.

"We could turn south with the wind and try to outrun them—maybe reach Crete."

Aëtius did not even consider such an option.

"Hortator, double that drum! Break your backs down there, slaves! All spearmen below the fly deck, half a side, and keep yourselves out of sight till I give the word. Bring my sword up, boy. Princes Theodoric and Torismond, to me on the poop deck—bring a few bowmen. Master, keep a steady course east. Give 'em the sun in their eyes if they try to come in behind or portside. No, you bearded Cretan loon, get below! We want none of your wretched fire balls now. We'll call you when the fight is over."

The princes and their best men soon appeared on deck, buckled and helmed. Aëtius's eyes narrowed at the helmet that adorned Prince Theodoric's blond locks.

"What in the name of Lucifer have you got on your head?"

The rest of the wolf lords, and Torismond, wore plain enough *Spangenhelms,* tall domed helmets reinforced with crossbands of iron or bronze. Theodoric, however, wore a helmet set with studs of colored glass which gleamed from the highly polished bronze. He removed it again, looking displeased.

"It's an inheritance of my family, always worn by the eldest son in battle."

Aëtius took it from him without asking. "Very pretty it looks, too. These glass settings will really help an enemy blade get a purchase with a downard blow. Cut straight in. Very handy. Why not just take off your helmet and offer him your scalp? On your knees?"

Theodoric looked sullen.

"This is no fighting helmet, boy." He handed it back. "Get yourself a plain iron hat with crossbands like the rest of your men."

"What should I do with this?"

"That?" Aëtius grimaced. "You can give it to your granny as a pot to piss in, for all I care. We're not playing toy soldiers now."

Torismond stifled his giggles. Theodoric returned below.

The rowers were tired and aching after two weeks at the oar, but now was the time they would have to work hardest. The wind dropped further but still the silent dromonds came on. Suddenly it seemed a cruel, flat calm, malevolent, and glittering sea. "Wine dark" indeed, thought Aëtius, clutching the stern post, watching the bosun haul the big rudder round; feeling the wind desert them. Blood dark, more like. "Wine dark" was Homer's lyrical view of it. Blind Homer.

The nearing vessel had a single bank of oars and a mainsail, like the *Cygnus,* but it boasted high parapets and a solid raised deck over the rowers to protect them from incoming missiles.

The master turned to Aëtius in consternation. "They'll destroy us in a missile exchange. They stand much higher, as does their sister ship coming in there."

"Thank God it's no battle group," muttered Aëtius.

"There may be squadrons in the area," said the master. "You heard what they did on the island of Zakynthos? Sent back sackfuls of heads to their king, Genseric."

"We're going to Constantinople. We have business there. I trust our rowers can still get up to ramming speed?"

"Ramming?" growled the master. "You're crazy."

Aëtius grinned, allowing him the impertinence. He knew the score. The stately, high-sided galleys of old were always vulnerable to ramming by low, skimming Liburnians and dromonds. But those sleek wolf ships were very vulnerable to having a huge boulder dropped onto their hull, holing them instantly. Naval warfare by dromond and Liburnian nowadays was all about keeping your distance and shooting missiles, bolts, fire arrows—those accursed firepots of Alexandria. Only a madman would still practice ramming as a tactic.

"Prepare for ramming," he confirmed. "But let 'em come in close first."

"Then there won't be enough distance to get up to speed."

Aëtius did not repeat orders.

"You think like an old legionary," said Prince Theodoric quietly, having overcome his sulks about the helmet.

Aëtius frowned. "Meaning?"

Thedoric looked at him respectfully but without fear. "Meaning, you want to get up close to your enemy, engage face to face, looking him in the eye, and stab him in the guts with your old-fashioned *gladius*. You think that's how a true-hearted man fights, and you think to do the same at sea. You want to ram and hole this pair beneath the waterline, right up close. But there are two of them, and they stand higher than us. Ram one and you will get stuck yourself. The other will come alongside and we'll be attacked on two fronts. Each pirate ship probably carries a hundred cutthroats. My wolf lords are valiant beyond words, but they are not superhuman. They will all be destroyed." The young prince braced his shoulders. "And I will not have them destroyed."

This haughty, blue-eyed prince in his gold fillet, an unsalted adolescent, offering criticism of his naval tactics . . . ? But Aëtius quelled his indignation. "Trust me," he said.

The second ship was a mile or two off now, moving in close astern. They were to be surrounded, as expected. But the *Cygnus* would surprise them. Never do the expected. Alchemical Alexandrian fripperies won no battles, but rather courage, discipline, and a dash of the wholly unexpected. Aëtius grinned. It was good to be fighting again.

Before boarding at Massilia he had ordered a big grappling iron and a couple of boarding planks from the naval stores. Now he commanded them to be brought up and laid at the stern of the ship, the grappling iron roped.

"The *stern*? But we're ramming at the bow!"

"Just follow orders, sailor." He went below.

They were magnificent men but they looked terrified, these Gothic spearmen, sea green and shaky. The massive clunk of the ram, the sounds of battle at sea, would terrify them. They were fine and powerful, but barbarian and undisciplined. Today they might die, here in these salt wastes far from home.

How could a sea death be a heroic death? Food for fish. It was not the Visigothic way. They looked to their princes and this commander, this Aëtius, the Roman beloved of King Theodoric, and saw that he did not have the aura of death about him today.

Prince Torismond appeared beside Aëtius.

"Trust me," said the general again. "Consider the regard I have for your father. There is no Christian king finer, and you are his sons. You are in my care." Would that King Theodoric cared so much for his daughter, he thought bitterly.

Torismond looked a little reassured.

He sent further orders to the master. "Unchain the slaves now. The instant we ram, pull them back from below. You understand? To the stern. Shift the ballast to the bows. Our foredeck will soon be smashed in from above by pirate missiles. Keep the wolf lords hidden until the moment I give the order. And ready your sailors to throw out the grappling iron."

"Where?"

"The second ship," said Aëtius patiently.

"How do you know she'll come anywhere near?"

"She'll come. Hook her in, then throw out the boarding planks."

The pirates must have been flogging their enslaved rowers nearly to death, their vessels came on so fast. The first was only half a mile off now, the second still two or three miles off but closing fast.

"Pull us up to full speed."

"We can't outrun them." The master was right. The first pirate ship was already turning, ready to cut across their bows.

"I don't intend to outrun them. I intend to engage them."

The rowers were driven harder.

From the nearing enemy ship, a couple of exploratory arrows came over the water but fell short. At the prow they could see her captain, narrowing his eyes. Very tall and whip thin, with long, lank hair, bleached fair in sea and sun. He was naked but for a thick gold torc round his neck, torn breeches and a wide sword belt, sword bare in his hand. More of his cutthroats sat along the yardarm with bows and arrows.

The *Cygnus* surged forward steadily, the pirate ship inexorably gaining on her, curving in tight. Away to their right was the little sunlit island of Melos. The Visigothic spearmen crouched below, beside the unchained slaves. The two ships closed slowly, amid the vast serenity of the sea.

Not taking his eyes from the enemy ship for one second, Aëtius said to the brothers beside him, "You can swim, can't you?"

They shook their heads miserably.

"Then today you might have to learn—either that or make sure we don't go down. Order your wolf lords well."

As she closed, they could see the pirate ship better: the *Draco,* with a saurian red dragon painted along the boards. Rufus squinted across to the second ship, which was giving them a wide berth, coming in astern; her prow was scratched with crude runes.

"The Vandal tongue," said Aëtius.

"It looks like '*Halfish*' or something."

"Haifisch—the Shark." He roared below, "Wolf lords at the ready!"

The master looked deeply unhappy.

Suddenly the *Draco* hauled round, her oars digging into the backwash, and came broadside on to this helpless fleeing merchant ship, blocking her off.

"These pirates must be just out of school," murmured Aëtius. "Ramming speed—*now!*"

Immediately the *hortator*'s drum below accelerated into a furious rhythm, and the bosun's lash whipped through the fetid air below. The slaves hauled on their oars, blistered and bleeding hands straining in one last effort, and the *Cygnus* surged forward, straight toward the *Draco.*

The pirates stared at the oncoming ship, dumbfounded. The *Haifisch* altered course again to keep up with it.

"That's it," muttered one old hand. "We're finished now. Good as sunk."

"Correct," said Aëtius, arms folded, smiling. He strode to the stern and dropped down. The wolf lords sat crammed along the sides of the underdeck clutching their spears in their huge hands, yet looking like men about to go into arena naked and unarmed, or to their execution. Aëtius nodded to them. He told them not to be afraid. He told them their one hope of survival now, and it was a good one. "Lay aside your ashwood spears," he said. "This is close-up sword work." He explained what they must do. "Imagine you're taking a castle," he said. "If you fail to take it, you drown. We all drown—food for the circling *Haifisch.*"

The wolf lords drew their swords.

The pirate ship wallowed and struggled, trying to turn again from this impossibly belligerent prey, even as her ragged archers let loose their arrows onto the exposed decks but hit nothing. The *Cygnus*'s bronze-headed ram, more decoration than weapon of war these days, drove on through the water like some terrible sea serpent, white ripples curling back over its length. The master bellowed down below, the lash flailed. They were but fifty yards off, thirty, twenty . . . The pirate ship staggered and lurched as they slammed into her amidships with a terrible splintering crash. It wasn't top ramming speed but it was enough. The ramhead punched straight through the bulwarks of the astonished *Draco,* and the sea began to pour in.

It was a pact of mutually assured destruction. Immediately, the enraged pirates began to lever huge missiles, boulders, and lumps of lead up over the high sides of the wounded *Draco* and drop them onto the decks of the pestilent prey below. One went straight through the oak deck and into the shivering rowing hold beneath. But the master had followed Aëtius's orders to the letter: the unchained slaves were already pulled back from their rowing benches. The timbers were smashed but no men were hurt. The wooden walls of that narrow world began to collapse and the dark waters surged in.

Torismond had a vision of the ship, a puny raft of life afloat on a black and infinite abyss, full of death, of creatures unknown, spawn of moonlight and black night. And this raft was being smashed to splinters beneath them. It was insanity. They would all die. But Aëtius had said to trust him. Very well. He drew his sword. War's no sorcery, and bravery alone wins battles. That was Aëtius's creed, as the prince was learning. Like his loyalties, and his haircut, hopelessly old fashioned.

The *Haifisch* was drawing behind them, determined to avenge the damage to her sister ship.

"Loyalty among pirates," sneered Aëtius. "Wonders are many! Throw out the grappling iron!"

The great barnacled claw rang hard upon the *Haifisch*'s sides and then fell back into the water. Instantly the sailors hauled it up and threw it out again. Theodoric needed no instruction to give them covering fire as surprised pirate archers tried to hit them. His own close band of half a dozen Visigothic archers returned far more aggressive fire, and the pirates ducked behind their bulwarks, as surprised as the crew of the *Draco* at this unexpected belligerence. They were supposed to be taking prey. Now the prey was taking them.

The grappling iron flew spinning out again, slipped against the planking and then one barbed tine dropped and stuck hard over the lip of an oar port. Perfect. Too low for a pirate to sweep down a sword blade to cut it away, even if any dared brave the Visigothic arrows. Already the pirates were beginning to wonder if loyalty to their sister ship was such a good idea. There was only a handful of archers on this enemy ship, plus that hard-faced Roman commander in his red cloak, who'd fetch a good ransom if taken alive. But still, the pirates felt ill omened. One of them was already nursing an arm struck with a white-feathered arrow. There was something they hadn't understood today.

A pirate stood up and loosed a javelin toward a sailor, but the nimble Libyan skipped aside and it stuck quivering in the deck. He pulled it free and lobbed it back. Not a serious throw, but the pirate ducked back smartly, cursing.

"Haul in!" roared Aëtius.

The sailors set their callused bare feet against the boards of the *Cygnus* and obeyed. Slowly, very slowly, the *Haifisch* began to drift in helplessly, broadside on. There was an angry cry from above, an order or warning from its captain. But it was too late.

There came another monstrous crash from the bows. The *Cygnus*'s splintered deck was holed again, and the mainmast began to lean forward. Water was flooding in below, floating the ballast of sand barrels. The ship groaned and began to tilt sickeningly forward. The mainmast creaked ominously.

"Haul for your lives if you'd live to see tomorrow!" bellowed Aëtius. Soon the *Haifisch* jolted against the poop of the *Cygnus,* which was raised up by the counterweight of the water pouring into her bows.

Raised up. Nearer and nearer to the high parapet of the pirate ship. The master breathed out slowly, his bafflement and fear at last turning into something else. The timbers of his beloved *Cygnus* were creaking and screaming, the poor vessel tearing herself apart at the seams, yet serving in her very death throes as an unexpected siege engine for boarding the hooked Shark at their rear. He felt a surge of hope, and sudden admiration for this obdurate Aëtius. Master general of the West, was he? Then maybe the West was in good hands.

"More ballast to the fore!"

A crazy order on a sinking ship under assault, but now the master understood. A couple of lithe, sun-blackened sailors scrambled below, leaping over the straining line of the grappling rope and rolling the last barrels down the steepening incline of the lower deck. The prow sank further in the water, the ram stuck into the belly of the *Draco* grinding her down into the depths with it. The poop deck rose further.

Aëtius grinned at the princes. "Think your wolf lords can vault that now?"

Theodoric nodded. "No problem."

"Then take it."

"Wolf lords!" The old Gothic war cry.

The magnificent warriors, needing no second bidding to escape the fetid and drowning darkness, driven by a powerful mix of fear and battle fury, came buckled and armored up the steps at a run, shining blades in hand. The pirates looked down in shock at this erupting tide of red cloaks and straw-colored plumes. What in Hell's name had they taken on? This was no ordinary ship. They would be lucky to escape with their lives.

With the ships locked together in their fatal embrace, the crew of the *Draco* had fallen silent and inactive. At the appearance of the wolf lords, however, they realized that the battle was on to take charge of the *Haifisch,* the only seaworthy ship left of the three. In an instant they were swarming over the sides of their own listing vessel and dropping down onto the foredeck of the *Cygnus,* now almost at water level. They tried to fight their way up, but the deck was slippery and sloped against them. Another foresight of Aëtius's. As they scrambled up, they were met by three men with drawn swords, two fair-headed adolescents and an older, gray-haired fellow with a certain look in his eyes which suggested he'd seen battle before. Soon the decks were more slippery still with Vandal blood. For a few seconds Aëtius, Torismond, and Theodoric manned this second front alone, swords sweeping and thrusting, cutting down the oncoming pirates with ruthless despatch, letting the slain fall back into their scrambling comrades. Then the Visigothic archers loosed arrows in from the sides, and the pirates of the *Draco* knew the day was lost along with their ship. Now they understood very well the temper of those they had so foolishly chosen to attack this bright summer's day. There was nothing left for it. They threw themselves into the sea.

The handful of scrawny pirates on the *Haifisch* were similarly outfought. Accustomed to taking harmless passenger vessels for kidnap and ransom, or fat, wallowing cargo ships laden with amphorae of oil and wine, they were stricken helpless. No match for the fifty Gothic wolf lords vaulting in over the high bulwarks, swords drawn, teeth bared, long hair flying. There was hardly a fight to be had, to the wolf lords' considerable disappointment. Though unable to swim, like most sailors, who superstitiously regard the skill as a kind of temptation to fate, the second crew, too, gave themselves up to the dark, still waters of the Aegean. Any who lingered were swiftly cut to pieces, their lifeless bodies following into the foaming pink brine.

There came a strange sound from behind, like the bubbling of a drain in a rainstorm, though far greater, more sonorous. The rumbling of some vast and nameless sea creature, perhaps. It was the *Cygnus* at last going down, joined prow to broadside with the *Draco* in fatal embrace. The masts of the two ships collapsed into each other like tired lovers. The timbers creaked, the decks were washed and swamped. From below decks on the *Draco,* anguished cries: the pirates had not troubled to unchain their oar slaves. And then, amid the cries of terror and lamentation, cries of desperate hope.

Aëtius glanced around. Torismond had vanished.

The slaves of the *Cygnus,* meanwhile, were swarming after the Gothic swordsmen to the safety of the abandoned *Haifisch.* Then came the sailors, then Aëtius and Theodoric, and finally the master himself, kneeling only to kiss the decks of his dying ship in time-honored tradition, before abandoning her to the seas.

Slaves were emerging above deck on the half-drowned *Draco* and rolling over into the water. Theodoric watched anxiously.

"Neither you nor your brother can swim, you say?" said Aëtius.

Theodoric could not speak.

"He's going to have to learn today."

The sailors pulled up the last of the boarding planks, and the little Libyan scrambled down the side of the ship, holding on by one hand and with the other slashing through the grappling rope that still tied them to the drowning ships.

Aëtius nodded admiringly. "If you weren't just a common sailor, I'd recommend you for promotion."

The sailor flashed a white-toothed smile. "A gold *solidus* will do instead, my lord."

Aëtius regarded him steadily. Then he slipped a hand inside his cloak and produced a big gold coin. He glanced down. It showed Valentinian himself, the martial emperor, dragging a barbarian by the hair. Around the rim it read, "Unconquered Eternal Rome, Salvation of the World." He flicked his wrist and the gold coin arced and flashed in the air and the sailor caught it.

"Don't believe all you read on it, though," muttered Aëtius.

At the prow of their fine new ship, a less than happy sound: Nicias wailing for his vanished alchemical chests.

"Shame," murmured Aëtius.

And last of all, paddling through the water like a puppy, breathless and ungainly but not actually choking or drowning, Prince Torismond, Savior of Slaves. Theodoric threw out a line and hauled him up. After that, the slaves of the *Draco* came scrambling aboard the heavily laden *Haifisch* as well.

"This is going to slow us up," grumbled Aëtius.

"We'll sell 'em at the next port," said Torismond, his eyes glittering excitedly. He shook the saltwater from his hair, thrilled to have braved the sea and survived.

"And spend all the proceeds on wine and girls, I suppose?"

The brothers just laughed.

They watched the two ships go down amid huge, slow bubbles. Further off, what pirates were still afloat circled, exhausted, or clung to broken spars. Aëtius ranged over them until he settled on the long, pitiless, expressionless face of the captain. He pointed him out to one of the Visigothic archers. The captain gazed steadily back, not moving, his pale hair plastered to his gaunt cheeks, his pale blue eyes fixed on Aëtius, his lips moving with the words of some ancient curse. The archer lined up his arrow and fired, and the arrowhead hit him between the eyes. His head sank back, his arms floated out beside him, and they left him there gazing heavenward, his mouth still open, the words of the curse still on his salt-white lips.

Some of the other pirates had begun to swim toward the captured *Haifisch*, their last hope, but at this they realized they would be speared in the water.

Aëtius sent the lookout up to the fighting top.

The lookout pointed in a direction just south of the sun. Aëtius vaulted up onto the fly deck and called to the swimmers across the water, twenty or thirty soaked and bobbing heads, "Be thankful we haven't slaughtered you in the water, as you deserve!"

The swimmers listened, agony on their faces.

"You might drown. You might fatten a few sharks. What does that matter to us? But if you swim that way," Aëtius flung his right arm out—"just south of the sun as it stands now, you just might make landfall. Let God decide."

One struggling novice swimmer cried out, "How far is that?"

"Maybe ten miles."

Rufus murmured something. Aëtius squinted again toward the horizon but could still see nothing. The lad's younger eyes had seen it, though. "Maybe less," he called out again. "Maybe only six or seven."

"We'll drown!" they cried. "You are condemning us to death!"

"On the contrary, I am leaving you to death—which you deserve—knowing that there is a small chance you may be reprieved. You're in God's hands. It's a good, flat calm. The sun is shining. There's blood in the water around you, and plenty of sharks nearby. You'd better start kicking.

"Hortator! Sound the drum!"

In the silence, the slow, renewed dip of oars, the gentle splash, and the low Liburnian began to move eastward through the small waves again, the water breaking in no more than a silver trickle round her bows. The wretched pirates watched the *Haifisch* depart, a sailor on board already reaching down to scrub out the barbaric name and paint over it afresh: *Cygnus II*. It had all happened with such startling speed, such ruthless efficiency. Then some of the more optimistic souls turned in the water, pushed their spars ahead of them and began to kick.

The master shook his head. "Caesar had his pirates crucified."

Aëtius grunted. "Caesar was a greater man than I."

Torismond sold his slaves at Thessalonica. Aëtius resented the loss of even those two hours, but there was no food or water left on board for them. The prince netted a bag of thirty solidi.

He grinned. "Quite a catch."

"And behold, I shall make you fishers of men," said his brother sardonically, eyeing the weighty leather bag. "Not quite what Christ intended though, I think?"

Aëtius roared with laughter.

It was quite a pleasant voyage after that.

5

YANKHIN

I, Priscus of Panium, heard of his arrival and rushed down to the Harbor of Julian to meet him.

He smiled at me. "And who might you be, old man? An aged mendicant, supplicating for alms?" He laid his hand on my shoulder. "Let us talk later. I must speak to the emperor even more urgently than to my old tutor."

"Divine Majesty. Master General Aëtius requests an audience."

There was a pause and a fumbling, while Theodosius seated himself upon his gilded wooden throne, and then he was admitted to the imperial presence.

"Aëtius. So far from home." His voice was as frosty as a Pontic winter, with a wind blowing down out of Scythia.

"Majesty." He knelt and kissed the hem of the imperial robe in formal *adoratio*, privately detesting the gesture, and stood again swiftly. "You have still no news from the field army under General Aspar?"

Startled to find himself so abruptly questioned by a mere soldier, even if he was a general, Theodosius heard himself stammering, "They—they have not yet engaged, no."

"And it is true about the VIIth at Viminacium? Entirely destroyed?"

"Such was the judgment of God. Also . . . also Ratiaria, downriver. That, too, has been overrun by these wretched *Huns*."

"Ratiaria, too? Already? The III Pannonia? How many men did that number? And the weapons factories?"

The emperor could not look him directly in the eye, those limpid gray eyes. He surveyed the mosaics on the wall to his left, desperately hoping to radiate the regal serenity of God's viceroy upon earth. "The III Pannonia, too, is destroyed, and the weapons factories are now in enemy hands."

Attila. He knew. Now he had ownership of the most important armaments factories in the East. *He knew.*

"Then I come to offer you urgent military assistance. I have cohorts remaining from the Ist at Brigetio, from the IInd at Aquincum, the XVIth at Carnuntum, the IVth Scythica at Singidunum. I know all are well trained—I appointed their legates personally. I could pull them back from the Danube frontier and attack Attila's flank as he rides south on Naissus."

"And if Attila should turn on the West?"

"Attila *will* turn on the West. But not yet. He will wish to neutralize the East first."

The master general spoke with such energy and conviction, as if he had been waiting all his life for this moment, this final confrontation. Theodosius understood then, with distaste, that Aëtius actually *enjoyed* all this . . . this war business. It gave him his sense of purpose and destiny.

"More importantly," resumed Aëtius, "I have—with the Emperor Valentinian's permission, of course—the core of the Western Field Army still stationed in Sicily, waiting for orders to sail for Africa. Two thousand horses and twenty thousand men, in peak condition, under command of my good general Germanus."

Theodosius turned aside and touched a handsome polished wooden cabinet as if for reassurance. "And why should I trust you in bringing such a powerful force into the heart of our domain?"

"Majesty?"

"We are not wholly ignorant, Master General Aëtius—despite the fact that we are known for our love of learning," he added sarcastically.

"I sense mistrust."

"You sense aright."

"Then let me speak plainly. Your enemy is Attila, King of the Huns, and none other. Not your cousin Valentinian, nor Galla Placidia, nor I. Do not look for your enemy among your own. Your enemy is far cleverer and more ruthless than any of us. He is also cleverer than you, Majesty, though he has read fewer books."

The emperor compressed his lips and stared hard and unblinkingly at Aëtius. What he saw before him, though he was no great judge of men, was a blunt and unlikeable soldier, without learning, refinement or even common courtesy; but an honest man, for all that.

"We have learned," he said, "that there were detachments from the Herculian Legion fighting alongside the Huns at Viminacium."

"Bogus! Do not believe it!" Aëtius smacked his fist into his palm, his eyes burning, and began pacing the room impertinently. "I knew it!" he said with peculiar exaltation. "The fight has already begun! The fight of intelligence." He wheeled on the emperor and barked at him as if he was one of his lieutenants. "Who brought you this information?"

Theodosius had already lost his chilly composure, despite himself. "My . . . my chamberlain. One Py—"

"Search his room."

Theodosius hesitated, then spoke to a steward.

Aëtius continued pacing; it was most disconcerting. He snapped at another steward to bring him a map. The steward fled.

"You said Naissus?" said the emperor with some puzzlement. "But Attila will be destroyed by the field army before he rides down on Naissus."

"Well," said Aëtius, inclining his head, "just suppose that he is not. Heaven forfend that so great a disaster should befall, of course, Your Majesty, but we must prepare for even the darkest eventuality."

"God is with us."

"I don't doubt it. But 'Trust in God, and keep a good hold on your sword,' my father, Gaudentius, always said."

Theodosius crossed himself. "Ever since we heard of the fall of Viminacium, the bishops and people have given themselves up to ceaseless intercessions to the Holy Mother."

"Good, good," said the uncultivated general, pacing about, his hands clasped behind his back, clearly not listening. The steward returned, trembling like a rabbit, and laid the map on the marble-inlaid table. Aëtius took one glance at it and turned to bellow at him. "Not a map of the *city*, you arse, a map of the empire—from here to the Danube! At the double!"

Again the steward fled.

"He is not a soldier in your command," protested the emperor.

"Damn right he's not, he's too bloody useless."

Theodosius rose to his feet, his eyes burning with indignation. Tall, though of feeble build, he suddenly appeared a much more imposing figure.

"Master General Aëtius, you forget yourself," he said crisply. "Soldierly braggadocio is all very well in the barracks, but you stand now before an emperor. I suggest you remember that if you truly want to help."

Aëtius was chastened. He treated Valentinian with respect and circumspection because he was so dangerous. But Theodosius deserved respect, too. He was not such a fool as some said, and his heart was good. They must work together.

"Majesty," he said with bowed head.

The trembling steward returned and laid out a far larger map.

Theodosius indicated Naissus. "And after this?"

Aëtius traced a line south, down the great imperial trunk road toward Constantinople. "He'll be after the imperial stud farms of Thrace, too. You should send men out to round up the horses and drive them south, across to Asia if need be. We can't let Attila get his hands on them."

Theodosius looked puzzled. "A horde of thieving horse rustlers are going to ride up against the walls built by my grandfather, Theodosius the Great? Ridiculous. Our walls are impregnable. All the world knows that."

"Attila's ambition knows no bounds. And they now have siege craft. Let me fall on their flanks, here." He jabbed the map. "We could ride through the mountains. If we met them there we would do great harm. Do you still have your Isaurian auxiliaries?"

The emperor nodded. "At Trajanopolis."

The Isaurians were little more than Anatolian bandits, but skilled at mountain warfare.

"The Huns have little understanding of mountains," said Aëtius, "where all their speed will be useless to them. They are plains nomads only."

"You still imply that the field army . . . will be defeated by this horde of transient looters, without law or reason. Ridiculous! Never before has this happened."

Aëtius spoke one painful word: "Adrianople?"

The emperor compressed his lips.

"Besides," added Aëtius, "never before have they been commanded by a man like Attila."

The steward returned, entering the room backward until the emperor's address allowed him to turn, and then falling at his feet. He held something in his hand. Theodosius stared at it in puzzlement. "Pytheas," he murmured in puzzlement. Then he passed it to Aëtius.

He examined it cursorily: a small gold ingot, stamped with the legend of Viminacium. Looted Hun gold.

"Attila pays well," said Aëtius dryly. "Judas only got silver."

"Pytheas," repeated Theodosius softly, shaking his head.

"He won't be the only one. You need to clean out your Augean Stables."

The emperor looked shaken. Aëtius's heart went out to him. Each day he reigned, this haughty yet gentle scholar must perforce learn more about the cruelty and treachery of men, and how even those he most trusted would betray him for the glamor of gold.

Theodosius made to walk away.

"Majesty."

He stopped.

"Not everything will fall."

After a while, Theodosius nodded, his back to the general. "Do what you think is needed." Then he lifted his robes and walked swiftly from the chamber.

Aëtius gave orders for the traitor Pytheas to be executed. His head, hands, and all the gold of Viminacium found in his room were to be sewn in a sack and delivered to Attila; no other message. At the last minute he changed his mind and called the man back.

"On second thoughts, we keep the gold," he said. "Why enrich Attila so that he can buy more mercenaries? Put some iron in the sack with the traitor's head and hands. And on a potsherd, write these words: *"Yaldizh djostyara, Ütülemek haşimyara."*

It was I, Priscus, to whom he dictated. I grimaced with distaste. I had heard but little of this foul language before. "An ugly tongue, my lord."

"Matter of opinion. A complex tongue in many ways, utterly unlike the languages of the civilized world. Their compound words, for instance. You know they have a word meaning, 'the noise a bear makes when walking through cranberry bushes?'"

"How ridiculous."

"I thought you admired Herodotus? Yet you hardly have his candor and curiosity about other peoples and cultures."

"Hm." I trimmed my nib. "So. These barbaric words. '*Yaldizh djostyara*' et cetera. Might I be so bold as to ask what they mean?"

"An ancient Hunnish proverb, which I learned in my boyhood—from the uncrowned King of the World himself." He smiled a wintry smile. "It means 'Gold for my friends, iron for my enemies.'" He stood up and went to the window, hands clasped behind his back. "So that Attila will know clearly who his enemies are."

"How will we find Attila?"

"At the end of the trail of destruction," said Aëtius, still with a smile not entirely comforting.

"And who will run the errand?"

"His own. Flushed from this palace like termites. Now listen to my instructions. The Hun word for fire is '*yankhin*.'"

In the silent middle of the night, numerous slaves erupted and ran about the palace, screaming the word at the tops of their voices. Naturally almost everybody, except perhaps those who were in bed with other men's wives, quickly emerged, bewildered and blinking, into the shadowy courtyards of the great palace complex. But here and there, one or two dashed with buckets to the nearest wells and fountains, or even over toward the Baths of Xeuxippus. They were immediately seized and, to their astonishment, interrogated fluently in their own sacred tongue by this newly arrived western general. Torture was not necessary. They soon confessed all.

Aëtius's ruse had smoked out six termites in all: four men and two women, one of them a midwife. She might have secretly poisoned a newborn child of the imperial family, but apparently she had always worked diligently. Perhaps her woman's tenderness had outweighed even her loyalty to the Lord Attila.

To these six, Aëtius gave the task of taking back the remains of the traitor Pytheas, and the iron.

6

THE CRUCIFIED

It was in the meadows outside the ruins of a once-great city that the six Huns expelled from the Byzantine Court found Attila's camp. They looked about them with something approaching horror. The midwife gave a little cry of despair, strange to hear. The city should have been nothing to her. During her time in the Christian emperor's palace, she had delivered children faithfully. Sometimes, like the others, she had sent back communications to her people about what she had discovered of palace life, defenses, fortifications, but she had also begun to feel settled. Then one night her dreams had been disturbed by cries of "Fire!" in her own tongue, and she had been exposed, along with the others, by running to the wells. Until then, her work was all of life new born. Here, meanwhile, life was being destroyed.

A pall of black smoke hung over the burning city, and drifted ominously to shadow the camp of her own people. They who had once been her own people, she thought, with a sick lurch at her own treacherous thoughts. Under a black cloud of death, in his plain tent, the Lord Attila. Great Tanjou. She had made mothers in the palace with her strong hands. Meanwhile, her Great Lord had been making widows.

One of the men dropped the sack before Attila's throne.

"What have you brought me?" asked the King, eyes glittering, chin resting in the cup of his hand.

"The remains of the traitor Pytheas, the eunuch," the fellow replied.

"Traitor? To whom?"

"To the emperor, Theodosius," he stammered. "He was found out. As were we."

"If he was traitor to our enemy, he was our friend. No? He was a hero of the Hun people!"

The six hung their heads wretchedly. They had no refuge on earth now.

Attila delved in the sack and pulled out the potsherd. He read out the Hun proverb: " 'Gold for my friends, iron for my enemies.' I know who sent this," he murmured. He looked up. "What was your judgment of Master General Aëtius? Did you meet him?"

They hesitated, then one said, "He is a man of forceful character, my lord."

"Is he? Is he?"

He pulled out something else: a putrid, blood-clotted hand.

A figure hovered near. It was Enkhtuya, the witch. Attila seemed to know, without looking, that she was there and what she wanted. Wordlessly he passed the foul object back to her. She hid it in her cloak and slipped away.

He looked back at the six. "They tried to kill me," he said. They were frozen with fear. They did not know what their Lord meant. "In my youth." He rubbed his beard. "The traitor Pytheas," he murmured. "Well, well." He surveyed them with glittering eyes. Then he decreed, "Negotiation is tiresome. Revenge is profitable. All shall pay." And with that he ordered the six to be taken outside and crucified, men and women both.

His guards bound the six and led them away.

As they passed by, a motley little figure in a tattered old buckskin shirt covered in little black stick men crouched beside the doomed procession, and held his arms over his head like a monkey sheltering from the rain, and cried out in a muffled though audible voice, "This funeral sky grows heavier by the hour!"

Toward evening an old warrior with fine gray mustaches and long white hair rode out and surveyed the six crude crosses bearing the six dead and dying fugitives. Their faces were blue-white masks of agony, their breathing like a tortured wind in a ravine. He rode back to his tent, found his long spear and returned and killed them all one by one. The last was a round-faced woman.

She should have been someone's wife. The agony left her face as the spear entered her heart, and her eyes closed in something like peace.

He got off his horse and cleaned his spear in the grass, then drove it into the ground and squatted down and looked away south over the low hills, his back to the bodies hanging like withered fruit on leafless trees.

After a time another man came and squatted not far off in the gathering dusk. For a long while they said nothing to each other.

Eventually Chanat murmured, "My dreams are becoming as crazed as yours, old shaman."

Little Bird hummed and tore grass.

The old warrior cupped his big bony hands round his ringing skull. His skull was thin as a bird's now. Old age was wearing him thin all over.

"It is not as it was before," he said with quiet disgust. He gestured over his shoulder at the crucified cadavers and the smoldering town beyond. "Look at our work."

"He is Tashur-Astur, the Scourge of God," said the shaman in his singsong voice. "A fool may argue with God, but God will not answer."

"This is God's judgment on wicked people? Do you believe that, Little Bird?"

The shaman looked away. He never answered a direct question for, as he said, how could he? He did not exist.

"I did not come here to scalp infants in arms," growled Chanat.

He remembered seeing Candac amid the smoking ruins of Margus, standing silent upon rubble and slaughter, staring, a look unfathomable on his strong round face. Looking about him perhaps in judgment before he chose to vanish.

Chanat gasped and clutched his side. A week ago, he had cursed the witch Enkhtuya to her face. The cramps in his bowels still hurt. Such pettiness they had come to. He thought he saw nobility itself ebbing away like the last of the sun on a winter's day. The cold and brazen light across the steps occluded by black cloud from some burning town.

Little Bird and Chanat both shivered.

7

PEACE AT LAST

Catastrophe followed hard on the heels of the small success of unmasking the spies. A brief and bitter communication came to the Imperial Court from Adrianople.

The Eastern Field Army under the command of General Aspar, *Magister Militum per Thraciam,* leaving from army headquarters at Marcianopolis, engaged the Huns on flat country near the River Utus. Overwhelmed by vastly superior numbers, however, and the speed and ferocity of the enemy, as well as their unexpected mastery of both artillery and the heavy cavalry charge, the six legions and all their auxiliaries were destroyed. General Aspar himself continued to fight with utmost gallantry on foot after his horse was killed under him, but eventually he, too, was slain.

It is believed that the Hunnish army is continuing to advance south.

In Constantinople, there was outright terror at the news. Now there was nothing but a few centuries of the Palatine guard, and scattered auxiliaries down at Trajanopolis and Heraclea, to stand between them and this demonic army of a million heathen horsemen. Who ate children's flesh, they said, and drank bat's blood mixed with wine. Some citizens fled across the Bosphorus to Asia Minor. Others prayed for twenty hours a day to the Holy Mother. All were infected with panic, as contagious as the plague.

Theodosius begged Aëtius for Western aid, and the general duly wrote again to Ravenna. But he warned that there would be little time and that, now Valentinian knew of the Huns' power, he might prefer to keep his legions for his own protection: frontier legions as well as field army.

The reply soon came by sea. There was to be no aid. Theodosius's curses rained down on his cousin's head.

"He will fall on us soon now," he said. "This Attila, God's punishment upon us. Yet in what have we so sinned? I do not know." He gave a deep sigh: the sigh of the foredefeated. "First he will devastate all of Moesia and Illyria, Thessaly and Thrace, and then he will fall upon this city. We cannot stand against him with only a few hundred ill-trained auxiliaries and the Guard. We will have to negotiate."

"We still have the walls," said Aëtius.

"Not all of us are behind the walls."

"True," said Aëtius. "In the provinces, the people must shift for themselves. But the city will be saved. And there will be recompense, I promise you. When Attila turns westward against Rome, he will not meet with such easy victory."

"You do not understand," said the emperor haltingly. "Not all the . . . imperial family is behind the walls."

Aëtius frowned. "The Princess Honoria?"

Theodosius smiled mirthlessly. "No, she is still in my sister Pulcheria's charge. I mean . . . the Empress Eudoxia."

The empress. Athenaïs. He had not allowed himself to think of that name for years.

"She is in Jerusalem?"

"Would that she were. No, she is visiting the convent at Azimuntium."

"I do not know it."

"A small hill town near the Pontine coast, of ancient Thracian origin. Indeed, it is proposed by some of our most eminent mythographologists that the site may in fact be etymologically cognate with that of the Homeric—"

"In the path of Attila?"

The emperor's voice dulled again. "In the path, as you say, of Attila."

"Why was I not informed of this before?"

"Your services were needed here—as indeed they still are. The Holy City must needs be defended even more than . . ."

"Even more than the empress."

"Do not speak with such quick judgment," cautioned Theodosius, his voice low but his gaze again fixed on the general. "I know you, Gaius Flavius Aëtius. You think yourself a man of very different mettle from mine. But an emperor's choices are never easy, especially in time of war."

Aëtius bowed his head a little.

"We have intelligence that the empress remains safe in the convent of Saints Perpetua and Felicitas, Virgins and Martyrs, behind the considerable walls of that venerable hill town. But the country round about is lawless, and the Huns draw closer daily. She will require an escort. I cannot spare the Imperial Guard, but I thought perhaps your . . . rubicund friends from Gothia?"

Aëtius smiled at the emperor's feline words. To a man like Theodosius, the Goths would forever be the barbarous immigrants who had caused the disaster of Adrianople, seventy years before.

"Very well," said Aëtius. "I will take my wolf lords."

"You will be back in one week."

Aëtius bowed.

He was on the brink of departure when more news came. Two Hun ambassadors had arrived from the camp of Attila.

The emperor's eyes lit up. "You see, we *can* negotiate! The empress will be safe. They wish to make peace."

"They do not wish to make peace. They come only to reconnoitre. This is a trap of Attila's. Do not trust him. Blindfold the ambassadors, do not let them see the walls, do not let them near anyone, do not let them speak except in a closed cell."

But the emperor was no longer listening, his whole being flooded with relief. Theodosius hated war, with a fierceness more usually found in men who have experienced the crimson foulness of the battlefield themselves. For in truth no man dies well who dies in battle. And hating war, he had already sent out emissaries to find the approaching barbarians and their terrible king, and sue for peace. What could he offer them? Land? Their own kingdom south of the Danube? The whole province of Moesia, even? So far, none of the emissaries had returned, but now he revealed this new twist to the general. Voices were soon raised.

"The emissaries have not returned, Eternal Majesty, because their crow-pecked corpses are even now hanging from trees all along the Egnatian Way!"

Aëtius's anger was barely controlled. In the West, as a letter from that good general Germanus had informed him, many of the lesser troops were already beginning to desert from the Roman side. News of the destruction of the Eastern Field Army on the Utus had already reached distant ears, and now the Western Field Army was also ebbing away. Terror, as Attila observed, is a powerful weapon; and very cheap. If only the Western legions could be embarked forthwith, Aëtius urged, and sail for the East, the very mission itself might steady them. Galla Placidia had tried to persuade her son of this very policy, but Valentinian and his advisers were set against it. The Western Army must remain for the defense of the West. Germanus wished his commander well, and trusted that the Huns in the East could still be resisted. Aëtius wrote back that for now he would have to trust in walls, not men.

Theodosius remained cold in the face of Aëtius's temper, and spoke of how all men in their hearts love reason.

Aëtius paced, and clenched his fists unreasonably.

"Is a man rational when in love?" he cried. "A woman when she is defending her child against some wild beast, armed only with her own rage, fighting off a ravening lion with her bare hands, or a puny knife she has snatched from the table? And she will triumph, too, for she fights for everything that she loves, whereas the lion fights only for his dinner, and will soon slink cowardly away."

"You have seen this?" asked Theodosius, wide eyed.

Aëtius suppressed a spasm of irritation. At times the learned emperor could be the stupidest of men. "I speak in a figure, Your Majesty. Reason does not reign supreme."

He tried to explain—rationally—what he knew and understood of Attila, and his idea of himself and his demonic destiny.

The emperor listened, brow furrowed. "But this is madness!" he said incredulously. "It is almost as if you are suggesting that Attila has no aim but to avenge the insults he suffered as a child—with vengeance in the form of purest destruction!"

"To destroy his enemies is the sweetest thing to him, and his enemies are all those he feels have insulted him and his people. The more he destroys, the stronger he becomes. If you buy him off with gold, that makes him stronger, too. It will not buy peace. Attila scorns peace, and loves power. Gold will only buy him more weapons, more armor, more warhorses, the service of freebooters and shiftless mercenaries."

Still the emperor looked perplexed and angry.

Aëtius approached him as closely as he dared, and fixed his eye urgently. "Majesty, you must imagine that Attila has sent you a message saying simply, 'We do not want anything from you. We want to destroy you.' "

"But it was on the orders of the Western Empire that the original attack on the Huns was mounted."

"And the Western Empire's turn will come. But it was an Eastern legion that executed that order, a legion itself now destroyed. Adam blamed Eve and Eve blamed the serpent. The Lord God punished them all."

"You are comparing Attila to *God*?"

"Not my comparison, Attila's own. Attila Tashur-Astur—'*Flagellum Dei*.' "

Theodosius pondered a moment, and then another party entered. It was Pulcheria, the emperor's absurdly pious and misleadingly christened elder sister, a sour-faced woman in her sixth decade. With her came one of her closest counselors, the lean, saturnine Chrysaphius, and a small, wiry man called Vigilas. She spoke quietly to the emperor, and a moment later Theodosius asked Aëtius to leave them. Matters had already progressed from the military to the diplomatic, he said smoothly, despite the master general's "pessimism" and "negativity"; further advice from him was now redundant.

The two Hun ambassadors were Geukchu, an intelligent-looking fellow in a fine silk robe, not in animal furs and skins as they had expected; and a quiet, very polite, bald-pated companion, Greek by birth, who introduced himself as Orestes. Within minutes, Theodosius felt he had mastered them. They brought the emperor some wonderful treasures, including a Cimmerian leopard in a cage; they paid him great respect, kissing the purple hem of his robe, and they said that yes, they would be happy to receive a Byzantine embassy in return. They were sure an accommodation could be reached in this unfortunate matter.

Behind them, Theodosius's eyes met the gaze of Chrysaphius, and the counselor, almost imperceptibly, nodded.

That night, Geukchu and Orestes dined and drank late into the night with Chrysaphius and Vigilas, and in the morning they took their leave of one another like brothers.

The emperor insisted that Aëtius lead the Byzantine embassy to the Huns, despite the general's lack of enthusiasm. He could combine the mission with escorting the empress home afterward. Chrysaphius and Vigilas would go, too, the counselor handling the actual negotiations; and he also sent his trusted clerk in consistory, modest Priscus, to record the historic meeting, along with a small retinue of guards. Aëtius wished to take the two Visigothic princes and their fifty wolf lords on the long and perilous journey, fully armed. The emperor grudgingly agreed. Those wolf lords ate like oxen in winter. It would be good to be rid of them for a while.

A note came to Aëtius from the Princess Honoria, smuggled out via a bribed slave, bribed in God knew what manner. The disgraced and dishonored daughter of Galla Placidia and sister of Valentinian, long held in virtual captivity in the women's quarters, she wrote mockingly that she, too, would like to ride out and meet this Attila. She thought he sounded interesting. Aëtius grunted with grim amusement, sniffed the delicate little note and found it was indeed perfumed, then screwed it up and tossed it into the nearest brazier.

And so it was that I, Priscus, rode out that day with the man I still thought of as my beloved pupil, upon the most perilous journey of my life. Sailing back and forth from Italy to Constantinople was bad enough, but this was virtually into the wilds of Scythia! I took a flask of very strong red wine, heavily sweetened, to keep me warm; and an extra woolen blanket.

Thus prepared, I took my brief place upon the stage of History, tentative, blinking, and for what I hoped would be but a short scene. The public theater is sufficiently unpleasant, what with the rotten fruit and the catcalls, but the stage of History is far worse, and for those who take their place upon it, the play often closes early.

I also took with me many scrolls to record this historic venture. In the night I dreamed that I was reading them over, and that I had called my account "A Journey Through the Thirteen Cities of the Ruined Lands."

We rode out that morning through the Golden Gate, heading westward along the shores of the Sea of Marmara on the ancient Via Egnatia, which people had traveled for six hundred years toward Thessalonica, and then over the Dinaric Alps to the Adriatic coast at Dyrrachium. But before Thessalonica we would turn north away from the coast and up into the hills. The wolf lords and their two princes rode the finest white Cappadocian horses from the imperial stables. That favor, at least, the emperor had allowed his allies, though they still mourned their own drowned chargers, lying deep beneath the waves and far away.

Under a late summer sky heavy with storm clouds, Aëtius was trying to keep other ghastly images at bay. The battle of the River Utus: is that how history would remember it—if at all? The Beginning of the End, far more surely than Adrianople, seventy years before. Six legions gone. Another at Viminacium, another at Ratiaria. Other cities destroyed since then, he was sure. He was glad he had not seen it, but he could imagine the scenes of carnage all too well.

They had mastered artillery and the heavy cavalry charge already. A bludgeoning bullock-headed charge: no lightly dancing, lethal arrow storms now, but a heavy cavalry, gleaming and newly armored from the armories of Ratiaria, thumping into the aghast Byzantine line and shivering it to splinters. Shards of shield wood and flying teeth, lost limbs, open mouths screaming silently, flailing, falling, trampled into the reddening mud. The Huns must have learned fast, clad in the laminar plate of their slaughtered foes, clutching long lances resting in slings and couched tightly under bulging biceps. Their squat muscled horses galloping in fast, a pummeling gallop with huge heads stretched forward and low, juddering into the Byzantine line like battering rams, men flung aside, horses' eyes rolling to the whites like those of horses gored by bulls, Roman horses rising up under the punch, staggering, toppling their own riders back into the melee, legs flailing, hooves turned upward, kicking, horses screaming, their lips curled back over long yellow teeth and terrible horse cries, the foul stench of blood and ruptured bowels, the earth slippery with loosed innards and gore, the horror. . . .

"Deep in thought, Master General?"

It was Prince Theodoric at his side, his voice light and young and jaunty. Aëtius said nothing.

"Worried about the Huns?" asked Torismond, equally brightly. "Never fear, the mighty Visigothic nation will vanquish them by Christmas."

"Mind your tongue, little brother," cautioned the more sensible Theodoric, glancing round. The Hun ambassadors Geukchu and Orestes with their small party of Hun warriors rode at the back of the column. "This is just us. Our father's people are not at war with the Huns."

Aëtius said softly, "They will be."

"Attila's aim is Rome," said Theodoric, "and Constantinople."

"His aim is the world."

"Well, I pray that this embassy fails," said Torismond.

Aëtius glanced sideways at his rubicund friend from Gothia. "It'll fail."

"And then I pray that we meet some of 'em out there!" he added eagerly. "A war party!" He even leaned forward in his saddle as he spoke.

"Pray that you don't," said Aëtius.

The threatened storm passed and we rode on west across the burning Thracian plains. Already many of the farms and homesteads were deserted. The people had fled, refugees stumbling back to the already overcrowded city of Constantinople, in dread of the approaching wrath. "The Huns are coming' was the whisper throughout all that country. "Flee for your lives. The Huns are coming." The people, too, had no faith in embassies.

One solitary man stood at the side of the road watching us pass, clutching his hoe like a spear. Then he called out sardonically at our band of sixty or so, "You're going to need a bigger army!"

We said nothing and rode on.

One night, as we camped, a snake appeared beside where Chrysaphius was standing. The counselor froze in horror, a townsman to his marrow, but in a trice the little fellow Vigilas had drawn a gleaming dagger from his cloak and skewered the snake through the head.

Aëtius regarded him curiously.

Later he addressed him casually in simple Gothic, and then Aramaic, but the fellow looked blank. He spoke only Latin and Greek, the former somewhat stiffly. A poor linguist for a diplomat.

"He is my personal bodyguard," said Chrysaphius defensively. "Let us concentrate on the task in hand, Master General."

Aëtius assured him that he was all concentration.

Sleeping out at night was bad, although, as it turned out, far from the worst horror that we would face. How I longed night after night for the hot baths and cool chambers of the Palace of the Emperors, overlooking the Sea of Marmara, silvered by the moon. Instead I went along, and saw things that I have never forgotten and would never have dreamed.

For the first time I saw with my own eyes the horrors of war. I, Priscus of Panium, obedient son, studious pupil, humble scribe in the Imperial Court of Theodosius II, and lately raised to the post of chief clerk in consistory. How tearfully proud my parents would have been, had they lived to see! I was never meant for the battlefield, and was a little fearful even of that more playful battlefield which lies between the opposing armies called Men and Women. I was happier, generally speaking—but for an occasional scampering visit to the local bawdy house on the Street of the Golden Cock just behind the Hippodrome—to keep myself to myself, and to stay peacefully and diligently among the scrolls and texts of the ancients, reading and writing and dreaming of other ages than this.

But now I was riding out to see the world as it is. I do not think that I have known the same peace of mind since seeing the world as it is. My dreams have been more vivid, and more troubled. In the old days I barely remembered my dreams at all, but now they come to me in the silence of the night, messengers and harbingers unsought. I have less of my old equanimity now. But perhaps I will be a better chronicler for it. There is no reason to think that Tacitus and Thucydides were happy men.

Of the things I witnessed, I asked myself, did the armies of Rome not commit similar atrocities? Yes, they did. Perhaps not on such a scale; perhaps not with such malevolent randomness or glee, perhaps with rather a dutiful grimness. But if you are the victim, does it matter whether your killer is grinning or grim faced when he cuts your throat? I tried to discern that the violence of Rome was a means to an end, committed to secure peace, stability, and the rule of law, but the violence of the barbarians was committed for its own sake, for the pleasure of terror, and as such would never cease or find satiety.

But I do not know any more. I do not enjoy the ordered comfort of such thoughts. I know little with certainty, and I can only record what I saw. At my age I no longer have opinions, only memory.

I had hope
When violence was ceas'd, and War on Earth,
All would have then gone well, peace would have crowned
With length of happy days the race of man;
But I was far deceived. . . .

And one battle looks much like another when you survey the corpses after.

Our journey was long and arduous, and I often slept in the saddle. I remember a violent storm, and fires of blazing reeds, detonated by the lightning and burning up even in rain. I remember weariness and disorientation, tiredness beyond measure, and the sun appearing to rise in the West one morning. A bad omen.

When we came to the ruins of what had once been a city, the omen was fulfilled: the first of numberless settlements, villages, towns, and cities we were to encounter, destroyed and utterly laid waste by the hand of Attila. The rich and golden cities of the Eastern Empire that would never again recover from his wrath. Through all the destruction, our two Hun ambassadors, our guides through this wasteland which their own people had created, seemed not a bit contrite. Guilt they doubtless regarded as a form of cowardice, like most barbarians. Only at a certain rest stop did the one called Orestes, Greek by birth—shame on him!—wave his hand over the void before us, and say softly, "You see now why it would be in your interests to negotiate." He almost smiled. Aëtius's face was dark with fury and he did not speak. Not for days.

The city was a blackened skeleton of its former self, a skeleton of wood and stone, flattened walls, arches, and buttresses broken off and hanging in space.

Like Philippopolis and Marcianopolis, it had been a bishopric, and the Huns had knifed and stripped its bishop and hung him from the walls.

"They would have spat in the face of Christ if they could," I muttered.

"As did the Romans once," said Prince Theodoric beside me.

I could think of nothing more to say.

A few had survived the firestorm and the arrow storm, and them we pitied most, for they must have envied the dead. Sick people sheltered beneath the broken walls of the churches. Rachitic or tubercular children, riven with coughing, held out their clawed hands to us for food, but we could not help. A small girl cradling an infant in her lap sheltered beneath a smashed stone altar table, dark eyes peering up at me through filthy hair. In a demolished side street, a mere pattern of rubble now, there was another huddle of children, lips withered with hunger, worm-filled bellies like sails before the wind. Near them, though they appeared mercifully oblivious, lay two adult corpses, scalped, their temples stained as if with some dark chrism. Here I tired and could no longer look at the sights of the city.

I rode over paving stones grouted with dried blood, my horse trampling over a tattered prayer book, an illuminated euchologion, torn pages turning to no purpose. My ears rang with sad litanies of mortal flesh and blood. My old pupil said, remounting and pulling his horse away, "And the emperor believes he can negotiate with this."

A little further on he stopped again. His head was bowed and his big, scarred hands gripped the front of his saddle. I saw to my astonishment that, although his shadowed face was set as hard and grim as ever, tears ran down his furrowed cheeks and fell in dark splotches on the saddle leather. Yet why should I be astonished? That was Aëtius to the core: the deepest passions, under iron control.

He turned in the saddle and looked back. The column of wolf lords in their scarlet cloaks was riding out after us, and the Byzantine ambassadors, and the two wordless, expressionless Huns. We were leaving the sick people and the starving children behind. Aëtius said, his voice trembling, "All we can do now, to help them, is defeat Attila."

I understood. He was almost asking me to forgive him for riding on and not helping, here and now. I nodded. It was agony, but there was nothing to be done here. We had no food, no medicines, no resources. The people were too sickly to move, let alone make it all the way back to the safety of Constantinople. In a few days they would simply . . . vanish. Their souls would be gathered in. I nodded again, I hoped consolingly. We must do the emperor's bidding and speak with Attila. Then we must ride back to the city. There were a million or more people there whom we could save. And beyond that . . . the rest of the empire.

The two princes reined in, flanking Aëtius on either side, behind them the powerfully built wolf lords Valamir and Jormunreik. No word was spoken but, as is the way of men, the meaning was plain. They rode with Aëtius: to whatever doom.

The two Huns were not addressed again.

We camped on a nearby hillside in the coarse tussock grass. We would rather have camped in the lush water meadows down by the river, but the water was befouled, and there were too many bones of the slain littering the country round about.

Over the following days we passed more ghosts of towns and cities, each as bad as or worse than the last. On the road we glimpsed trickles of frightened fugitives who fled from us into the woods before we ever reached them; and one old woman, who could not flee. It is terrible to see a mother wailing over her child, but worse still to see an old woman wailing over her aged husband, lying broken in the mud, snapped like a dry twig. He with whom she thought to live out her last quiet days.

After the devastated cities of the plain we ascended into low foothills and then rough, barren mountains, over mighty gorges, treacherous wilds barely touched by the magisterial hand of Roman law, where men dressed in sheepskin jackets tied around the waist with twisted leather, and women were safe only beside their own hearth fire. We traversed many rivers by dugout canoe, and villagers fed us on mead rather than wine, and on millet not wheat bread.

Later in our journey there were no villagers left. We could only forage like beasts.

We came to a fire-blackened valley, and among the still-smoking stubble there were other black shapes, not of sheaves but of men, women, children, infants burned in their mothers' arms, mothers clinging to their children, mouths open, black and charcoal. From such unimaginable weathering, we can only hope their souls do well to fly. In the night there was a downpour from a summer cloudburst over the valley, and in the dawnlight the bodies were ash gray under the rain, some of them no more than washed white bones showing like strange root crops through the folded gray mud half covering them like sodden earthen shrouds.

Our Hun guides remained expressionless throughout. The one called Geukchu only commented that this would be the work of their brothers the Kutrigur Huns, in their battle madness. But he did not say it in exculpation.

We moved on a way before we camped that night, but it was not far enough. The smoke from the campfires rose into the night air as we lay on our backs and stared into the heavens, dreaming bad dreams open eyed. Through the drifting smoke, the starry sky, those white celestial worlds where all things are pure and good, far above this sinful sublunary world so darkened by violence and wrath, and by the furious selfhoods of ambitious men. The wolf shall dwell with the lamb, and the leopard shall lie down with the kid, and the little child shall lead them, saith the Lord. And they shall not kill nor hurt in all my Holy Mountain.

But how long, O Lord? How long?

It seemed to us that the viper and his venom would outlast all our days; that the bloodlust of Attila might rise even to the heavens and stain the white radiance of eternity, as the heavy smoke rose from that blackened charnel field, thick and greasy from where the bodies still smoldered, a choking veil between our wondering upturned faces and those white celestial worlds now lost to our sight.

8

THE EMBASSY

At last we came down onto a broad grassy plain and there we saw stretched out in encampment, as far as the eye could see, the People of Attila. A city of leather tents beside a wide lakeshore; sunlight and slow plumes of woodsmoke and children's laughter: a tranquil scene.

Aëtius spoke at last, addressing the Greek. "So you have brought down your women and children again?"

Orestes' eyes were very pale blue. "Why not? There is no danger to them now." He gave his almost-smile again. "Your army is destroyed."

We had begun to set up camp on a small hill when a group of Hun warriors rode out to us and, with mockery and contempt, told us to camp lower down in the damp valley so that we should not overlook the tent of the Great Tanjou. We obeyed without a word. They also demanded that the wolf lords hand over their weapons. Prince Theodoric answered, with undiplomatic brevity, "No." After brief talk among themselves, they said no matter, the Huns had never feared any Visigoths yet, armed or unarmed. One of the hulking wolf lords, Jormunreik, growled at this barb, but his prince silenced him. The Huns said that the Lord Attila was out hunting, but would speak to us in time and galloped away, laughing.

When we rode into the camp toward the king's tent at its heart, I marveled at how many races there were. The great majority were horse-bound Huns, of course, stocky and immensely strong, sparsely bearded, with long black hair and mustaches; but there were also Greeks like our guide Orestes, and renegade Teutons, Thuringian chieftains in bearskins, even Celts. There were Africans, Spaniards, Syrians, many marked with the marks of criminals. They were fugitives from Roman law, consumed with disgust at the insipid life of the tottering empire, longing once more to be on History's winning side. There were more savage Huns who were heavily painted and tattooed and stuck with feathers, and wore their hair limed white in a stiff topknot; other people, who looked almost like Chinamen, their language unknown to us, camped a little apart. We knew what this meant well enough. All these people believed that victory over the whole Roman world lay with Attila, and their fortunes with him.

As we came near a large, plain black tent in the heart of the camp, a woman appeared from inside. And what a woman. Perhaps fifty years old, immensely graceful, with high cheekbones, a red silk veil drawn back over her slim shoulders, and wearing a diadem of astonishing richness, of hammered sheet gold ornamented with Indian almandites. I do not think the diadem was paid for.

We dismounted and bowed low. She was Queen Checa, Attila's wife. His first wife, that is—he had many more, and countless concubines. All round the central circle of the camp were huge wooden wagons, those ships of the steppes, laden with decorated copper cauldrons, rolls of the finest silks and stuffs, and even occasional marble statues. A smaller, lighter wagon, guarded by two burly fellows who looked like brothers, bore Far Eastern saddle ornaments, fabulous reins decorated with gold cloisons and Indian gemstones, Pontic crowns and oval Sarmatian mirrors; tethered to the wagon was a pair of gray riding horses branded with Turkic tangas. What a motley, magpie people, yet they had raided and looted their way across half the world.

Then word came to us. The Great Tanjou had returned. We unbuckled our weapons and left them in a heap.

Attila received us in his black tent supported on carved and polished wooden columns and hung with animal skins. He was seated on a barbarically carved wooden throne. The warriors about him were outlandishly accoutred in Chinese silks and fur headdresses, their cheeks scarred with blue tattoos, but Attila himself was simply dressed, with a hatchet in his belt. A powerfully built man of medium height, with the scarred cheeks of his people, muscular forearms corded with ropy veins, and messily scarred, I noticed, from fighting in many furious battles. He had a strong and bony nose, leonine eyes glittering beneath lowered brows, face weathered and wind furrowed, and he was leaning forward slightly, stroking his wispy gray beard, a glimmer of something like amusement in his eyes. But none of this captures the spirit of the man. He radiated a terrifying force, the kind that turns to fury in a moment. Being close to him was like trying to find rest on the slopes of Mount Vesuvius. Had he turned and looked at me, my eyes would have dropped away instantly. Few men could meet that gaze.

Chrysaphius bowed lowest.

"The Emperor of the East, the Viceroy of God, the Divine Theodosius, the King of Kings and Lord of Lords, and his subjects, the Senate and the people of Rome, wish upon you health, happiness, and length of days."

Attila smiled and said, "I wish upon the Romans whatever they truly wish upon me."

Slaves came forward and presented the gifts we had brought: furs and silver goblets, dates and pepper. Attila received them without thanks.

We dined on juicy steaks cut from the croups of grass-fattened horses, and freshly slaughtered sheep and cows, roasted whole. It would have been impolitic to inquire at what livestock market such excellent meat was purchased. We lay on couches, Roman style, drinking from the finest goblets. The Huns themselves sat cross-legged, or upright on benches. Attila ate only meat from a plain wooden platter. Conversation was stilted but innocuous. Attila spoke very little. Only when his young son Ellak—his favorite, so they say—was brought in to say goodnight to his father did the king show pleasure.

For the night, we were offered the choicest young female slaves for our comfort, a Scythian compliment, but one disdained by our leaders—somewhat to my chagrin, I must admit. Well into my sixth decade, the chains of lust had loosened but by no means fallen away entirely. And so after we had retired to our own tents on the hill, I wriggled my way back out again, and hurried after the retreating women in the darkness, at one point tripping in a marmot hole in my haste and very nearly doing myself quite an injury. The girls heard me and turned, and giggled.

Though they were all lovely to look at, one drew me in particular. A Burgundian she was, flaxen haired and as pretty as a flower. I took her by the hand and pulled her back to my modest little partition in the tent. In the dark I could barely see her features, but her hands were small and her lips were soft, and I confess I passed a happy night with her. In the morning, as she lay there only half covered by my side, she stretched sleepily and smiled and said that, although I was a very old man, I had not entirely failed to please her.

Aëtius passed me as we ate bread in the morning sunshine outside our tents, and nodded curtly as I munched. "You must be hungry," he said.

9

ORESTES

Among those I talked to in the camp was an apostate Greek picking stones out of his horse's hooves. When I asked him why he was there, he eloquently applauded the freedom he enjoyed among the Huns, compared with the iniquitous taxes, self-serving officials, and meddling laws of Rome. Once, he agreed, Rome might have represented a kind of freedom with dignity under the law, but those days were gone. Here a man could be truly free. "You think Attila a barbarian tyrant," he said sardonically. "But he does not oppress me daily, he does not survey my every action, he does not dictate my religion, he does not tax me to death. Indeed, he does not tax me at all. I follow him, he protects me. It is a simple and noble society; as Rome was once, perhaps, long, long ago."

"It is a society that feeds off others!" I protested.

"In that respect, at least," he answered, "it is just like Rome."

He was a very sardonic fellow indeed.

Of all the people in the camp of the Huns, aside from Attila himself, it was that other renegade Greek, Orestes, who seemed to me the most compelling and enigmatic. I was astonished, then, when I approached him later and respectfully asked if I might hear his story.

"My story?" he said softly. "Ah. Yes."

Perhaps Attila himself had encouraged him to tell me, for my chronicle. I shall never know.

We sat on stools in the shade of a long tent. No others were near. A small fire burned in a brazier. Orestes cast a handful of barley kernels across an iron tray.

"I was from Thessalonica," he began. "You know the history. You have heard of the atrocity."

I nodded. Indeed.

"My parents—" Orestes stopped again and smiled, a bitter smile. "The man who died eight years before I was born, he who should have been my father."

The barley kernels popped in the heat.

"I will start again." He drew breath. "Some twelve years before I was born, my mother was married to a man of Thessalonica. He was a ship owner, a wealthy man, also a man of taste. He had a library. He was a Christian but kept his counsel. In their villa on a hill above the great harbor, they had mosaics of Silenus, frescoes of nymphs and tritons, silverware decorated with images of Mars and Venus on a shelf beside a devotional to the Virgin. My mother described it all to me in later years. My mother was high spirited, mercurial. She was beautiful when she was young. Their house in Thessalonica was very fine. They had two sons, and then a daughter. They were a fine family. My family. Yet not."

He chewed some kernels.

"In the summer of 390, eight years before my birth, the great city of Thessalonica stood the mother city of all Illyria. The people of the city, we chattering Greeks, ever argumentative, volatile, full of life and bustle. And the city was well walled around, well garrisoned. The captain of the garrison was one Botheric, a German by birth. Among his slaves was a boy, a beautiful boy— you understand. One of the Circus charioteers loved this boy. He lured him home and raped him. Botheric had the charioteer thrown in prison.

"The common people of Thessalonica, who like the common people of any city love their sport before all else, and will forgive their sportsmen any crime, corruption or rapine so long as they perform well and give them pleasure—the common people were furious at being deprived of their favorite charioteer, the boy rapist. They rioted. Botheric and one of his most senior officers were spat on, dragged through the streets, butchered. You know what the mob is like when their moral indignation is up: all on behalf of a boy rapist. Emperor Theodosius the First—the *Great,* grandfather to both today's emperors—residing in Milan, heard news of the uprising, and in his fury ordered a punitive massacre. We know all about the Roman urge to commit punitive massacres of civilian populations, do we not? It is an old habit."

I said nothing.

"Only after the order was sent did the Christian bishops manage to persuade Theodosius to remit his bloody sentence, so against the teaching of Christ. He despatched a second message but it was too late. The garrison at Thessalonica, already enraged at the murder of Botheric, took their revenge with alacrity. In the name of their emperor, the games-mad people were invited to more games—a little joke. Once in the circus, the gates were barred and they were slaughtered, all of them, without distinction of age or sex. The carnage continued for three hours. Some say seven thousand were slaughtered that day, some say more than fifteen thousand, 'sacrificed to the *manes* of Botheric.' After the massacre in the circus, the troops spilled out onto the streets and continued their work.

"Among their victims was a father who pleaded with them, offering his own life for that of his wife and two young sons and his daughter. You have guessed it. My family. The troops were unimpressed. They killed the father, the two sons, the infant daughter, and the howling mother all together. Except the mother survived, wounded and bleeding, beneath the bloody corpses of her family."

He paused for a while, mastering himself.

"My mother survived. That is the correct word. She endured. She drank. She sold herself. When pregnant she administered her own abortions. Later she failed and bore another son. Miraculously, he was a healthy infant, grew to healthy adulthood. Later there was a daughter, Pelagia, always thin and weak. Her brother loved her deeply."

Again he stopped. I waited. He swallowed and started again.

"She, the mother, died when her children were still very young. She was no longer drinking, no longer selling herself. She was trying to care for her two children by unknown fathers. But she was so broken that not even her children could heal her. Of course not. There is no healing for what she experienced. The two children, then aged no more than six and four years old or so—they remembered their birthdays, but not the year of their birth—had no choice. The boy took his sister's hand and walked out of the wooden shack where their dead mother lay, and went down to the port, and sold himself and his sister into slavery. They were taken to Italy. Their owners maltreated them. They ran away. On a road going north out of Italy, they met up with a runaway Hun boy, a savage. A little while later, Pelagia died and they buried her in the mountains."

Another silence. I dared to look at him and his face was streaked with tears. But, when he resumed, by supreme effort of will his voice remained low and steady.

"As for the slaveboy and the savage, they stayed together through many adventures. The rest . . . The rest you know."

"Great God."

"As for Theodosius the Great, Archbishop Ambrose was so disgusted with the massacre that he refused to give the emperor communion, refused even to admit him into his cathedral. A brave act. Eventually Theodosius got down on his knees, and begged for forgiveness. The Christian Church had conquered the emperor.

"But you see why my feelings about Rome must needs be . . . qualified."

Yes. I saw.

10

THE VIPER

In my last encounter, I was summoned to speak with Attila himself. This came as a great shock to me. But he had heard I was the official Byzantine recorder, and so, as he said dryly, "History is in your hands." He wanted me to know some things—many things. We met after breakfast, and he was still talking, I was still writing, trembling less than at first, when the sun went down. Many of the things in this chronicle came from his lips: his boyhood, his struggles, his uniting of the Scythian tribes. It was a grand and terrible story, and the hours passed without my noticing. He expressed few opinions, and he asked no questions; but he answered mine willingly enough. One thing I wanted to know was his date of birth. I was there to assist the recording of the truth, as he saw it, and so he told me. At the end, he said I was free to talk to anyone in the camp, for he trusted his people's discretion; then he gave me a small gold coin and dismissed me. He never even asked my name. The coin was beaded round the rim, and bore a crudely stamped eagle. It was an authentic and very rare Hunnic *solidus*.

At dinner that night we were offered koumiss, the Hunnish drink made from fermented mare's milk and very strong. The wolf lords drank deeply as always, and yet even after their eighth or ninth goblet seemed barely affected. I, on the other hand, could feel a foolish smile spreading across my face after only the second goblet, and my loins beginning to stir and warm again at the thought of my flaxen-haired Burgundian girl. I wondered if it might be possible . . . again . . . tonight . . .

Then suddenly I was very sober indeed.

Attila had taken the floor in the middle of the tent. We paused in our eating. Everyone fell silent. It was time for his address to us; but not, alas, the address we had hoped for.

"We came together in peace and friendship," he began.

We all applauded, our collective dishonesty breathtaking. Our applause soon died away.

"But alas, our guests had other plans. For tonight,"—and he took some bread and broke it, in dumbshow blasphemy—"I am to be betrayed, and handed over to my enemies. Except that"—he popped a morsel of the bread in his mouth, though he reviled the stuff as fit only for farmers, and chewed as he spoke, his eyes glimmering, for he was enjoying this—"except that, unlike your god Christ"—he spat the bread out—"I have an *exceptional* spy network."

He was joined by his warlords, the clever Geukchu and the wary Greek, Orestes.

Aëtius beside me laid down his knife and said softly, "What is this?"

The weapons of the wolf lords were outside the tent, far away. Within the tent, Huns had already unsheathed their swords.

"He would not dare," I said.

"Oh, he would dare," said Aëtius, clearly unafraid. "But it would serve little purpose." He looked on, curious rather than afraid. Myself, I was already wondering how I might slip away to the privy.

Attila strode around the tent, his voice strong and commanding, his whole figure with the bearing of absolute power. Never have I seen such bearing—except in Aëtius. They were like brothers in that.

"Our guests, you see, these noble Byzantines, planned that I should be assassinated tonight. As if my death alone would save them. Ha!"

He was the only one in the tent, among a hundred, who laughed, albeit with a laugh as harsh and excoriating as sharkskin. Everyone else remained frozen.

"These two loyal servants of mine, the Lord Geukchu of the Hun People, and the Lord Orestes, born in the somewhat decayed city of Thessalonica, but now also, and honorably, of the Huns—these two loyal servants, I say, remain as loyal as ever. We do not have traitors among our people." His smile and his roving, burning eyes were equally terrible. "But in embassy to the fetid and benighted city of Constantinople, ruled by women thinly disguised as men"—at this, his warriors began to laugh, and relax—"they were inveigled into a plot to assassinate me, their divinely appointed king, in exchange for— what was it, my beloved Geukchu?" He was playing with us, with the whole situation.

Geuckchu smiled broadly, too. "Gold, Great Tanjou."

"Ah, yes, of course. Gold." He roved around. "My beloved Geukchu, one of the closest and most trusted among my Chosen Men, who has ridden by my side for nearly a decade, ever since the day I returned from exile to claim my rightful crown. My beloved Geukchu, who rode with me east into hardships and battles unimaginable, who stood by my side in the foulest blizzards and the fiercest arrow storms—this Geukchu, noble Geukchu, the Byzantines and their clottish emperor, Theodosius, the *Calligrapher,* and his barren sister, Pulcheria, believed could be bought off, and turned against me, after all this, with . . . *gold.*"

His warriors laughed and cheered, then fell silent again for their infallible king to continue. By my side, Aëtius was very still. Only once did he glance along the couches, to Chrysaphius and Vigilas. They, too, were very still. Vigilas's right hand was on his fruit knife.

"You fools!" roared the king suddenly, smashing his mighty fist down on a near table and setting the dishes sliding to the floor. His fury seemed to make the felt walls of the tent bat in the blast. "You Roman fools! As if any of my people would envy the trappings and tinsel that festoon your brothel of a palace! As if any of them would exchange gold for glory!" His voice dropped again. "It would not have been the first attempt on my life by the forces of Rome, a eunuch empire which prefers to slay its enemies by deceit rather than by bravery in battle. But you may be sure that, in consequence of this fresh attempt—the clumsiness of which would have shamed a child—our vengeance upon your heads will be only the greater."

He turned to Geukchu and held out his hand. Geukchu passed him a sword.

"Chrysaphius," he said, "beloved of the Emperor Theodosius, step forward."

The saturnine ambassador looked very pale. His eyes darted desperately around, and he stammered, hoping for support from his fellows, but there was none. At last he stood and walked uncertainly into the center of the circle, looking like he might faint.

"So," said Attila regarding him with lacerating scorn. "You offered gold to my lords Geukchu and Orestes, limitless gold, so that they would lead you and the assassin Vigilas into my chamber at some opportune hour, and murder me as I slept."

"My lord, I must protest, you have been grievously mis—"

The backhand blow Attila dealt him sent him reeling back three or four yards, before he crashed into a wooden trestle table amid a welter of sliding plates and food. Not one of our party or the wolf lords stepped forward to help him. Deceit and assassination were no part of the Visigothic armory, and, if the accusation were true, they despised him for bringing deep shame upon them.

"I did not ask you for your commentary," said Attila gratingly. "I am not questioning you, I am telling you, and your disgraced comrades here."

Two Hun warriors hauled Chrysaphius back and and dropped him at the feet of Attila. He lay there struggling for breath, blood flowing freely from nose and mouth after that colossal blow.

I glanced along at Vigilas. He had removed his hand from his fruit knife. It was hopeless. Across the tent, a dozen Hun arrows were trained on his heart.

"To resume," said Attila. "Geukchu and Orestes, for amusement, agreed to your stinking Byzantine bribe. They led you back here, where they promptly reported your contemptible plot to me. How we laughed together, my loyal men and I. And now . . . here we stand." He looked at the rest of us. Another man had got to his feet. It was Aëtius.

"Ah, Master General. You are about to tell me that you had no part in this plan. You knew nothing of it, and would not have approved it if you had."

"Correct."

"I already know that. Please be seated again." He looked down at the bloody-faced ambassador at his feet. "Tell me how much you would have paid your assassin Vigilas for killing me."

Chrysaphius breathed heavily and scarlet bubbles came from his nose. "Five pounds was mentioned, my Lord."

"I don't know whether you are brave or stupid," said Attila, "but you are still lying to me." He raised his foot and brought it down on the ambassador's bare ankle. Chrysaphius howled and tried to crawl away but could not. I winced and averted my gaze. The Hun king was pressing his whole weight down on that ankle, and I thought I could hear bones cracking. Cruelty like this demeans everyone: the torturer, the tortured and the spectators alike. Aëtius, too, was looking away. I quickly surveyed the Hun warriors around the tent. They were stone faced, expressionless.

"Vigilas was to be paid fifty pounds of gold," grated Attila. "A deal of gold, though"—he smiled around at his own little joke—"I still feel undervalued."

His warriors laughed.

He raised his foot and let Chrysaphius crawl free. The broken man, trembling all over, reached down to his shattered ankle, but it was too painful to touch. I thought I glimpsed shards of white bone showing through flesh. He wept. He would never walk without a crutch again.

Attila murmured something to Orestes, who went out, then said, "Step forward, Vigilas."

The little assassin did as he was instructed. He did not look afraid. A man of deceit and violence himself, he was accustomed to it in others, and knew exactly what to expect. But Attila was fond of springing surprises.

He drew his dagger from his broad leather belt and, instead of despatching his antagonist, tossed it to him handle first. Vigilas caught it deftly.

"Now," Attila said, "finish your work."

I was very afraid. The two men started circling each other, Vigilas armed, Attila not. Vigilas all furious concentration, Attila smiling, bare hands held out before him as if to swat away flies. What if Vigilas should succeed? The rest of us would all be slain by his warriors—and not quickly slain, either.

Yet Vigilas was determined to try. It was his nature. A different man might have used the dagger to cut his own throat, but he circled round the king, dagger held lightly in his right hand, his left arm extended for balance, his eyes fixed like a hawk on his prey. He knew he would have only one chance. The atmosphere in the tent had the skin-tingling tension before a storm. We could scarcely breathe. When the two men suddenly burst into action, like snake and mongoose, they moved so fast I could hardly tell what had happened. I think Vigilas tried to lunge forward, perhaps at Attila's neck, and the king moved fractionally aside—enough for the dagger to miss its target by a hair's breadth. He seized Vigilas's right arm, still outstretched, in his mighty hands, one hand clamped around the assassin's wrist and the other near his shoulder, raised his own knee, and brought the arm down. When it struck his knee, the elbow was turned backward and unable to accommodate the blow. The arm snapped in half with a sound that sickened me. Vigilas screamed, and this was a man who did not scream easily, I was sure. He reeled back, clutching his broken limb to his body, his forearm twisted away from him at a horrible angle, his elbow . . . I could not look.

Orestes appeared, carrying a small sack. He dropped it with a heavy thud before Attila.

"Now," said Attila, retrieving his dagger from the ground and reaching for the sack, "here is your gold. All of it." He opened the sack and showed it around and, sure enough, within lay the dully gleaming gold, all fifty pounds of it. "Here is your reward. You may have it from me, your intended victim. Only"—he smiled, and lifted that fifty-pound sack into the air with one hand, his arm muscles bulging—"you will carry it yourself back to Constantinople, without aid from man or beast." He set it down and looked over at Aëtius. "Master General, have I your assurance, as a Roman nobleman, that this sly and deceitful back stabber will return to Constantinople as I command it, under your watchful eye?"

Aëtius struggled for a moment. But this wretched plot had shamed them all, and the two conspirators were lucky to have escaped with their lives. "You have," he said.

Attila nodded. What a gesture, what theater! How magnificently scornful he had shown himself of the Byzantine plot. Never before had we faced an enemy like him.

There was one more gesture. Out of the corner of his eye he saw Chrysaphius trying to pull himself to his feet against one of the tent posts.

"Ah, no," he said, his voice almost gentle, stepping over to him, his dagger still in his grasp. "For you, coward as well as deceiver, there will be no return to Constantinople." He took the ambassador by a hank of his hair and pulled his head back and sliced the blade across his throat. He wiped the blade clean of blood on the dead man's fine court robes and stood again and smiled round at us broadly, his arms outstretched, his dagger still in his fist.

"My dear friends, I think our meeting in peace and friendship is at an end, is it not?"

Behind him, Chrysaphius's body was already being dragged from the tent, leaving behind it a shining trail of gore.

We returned to our tents without another word, our hearts full and dark.

Before we left at dawn, in the dull gray half-light, an extraordinary meeting occurred. Attila came to Aëtius. I watched from the shadows.

They spoke to each other without formality, as if they were old friends. A naïve observer might have thought Aëtius indeed a traitor, newly allied to Attila, there seemed so little tension between them. Then the Hun grasped Aëtius's arm as if with a mix of urgency and brotherly affection, and I heard his harsh, passionate voice.

"One of the reasons I exposed your treachery—the treachery of your master, the emperor in Constantinople last night—was to show you the rottenness of your world, your eunuch empire."

Aëtius said nothing, and did not try to pull free of Attila's clasp. His expression was deeply troubled.

"And your Valentinian, Emperor in the West, feebleminded son of that bitch Galla Placidia, he is still worse. He sacrifices cockerels, he studies witchcraft."

Aëtius muttered, "You, too, have witches about you."

"I do not claim to be Christian. Aëtius, your empire is tottering."

Now Aëtius resisted him. "The VIIth legion at Viminacium, they did not totter."

"They gave us a good fight."

"They gave you hell."

Attila's teeth showed in the gloom. "They fought like men. But for what? For a decrepit empire, a long lost cause? It is the time of new powers and other empires now. Rome's all done." His grip on Aëtius's arm tightened, and I heard his astonishing words: "Join me."

It was long before Aëtius responded; too long. His eventual response was only to pull away, saying nothing.

"You fool," said Attila. "You have already lost whatever it is you fight for." He remounted his horse. "Fly back to your city, fool. I am hot on your path."

11

THE BIRD CATCHER

We rode away south that morning in anger and shame. Behind us staggered a small, broken figure, carrying his cruel sack of gold.

There was nobility in the soul of Attila, that I could see. Aëtius saw it, too. But the darker traits of malice, tyranny, and vengefulness were overshadowing it, and ultimately it would be extinguished. His ruthlessness and avarice would destroy him as a living human soul. It has happened many times in human history. Already his nobility and grandeur were fading before his hunger for world dominion, his furious desire to seize and master life itself—a hunger which had also driven, in different ways, Alexander the Great, and Phidias, and Euclid, and even Sophocles. But such men as Sophocles and Phidias grow wise before they grow old, and let go of their hunger, and instead of wanting seize and master life, they fall down before it and kneel in silent wonder, understanding that they may never master or understand but only worship. Attila saw such humble wisdom only as inglorious defeat. He was ever one of the rebellious sons of God.

Attila's hatred of Rome was like a fire, blazing up and destroying some great, majestic basilica. But when the flames have finally devoured and destroyed that basilica and laid it to ashes, the fire also dies: it has nothing left to feed on. So his hunger was devouring his own self from the inside, engendering only more and more appetite in place of his youthful pride and fire.

And when there is only appetite, allied to the stubborn, implacable vindictiveness of old age, there is no telling what evils may ensue.

After only two days, Aëtius halted the column toward evening and looked over his shoulder. Far behind us was the hunched, misshapen figure of Vigilas with his sack. He was no longer moving. Aëtius galloped back, and I saw him lean from his horse, pull up the sack and rest it on his lap. Vigilas rolled onto his side in the road and was still. Aëtius brooded a moment, then dropped the sack in the road and rode back to us. None of us uttered a word in protest. We knew it was like a gift of Agamemnon's Greeks. *Timeo Danaos* . . . Let a peasant find it, an untold treasure, and bury it beneath an oak tree by moonlight for his old age.

Our journey back was long and wearisome, for we rode fast and relentlessly without Vigilas to slow us. We must take in the little town of Azimuntium on our way and find the empress, then retreat to safety behind the great Theodosian walls of the capital. There at last, I observed, we would be safe.

"Safe?" said Aëtius savagely. "As safe as a rabbit in his burrow, with a huge and ravening wolf just outside, his stinking breath in the very mouth of the burrow. How safe is that, do you think?"

I did not answer.

After crossing the plains at an exhausting canter, our horses flecked with white foam and drooling at the bit, we rode up into the cooler foothills of the Haemus Mountains and then higher, where there was still edelweiss growing among the rocks. We found water for our mounts, a runnel clear as crystal from a rock spring, and they whickered and drank deep and raised their heads again, refreshed. We had the finest white Cappadocian horses from the imperial stables—magnificent, though I say so myself—and the master general and Theodoric and Torismond rode at our head. It was no great force to turn and face a numberless horde of the enemy on our heels, but we could at least move very fast.

Behind us were over a million of the devil's own horsemen, so they said. Well, rumor always multiplies enemy numbers by ten. Aëtius had estimated Attila's fighting force to be a hundred thousand, which was still the greatest number that Rome had faced in seven centuries, since the days of Hannibal. And how had the strength of Rome herself fared in those seven centuries? Not well.

As for our chivalrous mission to rescue an empress, Aëtius kept his head bowed and did not speak of it. She whom he had not seen for . . . fifteen years, was it? Many battles and campaigns ago. That was how he measured out his life, in battles, not years. Too many battles ago he had kissed her, on a balcony overlooking the Golden City of Jerusalem. But that was many battles ago, and in another world.

We rode into deep pinewoods and the light grew dim and green. The horses harrumphed nervously, their hooves crunching over dry needles. The men patted their necks for comfort, none too comfortable themselves. Both horses and riders were creatures of the open plains. Woods meant darkness, witchcraft, and ambush.

Toward evening, having ridden as fast and far as we could into the falling darkness, we were looking for a clearing to camp in when Torismond said he had seen a leopard, high in the trees.

"There are no leopards in these mountains," Aëtius assured him.

"Alexander the Great hunted lions in the mountains of Greece," said the youth stubbornly.

"That was many centuries ago, brother," said Theodoric.

"Don't fret," said Aëtius. "You will meet with dangers enough without leopards."

As we lay that night beside the fire, one of the wolf lords stepped forward, driving before him at the end of his spear something he had captured, creeping around the outskirts of the camp. No leopard, but a crazed bird catcher. We regarded him with curiosity.

He had only one blackened stump of a tooth, and bright beady eyes darting to left and to right and missing nothing. His bare feet were glued with feathers as if he were turning into a bird himself, and he wore a straw hat garlanded with faded summer flowers.

"And you are?" growled Aëtius.

The bird catcher began to babble at once, speaking extraordinarily fast, like one who has not spoken with another living soul for months and years.

"I was a missionary of Christ, one of the missionaries of St. John Chrysostom sent out upon the eastern steppes to minister to the heathen there in their feathers and skins and preach them the gospel." He grinned, showing his blackened stump, shiny with saliva in the firelight. "But my friends would say, if I had any, they would say that I was driven mad out there by the indifference of the trackless, Christless wilderness. For you know that there is no law of heavenly love out there."

"What tribes did you preach to?"

"Ostrogoths, Monoglots, Monopeds, Huns, Hasmodaeans, Amazons with only one titt—"

Aëtius rolled over to go to sleep. "The man's insane."

"And now I trap my feathered brethren for meat and for feathering my own feet," continued the bird catcher. The princes and their wolf lords continued to regard him, this antic figure in the firelight, fascinated, half amused.

"And you see, of all the birds that I tear gently from their gluey lime-white perches there on the tree and drop into my capacious basket, wry-necked and forever after songless and silent, I sometimes take one that appeals to me and my curious whims and I let him go with his song intact and his neck unbroken. It is a fancy of mine. So may it be with you, my noble warriors, in the hands of the Great Catcher, as you ride out into the Christless wilderness against that terrible enemy whose hearts would turn you to stone if you could but see them. For though even the freed bird shall end in a basket all the same in time, yet do not despair, for not all are killed outright, not all lose themselves in the nighttime of my capacious osier basket. Some fly free and sing still. May you do the same, little brothers, for the Truth is nothing but all the little deeds of kindness that man to man or trapped bird ever did."

"You were a strange missionary," murmured Theodoric. "A shadow missionary, preaching the Fallen Christ."

The bird man glanced at him quickly and then went on, "Our stories are not completed in this world. There remains something far beyond, never to be known or named by the stumbling tongues of men. He who thinks he has it by the tail, and owns its name, is drowned in ignorance. Yet it abides. And even when in the latter days, which may be coming soon, the scroll of the world is rolled up and cast into fire, and the light of the sun is snuffed out like a candle, and all the universe comes to its natural and inborn doom, that

Being will still abide, brooding on in all its eternal majestic solitude, as before the world was made."

"Peace now, go," muttered Aëtius beneath his blanket, pretending to be asleep but in truth hearing the fool's words, for they had a kind of compelling power. But the bird catcher had more to say before we slept.

"In each man's heart lies his own truth, and there is no shaping it with eloquent words and reasons to fit your own more neatly. There was a bird's nest, a lark's nest, a little thing unregarded, and I trod on it unawares, and hearing the sound I looked down and saw a little mess of nest and blood and feathers and tiny sodden shapes of baby birds unborn. A little thing. It was then Christ died in me, never to rise again."

Some of the wolf lords looked hard at him. This was blasphemy. But the fool was oblivious.

"Those broken eggshells. The wind in the trees. The pitiless sky. Nothing changed. Nothing mattered. No solace came to me or bird. I scraped the remains of the eggs and tiny birds from my boots—for I wore boots in those days like a man—and heaped them up and scattered earth on them and blessed them, and then I walked on, and Christ no longer walked by my side. Never again. From that day to this I am no Christ worshipper nor missionary of St. John Chrysostom, sent out into the wilderness to baptize the Scythian heathen, but only a bare lone man, a birdman, a madman.

"And one day before very long now, I too will perch on a branch and be caught and trapped by one far greater than me, the oldest and the greatest god of all, his capacious osier basket unfillable and forever hungry for all eternity, no matter what goes in. Death is a portal, to be sure, but a portal to what?" He smiled and winked conspiratorially. "Some doors go nowhere."

Then they tired of the madman and, believing that his ominous words would bring them bad luck in this dark and forbidding place, on this uncertain mission already compromised and humiliating, they drove him away at spearpoint into the woods and commanded him not to return. He went whistling into the darkness like a bird at dawn.

12

THE PASS

The bird catcher's words cast a pall over the next day. As we rode up higher into the mountains for the pass that would take us down to Azimuntium, safely away from the open plains where our enemy in countless thousands once more hunted and laid waste, several of the wolf lords already wore bronze cuirasses under their long red cloaks, and tall, gleaming *Spangenhelms* nodding with flaxen plumes. The air was heavy and ominous, and we almost prayed for a rainstorm to relieve it.

We rode higher and higher, the country becoming lifeless and bare, only a few last twisted and stunted trees sheltering straggling sheep, then only thorns and faded brown heath. In the deep rocky chasms, the trickle of dark streams and ferns and mosses hiding from the light. We rode along one of these narrow, sunless defiles, its high, gloomy walls hung with sphagnum moss and hart's-tongue fern, thinking of ambush. But Aëtius did not fear ambush, not in the mountains. This was not the Huns' terrain. They would be fools to ride here, steppe warriors raised on the limitless plains.

The column of Visigothic wolf lords rode uneasily nevertheless, spears held lightly under their right arms, looking silently about them. They had seen dark things, these mountains of Thrace, home to mysteries since ancient times, where Orpheus was rent apart by his screaming maenads. As they rode down the narrow defile, the horses also silent and oppressed, picking their way carefully among the boulders and the rockfalls, hooves slipping sideways on slate-gray stones, the rain began to fall from the leaden sky and make the way yet more treacherous. The sky was a great iron lid on the world, and big raindrops struck silver bright on gleaming *Spangenhelms,* running in droplets down over the steep helmed sides and down noseguards and aventails, over stubbled and unshaven cheeks, brushed away, soaking into neck cloths, beading on scarlet woolen cloaks, trickling over mailed and plated shoulders. The riders sweated, despite the steely rain. Not a living creature did we glimpse. The rain came down more heavily.

Then the pass widened. We came round a broader turn and a light wind blew in our faces and there opening before us was a lake surrounded by bare rocky mountains, its pewter surface stippled with rain. The cliffs on our left broke down into massive tumbled boulders, while on our right they ran along the lake shore, the water lapping almost to the foot of the cliffs but for a narrow gravel spit. On the other side of the lake were more green hills and then crueller mountains beyond.

Aëtius sat his horse and took it all in.

"A majestic scene," pronounced Prince Theodoric.

Aëtius smiled indulgently. "But I can smell horses."

The prince looked puzzled.

"Many horses, and not ours. The smell of them blowing over to us across the lake. Look at your own, how her nostrils flare."

"I thought that was at the water. It's long since they drank."

"Well, don't let them now. Time enough to drink after. Ready your lances."

He ordered Jormunreik and Valamir to climb up to their left and scout. A few minutes later they came scrambling breathlessly down again, reaching for their armor even as they gave their report.

Yes, many horses. And many men.

"How many?"

"A few hundred," said Valamir, tying his long hair back into a ponytail and setting his tall steel *Spangenhelm* back on his head, ready for the fray.

Aëtius rubbed his unshaven chin. He doubted Attila himself was here. One of his generals would be leading. "This was no ambush. A scouting party, that is all. An accident of fate."

"A misfortune we shall face with direst fortitude," said Theodoric, sitting very straight in his saddle.

The lad was becoming more ridiculous by the moment, but still Aëtius did not mock him. He had been young himself once. "A misfortune for them," he said. "Poor, lightly-armed scouting Huns, suddenly running into a column of Gothic wolf lords in these desolate mountains. They are doomed."

The princes looked cheered at the thought. I was very anxious about it, myself.

"Doubtless they were only mapping passes through the mountains. A surprise for us. But a good soldier should not be surprised at surprises." He ordered the two wolf lords back on their horses, then rode out of the end of the pass and down to the lakeshore. And there, across from us to our left, was a milling horde of Huns, arrows to the bow.

Ahead of us across the lake, at the far end of the cliffs beyond the narrow gravel shore, was the second group. He looked back. Very well, then, three groups. Behind us, on the cliffs under which we had just passed, dismounted Huns lay in wait, spiky with bows. Others had rolled big boulders to the edge of the ravine and were waiting patiently for our flight. Retreat would be nothing but self-slaughter.

Aëtius did not hesitate. Already the party of Huns up on the cliffs were turning their arrows toward our defenseless backs, and over to the left the second group was doing likewise. There was one way to go, with shock and force. A small figure on a skewbald pony was at the head of the group before us, below the cliff face, still, watching. Then he raised his arm and dropped it, and the Hun arrow storm began, slicing through the rain. Arrows and rain crosshatched, making a cage in the air.

Aëtius ordered me to ride in the center, then twisted in his saddle and yelled to the column, "Shields on your backs! Spears couched low! Fast trot, keep formation. Full charge only when I give the order. Forward!"

The wolf lords were no fools, and few had not strapped their shields across their backs already, seeing that the heaviest arrow fire would come from behind. Then the column was trotting forward into the lake shallows, a Teutonic-style attack column of the kind they knew best, four abreast and twelve deep, with myself jostled unpleasantly in the middle, speechless with fright. This was not appropriate work for a clerk in consistory. No wider front was possible as we were squeezed between the steel-gray lake on the left and the black, shining cliffs on the right, the left-hand files riding their horses up to their bellies in the cold water, the right brushing their knees against the rockface. Arrows fell through the rain but to no avail: our shields were stuck like pincushions but our backs doubly protected by both shield and armor. We kept in tight formation.

Then Aëtius rose up in his saddle and flashed his sword in the gray air and bellowed with sudden ferocity and drove his rowelled spurs into his horse's flanks. Our disciplined trot turned into a canter, water and gravel kicking up beneath two hundred flying hooves, spurs driving into sodden flanks, chamfrons covered in silver beads of rain and misted with horses' breath. Then we were galloping, long ashwood spears couched low like lances, braced back against the rear horns of our wooden saddles. Two hundred yards to cover and the arrow storm thickening, a splash to the left and a cry to the right, arrowheads thocking into shield boards, men tumbling. But most kept low and our charge was lightning fast, and already the nearest milling Hun archers were wavering and breaking ahead of us, fingers fumbling on their bowstrings. This was not what they had expected or foreseen, this heavy cavalry charge embarked upon so lightly, so quickly, with such dash and conviction.

In a flash the last few dozen yards were covered, there was a glimpse of sun through the thick clouds, and suddenly our galloping horsemen were coming on like spangled wraiths through the rain and flying water, blinding with sunlight, and then crashing into the heart of the Hun pack and splintering them apart, their leader on his skewbald pony rearing and turning and making for higher ground.

Lost and uncertain among these alien mountains, the Huns were taken by surprise and by the ferocity of this attack from such inferior numbers. Mounted archers of the steppes, they could not gallop free and circle and come back with a low, level volley of arrows. Trapped between lakeshore and cliff, there was no room for their usual tactics. Where was the wind on the plains, where were the wide grasslands? Here there were only tall dark cliffs and steep mountain paths and jagged rocks and heavy rain, and this bludgeoning charge. There were ponies tumbling, stuck through the ribs, and lightly armored warriors impaled on the long ashen lances of the Gothic horsemen. Cries of men and horses mingled. Where they could, stocky ponies and their riders fell back and surged away into the low green hills in bewildered retreat before that calamitous attack. But many of the Huns were too close packed, the terrain around was too steep for easy retreat and they were beaten down by this onslaught of weighty metal and ashen spear.

The clash of arms, the bell-like ring of steel on steel, warriors flecked with drops of rain and blood, aghast Asiatic faces sliced open, stocky bodies riven through, and nowhere to move or fly, not even space to pull up an arrow and draw a bow in the impacted melee. The wolf lords rose up in the saddle, drawing their great two-handled swords from their back scabbards and slicing down into the helpless throng. Over the water, the other two Hun war parties held their fire, unable to risk killing their own, stricken and motionless, watching the ghostly carnage across the pale lake.

At last the bloody skirmish was done, and all the Huns either dead or vanished. On a flat rock high above them, turning on his skewbald pony, one of the Hun warlords looked down on the victorious Gothic column. Aëtius reined in his horse and looked up at him through the thinning rain. The warlord was expressionless, his cheeks ritually scarred, his iron-gray ponytail dripping. It couldn't be him. It couldn't be. The warlord drew a short shining sword and levelled the point directly at Aëtius. Aëtius gazed back, unmoving. Then the warlord pulled his pony round, sheathed his sword and vanished into the mountains.

We rode down to the lake at last and let our horses drink. The men drank, too, leaning back in their saddles, tilting their flasks. Then they dismounted and dragged down dry brushwood from under the shelter of some trees up a nearby valley, and burned their dead upon a pyre, pagan style, but with prayers to the Christian God. The rain slowed and stopped and the last of the day's sun leaked through and spilled molten copper upon the placid surface of the lake, and the funeral fires reflected in the water and dark smoke drifted away over the green hills. Then the column of wolf lords, forty-four in number, with their two princes and the fierce and now well-respected Roman general, remounted and rode up into the hills above the drifting smoke, knowing that the Hun war party might attack again at any time. There would be no sleep nor rest from riding tonight.

13

AZIMUNTIUM

It was late into the night when we came to an abandoned stone farmstead on a high plateau, with a half-broken stock wall. Aëtius gave the order to dismount here and take our rest, with sentries posted. We made a single small fire within the shelter of the wall and rolled ourselves in our blankets.

As if to honor their dead, the wolf lords recited in low voices the lays of their people. Long wanderings of their doomed and tragic tribe, driven from their ancient homelands in icebound Thule by a still more warlike people they called the Sweotheoden. Then half-destroyed by nameless Easterlings in Hrefnawude, or Ravenswood, in a great and terrible battle when the arrow storm pelted the shield wall in the dark pine forests of that land, a battle etched in the memory of their bloodstained lays. They fled east and then south to the shores of the Scythian Sea, and then westward again like autumn leaves, to find their final heartland in sun-warmed southern Gaul.

At dawn, after only two or three hours' sleep on the hard ground, we arose and smothered the fire and rode on. Coming to the edge of the plateau we looked down, and eastward across the burning plain below we saw a hill town shimmering in the hazy morning air, set atop a single cone of golden rock amid the waterless flatland.

Azimuntium.

We had thought to come here having made our peace with Attila, though

Aëtius always knew it would never happen. The emperor had expected us to come peaceably to Azimuntium, at a relaxed and serene pace, having seen Attila slain behind us and the Hun threat dissipated for good. I could still hardly believe such clumsy stupidity. We had tried to assassinate Attila himself! How we would pay for it in time. The whole world would pay for it. But we would be the first to suffer. Now we had to bring Her Majesty home urgently, ourselves already battered and reduced in numbers, with the darkest clouds rolling toward us, just over the horizon.

We rode round the edge of the plateau and down a narrow valley where a limpid brook flowed over rockfalls from pool to pool, and small trees grew and birds chittered, and eventually down and out onto the plain along a dirt track toward the town. We broke into a fast trot again here. The sun moving across the sky was our constant bane. Time was against us. Aëtius sent outriders far to our left and right, but they could see nothing, and on a plain like this, a hundred thousand horsemen would kick up some dust. After a while, though, approaching us from the northwest we saw a small band of vagabonds, mounted and spiky with spears. Aëtius reined in and we waited, the sun blazing down on us as if in angry warning.

Eventually the band came near, not slowing in their approach nor showing any sign of fear. There were but four of them and they made a motley crew. There was one youngish fellow, very scarred and bruised, a deserter perhaps; an arrogant-looking easterner with long black mustaches; a grim-faced older fellow with cold eyes; and a fat, grubby oaf with a scarecrow thatch of hair, whose poor horse looked ready to collapse beneath him. None was clean-shaven, and all carried weapons and wore looted Roman armor. Aëtius rested his hand on the pommel of his sword. He detested looters of slain soldiers. Battlefield carrion crows.

"Where did you come by that armor?" he demanded peremptorily.

The four slowed and reined in. They seemed in no hurry to reply.

"Answer me, damn you."

The fat oaf, quite unafraid, looked round at his three bandit comrades and grinned. "Well, I should say we came by it at Viminacium."

Aëtius's hand tightened on his sword. He had executed looters on the spot before now. "Viminacium was destroyed."

"Quite so, your lordship, though not without a struggle, I should say, if you wanted to go and inspect the ruins, what's left of 'em. And it's bye bye to the field army, too, from what we heard on the road, over near the River Utus. Six whole Eastern legions gone up in smoke. Still, I always did say the Eastern legions wasn't no match for the Western lot. Not that we been over River Utus way ourselves. There's a few Huns about here and there these days, so you want to keep a low profile if you take my advice. Of course, if you'd rather—"

"Shut it."

Knuckles subsided into injured silence.

"So you admit it? You are common looters?"

Neither "common" nor "looter" could be tolerated by Arapovian. He snapped back crisply, indicating Knuckles, "This one's birth was not of the noblest, it is true, though beneath that ape-like exterior he has a noble heart. But I am Count Grigorius Khachadour Arapovian, the son of Count Grigorius Nubar Arapovian, the son of—"

"Oh, 'ere we go," sighed Knuckles. He shook his head at Aëtius. "I hope you're not in a hurry, though you look like you might be. Now you've got him started, we'll be listening to the names of his forefathers till tomorrow nightfall."

"Silence, both of you."

Knuckles ignored him. "We're from Viminacium."

"No one survived from Viminacium."

The legionary looked around at the other three and grimaced with downturned mouth. "Well, comrades, seems like we must be fucking ghosts of ourselves, then—thought I was feeling a bit funny." He looked back at Aëtius. "Ghosts can't commit crimes, *sir*. If there weren't no survivors out of Viminacium, we're the walking dead. And if we're the walking dead, we ain't no looters and we don't belong to no legion except the legion of the damned."

It was impeccable logic.

Aëtius's hand on his sword hilt relaxed again. Though these four were as irritating as hell, he began to sense they were indeed no ordinary looters, and spoke the truth, or something like it. He threw his cloak back over his right shoulder to show his general's epaulettes. The scarred young fellow and the cold-eyed older man immediately sat straighter in their saddle and saluted.

Aëtius smiled grimly. "So you are deserters, not looters."

Still holding his salute, the older man rasped back icily, general or no, "We are no deserters, *sir*. There was nothing left to desert from."

Aëtius eyed him. "Name, rank and legion."

"Marcus Tatullus, centurion, primus pilus, the VIIth Legion, Claudia Pia Fidelis." He spoke these last words with exaggerated emphasis, his gaze fixed on Aëtius, a look of agony behind his deep-set, unblinking eyes.

Likewise still holding his salute, the younger scarred fellow loudly pronounced the legionary motto, "Six times brave, six times faithful."

"Make that seven," said the centurion. His voice sounded strange.

"Gaius Malchus," said the young fellow, "cavalry captain, VIIth Legion, sir!"

Aëtius began to understand, though it was hard to believe. He felt a flood of emotion within him, and fought to control it. He looked at the last of the four, the thatch-haired troglodyte. "And you?" he said, more quietly.

"Anastasius, sir, son of the whore Volumella, one of the most noted whores on the Rhineland frontier in her day. Though most people call me Knuckles. I believe it suits me better."

Aëtius couldn't help but smile, though his heart was heavy with emotion. "And your rank?"

"An ordinary boot, obviously, sir. Of the lowest possible class, and common as muck in a cowshed."

Aëtius looked them over and saw them anew. I saw his breastplate heave and I knew his great heart shook. These were no common men, sitting their horses battle scarred and travel stained, unspeakably weary, and yet not broken. These were the backbone of the old empire, and with such the empire would live to fight again.

"You survived Viminacium? You fought against the Huns there and survived?"

"If you could call it surviving," said Knuckles.

"You survived," affirmed Aëtius. "Ride with us."

"You're headed back to Constantinople, I take it, sir?" asked Malchus.

Aëtius nodded. "Via Azimuntium, that hill town yonder. To provide escort home for the Empress Ath—Eudoxia. She is in residence at the convent there."

"The *empress?*" Malchus whistled. "The Huns are all over this plain. From what I've heard, they're operating in at least four different battle groups."

"At least," said Aëtius. "We've already met one of them—only a thousand men or so. Yes, they're everywhere. And," he smiled grimly, "they are no more favorably disposed toward us than before." He turned back and raised his hand. "Column: fast trot!"

As an officer, Malchus rode just behind Aëtius, on his shield side. Tatullus rode behind him, and Knuckles and Arapovian brought up the rear. The wolf lords whispered among themselves, and soon it was known throughout the column that these four were the sole survivors of a terrible battle with the Huns, which had seen over a thousand Romans slain. Some of the Visigoths could not help glancing round at Knuckles and Arapovian and seeing those ragged wanderers with new respect. The wolf lords admired nothing so much as valor in battle.

Knuckles nodded back at them. "Got a biscuit?"

One of the wolf lords grinned and rummaged in his saddlebag and threw him a hunk of stale bread. Knuckles caught it in his huge paw and began to gnaw it with a certain awkwardness as he trotted.

"So I got a noble heart then, have I?" he rumbled, spraying crumbs at his companion beside him.

Arapovian rode looking straight ahead, aquiline features expressionless. "Accept the compliment graciously, and do not expect me to repeat it."

"I don't do graciously," said Knuckles, "son of a whore like me."

"I believe," said Arapovian, "though I do not understand it, that you are almost as proud of your ancestry as I am of mine."

Knuckles snorted with laughter, and bread crumbs flew out of his nose.

Azimuntium was a town of less than a thousand souls, though its numbers were now swollen with terrified refugees. Thick walls ringed it round, built into the jagged bedrock, and a steep cobbled ramp led up to the stout wooden gates. Once the column was within the gates, a great cheer went up from the people, as if we were come as liberators. Little did they know. Aëtius could not look them in the eye. Our mounted column snaked up a narrow cobbled lane to the Upper Town, high-battlemented gatehouses marking the way. It was a fine defensive site.

The Lord of Azimuntium, Ariobarzanes by name, met us at the entrance to the courtyard of his tumbledown palace. He was a weak old man in a less than spotless gabardine, supported on a vine staff, crouched in the wooden gateway with an ancient hound at his side.

"The empress is in the convent," he said. "She is finishing mass."

"There is no time to finish mass," said Aëtius. "We ride out immediately."

"She left strict instructions."

Aëtius cursed under his breath. Then he ordered lookouts posted on the walls.

"The enemy are near," said Ariobarzanes.

He turned sharply. "How do you know?"

"Ask any of the refugee shepherds in the town." He waved a hand knotty with purple veins. "Shepherds without sheep—the Scythian heathen have taken them all. May the Lord of Hosts defend us."

And cold steel, thought Aëtius.

"We also hear they have razed Philippopolis."

Aëtius said softly, "The entire city?"

Ariobarzanes tilted his head. "The entire city. The Flower of the River Hebrus. The waters of the river ran red, and the savages hung the body of the bishop naked from the walls." His watery eyes searched Aëtius, and his voice trembled. "I tell you, Christendom has never before faced an enemy such as this. They will raze the world flat."

"He who lives longest will see the most."

And they were standing there, kicking their heels while the empress finished saying her *Kyrie* and her *Agnus Dei*. It was madness. He sent his new centurion, Tatullus, to demand entrance to the convent. Tatullus returned, saying that his way had been barred by nuns.

"Nuns," breathed Aëtius. "In the Name of Light!"

Frustrated, he went down to the Church of Saint Jude, with a long, low hospital building behind. In the gloom, a very tall, thin old man with an unkempt beard was striding about, ordering the shutters to be thrown open and pots of fresh flowers to be brought in. "End of summer, but anything you can find!" his voice boomed down the room.

There was a single middle-aged woman bustling about to do his bidding, and two plump older men standing in one corner arguing. In another stood three of the Visigothic wolf lords, their wounds from the skirmish in the mountains freshly bandaged, looking uncomfortable. In one of the eight narrow beds along the wall lay an old peasant, eyes glazed, mouthing to himself, and in another was a tired-looking woman, having recently given birth, her newborn at her breast. Sickness always made Aëtius feel uncomfortable and he moved to leave, but something about the commanding old man held his attention. He frowned.

"You, man," he called out. "I remember you." The old man turned and regarded Aëtius vaguely. "I remember your face. But it was . . . many years ago. What is your name?"

"I thought I might be of use here," said the old man with airy evasiveness. "I came to Azimuntium to examine some remarkable old texts in the synagogue here, you know, dating from the time of the Maccabees—"

"Do not play games with me. Where have I seen you before?"

"I have been around a bit," he continued, still airy. "In an empire of a hundred million souls, a few second meetings are not unlikely. All is for the best, et cetera. Now, where did I put that ewer?"

Aëtius stepped up to him and held him. "*Your name.*"

The old man looked fractionally down at him, he was so tall. His eyes were deep set and serious now. "My name is Gamaliel."

Aëtius stared. "It was you who came to the camp of the Huns, with that British officer, in search of his son. It was you. Spinning tall tales of how you once knew Aristotle."

"I am a citizen of the world."

"But that was years ago, decades ago. You've hardly aged—well, not much. How old are you?"

"Older than you and younger than Methusaleh," said Gamaliel blithely. "Nuts and berries, nuts and berries. But I eat very little. Now, madam, please will you open those shutters?"

At this, the two men arguing in the corner approached.

"Forgive us for interrupting," said one. "We are trained medical men on our way back to Constantinople."

"Seeking shelter here from the rumored horsemen of the steppes," said the other. "Though not afraid, we are careful."

"Not a good place to seek shelter," muttered Aëtius, still half lost in memories of his own boyhood. "They'll be here before we finish yakking."

One of the men regarded Aëtius with alarm, but the other drew in breath and addressed Gamaliel.

"As a strict Pneumatist of the Alexandrian school, founded by the revered Athenaeus of Attalia, in Pamphylia, as I'm sure you know, himself a pupil of the stoic Posidinius of Apamea, a purist of the noblest standing, in the face of multifarious insults and contumely from those wayward and contemptible Episynthetics, those magpies of medical learning, led—or should I say misled?—by that scoundrel Leonidas of Alexandria—"

Gamaliel who had begun his examination of the ailing peasant, but the two learned doctors followed him over.

"Your point being?" interrupted Gamaliel, a little testily.

"My point being, my dear man," said the doctor, "that this demand of yours that the shutters be opened, on, I take it, grounds of *fresh air,* is, I'm afraid, woefully ill advised. Such fresh air might be fatal to a man in this one's condition," he indicated the old peasant, "although with brief perscrutation I can see that he will shortly be in the grave, come what may. However, since we must abide by our Hippocratic oaths until that melancholy end, I refer you to the teachings of the Alexandrian Pneumatists, who have made it very clear that the *pneuma*—that is, the vital breath—being not the whole soul, but rather only the *potentiality* of it—"

Another woman brought in a jug of late flowers. Nearby, Prince Torismond appeared and was saying something to Aëtius about a large dust cloud to the north.

"—a compound," continued the erudite man of science, "of varying proportions of air and fire, the vehicle of cosmic *sympatheia,* and in truth quite unlike that preposterous agglomeration of indivisible Democritean particles hypothesised by the Peripatetic Atomists . . . The *pneuma,* I say, is the seat of corporeal vigor, from which flows the vital breath throughout all the nerves and vesicles of the body. And the *pneuma* is only diluted, perhaps fatally, by the admixture of lifeless outdoor air—"

"Fascinating," murmured Gamaliel. "Hold out your tongue," he said to the old peasant.

Behind them, Aëtius swept from the room.

"However," said the second doctor, "notwithstanding my colleague's animadversions upon my own school, for I am myself an orthodox Peripatetic Atomist, having participated at Athens, Mother of Learning, in the experimental decapitation of both eels, goats, tortoises, and grasshoppers, I can assure you, as against the doubtless well-intentioned but hopelessly misguided teachings of the Alexandrian Pneumatists, that it is the head, and not the *pneuma,* which is the seat of the vital power, and it is the crowding of atoms to the head which causes all manner of night sweats, interferences of vision, and spasms of the bowels."

Gamaliel frowned. "What are you saying? We should cut his head off?"

The Peripatetic Atomist smiled indulgently at the old fellow's foolish jest. "My dear man, I am saying, in short, that in a man of his late years, doomed to expire shortly as he is, his body is too soft and relaxed, his atoms are slowed and weighed down with too much moisture, and he needs must be condensed."

The pregnant woman in the bed behind them groaned.

"Condensed?" scoffed the Alexandrian Pneumatist. "On the contrary, the atoms of his *pneuma* are already too condensed. They need to be more spaced apart. This can be achieved by moderate suffocation, or else by bleeding with leeches."

Gamaliel regarded them. "Gentlemen, when you see a ruddy man, full of air and fire, does he seem to you strong or weak?"

"Strong," admitted the Atomist.

"And when you see a man as pale as whey and obviously of thin or little blood, as this one, does he appear to you strong or weak?"

"Weak. But, sir, the learned Galen—"

"Oh, bugger Galen!" snapped Gamaliel impatiently. "Now gentlemen, I could listen to you all day, but I must be about my work. Madam, all the shutters open, if you please. And boil some water. A large vat, yes."

"Water!" exclaimed both doctors. "Too much moisture, too much softness! Highly dangerous!"

"As for this one," said Gamaliel, turning to the woman, and then bending down to her kindly, "how old is . . . he? She?"

"Near a week since, sir," she gasped. "She."

"A blessing," he said, then turned to the nurse. "Find some mouldy bread, rye if possible."

"We have made our examination of this one already," said the Alexandrian Pneumatist, "notwithstanding her protestations of modesty—always amusing in one so lowborn. She suffers from a filthiness of her uterine matter, which is not all ejected. We recommended an application of dung, ideally of swine, being the foulest of dungs, on the sound principle that filth drives out filth."

"Absolute twaddle," said Gamaliel, washing his hands. "Mouldy bread is what she needs. Mouldy rye bread."

Both doctors laughed with disbelief. "My dear sir!"

"You know about ergot, the fungus that grows on rye grain? Reappears in the loaf afterward, if left to go mouldy. Mildly toxic, yes, hallucinogenic, yes, but also a powerful emmenagogue. Stimulates contraction of the uterine muscles. Now, out of my way. Swine dung indeed!" He pushed the open-mouthed doctors aside and bent down to talk to the woman. To the doctors' even greater astonishment, he wasted his time actually explaining to this unlettered peasant what treatment he would be administering to her, and why. He explained to her gently and patiently that the mold would make her feel a little sick, a little light headed and unwell, but within a day it would make her better. The woman smiled faintly.

"This is quite wrong, a gross categorical error," said the Pneumatist. "A woman's afterbirth is not mouldy, it is filthy, and must be treated as such."

"Filthy?" said Gamaliel, standing straight again. "Nonsense. You could cook it and eat it quite happily. Very strengthening. In fact, you could eat it raw if you really wanted, nice and fresh."

"The man's mad," they muttered, and they backed away, appalled.

Gamaliel smiled and moved on.

Up on the walls, five men were on lookout post: Prince Torismond with his two Gothic wolf lords, Jormunreik and Valamir, and two of the survivors from Viminacium, Knuckles and Arapovian. Rumor had spread that the empress had been taken ill earlier that day, and was treated by an old Jewish doctor. A couple of other learned medical men from Athens and Alexandria had also been in attendance, arguing furiously about the empress's *pneuma*. And all this time, the clouded horizon came nearer.

"Doctors!" opined Knuckles. "Don't give me fuckin' doctors. Translate stuff, that's all they ever do. Translate what you tell 'em into Greek and chuck it back at you. What's this *pneuma?*"

"Breath," said Arapovian, watching the north over Knuckles's oxlike shoulder.

"There you are, then. You go to a doctor, and you tell him you got a sore throat that won't shift, and he tells you to poke your tongue out and he peers down your gullet, and then he pronounces, 'Ah, yes, my good man, now what you have there is what we doctors call *laryngitis*.' Which is just Greek for 'sore throat.' And you think, But I just told you that, you ass! And he says, 'That will be one fine gold solidus for my invaluable diagnosis, if you please. Next client!' "

Aëtius appeared beside them. "What is it?"

"A dust cloud," said Arapovian, "a few degrees west of north. And growing."

The wolf lords rumbled that they could see nothing, leaning their great copper-banded arms across on the top of the wall and gazing out into the twilight. Aëtius could see nothing, either, but the easterner had the eyes of a hawk. If the Huns were on the horizon, from this height, maybe a hundred feet above ground, that would be—he did a quick calculation, learned decades back from his old tutor—twelve miles off, perhaps a little more. Even slow-moving cavalry would be here in three hours, and the Huns did not move slowly.

It was time they left, with nightfall to hide them.

14

THE EMPRESS

I n the gloom of the convent chapel, there was a priest intoning the ancient litany, and, kneeling before him, a woman in white, veiled in keeping with the teachings of the Church, and, either side of her, two veiled handmaidens. The priest looked up, his expression angry.

"The sacraments have been administered?" demanded Aëtius.

"Who are you, and how dare you interrupt the holy mass?"

"I see they have. Shut up your gospel, Father. The service is finished. It's time for the empress to leave."

Immediately one of the handmaidens stood before him. "Night is falling, and the empress is in no fit state to leave."

Aëtius frowned. Two other of her handmaidens helped her to her feet. She turned. Through the dim gauze he saw a woman who looked old but once beautiful, her eyes still large and luminous. In truth, she was only in her middle forties. She looked at him and clutched one of her maids.

Aëtius's heart sank. "Take her to the hospital," he ordered.

There was a moment of hesitation, then the empress bowed her head and her handmaidens led her away.

———

Athenaïs lay in a fever, very pale, her broad brow damp with perspiration. Gamaliel sent out for some fresh willow leaves. He said an infusion would help, but it would take time, and she must drink boiled water. His cures struck those around him as mad. Heat should be used to drive out heat, surely? The empress should be laden with blankets, and given strong spiced wine. But they did his bidding, under the stern eye of Master General Aëtius, who seemed to have some connection with this bearded and peculiar ancient.

The general was hovering in the door of the hospital, about to leave, when the empress summoned him over. For a moment, her fever seemed to clear. She gave him a sad smile.

"What kept you?" she said. She might have been referring to his whole life.

He looked at the ground. "I was needed elsewhere."

"And still are?"

He looked troubled. "We must leave when we can. There isn't much time."

"Do not leave," she said, misunderstanding. She reached out a trembling hand. "Stay."

A nurse lit a candle for her bedside. After a moment, Aëtius called for a chair to be brought.

In the night she was feverish again, talking in her delirium, repeating an old rhyme: "Many a couple love one another, Though they never come together, Nor shall know each other's name ever."

Suddenly she half sat up and stared at him. "Let us ride away."

"We will," he said quietly, "once you are well."

One of her handmaidens eased her gently down again.

"Far away," murmured the empress. "Do not let the angel of history harry us to the bitter end."

The handmaiden looked awkwardly, questioningly, at the general. He nodded her away.

"Somewhere there is escape from it," Athenaïs murmured, barely audible, her dark hair streaked with gray and plastered to her face.

"You should rest now," he said. And then very carefully, with gross presumption by all the rules of court etiquette, he reached out his big scarred hand and stroked the hair back from her cheek. He took up the damp cloth on the edge of the bowl beside her and pressed it to her brow. She breathed in deeply, seemed calmer again.

"Somewhere there is escape from it," she repeated softly. "Somewhere we might awake one morning out of the clutches of this nightmare."

He did not want to hear her words, but he could not leave her.

"In two or three generations' time, all this will be at an end." She was looking intently at him again, and he could see she knew who he was. She was not so delirious. "Rome and her empire . . . These things are at an end. Can you not see, Aëtius? In two or three generations' time, these things will be only glorious memories in the minds of old men, monks, and scholars in their chilly skylit cells, dreaming of the Golden Antique Past, and of the Kingdom to Come, and of Christos Pantocrator who will descend from heaven and spirit their souls away to a far, far better world than this. And why should they not dream? For the present will be nothing but dust and darkness and ashes. The lights are going out all over Europe, the darkness is coming. Only in a few isolated places will the flickering candles be kept burning. But the strong, brave dream that was Rome in her might and youth"—she clutched his wrist with one hand—"and her centuries of confidence and pride . . . they are gone. It is done, and only darkness and ignorance remain."

Gently he released her grip and laid her arm back beside her. In the corner, in the gloom, her handmaidens were watching.

"The barbarians pour over the borders," she murmured, falling into oblivion again. "Or else they invest the empire from within, and in a dream people stagger on, the living dead, their civilization long since finished, believing in nothing. A ghost culture kept going only by comfort and illusion and wealth."

They said the prophecies of the dying were the most powerful of all.

When Gamaliel returned, Aëtius leaped to his feet and went to him. They spoke quietly in the shadows for a while, then the old physician mixed up more of his willow-leaf infusion, and added other ingredients from two more vessels. One of her hand maidens held up the empress's head and she drank and then she slept.

Aëtius would not leave, though he looked worn out.

"You want me to assure you that she will live," said Gamaliel.

Aëtius said nothing.

"Well," said the old man. "You know the cynical old saying: '*Ubi tres physici, duo athei*—where there are three doctors, there are two atheists.' But

I am the third of them. God is with us, in ways we cannot even imagine." He laid his hand on Aëtius's arm. "A leader of men needs sharp wits, which means good sleep."

Against his will, Aëtius followed someone else's advice for the first time in decades.

15

THE CAPTIVE

The general was shaken awake only a few hours later.

"There are campfires burning all over the plain." It was Prince Theodoric.

He flung his cloak round him and they hurried outside, onto the walls. It was a pitch-black night, with no moon and thin skeins of cloud dimming even the stars. Someone offered him a torch to see his way but he damned him for a fool and told him to put it out. And then they were on the walls of Azimuntium, and the plains all about them were a sea of blackness studded golden with myriad campfires, like a fallen starlit sky.

"So," he nodded. "They have come."

"The demand has been delivered already: an arrow over the gates."

"Let me guess. Surrender or die?"

"In as many words," said Theodoric. "What do we do now?"

"A small hill town and a column of forty spearmen, facing a Hun battle group of thousands? We ride out and attack 'em, of course."

Theodoric looked unconvinced. They watched the flickering campfires for a time, then Aëtius gestured at the nearest. "How far out are they, would you say? The nearest?"

"Hard to tell by night. Not so far."

"Choose four of your best men. Mounted."

"Myself among them," interrupted Arapovian.

Aëtius's eyes narrowed. "You are as good as the wolf lords?"

"Better. I survived Viminacium."

He grunted. "Prince, take three of your wolf lords, and this one. Ride from the postern gate. The night is very dark. See if you can take a captive out there. Do not endanger your lives, not for one moment. Do you understand?"

Theodoric nodded and the four departed for the stables below.

The postern gate was opened without a sound, and left open, spearmen ranked inside. The four rode out at a walk with their horses' hooves and muzzles bound in sacking, praying that the beasts would make no other noise, no friendly harrumphs to the horses of the Huns among the black felt tents. It would be pure luck if they did not. The riders wore dark cloaks, no helmets, and rode with their faces streaked with earth and bowed so as not to catch any light. The only weapons they dared carry were whips.

An old warrior stood in the darkness beside his tent, his campfire long since burned out. The four riders stopped in the shadow of a slight depression. The old warrior was naked to the waist, belting up his breeches. Arapovian dismounted, moved round behind him and dropped a cloth bag over his head and gagged him before he knew what had happened. The next tent was a mere ten yards off but the occupants were already sleeping, and the four made no sound louder than a mouse in a cornfield. In their haughtiness the Huns had not posted a single lookout.

They bound their captive with their whips. Another, smaller figure came out of the tent behind so they felled him and gagged and bound him likewise, and then pulled them back to the town behind their horses. The old warrior struggled mightily and threatened to cause trouble, so Jormunreik knocked him cold with a mighty fist to the back of his neck, and then they dragged him along peacefully enough in the dirt behind them like a travois. It was all done in two or three minutes, the postern gate latched and bolted again, the prisoners shaken back to consciousness and hauled up to the gatehouse for Aëtius's inspection.

"*Asia konuşma Khlatina,*" growled the old warrior, his head still covered. "*Sizmeli konuşmat loung.*"

"Oh, I'll wager you speak Latin very well," said Aëtius evenly. "As I speak Hunnish." He glanced aside. "Light more lamps."

They sat the two captives on stools and pulled off the first bag from the smaller warrior.

"You've brought me a woman," said Aëtius, glaring round at them. "You dolts."

Prince Theodoric began to protest at this unchivalrous attitude, but Aëtius silenced him. "Don't add to your doltishness," he snapped. "It's the Huns who don't value women, not I. They'll laugh in our faces if we demand favors in exchange for this one." He held the lamp up to the woman's face. Dark hair, olive skin, a long, narrow face: she was no Hun. "My apologies for any rough handling," he said more gently. "Where were you captured?"

"Philippopolis," she said. "My husband—"

"Calm yourself. You are free now."

She tried to speak again, but another voice interrupted.

"Leave her be," it growled. "She is a good ride."

They pulled off the other bag to reveal an old warrior with fine long gray hair and oiled mustaches, his naked torso copper in the lamplight, as lean and hard as that of a man half his age. His arm muscles bulged and strained against the whip.

"You are in no position to give orders," said Aëtius. "And I have no desire to know about your carnal preferences."

"Astur curse you," spat the old warrior. "Cut my throat and have done. But know that I have no fear of you or your women, who sneak about in the night like pigeon-livered slaves."

Jormunreik stepped nearer to him, but Aëtius held up his hand. He was beginning to enjoy this obstreperous old warrior's company. Then Arapovian came forward, examining the old warrior's face more closely.

"You were at Viminacium. You met us on the road."

The Hun glanced up at him, uninterested.

"You said the next time you met us, you would kill us." Arapovian's eyes glimmered with cold mirth. "Well, here we are."

The Hun bared his teeth.

Arapovian turned to the general. "This one is compensation for the woman. This one you can bargain with. He is a khan."

"You, your people will bargain for," said Aëtius. "What is your name?"

"I am the Lord Chanat, son of the Lord Subotai. In my youth I once visited your Ravenna, doing the bidding of King Ruga. I have never forgotten your city."

"Indeed?"

"Indeed. The foul stench of it stays in my memory still—worse than the stench of these sneak-thief women standing about me now."

Aëtius grinned. "If you think Ravenna smells bad, you should try Rome."

Chanat scowled at his flippancy. "In those days, the Romans tried to kill King Ruga's nephew, the boy Attila."

Aëtius nodded. "I knew him once. We rode together."

Chanat looked momentarily puzzled as he scrutinized the Roman.

"From what I have heard of those days," said Aëtius, "it was not so simple. King Ruga was not averse to his troublesome nephew . . . disappearing, one way or another. And he was very fond of Roman gold."

"You lie!" Chanat struggled against his bonds, but Arapovian snatched at his whip and tightened it.

"Ancient history," said Aëtius, waving his hand. "Is King Attila with you now?"

"You think I would tell you if he was?"

"Not really. We'll find out soon enough."

Chanat snarled. "Now Attila Tashur-Astur is our King, and a Great Tanjou, and you tried to kill him again, in your sneak-thief, womanly way, to cut his throat as he lay sleeping, as you visited us in pretended peace and friendship." He leaned forward and spat. "You failed, of course. At all times, Astur watches over him. Nothing can stand against him. And now he has come to kill you." He looked around. "All of you."

Aëtius ignored him. "So. We have ourselves a Hun khan, as well as one of his captured concubines."

"I have seven wives," said Chanat with dignity. "But it is long since I have known them."

Aëtius considered, then ordered Chanat taken to the dungeons. To the woman he said, "The sisters in the convent will care for you."

The woman looked after Chanat with something like agony on her face. "My lord!" she cried. Then she turned desperately to Aëtius. "I will stay with him."

"You . . . you would go to the dungeons with him?" Aëtius frowned. "But you mentioned a husband?"

She spat. "A pig."

Chanat turned in the doorway, a grin of triumph on his broad, high-cheekboned face.

Aëtius said, "I've heard of ravished maidens in old tales falling for their divine ravishers, but this is ridiculous."

"Your women would rather go with us, eh, Roman?" crowed Chanat.

Aëtius waved his hand irritably. "Take them away."

At dawn, he sat his horse at the gate, with Prince Theodoric and two of the wolf lords. Lord Ariobarzanes came down the cobbled street to wish them well. He stopped beside Aëtius. His old hand shook on his walking stick, but his voice was even and his words uncompromising.

"Not one breath of surrender, now," he said. "The men of Azimuntium do not surrender. Never, ever, ever. Remember our demands. We want our flocks and our herds returned to us, every single animal they carried off, and the shepherds they have enslaved. When that is done, their captive will be returned to them, this Chanat, and then the Huns may ride back to their own land unmolested."

Aëtius smiled. He liked the old man's attitude.

"All barbarians are the same," said Ariobarzanes, "They despise weakness, they admire strength." His voice dropped to a mutter. "As old Rome did once."

Aëtius kicked his horse forward and they rode out, unarmed, under a fluttering white flag of truce.

A gang of Huns on motley ponies immediately rode with them, arrows to the bow, aimed at their hearts.

"There is no need. We have no weapons," said Aëtius.

The Huns' faces were expressionless and the light in their eyes burned hard and their bows did not waver. They were small compared to the wolf lords, riding half naked, their arms and chests pure strength and sinew.

"Who is the leader of your battle group?" asked Aëtius.

One of the warriors indicated a black tent and grunted. They dismounted and were herded in. There in the half-light of early morning, beneath the smoke hole of the tent, on a plain wooden stool sat the Lord Attila.

He regarded them steadily. The atmosphere was very different from that of the embassy—the supposed embassy.

No word was spoken for a time. And then another figure entered, a small, .

antic shaman with ribbons in his hair. His cheeks were very smooth and boy-
ish but his eyes were old and cunning, and his hair bound up in a topknot
was tatty gray.

"The years roll back, Little Father," he murmured, coming close to Aëtius
with careful steps and staring at him. "This fine old warhorse, I have seen
him before, a young colt in the fields of the Huns." He glanced back at Attila.
"He drew a sword, white boy drew a sword."

Attila's glittering yellow eyes never left Aëtius's face, but now he waved his
hand and told the shaman to be silent.

"Where it chatters, Little Bird, water's but shallow."

The shaman disregarded him, and began to caper more and more, though
slowly, an arthritic old clown on tired legs. "The years roll back, the years roll
back. Yes, your uncle Ruga of blessed memory, uncle nuncle was he, he struck
you to the ground, you were always a terror as a boy, scarce out of the womb
and cut from the caul you were trouble. O Terror of the World, Great Tanjou,
my Lord Widow Maker, Scourge of God and all your other magnificent titles
which I forget now, he struck you, Uncle Ruga did, and white boy drew a
sword in your defense. You hunted together, you frolicked, you did, on the
sunny plains in your youth." Little Bird paused for breath. "I remember that
big boar. Huge it was, and rancid tasting by the time you dragged it home.
What joker gods look down! He was your friend, this one. Now look at you,
like two old buffalo fighting over the herd!"

There was a long silence, and then, as if he could not speak a word directly
to Aëtius, Attila turned instead to Prince Theodoric.

"So, a Visigoth prince once more in the camp of the Huns. I did not have
the pleasure of making your acquaintance when you made your . . . *embassy.* I
had other things on my mind, my impending assassination and so forth. Your
name, *boy?*"

The prince told him.

"What verminous company you keep. Your men slew many of my men in
the mountains."

"We were attacked."

"My heart bleeds for you." Attila's eyes glimmered. "You would make a
precious hostage, would you not? Why should I release you?"

"In exchange for your Lord Chanat," said Theodoric. Aëtius clenched his
hands behind his back. *Yes.* The boy was doing well.

"So," rasped Attila. "You ride with the Romans now?"

"My brother and I and our retinue ride as the friends of Aëtius."

"Friends and assassins?"

"I knew no more of that low plot than did the master general here."

"How many men left in your retinue?"

Theodoric smiled. "Enough."

Attila smiled, too, differently.

"The Visigothic nation remains neutral," said the prince.

Then Attila leaned forward, and his eyes burned, and all in the tent felt the ferocious power that was in him. His voice changed and his face darkened. He fixed the boy with his gaze. "You should ally with us. You should know which way the wind of history blows."

There was a silence and then Theodoric replied, with audible contempt, "My people ally with the Huns? I think not."

Attila sat back again. "Have a care, boy. I could send you back to your father as a barrel of chopped flesh."

"Then you would have the entire Visigothic nation against you, as well as the legions of Rome."

"The Huns have dealt with your nation before. Have we not harried you across all of Europe, from the shores of the Sea of Ravens westward? You ran from us as if you were trying to catch the setting sun, wailing like women!"

The boy's blue eyes blazed, like fire seen through ice.

Control yourself, lad, Aëtius willed him. *He is only testing you.*

When the prince spoke again his voice remained calm. "You did not deal with us well in the mountains. The Visigoths will flee from you no more. The next time, like the last, we will turn and fight."

"That is not your decision, *boy.* Your father still rules the Visigoths, does he not? Unless you intend perhaps to usurp him?"

Now Theodoric had the measure of Attila and his games. Calm was strength. He only replied, "Return the stolen flocks and herds to the people of Azimuntium, and the kidnapped shepherds, and we shall return your Lord Chanat to you. Then we shall ride away south."

Attila stroked his beard awhile and pondered.

Someone else came into the tent, without requesting permission, and the little gray-haired shaman whimpered and fled out of the back. Even Aëtius blanched when he glanced at the newcomer. This was a Hun witch.

She was very tall and thin, her chest flat and bony, her face like that of a corpse, her hair dyed an unnatural tawny red. She wore a sloughed snakeskin round her throat, and though she was very dark skinned her eyes were a pale blue. Everything about her was wrong. She strode over to Attila and spoke in his ear, her voice a strange, high insect whine. Aëtius thought he caught the name of Anashti, the moon goddess. As she spoke, she looked at Theodoric and showed her teeth. They were filed. Aëtius knew what she was saying, and hoped Theodoric didn't. The lad was holding his nerve well so far. She was speaking of the deep, strong *mana* of sacrificing the first born, especially the first born of a king, and she held out a wooden cup.

Attila looked at Theodoric. "Would you care for wine?"

Theodoric did not hesitate. "I would not. It is poisoned."

The king laughed a harsh laugh. "You are not the greatest fool I have ever met. Yes, it is poisoned. You would have died in agony." He waved the witch away. "She is a jester, is she not? But she has no notion of politics and power. She thinks it can all be done by spells."

They remained silent. Then Attila stood.

"Lord Chanat is worth many sheep. And I like men brave unto folly. Sometimes." With those words he turned at last to Aëtius, and handed him a note. "Take this to your pig of an emperor. You and I, we will meet again."

"On a battlefield?" replied Aëtius quietly. "After a battle's end? After the deaths of countless thousands of men?"

"Life is sacrifice," said Attila. "The world is an altar of sacrifice."

Attila kept them waiting all day and on into dusk.

Aëtius stood tirelessly on the battlements, waiting. The moon was not yet up, but he could imagine it glimmering across the Euxine. Sea to the east, and shining blue white on the snowy flanks of the Caucasus, and silvering the Danube delta, and that haunted White Island there where Achilles and Helen lived. Sailors said that they heard the sounds of their lovemaking as they sailed past, and saw Achilles' swordplay like a ghostly flame high in the rigging.

Then Gamaliel came to him. The empress grew neither stronger nor weaker.

Aëtius said nothing.

"And Attila? Do you trust him?"

"Not one inch," said Aëtius. "I know him of old. But horses can't gallop up walls like these, and I saw no siege engines. Even this little town would be hard to take without siege engines."

"You observed well."

"One of the reasons I went to parley: to check out the camp."

Gamaliel was amused. "But this is only one battle group."

"One of many. The others will have the engines."

"And where are they?"

Aëtius looked bitter. "Ask the citizens of Sardica, of Adrianople, perhaps even of Thessalonica. They will be fully experienced in the Huns' use of siege engines by now, and there is nothing we can do to help. The East has no army to speak of, only the last of the Imperial Guard, and any odd Isaurian auxiliaries we can round up to resist the attack on Constantinople itself."

"That is coming?"

"Oh, yes. That is coming."

After a pause to digest this black news, Gamaliel said, "I used to pray that men would love God more than power." He paused. "I am still praying."

Aëtius only grunted.

Gamaliel said, "Do you remember the other boy with you in the camp of the Huns?"

"The Greek slave Orestes." He nodded. "He is still there. Older and balder."

"No, the Celtic boy, Cadoc, the son of that good officer Lucius."

"My God," said Aëtius softly, sad and still with memories. Never look back, they said, Not if you want to stay strong. But now . . . "I remember him, just." It seemed so long ago. Such length of time, and all so greatly changed. He ached with unaccountable longing. What is that longing? For another world.

Then he straightened his shoulders. No. There was more to be done.

As if reading his thoughts, Gamaliel said, "Things are coming to a great conclusion. An age of the world is ending, another is being born, and we are its unlikely midwives."

There was a stirring out in the dusk. The Huns were mounting up.

"Riddle me no riddles, please," snapped Aëtius. "I've enough to think about."

"Do you remember the Last of the Sibylline Leaves? They are important. That boy, Cadoc, and his father Lucius before him, they are the last who remember them. The parchments were all destroyed, all but one, saved by General Stilicho himself. Lucius and Cadoc, in far and forgotten Britain, they are the living Last Sibylline Leaves."

Aëtius was tiring of the old man. "I don't believe in sibyls and prophecies and spells. They are the things of childhood. I believe in a line of good infantry—or a column of Gothic wolf lords, if it comes to it."

"Nevertheless," said Gamaliel, "the Son of God was born under a star descried by eastern Magi, was he not? And of a virgin? According to the ancient Jewish prophecy?"

"There's religion and there's superstition. Don't confuse the two, old man. 'By their fruits ye shall know them.'"

Gamaliel raised his bushy eyebrows. Then he changed tack. "This Attila, he is a superstitious man, is he not?"

Aëtius hesitated. "He has shamans and witches about him, yes, though he pretends to scorn them."

"You know he believes. His people believe in him, too, for now, and that he is the son of Astur, the All-Father, and possessed by the bloody spirit of Savash, their god of war. This is a struggle not just between armies, but between what people believe."

Torchlights were moving over the plain. Aëtius strode to the edge of the battlements to order the wolf lords to stand ready.

"Remember the verse," urged Gamaliel after him. "'Four will fight for the end of the world, One with an empire, One with a sword, Two will be saved and one will be heard, One with a son And one with a word.' And also the verses about a King of Terror from the East—"

"Balk the main gates!" roared Aëtius.

"Sir!" replied one of the men down below. It was the centurion, Tatullus. "Listen to that!"

There was a kind of muffled movement, a tramping, and then he could hear it: the baaing of sheep.

Attila always admired the brave and bloody minded. The men of Azimuntium had triumphed.

After the herds and the flocks had been returned, along with the captured shepherds, filthy but well enough, Aëtius ordered Chanat brought up from the dungeons.

The old warrior glared at him. "A horse."

"You Huns have horses enough. You can walk back to the camp."

Chanat growled, "Slaves walk."

Aëtius turned to the woman. "And what about you? Will you return to your lawful Christian husband, or do you wish to go with this aging barbarian?"

The woman gave Chanat a look that said it all. Chanat grinned. "I take the woman instead of a horse. She is slow but comfortable." The woman bowed her head in shame, but stayed by his side.

Aëtius sighed and looked away. "Open the postern gate."

"You have no courtesy, Roman, no hospitality for your guests," said Chanat as he departed.

"You weren't a guest, you were a prisoner."

"But I think we shall meet again. Maybe on some bright, bloody battlefield, and it will be a glorious death for both of us. But you should ride away quickly now. The shadow of Astur follows you over the earth, and we, too, are riding south. The next time we meet, the Lord Attila may not be so accommodating!"

After the gate had closed on the pair, Aëtius turned to his wolf lords. "Saddle up fast."

He insisted that the empress ride in a carriage, but she well knew what threat lay over them, and that time was against them: not just this party, but the entire city of Constantinople. She rode on a horse, clutching her reins, pale and silent. Lord Ariobarzanes came down to bid them farewell, grimly satisfied with the return of the sheep and cattle, and swearing that if ever the Huns appeared in his domains again, the men of Azimuntium would destroy them. Finally, the old Jewish healer or whatever he was came and spoke to him. Aëtius asked him to ride with them, but he said that his path was by another way. His arms were full of ancient scrolls which he had taken from the synagogue, fearing that they would fall to the Huns, to be used for lighting campfires. As if one man could gather all the scrolls of the ancient world and save them from the fire to come.

Aëtius had other things to think about, such as checking their provisions, exchanging a half-lame horse for a better one, and deciding what route they should take before the path of the oncoming whirlwind. But still Gamaliel followed him, shambling around the courtyard of Azimuntium before the gates as the wolf lords and the empress's retinue assembled, tripping over the tattered hem of his old gray robe, talking of the Sibylline Leaves, which were destroyed but not yet silent. He told the general to remember the prophecy recorded by Livy, that Rome would stand twelve centuries plus six lustra, which period was soon coming. And the king who destroyed two kingdoms. All is not all that it seems. The story is not yet finished. Is it ever? Which is the real, time or eternity? In dreams there is no time.

Aëtius peered into a pannier, checking grain, finding the old man very distracting.

"Last night," said Gamaliel, "perhaps you dreamed of your boyhood again. You were back at school under the stern eye of the *magister*."

"Dreams play us false," snapped Aëtius.

"Did the dreams of Pharaoh play him false? Or Nebuchadnezzar? God speaks in dreams. The wise man listens and attends. Have hope, Aëtius. Have precious hope."

Aëtius mounted, called for the gates to be opened, and turned back to look over the column. So feeble, so few in number. The wolf lords with their banners floating in the breeze . . . the empress with her dark, pained eyes. Then he muttered to Prince Theodoric at his side, "Time to go. Attila will be hunting us. The game has begun."

"He thinks war a game?"

"He thinks all of life and death a game. Forward!"

16

THE SOLITARY CITY

Elsewhere, all over the Eastern Empire in those days, the armies of the Huns roved unchecked, destroying all in their path. The shadow of Astur was indeed over the earth. The clumsy attempt on Attila's life would be paid for with the lives of thousands.

At the seaports of the Adriatic, refugees took ship and fled west, spilling out of ramshackle boats and making landfall along the Italian coast. Stories of devastation soon reached the horrified ears of the Court of Ravenna, and Valentinian, rather than leading the Army of the West to face Attila in a last, desperate attempt to halt him, as a man of a different stamp might have done, ordered his finest legions to huddle uselessly about him, camped on the debilitating summer marshes, while his Eastern brothers burned.

Attila and his horde left Moesia, Macedonia, Illyricum, and Thrace nothing but scorched earth. They razed to the ground the cities of Nicopolis and Marcianopolis and the great regional capital of Sardica. Their fury and their appetite for destruction knew no bounds, and they slew all they found. They destroyed Philippopolis, and Adrianople, and Edessa in Macedonia, and on the Euxine coast the lovely cities of Salmydessus, and Apollonia, and Tomi where Ovid in exile once wept. On the Aegean coast they destroyed Amphipolis, and the great port of Thessalonica, taking all that city's rich stores of silver and lead away in their huge covered wagons. Some of their war parties rode on further, as if unable to rein in, and laid waste to Thessaly and even ancient Hellas itself. They found Corinth and Athens deserted, but destroyed many of the finest monuments of those revered cities in vengeance. Their victims numbered in the thousands, tens of thousands. The stench of rotting bodies was always on the wind.

Constantinople, the sweetest dish, the Red Apple as they called it, was left till last. The walled city of Constantine, the New Rome, was all that stood between the Huns and the treasures of Asia: the teeming millions of Syria and Egypt, the cities of Nicomedia and Ephesus and Antioch, the ancient centers of Christianity, far greater and more populous than any the Huns had yet devastated. As the terror of the coming storm increased, so, too, did the slow and horrified realization that this was a storm which would not cease. Constantinople once taken, the Huns would cross the straits of the Bosphorus, and the rest of the world would be at their feet.

The Byzantines had visions of the Huns riding their rough ponies into the very Church of the Nativity in Bethlehem, or the Holy Sepulcher in Jerusalem, laying waste the site of Calvary and man's redemption itself. Huns traversing the desert east and besieging far Damascus; crossing the Sinai and trampling the rich corn lands of Egypt, burning and flattening Alexandria, barbarous steppe horsemen amid the immemorial pagan temples and palaces of that ancient kingdom. Huns riding across North Africa, via the burning shells of Cyrene and Leptis Magna, and on to Carthage, meeting up with their Vandal allies under Genseric. There was no limit to the destruction they might wreak.

Constantinople must stand; even though her sister Rome would not stand with her.

I, Priscus of Panium, have seen the Hunnic destruction with my own eyes, and I have also read other chroniclers. Callinicus tells us that "More than a hundred cities were captured. There were so many murders and bloodlettings that the dead could not be numbered. For they took captive the churches and monasteries and slew the monks and maidens in great quantities." It was amid this impious slaughter that the mythic terror of the Huns was born. As Attila observed, terror is a fine weapon, and very cheap; and panic travels faster even than galloping horses.

That other noble chronicler, Count Marcellinus, wrote simply of that year of catastrophe, "Attila ground almost the whole of Europe into dust."

There was one small town in those days, however, which did not fall. Tragedy did not visit it, History passed it by. It remained humble and un-remarked, a common, ordinary, unheroic little town. I mean the town of Panium, standing there on the green hillside, valerian and stonecrop grow-ing in the cracks of its ancient golden limestone walls, and the bell tower of the church peeping above. It had stood thus for many centuries, and it will stand for many centuries more, its people placid and unknown, goat bells sounding in the olive groves, cicadas chirruping in the sun-dried grass. In the evenings the old men still gather in the courtyard by the well to gossip and to drink the thin red wine. Just a simple green hillside, a little town of shepherds and farmers, a single half-literate priest. No, His-tory never visited Panium, and it remains there still. It has no stories, for it has no scars.

Aëtius took a gamble and rode directly back to the capital down the open road. The Huns did not snap at his heels. Indeed, there was no sign of them. They were waiting, looting, slaughtering through all the surrounding land, leaving Constantinople alone in mournful isolation, her provinces cut from her like limbs and destroyed in the fire. "*How doth the city sit solitary . . .*" Aëtius rode at the head of the column, face set, expressionless, never so alone. Athenaïs ached to see him.

This waiting, this torment, was also directed at him, as he well knew. At-tila's games, his complex furies and hatreds. He is isolating me, saving me till last, too, he thought. As if I have somehow betrayed him, and my betrayal is the worst, and must be punished the most.

As they came across the flat plains past the last outlying and deserted farmsteads, and saw the great brick-banded Theodosian walls ahead of them, and the domes and spires of the city within, it seemed as if they were arrived at a dreadful judgment and reckoning, entering upon some vast stage set di-rected by History herself, and they were only actors, their speeches and desti-nies already written. Through late orchards they came, fruit falling from the trees ungathered, abandoned monastic houses, past Maltepe Hill and the shallow valley of the Lycus and, all defenseless, the forlorn and foredoomed

Church of Theotokos, its precious furnishings and icons already taken by the priests and hurried within the safety of the walls.

There was a brief and bitter meeting between the emperor and his general. Theodosius was aghast that the assassination attempt had failed. Vigilas? Dead from exhaustion. Aëtius told him of Attila's little joke with the fifty pounds of gold. And Chrysaphius? Aëtius did not spare the details. It was time this stupid but well-intentioned man began to understand his enemy.

"Attila cut his throat in front of us. Before that he tortured him a while. Broke his nose, smashed his anklebone underfoot and so forth."

Theodosius held his hand to his mouth, looking at Aëtius indignantly for having exposed him to such truths.

There was worse. Aëtius produced the note Attila had given him.

To the Emperor of the Eastern Romans, slave, liar, coward, and traitor. It is a wicked slave who conspires against the life of his master. You have forfeited your position and the Will of Heaven has henceforth placed you in my hands. We are coming to collect the debt you owe us. Attila, *Tashur-Astur.*

Theodosius looked on the verge of hysteria, but gradually calmed himself again. "We must buy him off. It is our only choice."

"You cannot buy him off. He will take the gold and then attack you anyway."

He paced and fretted for long minutes. Finally he said, his voice quailing a little, "Can this city truly withstand the might of the Huns? With our own armies destroyed, and the help of the Western ships and legions . . . withheld?"

"Yes. I believe it can."

Thedosius looked sorrowful. "All my best generals are slain: Aspar cut down at the River Utus, Solimarius hunted to death like a dog by a Hun war party in the Chersonesus, Zenobius—his earthly remains—perhaps somewhere in the ashes of Thessalonica, which he died trying to defend with a handful of mercenaries. And so you see . . ." He opened his hands helplessly. "The city is yours to defend. I commit it into your hands. Do what you must."

He hesitated a moment longer, looking at Aëtius as if not seeing him, and then retired to his private chambers.

Outside the audience chamber, Athenaïs joined Aëtius.

"Your Majesty is in better health again?"

She smiled and did not answer. Instead she said, "The emperor is a good man."

"I know that," said Aëtius. "No Valentinian."

"That is treason!" Her tone was not entirely serious.

He grimaced. "Theodosius is all sweet reasonableness and gentle light, I know. But he has poor night vision. His wide eyes do not penetrate into the dark places either of the world or of men's hearts."

"Whereas you have good night vision."

"Plenty of practice."

The empress sighed. "He believes that all men are essentially like himself. A great folly, perhaps."

"A great folly for certain. Reason is weak, and unreason has unimaginable power against it: the power of ancient and irrational forces."

"Those powers burn strong in Attila."

"Strong as the sun." Aëtius laughed harshly. "And the emperor, God save his Imperial Majesty, believes that he can negotiate with him. Can you negotiate with the sun?"

There was a silence, then she touched his arm and said his name.

He pulled away. "Excuse me, Majesty. I have work to do."

There was still no news of the approaching Hun whirlwind, but the air was thick with heaviness and dread. It would not be long now. And so, amid signs and portents and the panicked babbling of crowds and self-appointed doomsayers in the choked streets of the capital, Aëtius set about preparing for the coming onslaught.

He surveyed the city's walls from the Sea of Marmara to the Golden Horn, wondering again at their colossal strength: squared stone facings of tertiary limestone, founded in bedrock, with mortared rubble for infill. The towers were built as separate structures, a masterstroke of that great overseer of the

work, the Praetorian Prefect Anthemius, back in 413. An assault on the walls
or settling of their foundations would do no harm to the towers themselves.
And they were so massively built that even the largest artillery machines
could safely be operated from their rooftops without damage to the structure
below them. He inspected the artillery as he went, approving the low-slung
onagers and the multiple arrow machines with grim satisfaction. He even approved a couple of newfangled machines supposed to hurl detonating fire pots.
None of the men operating the machines looked much good at hand-to-hand
fighting; they were city guards and technicians only, but they would do. He
inspected them all and gave praise or censure where due. Each artillery bat-
tery that he inspected, and spoke to of the coming attack, he left more som-
ber and more resolute than before.

The two Gothic princes in his party were awe struck by the walls: that
feat of engineering which they had often heard of but had dismissed as exag-
geration. Torismond leaned out from Military Gate V, overlooking the Lycus
Valley, taking in the multiple defenses of the city before any attacker could
even begin to scale the primary walls, starting with the outer ditch sixty feet
wide and thirty feet deep. He paused and turned to Aëtius, looking puzzled.

"Sir, I can hear something."

Aëtius nodded. "Keep watching."

A light wind arose from the bare stone below, then as if from underground, there came a low, rushing sound. There was a trickle of water across
the dusty facing of the ditch below, then a sudden, mighty onrush of waters,
foaming in from the sea, where the sluice gates had been opened on Aëtius's
orders. The princes whooped with glee. Within minutes the great moat was
flooded to a siege depth of twenty-five feet. The seawater settled and stilled,
glinting and opaque.

"The Huns don't like water," murmured Theodoric.

"You see that the moat is divided into segments," said Aëtius, "rather than
being a continuous ditch. Why?"

Torismond frowned. "I'd have thought that weakened us. Those dividing
walls—the Huns can come across them on foot."

Aëtius snorted. "One at a time, single file. We can pick 'em off easily
enough. No, those dividing walls are Prefect Anthemius's most brilliant device
of all. What will the Huns do when they first encounter the aqueducts outside
the city?"

"It had crossed my mind," murmured Theodoric. "They'll destroy them."

"Poison them, block them up, break them down, whatever. Quite so. But, firstly, every one of our cisterns will be filled to the brim before then. Secondly, those dividing walls below you conceal further underground aqueducts. The Huns will never realize. Our water supplies will continue, if severely reduced, even with our great arched aqueducts destroyed."

The princes gaped at such ingenuity.

Having crossed this first obstacle, by swimming or boat, pontoon or cumbersome infill of timber and brushwood lashed together, the attackers would have to scale a low crenellated wall and then face an exposed terrace thirty feet wide. This was the first killing ground, bare under the sun before another, higher crenellated wall, seven feet thick, thirty feet high and with ninety-six towers along its length. Even the most skilled artillery attackers, utilizing the most minutely calculated trajectories for their missiles, would find it virtually impossible to hit this second wall at its foundations and effect any serious damage. Should the attackers succeed in scaling the second wall, they would face another broad, cruelly exposed terrace, wider still than the last, and then the final obstacle: the walls themselves, beyond compare, no walls in the world higher. Sixteen feet thick, a sheer forty feet high, and with a further massive ninety-six defensive towers. Not even Babylon's walls at her apogee could rival the walls of Constantinople; walls whose broad tops, Herodotus tells us, the young men of ancient Assyria used to race around at evening time, in chariots drawn by four horses abreast. A thousand years ago.

Aëtius observed the princes' faces now shining, all youthful confidence and eagerness for battle, and reminded them that the Huns would have learned much in the siege and destruction of dozens of former cities. There was also disease. There were also food and water shortages, with the city's swarming populace swelled further by refugees. They could expect no help, no relief forces, no lifting of the siege by outside agency. There would be no mercy shown if the city fell to Attila, only the same universal massacre that he had perpetrated before.

"And we have no defensive forces to speak of," he added.

"We have artillerymen, and the wolf lords."

"Forty-four wolf lords, yes. Two centuries of Imperial Guard, some auxiliaries. Attila's army could be a hundred thousand men, and he has the whole of Thrace and Moesia behind him for looting and forage. We have failed to disrupt a single supply line. Neither his men nor his horses will go hungry, even as winter approaches. We have only what is already within the walls. And perhaps a few hours to prepare ourselves for the assault."

The princes looked very different now, but Aëtius had no remorse. The truth must prevail.

As if to confirm his grave diagnosis, a centurion appeared before them and snapped to attention. It was Tatullus. Only the third centurion in the entire city, and already appointed Aëtius's second-in-command.

"Sir. Manpower report."

"Proceed."

"Sir. Two centuries of Palatine Guard stationed beside the palace, a hundred and sixty men, on orders to remain there. Four survivors from the VIIth Legion, including myself, sir. Two auxiliary *alae* of Isaurian mercenaries, loyalty uncertain, numbers severely reduced, survivors from Thessalonica and Trajanopolis. Total head count, around eighty. Currently barracked off the Forum of Arcadius. Full complement of city watch, couple of hundred, untrained, armed with staves. Able enough to police a crowd but in battle couldn't fight off my granny, sir. Artillery operators, unarmed and unarmored, untrained in any hand-to-hand, but full complement. A machine on fifty-six of the ninety-six towers. No specialist archers, sir. No—"

"No archers? In the entire city?"

Tatullus remained expressionless. "No, sir. None."

Aëtius compressed his fists. "Very well. Continue."

"That's the manpower report, sir. No cavalry. And that's it. Apart from civilian population, around a million, plus further forty or fifty thousand refugees."

"And forty-four Gothic wolf lords," said Theodoric. "Archers, spearmen, swordsmen."

Aëtius brooded. Around three hundred fighting men in all. "Billet all refugees on existing households—none to be camped rough in the streets, do you hear? The city is to be kept scrupulously clean. No handouts from the state granaries until I give the order. Have the city watch oversee it. Order the auxiliaries to the walls. And your three men along with"—he turned to Theodoric—"your wolf lords."

A hundred and thirty men, including eighty mountain mercenaries from the wilds of Cappadocia. Christ have mercy. The Palatine Guard must be released to fight on the walls. He sent an urgent message to the palace.

Almost immediately, there before him was another messenger, his face white and taut. One of the palace staff.

"Have I the honor of addressing Master General Aëtius?"

"You have. Speak, man."

"Esteemed sir, ships have been seen passing eastward through the Hellespont and coming this way. A small party crossing to Chalcedon saw their sails over the Propontis and courageously turned back to warn us."

Aëtius's blood ran cold. "Ships? How many?"

"They said . . . they said, 'a flotilla,' sir. A large number, not precisely counted."

"But, but," interrupted Theodoric, looking bewildered, "the Huns may have mastered siege craft, but they have no naval forces. Impossible."

Aëtius turned on him so fiercely that the prince almost quailed before him. "When is your sister—what's her name?"

"Amalasuntha."

"When is the poor maid to be married to the son of Genseric?"

"I, I have no idea, sir. I . . . She is already betrothed to him . . ."

The poor girl. A child, a light-footed, laughing child when last he saw her in the Court of King Theodoric at Tolosa, throwing her slim arms round her father's shaggy old head. Now a mere pawn in this catastrophic game of *latrunculi,* which was becoming a war for the fate of the world.

"Pray God she is not yet sent to Carthage."

"But . . . the Vandals are our allies. We have sworn ancient Teutonic oaths of blood loy—"

"Too late, boy. Those are Vandal ships crossing the Propontis toward us. Those are Attila's allies. We are now at war, we and Genseric, and your father will soon have to choose on which side he stands. We will get no supplies or reinforcements from the sea now." He turned to the messenger and rapped out the latest sketch of the situation for the emperor, unsparing in its direst details.

"What of the Byzantine navy?" asked Torismond.

"No manpower. No marines. They died with the field army on the Utus. I've given orders for the ships to be scuttled to block the Golden Horn."

Theodoric crossed himself. "If it is true that the Vandals have allied with the Huns . . ."

"It's true."

"Then my father will have blood for blood."

"I pray it may be," said Aëtius. "I've said it before: your people may yet be Rome's last hope."

The messenger returned breathless from the Imperial Palace only a few minutes later. The Palatine Guard had been released for duty on the walls, and the Divine Emperor Theodosius had retired into his private chapel to hear mass and to pray. He wished to receive no further communications from Master General Aëtius until the victory was won. Until then they must trust to God and his Holy Mother.

Tatullus brought two men to him, very different in appearance. One was clearly the Captain of the Guard, doubtless the firstborn of one of the noblest and most aristocratic families in Constantinople: a tall, handsome, slightly arrogant-looking fellow in his darkly shining black breastplate, his helmet with its dark crest cradled under his left arm. He saluted smartly. He'd be eager for battle and glory, this one, chafing at having to remain behind in the city barracks as the emperor's personal bodyguard. Now was his chance.

"Captain Andronicus, sir. First Commander of the Imperial Guard."

"Your men fit and ready?"

"As ever, sir."

"They'd better be. How's your arithmetic, man?"

"Arithmetic, sir?"

"You heard aright. The Theodosian walls are around three miles in length, from the Golden Horn to the Sea of Marmara. You have a hundred and sixty of your own men, plus eighty auxiliaries."

"And a column of Gothic horsemen, I heard?"

"They're my close guard. It will be an easy calculation for you to space your men evenly along the walls. Yes?"

Andronicus looked distant for a moment, and then grinned. "Three miles . . . some six thousand paces. Six thousand divided by two hundred and forty is . . . a man about every twenty-five paces."

"Quite so. Not a lot, is it, soldier?"

"It's not, sir."

"Your men are going to have a hot time of it."

"Never fear, sir. My men are as highly trained as any in the empire."

Highly trained, yes, and an elite; but little used. Maybe that would be a good thing. They would be eager to test themselves.

"You'll have noticed, too, soldier, that there are three defensive walls west of this city. If we manned them all, what spacing?"

"A man every seventy-five paces, sir. Too little."

"Quite so. Even manning two walls would be overstretch. We can man only the inner wall. No chance of defense in depth this time. In other words, your men are going to have to hold their nerve like veterans, because in a few hours' or a few days' time, however long our enemy in his kindness and consideration allows us, a hundred thousand Huns are going to come across the moat and over the first wall, virtually unopposed but for what our artillery can do. Then they're going to come over the second wall, still virtually unopposed. Only at the third and last wall will you have your chance to fight. A man every twenty-five yards. Does the immensity of our task impress itself upon you, Captain?"

The handsome *miles gloriosus* grinned again with satisfaction. "Can't wait to get stuck in, sir."

"Your men aren't professional archers, is that correct?"

"They can handle a bow, sir."

"Very well. Now get 'em up there. I want the guard stationed from the Marble Tower in the south, right up to St. Romanus Gate. North around the Blachernae Palace down to the Charisius Gate, station your auxiliaries. The city watch will be in reserve at key points if things get desperate."

Andronicus curled his finely chiseled lip disdainfully. Desperate indeed. The indignity of having to fight alongside those peasants, with their staves and billhooks!

"And the Lycus Valley, and Military Gate V, sir?"

The weak point, the crunch point, where glory would be won or lost and the fate of the city decided. "My Gothic allies," said Aëtius. "But don't worry, soldier. We'll all end up fighting there sooner or later, I don't doubt."

He turned to the other man, a squat, burly figure with a bushy, unkempt, salt-and-pepper beard. "And you are?"

He did not salute. "Tarasicodissa Rousoumbladeotes."

Aëtius grimaced. "Say that again and you'll give me a headache."

Andronicus grinned. The bearded chieftain did not.

"And salute your commanding officer when he first addresses you," snapped Aëtius. "Tarasicodissa Rousoumbladeotes."

He spoke the name perfectly, after one hearing. Few men had ever achieved that. Tarasicodissa Rousoumbladeotes saluted.

Aëtius nodded. "Very well. From now on I'm calling you Zeno, so you'd better get used to it. You hear me?"

"I hear you."

"You and your Isaurian tribesmen are far famed for banditry, in your Cilician mountains." Zeno glowered. "But here you'll have the chance to win a higher renown. Your eighty will hold the walls of the Blachernae Palace until the Huns are destroyed. Yes?"

The chieftain nodded.

"Now move, both of you. There's work to do."

Despite the manning of the Walls—or perhaps because of it: the results were so visibly thin—the atmosphere in the city grew more hysterical by the hour, as the day slid into dusk. Twice a cry went up from a church or palace tower that a mighty host was approaching from the west, and twice it proved to be false. The second time, it turned out to be a great, dark cloud of rooks. Aëtius sent word that any more false alarms would result in flayed backs.

There also came news that a boy had seen a vision of the Virgin on the walls, bearing a flaming sword, ready to fight alongside her beloved and faithful people for the Holy City of Byzantium.

"Probably just bad wine," said Tatullus, unmoved, gazing steadfastly out into the twilight.

"On the contrary," said Aëtius. "A miracle." He told the messenger to spread the word.

"Sir?"

"Spread the word, damn you! The Virgin has been seen on the walls. Take the fellow round, give him wine to loosen his tongue, encourage the visionary in him. Find others who can corroborate his story. Move."

Tatullus grinned into the darkness. The master general turned everything into a weapon against the enemy, even pious delusions. Then he frowned. The rooks were coming back out of the twilight, circling again, as if unable to settle in their treetop colony.

Aëtius joined him. "They are infected with the general panic of the city," said the general.

"In the street below," murmured a nearby voice—it was Arapovian, characteristically not requesting permission to speak before commanding officers—"I saw a cat curl up and try to sleep, then leap up again with its tail straight out. And . . ." He hesitated, hardly daring to impart more bad news. He had seen one city fall to the Huns, and had stood in despair amid its ruins. He did not want to see another. Not this city, too.

"Go on, man."

"This afternoon I saw my cup of water shake when I stood it on the wall. I saw its surface ripple."

Tatullus stiffened. The rooks circled and cawed. Aëtius whispered, "Oh, no. Please God, no."

"I know the signs: they are common in my country. The cat, the ripples, those rooks . . ."

"No." Aëtius laid his hands flat on the top of the battlements. Suddenly these mighty walls seemed things of gossamer.

Arapovian nodded grimly. "There is an earthquake coming."

17

THE WALLS

In the night it began to rain. They could not sleep, sheltering in the lee of the walls. If Arapovian was right, they should be sheltering in the open forum. Or, irony of ironies, out beyond the city walls, on the open plain. There they would be safe from the earthquake, only to be devoured by the Huns. Damn it all, damn the rooks, and damn that cat.

Aëtius slept briefly, breathing rapidly through a nightmare in which he was walking alone on a desert shore, with a monstrous shark cruising through the waves on his left, and on his right a ravening lion coming through the dunes toward him, eyes glinting and yellow. If he kept wading through the waves at about waist height, neither lion nor shark could quite reach him. But they followed him along on either side, deathly companions, knowing he would tire long before they did. . . . He awoke with a start, needing no seer to interpret the dream for him.

A one-eyed storyteller loomed out of the night, bareheaded, hair plastered down, bloodshot eye red rimmed and shining.

"Oh, no more madmen and their tales, *please,*" said Malchus.

But the storyteller wanted them to know that the Seven Sleepers of Ephesus had awoken. The end was indeed coming near.

Wearily, they asked him to explain. Squatting down before them in the pelting rain, he said that generations ago, when the Emperor Decius was persecuting the Christians, seven noble youths of Ephesus concealed themselves in a cave in the nearby mountains. Decius ordered the cave to be sealed and left them to their grim fate. There they had slept unharmed and protected by God for one hundred and eighty-seven years. Then lately, the slaves of one Adolius, who owned the cave, came to take away the stones for building. The sun flooded into the cave, and the Seven Sleepers awoke, thinking only a single night had passed.

They sent one of their number, Iamblichus, into Ephesus to buy bread for their breakfast. He came down into the city, amazed by the sight of a huge cross over the main gate. He offered the baker a coin of Decius, speaking in an antique fashion and peculiarly dressed. On suspicion of possessing secret treasure, Iamblichus was dragged before a magistrate in the basilica. Inquiry established the astonishing facts. All went to see the cave—the magistrate, the captain of the guard, the city prefect—and all was as Iamblichus had told them. With that, the sleepers blessed their visitors, departed back into the cave, rejoicing that they had lived to see the Triumph of the Cross, and peacefully lay down and died.

There was silence but for the pelting rain. A stray dog pattered through the downpour. It was an eerie story. At last Malchus offered the man a coin, but he said there was no need. The end was upon them now. He fixed them with his single bloodshot eye. "The Lord care for all souls," he said softly. " 'This ae night, this ae night, Every night and all, Through fire and sleet and candle heat, Then Christ receive your soul.' "

A night bird called in the darkness above the walls. And then the earth began to tremble.

As they ran, they heard a great howl from out of the darkness, all the more terrible for being the howl of a man of steel. It was the general, at last giving way to despair.

The earthquake lasted perhaps a minute at most. A deep rumbling in the earth, the ground shifting beneath people's feet, animal cries of pure terror. Within the houses of the rich, mosaic floors creased and crumpled, candelabra trembled and were still and then flung down. Precious stained glass in the churches cracked and then exploded. Walls shuddered and shed their plaster amid clouds of dust. Stones fell and bodies were brutally laid out below.

All through it and for hours afterward, the autumn rain fell ceaselessly.

Whereas the city had been in a state of silent, pent-up hysteria, now all chaos was let loose. In the drenched midnight the bells of the churches of St. Irene, and the Apostles, and the Chora Monastery, and the great basilica of St. Sophia Augusteion rang out, as if to summon the people to judgment. The bells of the Apostles suddenly went silent, and then there was a terrible clanging crash. The quake had weakend the bell tower, and it had collapsed. Four bell ringers were laid out dead.

The streets turned to mud, the animals were maddened, wailing people ran to and fro with blazing torches. Some made to escape from the city altogether. Even in the pitch-black night, in the driving rain, they fled down to the half-ruined harbors, pushed past the few guards there, and piled into little boats. Some even tried to swim across the Bosphorus. But the currents were strong, the waves were wild and clashing after the shaking of the earth, and the next day the sun rose on the sight of many hundreds of bodies washed up along the silent golden shores of Asia like strange seaweed. The first offerings.

From the depths of his despair, somehow the master general stirred himelf and found the strength and resolution to go on. He gave orders that no more were to pass. All remaining boats down to the smallest dinghies and rafts were to be smashed, and even the smallest harbors of Julian and Constantius and St. Mary Hodegetria were to be blocked up. The general was ubiquitous on his white horse, one moment down at the Hippodrome, clearing out the many refugees there and billeting them in existing households, the next inspecting the cisterns of Aëlius and Mocius, thanking God that neither had been ruptured in the quake. For good measure he took time to excoriate their overseers and insist the great tanks should be at their highest levels—especially in this damned rain.

He hectored the city watch at the end of every street, struggling to contain and appease the hysterical people. He addressed the populace at times, sitting his white horse, and they grew familiar with the sight of him. He told them to return to their homes and keep calm. This was their best hope now, in a city unmanned and soaked and half ruined by earthquake. Outside the walls their fate would be far worse. Then he was riding north and overlooking the Golden Horn, his horse picking its way through the rubble of collapsed shacks and stalls and even whole stone houses. He nodded with approval that at least one order had been correctly carried out. The normally placid waters were still ruffled from the aftershocks, and drummed into a dark mist by the

rain, and spiked with the masts and timbers of half-sunk boats, an impass-
able obstacle course. Even more importantly, the Great Chain had been laid
across the mouth of the Golden Horn, from the tower just below the Acropolis—
mercifully still standing—to the oppposite side, locked onto the sea walls of
Galata. No ship could break through that chain.

Let the Vandal ships come, he thought grimly, through quake and storm.
They'll get nowhere. All our attention will be on the walls. Then he reflected
a moment, and sent an order for one, just one, artillery machine to be released
from the walls of Theodosius, whichever was furthest from Military Gate V,
and brought down here to be stationed on top of the towers of the St. Barbara
Gate, overlooking the chain. If the Vandal ships do cluster here like the amateurs they are, he thought, at least we can take a few vengeful potshots at
them. Good for morale.

Then . . . the walls. He turned with a heavy heart and rode west. As he
came round to the Charisius Gate, he saw the worst. The walls were half ruined. In places, the sections between the towers were no more than head height.
The rain slowed and stopped and the sun came out abruptly, mist steaming off
the piles of broken masonry.

He climbed one of the towers and saw that the great inner walls had suffered most. Accursed luck. But one small consolation: the moat didn't seem
to have been ruptured. It still held twenty or thirty feet of water, now covered
with a fine spray of limestone dust from the shivered and shaken walls.

He rode the three miles south with the Visigothic princes, and Tatullus,
and Captain Malchus. The Isaurian chieftain, Zeno, came down to say that
the walls of the Blachernae Palace had barely been touched. But beyond that
things were terrible. Tower after tower had shivered to rubble, jumbled piles
of brick and stone, the bright marble of the proud gateways grubby red with
brickdust. Broken statues lay face down along with broken people. What the
most skilled and powerful besiegers could not have achieved in a month, nature
had achieved in a minute. All rode on silently, thinking the same thoughts.
God has turned against us. We have been judged.

"Check with the outriders," was the only order Aëtius could give.

By the time they reached the southern end of the walls, they had counted
fifty-seven of the ninety-seven towers damaged or fallen, and almost half the
walls likewise.

"Find me the easterner," he ordered.

They sat their horses. The September sun shone down. Flies buzzed over puddles in the humid air. Not a word was spoken. Then Arapovian came. He saluted.

"So, easterner," said Aëtius. "With your intimate knowledge of earthquakes, tell me: if the Huns are fifty miles off, will they have felt it?"

"I do not know, sir. If they are more than two hundred miles off still, then perhaps not."

Aëtius brooded. The aqueducts still flowed, had not been destroyed. There might just be a chance.

He spoke more thoughts aloud. "The moment they feel it, for them it will be Astur shaking His enemies to the ground. It will be our righteous punishment. And they will be here at the gallop. But it is just possible—just—that they are still unaware of our calamities."

"Then what do we do?" asked Tatullus. "Other than fight to the death?"

"Other than fight to the death," said Aëtius, "a destiny which most certainly awaits us, we rebuild the walls."

The men stared at him long and hard.

"There are a million people at hand, doing little at present but wailing and praying. We put them to work. Any fool can learn to build a wall."

His eyes roved over a section still standing, and settled on an old tombstone which had been used to balk a weak point. *To the memory of Crescens,* read the crude lettering, *"oil dealer from the Portico of Pallas, born at the mouth of the Danube, lifelong Blues fan."* Nearby on the wall itself was a scrawled graffito. *"Up the Greens!"* it read. *"The Blues be crushed!"*

Aëtius's face settled again into its old, deep-graven resolution. "Get me two teams," he said. "Everyone in this city is almost as mad about chariot racing as they are about the Holy Mother. Everyone supports either the Greens or the Blues. Order all the Greens to assemble at the Marble Tower. Order all Blues northward to the Chora Monastery. Order every mason in the city to oversee them. Let us have a competition." He surveyed their dumbstruck expressions. "You are thinking this is no time for games. On the contrary, this is exactly the time for games. The spirit of competition between Greens and Blues is a wonderful thing!" He added wryly, "When they're not slaughtering each other in the streets."

His men continued to stare.

"Move!" he bellowed.

From the outriders came news that no enemy had yet been sighted. Water still flowed into the cisterns from the great aqueducts. It was a miracle. The earthquake had been a calamity, but now, it seemed, God had changed his mind. The God who blasts and blesses in one breath.

As He had stayed the sun in the sky for Joshua, so He seemed to be staying the advance of the Huns. Had they attacked now—had they known—the city would have been theirs in hours.

And so the citizens of the Holy City of Byzantium, men, women, and children of every station, turned stonemasons and builders. The children carried buckets of water and small pouches of clay and sand. Older men and women mixed the mortar. The stongest men, overseen by experienced masons, retrieved what solid stones they could find and began to re lay them. Crude cranes were improvised from fallen timbers, from collapsed houses, or from bundles of wooden scaffolding tied with rope. Mules were yoked and worked hard, but none was worked to death: their strength was too valuable to squander. On the remaining towers, the guard and the auxiliaries, the wolf lords and the artillery scanned the horizon ceaselessly. Nothing came. The aqueducts still flowed. It was a miracle.

Aëtius ordered water for the workers, but no food. "We eat at nightfall, not before. You can work all day on an empty belly. Just keep the water coming." Yet when nightfall came, after snatched mouthfuls of bread and meat, many continued to work by torchlight. Sweating, begrimed faces were lit a fiery red, like those of workers in hell.

"These Byzantines," growled Tatullus, grudgingly impressed, "I thought all they ever did was pray and argue theology."

After a little snatched sleep that night, Aëtius received a message toward dawn from the overseer at the Cistern of Mocius. He went to inspect. Citizens were filling their pails from the opened spouts at the base. The overseer greeted the general respectfully, shooed the people back, shut off the spouts, and then asked him to climb the steps and look into the cistern. Aëtius did so. There was no more inflow. He looked down questioningly.

"The Aqueduct of Valens," said the overseer, "supplies this cistern."

"But it's been shut off?"

"It's been shut off," said the overseer.

So. They were not far away now.

He went to look at the walls, and could have wept. People lay open-mouthed in the dirt, beyond exhaustion. And the walls . . .

Unlike the people, the walls were far from finished.

It was then that the men of the Church showed their mettle, their faith in the protection of Christ and his Holy Mother never wavering. They brought the most Holy Icon of the Hodegetria, She Who Leads the Way, painted by St. Luke himself, out into the streets from the Church of St. Savior in Chora near the city walls, mounted the icon on a wooden pallet, and processed through the narrow streets, swinging censers, chanting penitential psalms. Black-robed priests and cantors and barefoot laity alike sang the haunting quarter tones of the ancient hymns, walking beneath the swaying icon, gilded and jeweled and decorated with fragments of the True Cross. Elsewhere in the city, bishops in brocade vestments raised their croziers in blessing, and deacons sprinkled the faithful with holy water from bunches of dried basil.

They raised the mummified figure of St. Euphemia from her open casket and paraded her around the streets in blessing, her head like a dried melon. Bands of Syrian monks emerged from their monasteries, chanting their long litanies to the crucified Christ and calling the faithful to labor again, proclaiming that *"Laborare est orare,"* and telling them that the Lord of Hosts was with them. Swelling music came from the interior of every church in the city that morning, the doors thrown open so that the magnificent chants and liturgies of the Roman Church should be heard, surging forth like a tide out of those vast basilicas covered in glimmering mosaic, hung with silk embroidered tapestries and thousands of oil lamps in massive silver candelabra.

True faith moves mountains. The people roused themselves and worked on all that day. It was a Sunday, but today, of all days, God would pardon them for breaking the Sabbath.

A work gang of Greens, dust-caked youths, came to Military Gate V and asked how the badly damaged Porta Aurea, the magnificent Golden Gate built by Theodosius the Great, should be repaired. Aëtius said, "A soldier fights best whose armor is so highly polished that it gleams like silver in the sun."

So, even with the hordes of Attila riding down on them, these untrained youths reconstructed that gleaming wonder of white marble and gold, just as it had been. The four vast bronze elephants were raised up again, one of them repaired in a nearby forge, and set atop the gateway. Even more inspiringly, the two winged victories were set up again in their proper place, a little battered but facing boldly out over the surrounding plains, wings outstretched. Hundreds of people took it in turns to work at a furious rate and then to rest, and by nightfall the gate was more or less as it had been before the earthquake struck. There was huge rejoicing among the Greens at their feat, their spirits soared, and they danced and sang hymns and psalms of praise spontaneously in the streets below. Rumor of the achievement reached the ears of the Blues, whose work rate redoubled in envious emulation.

It was Prince Theodoric who first made the observation to Aëtius, regarding God and his mysterious ways. Aëtius nodded, at last almost allowing himself a smile. When the Huns attacked, the walls would not be as they had been. But they might just be enough. Aside from that, the achievement of the people of the city had put more spirit into them than they ever had before. Action makes men brave, inaction makes them timid. The earthquake might have damaged the walls, but perhaps it had been a blessing in disguise: a very heavy disguise. It had fired the citizens with a peculiar new ardor. Now they waited for the fight to begin with the eagerness of that hot-blooded Captain Andronicus. Aëtius felt for the first time that he and his few troops did not stand alone. They had a million people behind them. It was a good feeling.

At last, at the end of that Sunday night, the Blues and the Greens came together at the St. Romanus Gate, and there was no enmity left between them. They had achieved wonders together; besides, they were too exhausted for enmity. They embraced like brothers, and then sat in the dust, sweat stained, coughing and aching, plastered ochre with stone and brickdust, and with barely the energy remaining to eat and drink. Then their beloved Patriarch Epiphanius came out to them, and preached to them from the Book of Ezekiel, having instructed that the same text be preached in every church and in every public place throughout the city.

He preached upon Gog and Magog, the demons in Ezekiel's vision, who came from the north, and he said this time was come, and Gog and Magog were upon them. But the Lord of Hosts would not forsake his people of Israel.

"'And thou, Gog and Magog, shalt come from thy place in the North, thou and many people with thee, all of them riding upon horses, a great company, and a mighty army; And thou shalt come up against my people of Israel as a cloud to cover the land; and it shall be in the Latter Days, and I will bring thee against my land, that the heathen may know me, when I shall be sanctified in thee, O Gog, before their eyes. And against my people, thou shalt not prevail.

"'Though the mountains shall be thrown down, and the steep places shall fall, and every wall shall fall to the ground; yet I will call for a sword against the Prince of the North throughout all my mountains, saith the Lord God. Every man's sword shall be against him, and I shall plead against him with pestilence and with blood, and I will rain upon him, and upon his bands, and upon the many people that are with him.

"'For behold I am against thee, O Gog, the chief prince of Meshech and Tubal. And I will turn thee back, and leave but the sixth part of thee. And I will smite thy bow out of thy left hand, and thine arrows from thy right. Thou shalt fall upon the open field, saith the Lord God: for I have spoken it.'"

At these words a great shout went up from people: *"The Lord of Hosts is with us!"* and Prince Torismond said he felt as if he was living in the time of Joshua and Gideon and David and the mighty men of old.

18

A HOLY MAN

Aëtius moved swiftly with his new and unexpected civilian army. He divided them into citizen companies, and immediately an esprit de corps seemed to spring up within each of them. He appointed half of them to man the walls, and the rest as reservists at four stations behind, ready to fill any gaps at short notice. Their missiles were stones and rubble, their weapons any iron tool they could lay their hands on—spade, hoe, or pruning hook—but their expressions were soldierly and grim.

"This will be a crude fight," Aëtius told them. "But that's fine, since you will be crude fighters." They gave a great, self-laudatory cheer. "You will be up on the inner wall. The two lower walls before you will be undefended, and the savages will come pouring over them like a tide. How will you react? I'll tell you how you'll react: you will empty your bowels at the sight.

"Then there will be a man climbing up the wall to reach you and kill you. He will have a shield on his back, a spear, a sword, and a dagger, and he will have killed many, many men before you. He will have their flensed skulls decorating his horse, and he will mean to have yours likewise. There will be constant arrow fire coming in from his comrades beyond, and they are perhaps the finest archers in the world. But you will be standing above him, behind strong stone battlements, some of which you have built with your own bare hands." Another cheer, a little more sober than before. "You are protected

by the wall. He is not. You must kill him. Strike once and once only. Beat
him back, dash him down, brain him with your first, measured blow. Then
duck back for cover. The Palatine Guard will be among you, and you will
obey their every order. You need no more training. Now go to your stations
and do your duty."

Then suddenly this least martial of cities, this religiose New Rome with
its ceaseless liturgies and tangled theological debates about the true nature of
the Triune Christ, was an excited hubbub of brazen trumpets and marching
hobnailed boots. Theodoric said the Byzantines were turning into Spartans. It
was an extraordinary feat, and no one seemed to know who was responsible.

Tatullus said to blame it on the earthquake.

Aëtius said to blame it on the power that made the earthquake.

Around midmorning, news spread that the outriders had come in. The Huns
had been seen: they were no more than ten miles off. Eyes strained over the
battlements, sweaty hands gripped shears and pruning hooks, shaking hands
struggled to place a last few loose rocks on top of the jagged walls. There was
no more excited cheering.

A wild-eyed holy man began another sermon, declaiming to the women
and children gathered in the great square around the Church of the Holy
Apostles. The text was from Deuteronomy: " 'The Lord shall bring a nation
against thee from the ends of the earth. They shall be as swift as eagles, a nation whose tongue thou shalt not understand. A nation of fierce countenance,
they shall besiege thee in all thy high gates, until thy mighty walls come
crashing down wherein thou trustedst. And thou shalt eat the fruit of thine
own body, and the flesh of thy sons and thy daughters which the Lord thy
God hath given thee, in the siege and in the straitness wherewith thine enemies shall distress thee.' "

It was an ill-chosen text and, somewhat to the preacher's surprise, the
people promptly turned on him. Only a few days before they might have listened, and wailed, and crossed themselves, but now a woman whacked the
ill-advised doomsayer about the head with the flat of her washing paddle, and
he fled howling into an alley, pursued by an angry mob who soon caught up
with him and gave him a sound drubbing. Among their number, rumor had
it, there was even a black-cassocked deacon or two, putting in a sandalled kick.

Night fell again on the lonely, resolute city. Some still worked on, trying to build up the walls as best they could, but the masons all agreed they were as solid as they could be made in this short time. Only after darkness cloaked the land did they see from their walls and towers the numberless fires that burned out there in the desolate countryside. The last farmsteads, a few isolated chapels, hayricks, and barns, put to the torch by men on shaggy ponies, their reins and saddle straps decorated with scalps and skulls and severed hands.

In one of those forlorn chapels, barely more than a hermit's cell in the woods, with whitewashed walls, a stark stone altar at one end, and a crude little wood-panel icon hanging above it, a single holy man had lingered when all others fled. He said he would go as a martyr to heaven to be with his Christ, and spoke as if he was tired and longed only for sleep.

Now he knelt before the altar and prayed to Christ, even as the wooden door of the chapel swung open behind him and he heard the tramping of horses and the low laughter of men. First in the doorway was a man with a dagger in his hand, gleaming yellow eyes feasting hungrily on the helpless sight before him.

Behind him, Orestes spoke with urgency. "Do not delay here. This earthquake we have heard of, it will have done damage."

But Attila lingered, smiling.

Finally the priest turned, and crossed himself at what he saw. Attila strode into the chapel. Orestes lowered his eyes, his hand still on the doorhandle.

"You tried to assassinate me," said Attila gratingly to the startled priest, who was already shaking his head. But he did not kneel or plead for mercy. He only reached out and took down the little icon, and held it to his breast. Attila fixed his gaze on the bewildered priest, his eyes burning. "Vengeance upon vengeance. Those Roman rats would not even face me in the open field. They sent an assassin, a viper, to me in a putrid basket. Now they will feel my fierce anger, now we spare not, now all will pay for Rome's cowardice and weakness. I rejoice that they have angered me, anger is such a sweet fire!

"When I ride away south you will breathe again, Christian pig, and think that this is over. But it is not over. After I have destroyed Byzantium and laid it waste, and metamorphosed all its precious treasures into faithful mercenaries"—he showed his teeth—"I will come back and find you, eunuch priest."

The priest shook his head. The man was mad. He made no sense. Behind him, one of his companions, a bald, fair-skinned fellow, was calling him, but he seemed oblivious, rapt in his own words and imaginings. He even trembled a little in his mad passion.

"Hear me, priest!" roared the Scythian warlord, "and know how Attila punishes craven assassins! I will destroy Constantinople. I will not enslave its citizens, I will slay them, and on the ruins of the city I will build a pyramid of a million human skulls. And there is nothing you can do." He turned back to Orestes. "See how the poor Christian pig clutches this daubing of his little god, as if for protection." He faced the holy man again. "Pray to your God? Who, this pale Christ?" He seized the icon from the man's grasp. The priest tried to hold it, but Attila knocked him reeling with a casual bear cuff.

"My lord," said Orestes again, with feeling in his voice. "We are wasting time here."

Attila no longer heard him. He stared down intently at the icon in his hands. "Your bleeding and tortured god, is he so powerful? He does not look so powerful to me. How many battalions has he?" He raised his dagger. Behind him, Orestes had vanished. "If he is god, let him strike me dead now as I mutilate him." He slid the tip of the dagger under the delicate gold foil of the icon, and the priest groaned. "What, this is the Son of God? Why does his almighty Father not stop me? Is this blasphemy?" He gouged the dagger point into Christ's right eye—the priest howled—then his left. Then he dug it into the emaciated hanging body, blue white and stretched in his dying agony. "You say this is a holy icon. It seems to me your God is very feeble." He pulled his dagger free and dropped the mutilated image to the floor. He smiled. "It seems to me you should get yourself another god, for this one, too feeble even to intervene and stop the mutilation of his only son, will surely not intervene to save the stinking city of Constantinople."

The priest was on his knees, retrieving the icon from the floor and cradling it, weeping. Attila kicked him hard in the ribs and sent him sprawling, retching for breath. Then he stuck his dagger under his belt, strode out into the night, vaulted onto his horse and kicked it forward. Orestes spoke no more.

Instead Geukchu came and rode by his side, and at his other side rode the witch Enkhtuya.

"The earthquake we have heard of," said Geukchu in a low, sinuous voice, "surely Astur is with us! It is as if, my lord, you had planned it all yourself."

But even at this stage Attila still disliked flattery, and he only murmured a couplet from some ancient Persian poem. "*The spider weaves the curtains in the Palace of the Caesars, The owl calls the watches in the Towers of Afrasiab. . . .*'"

They rode on, and night closed around them, and in the woods behind, as if in answer to those melancholy lines, there were only the sounds of a lych owl and of a solitary holy man weeping in his cell for the sins of all the world.

19

THE REFUGEES

Aëtius stood on the walls beside Military Gate V. Near him stood the lean, ancient figure of Gamaliel.

"You again," was all Aëtius had said sourly to him in greeting; but he had put him in charge of the nearby Emmanuel Hospital, all the same, and ordered the monks there to do his bidding. There would be plenty of work there soon enough, and this old trickster seemed to know his stuff.

Below in the street children were playing, happily oblivious for a moment of the world and its shadows. People of all ages sat awake through the night now, huddled around fires, talking. The children sang an ancient nursery rhyme:

Tortoise, tortoise, what's going on?
I'm weaving Milesian yellow and yarn.
How did your father happen to die?
Fell off his white horses and drowned in the sea.

It seemed an ominous rhyme. In a sudden flash, Aëtius pictured himself dying. A sign of old age: young men never imagine they will die, but now he felt all too often the stab of a dagger or a spear in his belly, saw himself lying in a blood-soaked hospital bed, arms outstretched in supplication but slipping away, the battle still raging on the walls. He hoped this was no foreseeing.

Tum magna sperabam, maesta cogitabam—Then greatly I hoped, but sadly I thought.

Gamaliel was talking about the Hun pantheon, as if delivering a lecture. He said the gods were fighting a battle among themselves by proxy.

"The Hun gods fight well, and fight dirty," muttered Aëtius. "Astur and Savash and the rest. Attila believes in them as he believes in himself."

Gamaliel turned to him gravely in the darkness. "Men believe in a god who is a reflection of their own hearts. Dark heart: dark god."

"Then whose god is true?" said Aëtius.

"Whose heart is true?"

Another was brought to him in the night, led by Prince Torismond, looking distinctly amused. It was the Cretan alchemist, Nicias.

Aëtius growled, "I thought you were in Antioch, or Alexandria."

"I was," said Nicias woundedly, "collecting together another set of alchemical equipment—and very costly it was, too. Then I returned here to experiment upon the, ah, premortem dismemberment of tunny by alchemical means."

"You've been blowing up fish?"

"Precisely."

"You alchemists are strange."

Nevertheless, the man of science assured him that, after further unplanned experimental outcomes—Aëtius noticed that Nicias still had no eyebrows to speak of—a happy conclusion had finally been reached, when a large tunny was simultaneously exploded and incinerated, while *still in the water.*

"A miracle to behold, I'm sure," said Aëtius. Not without some misgivings, he gave Nicias permission to station his wretched firepots and God knew what else on the towers of the Gate of St. Barbara, overlooking the entrance to the Golden Horn. He could take command of the single artillery machine there, and hit anything that moved. Vandal warships, ideally.

"Oh, and if you see any ships bringing Western legions to help us, let me know."

Nicias looked puzzled. "Is that likely?"

"It is not. Now scram."

The alchemist scuttled off.

"The next thing we hear," said Aëtius, "he'll have burned the imperial palace to the ground."

Torismond grinned.

The sun came up on the third morning after the earthquake, and the autumn mist gradually cleared from the country around. But away to the west there was a section of the horizon that did not clear. That was not mist but dust.

They were coming, in their countless thousands.

Along the walls, Aëtius saw to his horror, the empress herself was processing with some of her ladies' maids, talking to the soldiers, doubtless wishing them well and the blessings of Christ upon them; all grace and comfort. But this was no time for such things. This was a time for hot fire and cold steel. Aëtius marched over to her.

"Your Majesty, I must insist that you return to the palace immediately. This is no place for you now. Besides," and his voice was harsh, "you're getting in the way of my men."

She regarded him evenly, no fear in her eyes. But then she had never seen the Huns fight. There would be fear soon enough, with all hell unleashed.

"Master General," she said, "you govern your little domain here like an Oriental despot."

Even now, she was playing with him. He felt his anger rise. This was no time for games. She had no idea how bad the situation was. She knew *nothing*. He swore foully and said that if she didn't get off his walls he'd throw her off himself. At last she reacted, her eyes wide with astonishment and even disgust, and seconds later she and her retinue were hurrying back to the steps and down into the city.

Behind her he roared again, this time to his troops: "Bar all the gates! You've got five minutes!"

"Sir," said Tatullus, pointing, "there are still refugees coming in ahead of them. Look."

Aëtius looked. Against the long, low terracotta horizon that was the Hunnish horde and their siege engines, there came a few dozen last stragglers hurrying across the plain. Behind them, catching the eastern sun, arose a gigantic cloud the color of old blood, and in its midst the watchers on the walls saw the huge shapes of what they most feared: siege engines.

They must lock everything down. This would be terrible, a battle they must win, with all of Asia cowering helpless behind them, dependent upon them. But they could not possibly win. Not alone. Aëtius knew that, Tatullus knew it, all the men knew it. The fate of half the world was in their hands, and they would fail it. But they would go down fighting in fury.

Yet here were refugees from the outlying villages, humble peasants, fleeing to the walls for shelter from the coming storm. Stumbling in cracked earth, a few pitiful possessions hauled in sacks, mothers clutching infants, children trotting, so weak and undefended, glancing back into the mouth of hell. Asses heavily laden, usually such wise and philosophic creatures, bellowing and cantering, their big eyes terror stricken, eyes rolling back to the whites.

The kind of decision kings and emperors make every day, thought Aëtius bitterly. Which innocents shall I condemn to death this morning? Whom shall I damn and whom shall I save?

The first horse warriors were minutes away, galloping with all savagery. They would fall on the refugees like scythes.

Already some of the refugees were outside the bolted gates, wailing for entrance, but there was no help for them now. Some lay in despair where they fell, in the very shadows of the walls, and never stirred again.

"Let them come," said Aëtius quietly. "There is room for all." He remembered the mad bird catcher in the woods. Room for all, in death's capacious basket. "Open the gates!"

"But, General, the enemy are—"

He was already striding toward the steps himself. "Get that gate open, and bring me my horse. Wolf lords, to me!"

In a moment the thick crossbar was raised and the massive iron-banded gates were being dragged back. Aëtius vaulted onto his white horse and it reared up, champing at the bit. Behind him the wolf lords mounted likewise, their horses packed together, jostling, shields and scabbards clanging, short cavalry bows clamped in their right hands, reins in the left.

The empress was watching from the bell tower of the nearby Church of St. Kyriake. Then she looked away, as if no longer able to bear the danger, or the evidence of what kind of man he was.

Aëtius and the column of a mere forty-four streamed through the middle wall and then the outer, over the hastily lowered drawbridge and away onto the plain, looping out round the dumbfounded refugees like sheepdogs rounding up the flock. Immediately the people picked themselves from the dust, barely able to believe such a redemption, and hurried over the draw-bridge into the welcoming arms of the city. The wolf lords formed a galloping circle, their ancient steppe-warrior formation as if written into their blood, lowering their bows outward toward the red cloud away to the west. Before it they could already see the nearest ranks of horsemen. The wolf lords them-selves were now well within range of a volley from those lethal, high-sprung Hunnish bows. But something had happened. The Huns had slowed and stopped. Somewhere their leader had brought them to a halt, as if to take in the poignant scene before him.

Attila grinned. What a scene of bravery and manliness! What touching salva-tion for these wretched, earth-grubbing peasant farmers, as they stumbled gratefully within the walls. Let them stumble. The walls would come down soon enough anyway, and the refugees have to face the terror of the Huns all over again. And then there would be no salvation for them, and their skulls—large and small, one and all—would soon take their place in the biggest pyra-mid of human bones the world had ever seen. So Astur's justice would be done, and all mankind would tremble.

Aëtius slowed, too, seeing what had happened. It did not surprise him. He ordered his wolf lords to range up and save their energies. Away to the north more figures arose from the earth itself. In dusty travel-stained garments, like creatures out of the apocalypse, more refugees who had been sheltering unseen down in the Lycus valley came running toward the open gates with stricken faces. It seemed that Attila would let them all pass. His games.

Attila sat his horse and watched from less than an arrow's range. The dust they had raised fell and drifted among their horses' hooves with the gentle breeze, and the army of the Huns for the first time became visible. It was in-deed numberless as the stars.

The watchers on the walls looked out over it and knew that they were to die soon. Some groaned and turned away. The citizen bands, especially, looked ready to desert the walls altogether, but the Palatine Guard marched among them and rallied them, saying to trust in God and the walls.

Beside Attila sat the witch Enkhtuya, her teeth and mouth stained red with berry juice. Many of the Hun horses, too, beside their usual charnel decorations, had their pale manes and tails and fetlocks stained berry red for this titanic battle, as if they had already waded deep in blood. They champed and stepped high at this abrupt interruption of their advance, as if even they were touched with bloodlust. But Attila, at that moment at least, was touched by something else. Curiosity, perhaps. A little sardonic shadow of a smile as he watched his old friend, companion of his boyhood, the light to his shadow, Aëtius, moving among the fleeing crowds, helping them home.

Like Jesus among the poor; like Jesus feeding the five thousand. His smile grew fiercer.

Enkhtuya purred beside him. "See how his heart is sorrowful. How he has compassion upon the destitute and wretched of the earth."

Attila's expression was violently conflicted, as if he hated his enemy more than ever because he was forced to admire him. As if he felt his coiled inner strength might begin to melt because of it.

"Drop some arrows on them," he said.

Conscience prevents cruel deeds. But cruel deeds regularly practiced cancel conscience. Enkhtuya stroked her twisted snakeskin tore and the arrows began to fall.

From the walls went up a feeble shout of warning as the sky behind darkened with ten thousand arrows, arcing up like a midnight rainbow. But it was too late. The arrows fell in a murderous shower and many of the stumbling refugees were struck down. Screaming broke out, panic and confusion. Some of them even began to run away from the walls again, thinking in their terror and bewilderment that the defenders of the city had shot at them. The wolf lords immediately raised their shields and moved into a circling gallop again. A few slung their shields across their backs, nocked arrows to their bows and loosed them at the Hun lines in return. A paltry reply to such an onslaught, but it showed of what mettle they were made.

Aëtius wheeled his horse round, white and speechless with rage. He galloped out past the milling refugees and drove them back toward the open gates of the city, at last managing to shout instructions at them, saying that the walls were their refuge, and the arrows were coming from the Huns. He scooped up a fallen child, a little girl of no more than four or five, whose forehead had been sliced open by a flying arrowhead. The wound was not deep but she was blinded with blood and tears and was screaming. He slung her across his lap, laid his hand in the small of her back and told her to stop squirming. Then he pulled his horse round again and rode out in front of the circling wolf lords and reined in and stared. He did not speak or move, not even when another iron shower came overhead. Several fell about him but he was not hit. He stared like a lost traveler on a lonely moor, staring into the rain.

Attila raised his arm and the arrow storm ceased again. Aëtius's stillness spoke more than any enraged shouting or shaken fist could have done. Behind him came the cries and groans of wounded people, struggling to their feet, trying to make it to the city. Ahead of him across the half mile of burned plains and abandoned farmsteads, the hundred thousand horsemen and their lord, his arm still raised. Across that half mile the two men regarded each other.

"Well," whispered Attila, "you Romans know all about the Massacre of the Innocents."

His arm dropped, and the sky darkened again.

Aëtius wheeled his horse, holding the terrified girl across his lap, and galloped for the walls, arrows thocking into the ground around him. Ahead of him, the people stumbled home.

Aëtius slipped from his horse as the gates were slammed shut and barred behind him. He pulled the girl down, swabbed her forehead and face with the edge of his tunic and squatted before her. She suddenly looked too shocked to cry.

"What's your name?"

She shook her head. He squeezed her thin shoulders.

"Euphemia," she whispered, barely audible.

"Were you with your family, Euphemia? When you were hiding out there?"

She nodded miserably. "My mother," she whispered.

"Did you see her running into the city?"

She shook her head.

Aëtius rose and handed her over to one of the other refugee women, with instructions to reunite them if she could. The wounded should go to the Emmanuel Hospital; one of his men would take them there. Then he raced back up the steps to the top of the walls, and down to the Gate of St. Romanus. The enemy were coming nearer, and already Attila's gaze, he could see, was fixed on the lowest point in the defenses, where the wall ran down into the Lycus valley and up again, overlooked by Military Gate V to the north. On its summit he could see the nodding horsehair plumes of the wolf lords, and the long spikes of their spears. They would need them soon.

Attila rode slowly across the plain beneath the noonday sun, along with his generals, gazing all the time at the walls. It was too far to see, but Aëtius liked to think his expression was one of misgiving. His spies and intelligence agents would have given him every detail of these titanic defenses. Nevertheless, this was the first time that the Hun leader had set eyes on the walls of Theodosius for himself. Surely the sight must cause him some consternation? It was no one-walled legionary fortress or cathedral city that he faced now.

Aëtius summoned the Armenian. "Screw up your eyes, Easterner. Tell me you can see the Great Tanjou, and tell me he looks worried."

"I see him," said Arapovian. "We have met before, remember?"

"And tell me he looks worried."

Arapovian grimaced. "I have read more expression in the cliffs of Elbrus."

Aëtius grunted. "Drop an arrow on him?"

"Too far. Besides, the last time I tried to shoot him, I got this." He dragged up his sleeve and showed the general the scar.

Aëtius laughed. "You tried to shoot Attila?"

"He rides at the front of his men, without fear. It was an order of Sabinus, the legate at Viminacium."

Aëtius looked grim again. "That Sabinus was a good man. Now, back to the tower."

He remained alone and brooded a moment on the assassination attempt. Treacherous and underhand though it was, it might have worked. Even now, as the siege began, if they could but hit Attila, weaken him in any way, the faith of his myriad hordes in his god-given power would begin to falter. That was their best hope. To defeat such an army as this in open battle . . . it was not possible, not with what few forces were left.

The fall of everything he believed in was very close now. It gave him desperate strength. He began to tour the other towers again, to inspect the artillery units, to rally them. His exhaustion and sleeplessness meant nothing to him. There was no point in saving himself. For what? For the nothing that was to come?

20

THE GREAT SIEGE

As Attila approached the Golden City at long last, the walls rose higher and higher before him, like a monstrous triple wave of stone. Of course, he knew the details, the measurements, and he had planned his attack minutely. But seeing the walls in the flesh, as it were, even he fell silent for a while.

Riding beside him, Orestes observed that, whatever the earthquake damage might have been, the walls and even more crucially the towers had been fully repaired. There were no major cracks to be seen, no promising crevices running from battlements to foundations.

"And there"—he pointed at the brickwork around the Gate of St. Romanus—"that tower must have fallen half away; you can see where it's newly built. Yet it's as strong as ever again. We should not have delayed."

Attila stopped and turned on him. "You question my choices, you accuse me of delay, even of cowardice?"

Orestes was unimpressed. "I question our delay in attacking. We have made our task harder."

Whatever Attila might have growled in response was lost, as Aladar abruptly pulled his horse back and it reared. "Arrows coming in!"

It startled them, the arrow shower from the wolf lords, even though it fell short. Attila ground his teeth and they fell back further. Then he wrenched his horse round in a fury, the poor beast almost rupturing its neck, its mouth cut by the bit.

It was time. The late-afternoon sun was falling behind them in the west, beginning to glare red into the eyes of the defenders on the walls.

"Bring up the engines!" he bellowed. "Either side of the valley! I want the wall there down by dark! Tonight, Byzantium burns!"

The key defensive artillery units would be on the gate towers overlooking the low-lying Lycus valley: Military Gate V to the north and, beyond it, the Charisius Gate, which led out to the cemetery, for which reason it was also known dryly among the people of the city as the Polyandriou Gate: the Gate of Many Men. For many men passed out of it. All men, in time.

South of the valley was the Gate of St. Romanus, and south of that was Military Gate IV. These would be the crucial points from which the Hun siege towers might be attacked and destroyed as they approached, before they could do serious damage. Aëtius took his stand on Military Gate V, sending the wolf lords below to man the walls, telling them that they would see any missiles coming in well enough. "So make sure you duck."

The engines on the broad platforms of the two gate towers were the best he could find. Less crucial towers, especially toward the Blachernae Palace, had been left without artillery. Here at the weak point of the Lycus valley was where the fighting would be fiercest. Each gate tower had two multiple arrow firers, two small but powerful onagers, and a finely made transverse-mounted sling which could hurl rocks, balls, or even those wretched new-fangled firepots if need be.

Half a mile off, the siege engines were coming, drawn by captured slaves. Dispensable flesh. Hun horsemen galloped around them, flailing their long whips. Attila knew how short of manpower his enemy were and so, predictably, he was attacking on as broad a front as possible. There were as many as twenty siege towers moving slowly and inexorably toward the walls, and half sheltered behind them, there were rams under steep, protective wooden tortoises.

A deep, coarse voice called up from the walls below: "Permission to speak to the master general!"

Aëtius stepped over to the battlements and glanced down. It was that brute Knuckles. He'd managed to arm himself with a club with a great lump of lead solder stuck on the end.

"At Viminacium, sir, the enemy had fixed up their engines without wide enough skirts to protect the wheels. They might not have learned."

Aëtius squinted into the falling afternoon sun. Yes, they had learned. He nodded down to the big Rhinelander. "Ready with your club, man. You're going to need it."

He stepped back, speaking quietly to the artillerymen. They were no fighters, but they were quick and deft with their machines. The engines rolled nearer. They waited, a kind of silent screaming in their ears. A young lad wiped his upper lip. Sweat glistened there again almost immediately. Behind them, the city was eerily still, the streets and forums deserted, everyone indoors, crouching, huddled, praying. Even the emperor himself, God's anointed, was crouched and praying, too.

On the wall in front of Aëtius stood a bowl of water, calm as a millpond. The machines rumbled nearer. The horizon was dark with horsemen, The sun shone steadily, indifferently, upon all. This curious battle between these tiny creatures on the surface of the earth. And then a flash of sunlight on the bowl. Aëtius glanced down, not breathing. It flashed again. Not on the bowl. Glancing off the water, as it rippled in response to some mysterious subterranean disturbance.

The artillerymen were suddenly terrified, hands shaking, mouths open, staring around wildly.

"Oh, no, not again," muttered one of them, his voice low and desperate. "Not another quake. It will destroy us."

But the general was eerily calm. He summoned Tatullus.

"You see any animals panicking, Centurion? Any horses stampeding out there?"

Tatullus's hard eyes scanned the plain below. "No, sir."

"As I thought. Relax, men. Look to your machines. Centurion, spread the word. It's no second quake. On the other hand, don't relax too much. It means the Huns are mining under the walls."

Tatullus started.

"No time for theatricals, Centurion," said Aëtius dryly. "Get running now. Bowls of water all along the battlements. We need to know where the bastards are tunnelling in. These'll tell us every time they knock out a pit prop and there's another rockfall."

He called a runner over. "To the northern walls. Bring back half the Isaurian auxiliaries with their leader. Zeno. At all speed!"

The runner ran.

To another messenger he gave orders for the heaviest weights that could be found dragged up onto the walls at intervals. Marble column drums, if possible.

One of the siege engines was very close to them now, and another just south of the valley was approaching the moat.

"This one," said Aëtius, indicating the nearest. "Concentrate all your fire on the top. Imagine it's the head and slice it off. Take aim." He glanced down the other side. The wolf lords were ready with their bows.

The second tower nearby was behaving strangely. The entire front section seemed to be collapsing. Aëtius realized that it was indeed collapsing—to crash right across the moat and form an instant drawbridge. It landed with a mighty smack and a billowing of dust. The men inside immediately abandoned the exposed remainder of the dummy tower, and from behind them a tortoise approached with a bronze ram head shining evilly under it. Aëtius leaned out over the walls. The improvised drawbridge was aligned directly to the Gate of St. Romanus. So the enemy were battering, mining, and scaling the walls simultaneously. It was going to be an eventful day.

"Where are those damned mountain bandits?"

He sent word to the citizen militia to thicken up numbers within the Romanus towers. That ram had to be destroyed. If not, it would quickly take out the lower and the middle wall, then a siege engine could roll in behind it right up to the inner wall, and they would be truly *in cloaca maxima.*

Zeno appeared. Tarasicodissa Rousoumbladeotes. He saluted smartly this time.

"Not much happening on your end?"

"Sir. You said about mining activity. I reckon we're getting most of it, under the Blachernae Wall."

Aëtius nodded. The ground was softest to the north, near the Horn. But how did Attila know? Ah, he knew everything.

The din of battle and the clamor of frightened men arose behind them. Aëtius raised his voice. "You know about mining?"

"Some."

He coughed angrily on a lungful of dust. "There's a transverse passageway running from the palace cellars out beyond the walls. The Guard will show you. From there you'll have to countermine for yourself, left or right, depending on where you reckon they're coming in. Got it?"

"Sir."

"I don't think the Huns know much about mining, but you never know. And we're still not sure who their auxiliaries are these days." A massive punch from an onager missile struck nearby. First strike. Zeno flinched. Aëtius didn't. Dust clouded the air around them, but Aëtius yelled through it, "Like whatever bastards are operating their onagers right now. And I don't have to tell you what would happen if they made just one good tunnel into the city."

Zeno nodded. "There'd be a hundred Huns inside within a minute."

"And a hundred every following minute, too. It would bring us down as surely as the biggest missile strike. So it matters. Get to it. Find the tunnel, kill everyone inside, and then bring it down behind you. Go!"

Already the first small bands of tattooed horsemen were galloping in below, yowling, turning, and threading their way among the giant protective siege towers and loosing off little, lethal arrow storms for good measure.

It was time to fight back.

Aëtius shouted to the wolf lords and they let their arrows fly. It was a loose volley but one arrowhead struck home perfectly, a Hun warrior flying forward over the head of his crumpling horse and rolling into the dust. One of the wolf lords, tall Valamir, immediately strung another arrow and took aim, meaning to take out the warrior for good while he was briefly a stationary target. But before he could let fly, a second warrior galloped up and the fallen horseman vaulted to his feet, seized the back of his saddle, pulled himself up and they galloped clear. All in a single, faultless movement, almost quicker than the eye could see. Valamir slowly released his bowstring again, saving his arrow. He and the master general exchanged glances. Christ, those horsemen moved fast.

From away to the left came the doom-laden thump of a mighty onager missile hitting the outer walls, a puff of limestone white dust rising into the air. Another hammer blow, and even Aëtius momentarily clenched his fists. How would the hurriedly improvised walls survive against such a hammering? And how the hell could the Huns have become such good artillerymen so soon? Surely they had Vandal auxiliaries, renegade Teutons? One rumor even said that deserters from the lesser Western legions had gone over to them, believing the future lay with the Huns. Aëtius refused to believe it.

And then much, much worse. A concerted volley of missile strikes, huge boulders fired from machines still behind the siege towers, barely glimpsed yet, their titanic loads arcing in high and raining down calamitously all on the same point. That was skill. Men were crushed without even the time to cry out, and when the dust slowly cleared the outer and middle walls were already flattened across a whole stretch of the Lycus valley. The siege engines began to advance. This battle wasn't going to last the night. To confirm Aëtius's worst fears, instantly another volley of onager missiles hit the walls further along, taking them down in a dozen blows, a ruthless pummeling. Everything would depend upon the inner walls.

From below came desperate cries at the sight of the ram approaching the St. Romanus Gate. Tatullus was roaring, asses screamed as they dragged heavy loads, bringing up more ballista missiles; there was a clatter of running hobnailed feet, the rush of citizen militia with their pitiful wooden staves. In the hazy distance, a monotonous beat on a barbaric oxhide drum.

Aëtius raised his hand, and the tower commanders all along the walls read the signal and did likewise.

He hesitated and sent a prayer like an arrow heavenward.

He dropped his arm. "Fire!"

The artillery units initially wasted their missiles trying to take out individual galloping horsemen as they darted in across the broad terrace beneath the walls howling like animals, arched back in their saddles, grinning up at the shaken defenders behind their battlements, baring their berry-red teeth. Aëtius was onto them immediately, striding over, shoving Imperial Guardsmen out of his way to reach them, roaring up at the next tower.

"The horsemen may look frightening to you, soldiers, but they're not coming in just yet! They're trying to distract you. So ignore them! Take out the siege towers, you hear? Kill the siege towers!"

Tatullus echoed his commander's orders all along the walls in finest centurion style, with just as much volume and some extra color.

"You heard the general, ladies! Hit the fucking machines! I see any unit wasting missiles on those malodorous fucking horsemen out of Scythia, I'll break your fucking legs!"

He bore down on a single hapless artillery unit atop the Romanus Gate, and they quailed before him. They were good technicians, but they'd never felt the hot blast of a centurion's angry breath in their faces, and it focused their minds wonderfully. As Tatullus well knew, it was essential they feared him more than the enemy. He seized one fresh-faced youngster by the scruff of his neck and flung him back against the wall with the might of his right arm alone. The youngster gasped and cowered.

"Now get back on your fucking machine and line it up there!" Tatullus screamed, spit flying in their startled faces. "You can see the target, it's not exactly shy. *There!*"

Indeed, the attack tower was already looming over them, the rubble field of the collapsed lower walls already having been traversed with quick-laid planking and lightning-fast winching from the darting enemy.

Further along, more Huns were attacking without the complication of artillery. Aëtius spotted them immediately.

"Escalade!" he yelled in warning. "Wolf lords, to me!" and he dashed southward to the section being breached. A swarm of half-naked Hun warriors had rolled from their ponies to race across the moat on a dropped pontoon, the stretch of water proving as much of an obstacle as a broad puddle. "Complain about it later," Aëtius growled to himself. "Shout at the devil."

Jormunreik and Valamir ran with him, arrows already nocked to the bow.

"Station here," said Aëtius. "Hit them on the flank as they come across." He ran on.

The Huns came scrabbling over the collapsed lower walls, tripping and stumbling in the limestone rubble of their own creation. Immediately a short, hard volley of Gothic arrows slewed into them from the side and, close packed as they were, found many a target. But countless more warriors came on behind, daggers clamped between their teeth as they scaled the ruined walls, using their gleaming Hunnish *chekans* or cruel spiked hatchets to dig into the stone like climbers.

Aëtius ordered Captain Andronicus up with his century, and strung them along the battlements. "Escalade," he said by way of brief explanation. "Get ready to wash your spears."

The Gothic wolf lords kept up relentless volley after volley of long ashwood arrows, cutting into the flank of the advancing horde, but it barely slowed them. Somewhere back across the crowded plain Attila would be sitting his scruffy skewbald pony, oblivious of the deaths of individuals, his own, or the enemy's, and dreaming only of conquest.

Already the advancing Hun foot soldiers were across the exposed terrace below the inner walls. The defenders' arrows and even the wild stones and improvised missiles hurled by the citizen militiamen took a terrible toll on exposed heads and bodies, but they moved in a swarm, as planned and concerted as a colony of ants. A wily old warlord was with them, Geukchu, having crossed this far on a white horse, and he rode among them giving calm orders. The defenders tried again and again to take him but he seemed under magical protection. Faster than the eye could see, some six or eight Hun marksmen stood back from the swarm and fired small grappling hooks carrying the thinnest ropes of knotted hemp straight up into the air, only falling back when they were just across the battlements, perfectly pitched.

"Cut 'em away!" roared Aëtius. "Don't let 'em get up!"

The Palatine Guard followed his orders, but as soon as they leaned out to slash at the ropes, in came the Huns' covering fire. It was devastating: an instant barrage of three or four hundred arrows, immaculately aimed, scything in over the top of the wall and into the chests and faces of the desperate defenders. Men screaming, flailing, faces crimson, hands clutched to eyes and throats. Andronicus himself was stuck with an arrow in the shoulder, sinking down, snapping it off gasping. "Bastards," he murmured. There had to be more of a fight than that.

"Take them out!" roared Aëtius, desperate. "Kick away the hooks! Citizen militia, move down!"

But already the hooks were deeply lodged by Hun warriors coming up the ropes, not one of them cut. Knuckles saw the first Hun appear along the walls, and lumbered over to cave his skull in. But the Hun moved like a spider, vaulted over the battlements, dagger between his teeth but not even standing his ground to fight. You don't take a fortified city with an escalade of one. Moving at blinding speed, he kicked out and loosened the tough little grappling hook from the wall where it had lodged, checked that the rope it hung from was looped only once, nice and loosely, round the back of the merlon—Knuckles was upon him, swinging his club at the half-shaven and unhelmeted skull with a blow that would have killed a horse—and the warrior was gone. Not even looking, holding onto nothing but the little hook two-handed, he vaulted back over the walls to the ground below.

technically within the city, but with no access yet to a descent. Beyond, Aëtius could see the stricken, uncertain faces of the Imperial Guard, looking
across to him. What was he *doing*?

He was waiting.

Near him, Theodoric waited, too, long sword drawn.

"You'll use that to thrust."

"I will," said the prince grimly. "No room for cutting blows."

"Quite so." He roared down the walls to the Guard, "Hold it still!"

"You want the Huns densely packed," murmured Theodoric.

"You got it."

A few more agonizing moments, the Huns hardly able to believe that they
had taken an entire stretch of wall, and behind them more and more of their
comrades coming up the nets unopposed. To their right, one of their rams
was splintering in the gates, and the platforms of the gate towers themselves
would soon be flooded with more of their comrades from the approaching
siege tower. The city was as good as won.

Then they heard that hard-faced Roman general roar, "Now!"

From behind the Imperial Guard, holding the line rigid with fear, came
the sound of something creaking, being winched and lowered. Andronicus
told his men to brace themselves. They had their orders. Forward face.

It was Tatullus who led the rearguard attack, along with his old soldiers
from the ludicrous remnant of the VIIth, Knuckles and Arapovian and Malchus, and some of the hardier of the citizen militia, including a blacksmith
still in his apron and wielding his hammer for a weapon.

The Hun siege tower was built with a high drop bridge which would soon
fall across the battlements and admit a party of ferocious warriors with squat
round shields and short curved swords onto the high platform of the gate
tower, from where they would command the walls and worse, the steps leading down. Crazed with bloodlust and dreams of Byzantine gold, they were
unlikely to give up their position once they had taken it.

Tatullus faced the approaching siege tower with his billhook lowered. He
bellowed for more men at arms up here. These bird-brained artillery novices
had left it too late. This tower was going to get bloody very soon.

But the primal instinct of raw fear had finally galvanized the unwarlike
artillery technicians. In a few seconds of astonishing deftness, they had raised
the trajectories of their machines to face the head of the tower, not ten feet off

the walls now, and let loose. Serried metal bolts shot forward out of each shivering machine, flat and lethal, at speeds of more than fifty or sixty feet a second, or so the mathematicians of the imperial workshops had calculated. Those huge, straining torsion ropes could store an astonishing power. The flight of bolts drove straight through the raised drop bridge and anyone within. The sling balls simultaneously slammed into the side timbers, causing less damage to the occupants but at least as much terror. Rapidly assessing the situation, the slingers forsook their machines, took flaming pots and brands in their hands, and lobbed them across onto the roof of the siege tower, where they exploded into fire balls and began to burn the overhead timbers.

Tatullus almost guffawed. The artillerymen's initial dithering incompetence had actually drawn the Hun attack tower in too close, only to be suddenly blasted with this volley of heavy steel bolts at almost point-blank range, and then set afire to boot.

"And again!" he yelled, thumping his billhook furiously on the wooden deck. "Give 'em hell!"

Sweating with effort and dread, sweat both hot and cold running together, blinded until they wiped their faces clear with stained neckerchiefs, the artillerymen strained back on the well-oiled winches and reloaded the arrow firers, so finely manufactured and gauged by the best engineers and technicians in the city's Imperial workshops. They slotted in a new set of bolts, whose cross-ply steel heads no armor in the world could withstand, let alone mere timber walls, while Tatullus bellowed down to the citizen runners to bring more. The torsion ropes twisted and screamed, the nearest arrow firer swiveled on its base toward the siege tower, like some terrible steel animal with eyeless gaze, and then the bolts erupted from their ports again and drilled into the blank face of the tower. Inside there were more screams signifying carnage. The drop bridge had paused in being lowered, barely open.

"Fuck it," growled Tatullus. They had only killed the operators, when they wanted to get inside and slaughter the rest of them. He sensed a crazed stratagem and an invaluable morale booster rolled into one. Off to the south, another tower was disgorging its occupants onto the undermanned Military Gate IV, with only citizen militia to oppose them; likewise a further one on the Rhegium Gate. Below came another thump from the ram. There would be more work to do elsewhere soon enough, so they needed to get this finished.

"Let's get that drop bridge down now so we can cut 'em up inside! Knuckles, and you Parsee fancyman, get with me!"

Then he was up on the battlements and jumping, flying out across the gap between wall and tower, slamming into the wooden sides, clasping the rim of the drop bridge in his left hand, his right bringing his billhook back and ramming it repeatedly though the splintered front timbers and stabbing anyone who stood inside. Then he slashed overhead at the ropes of the dropbridge with such determined swipes that the ropes bristled and frayed in moments. The bridge fell with a mighty crash, Tatullus still hanging beneath it, forty feet above the ground and with Hun archers below gazing up, already nocking arrows to the bow. With the agility of an adolescent acrobat, this centurion of twenty years' service was back on the bridge like a cat, even as the the arrows thumped into the timbers beneath his feet, his billhook flailing in the open mouth of the tower head, holding the drop bridge alone for a moment. Then Arapovian and Malchus and Knuckles were with him again, the four survivors doing what they did best, fighting shoulder to shoulder against impossible odds.

The Hun ram drivers felt the gates suddenly heavier under the blows. The gang master galloped around lashing at them, but it was no good. Inside the city, the quick-thinking Isaurians under Zeno had realized what was happening and balked the gates with anything and everything they could find. Barrels of sand, rocks, massive timber props and, best of all, a wagon laden with stone. The ram could hammer away all it liked; it wasn't going to come through the Gate of St. Romanus any time soon. And as long as the Huns were still trying . . .

"Back to the walls!" growled Zeno, seizing one of the *mattiobarbuli* or weighted darts from behind his shield grip. The ram drivers would soon be targets themselves.

The tower head, prised open, exposed and blazing, revealed a mass of startled warriors ready to leap onto the city walls. A breeze blew, a breath of God's mercy, and the heat from the rooftop blaze gusted away from the defenders, dark smoke drifting away west over the mass of the Hun army out on the plains beyond. Somewhere, sitting his horse, Attila would see this: one of his attack towers already burning. The first setback. Soon there would come news to him of the ram's difficult progress, and then news of the mining operations having been shut down by an unexpected and ferocious underground attack.

There was a momentary stillness while Tatullus and his three men stared at the twenty Huns packed inside the tower head. Then they roared the old cry, "Six times brave, six times faithful!" and charged in.

The Huns were packed too close within the wooden walls. They were expectant, sweating, their red and black war paint already running in greasy streaks across their faces, trembling with battle madness, fire roaring above their heads, desperate to be out and free and fighting; ready to erupt across the drop bridge and fall on those thinly defended battlements like wolves. But they would never get that far. They were trapped in their wooden cave, backing up against tightly nailed timbers which their own slaves had built not days before. The din of battle was all around them, but immediately before them in the late afternoon sunlight stood the terrible figure of an iron-hard Roman soldier, of the kind they said no longer existed.

Pale blue, emotionless eyes burning like hard gemstones, a tight-fitting steel helmet like a bare metal skull, a long noseguard running down between those deep-set, implacable eyes, the Roman swung a monstrous billhook left and right like a scythe through dry grass. The warriors with their short swords couldn't get close to him, and none of them had brought bow and arrow. They cursed and howled, caught between the blazing fire above and the murderous blades before, limbs lopped off, arteries severed, chests and bellies opened and spilling, the enclosed space an infernal abattoir, a place of fire and blood. Behind the billhook came a huge man wielding a club, and an eastern swordsman, and some civilians and a couple more hard-looking soldiers in black armor. The Huns stabbed and fought as desperately as trapped rats, and one even made a dash for the edge of the drop bridge and hurled himself to a kind of safety forty feet below. But even as he leaped, the eastern swordsman slashed his weapon in a wide arc and cut him across the backbone, so that when he fell to earth below he was already dead. It was hopeless. Within a minute or two the Huns lay slaughtered in heaps within the tower head. Two of the Palatine Guard lay with them.

Along the wall the gathered Huns faced a jaw-like attack at both ends from the long spears of the wolf lords on their left and the Palatine Guard on their right. Their own numbers were vastly superior, but they realized in panic that this would not help. They were as good as trapped along the wall, and could offer no broader line of battle than the battlement walk allowed. They had packed themselves too tight. More and more warriors were still coming up the nets behind and squeezing through the embrasures to enter the fray, but there was barely space for them to drop down the other side, let alone swing a *chekan* or sword. Now suddenly there were disciplined forces hitting them either side, long spears lowered to gut height, forcing them together more closely still. Then the killing began, even as the Huns were still squabbling among themselves.

Inside the siege tower, Arapovian thought for a moment that his centurion had gone insane for, having slain all living men before him, he was attacking the rear wooden walls of the tower, jabbing at them ferociously with his mighty billhook, splintering timbers and kicking them out into the air where they wheeled and fell free, until the protective tower head was half destroyed.

"Pile in, you idle fuckers!" he yelled. "And you, blacksmith, get your hammer in there. I want this wall smashed down."

Still not understanding they piled in as ordered, the blood-boltered centurion still muttering about morale, eyes gleaming through a mask of other men's gore. "Good for our morale, bit of a downer for them." And as he kicked out the last of the rear timbers and exposed the tower head to the setting sun, Arapovian understood. Tatullus began to hurl the slathered bodies of the Hun warriors out of the tower head to the ground a long way below.

Knuckles booted the corpses out with his great feet, grumbling that they'd be under attack again at any moment. But it made a horrible and telling spectacle.

From the main Hun lines across the plains, from their restless horses, the waiting warriors saw comrade after slain comrade, the bodies of fathers and brothers and sons, mutilated and hacked to death, come wheeling back out of the attack tower, a grandstand view of savagery fully visible to all. Corpses flung out and falling, spraying gore from cut and missing limbs, crashing onto the besiegers below and pulped upon the hard ground.

Aladar rose up in his saddle on his fists and roared out at such theatrical cruelty. "Vengeance will rain down on them like blood!"

Attila said nothing but the set of his face was grim.

"Let them come and take their comrades home," growled Tatullus, throwing out the last of the slain. "Any come near, we destroy them."

It was foul and unforgiving, but it was the first hint that day that not everything might go the way of the heathen.

The other two attack towers further down the walls had been smashed and burned before they could drop their bridges. At the same time, the packed Huns who had gained the walls by escalade had been rolled up from either end in the furious two-sided onslaught, and their bodies tossed back over the walls. The net ropes were cut and dropped down after them, and the citizen militia thought to pour boiling oil down on them and then throw flaming brands after, so that the nets couldn't be used again without long and tricky repairs.

At last the walls were cleared. Hundreds of Huns had died that day, as many from falling as from fighting. Not one of them made it past the inner walls. Their mining operations had been ruthlessly sabotaged, and none of the attack towers had made it. Aëtius collapsed at last in the shadow of the battlements, pulled his helmet off and swiped the sweat from his face. His arm was almost too tired to lift. Spread out before him was the city they had fought so desperately to defend, the sinking sun gleaming on its myriad golden cupolas and spires. The Holy City of Byzantium. He smiled.

"My brother," said Torismond nearby, gasping. He pulled at Aëtius's arm. Aëtius wrenched it free again with weary irritability. "My brother," cried the prince more desperately, nearly sobbing. Suddenly Aëtius was alert again, dragging himself to his feet. The princes had fought as fiercely as any today, and their wolf lords had been crucial.

"Where is he?"

Torismond sobbed that he could not move. His arm . . .

"Come on," said Aëtius. "We'll get him to the Emmanuel Hospital."

Theodoric's wound was ghastly. Without analyzing why, Aëtius demanded the old trickster medic, Gamaliel. The hospital was not even full, the defenders' casualties had been so few. The old man came hurrying, gray gown gathered up round skinny white ankles. Aëtius and Torismond started talking at once, but he ordered them to be silent.

The wounded boy lay on his back, his face white as chalk, his forehead beaded with sweat, drifting in and out of the faintest consciousness. Gamaliel gently unwrapped the filthy rags used as emergency bandaging, saying nothing.

"He killed six or seven at least," said Torismond. "One burly fellow must have been twice as broad in the shoulder as my brother. Theo drove his sword right through him. But as the fellow died, he brought his sword down on Theo's arm and . . ."

He broke off and buried his face in the crook of his arm. Aëtius laid his hand on the boy's trembling shoulder.

Gamaliel said, "In amputation for gangrene, the crucial thing of course is to remove more bone and leave more soft tissue for better healing."

Torismond looked up, eyes bright with tears.

"However," said Gamaliel, "the boy is young, and God is merciful. It may not come to amputation, we cannot be sure. As the First Hippocratic Aphorism states, 'Life is short, art long, opportunity fleeting, experience fallacious, and judgment difficult.'" He smiled gently at the two exhausted soldiers and added softly, "I have always thought it a good guide to life in general. However," and his voice grew brisk again, "before resorting to the crude science of amputation, we shall trust to vascular ligature—unknown either to Hippocrates or that fool Galen, but widely practiced among the physicians of India—as well as the liberal application of egg yolk, rose oil, and turpentine, and those two great healers time and hope."

He said to Torismond, "You must sleep, boy. You can sleep here. When you wake again, talk to your brother. Even if he is unconscious, talk to him. Do you play a musical instrument?"

Torismond looked baffled. "A lute. Badly."

Gamaliel turned to Aëtius. "Get the lad a lute." And to Torismond he said, "Play the lute to him. Even badly."

There was one final chapter to this grueling day. Tatullus had roped up the half-destroyed siege tower with a couple of huge iron hooks, and with ropes long enough to reach the ground. A team of oxen waited in the cool of the evening shadows, nodding their heads. There was the sound of a whiplash, and the oxen were driven forward. The two mighty ropes stretched taut from the tower. The oxen bellowed under the lash, their hooves scrabbled. Dozens of citizens seized the quivering ropes as well, hauling as in a neighborhood tug-of-war. The huge siege tower creaked, tilted fractionally. Below it, still ramming under orders but no longer with any hope, the Huns glanced up and saw what was coming. The tower tilted further—a little further—and then the meridian was past and gravity did the rest.

Like a monstrous tree in a forest, felled by giants, the unmanned tower fell sideways with dreamlike slowness and crashed down onto the ram tortoise, smashing both itself and the tortoise to matchwood in twin destruction. The ram team had pulled away in time and not one was injured, but for their fighting spirit it was the last straw. They retreated and ran, along with the surviving warriors around them, back over the smashed middle and lower wall, crowding together to cross the pontoons. In their desperation some even flung themselves into the water.

In final farewell, the wolf lords knelt calmly at the battlements, unslung their bows and took out more of the fleeing enemy, one by one, silently and without mercy. No volleys, but a lethal, individual killing. For the besiegers, now in full flight across the plain, it was the first defeat they had ever tasted. When they reached their own lines, they heard that the Lord Attila had retired to his tent.

21

NIGHT AND RAIN

Aëtius was too tired to eat, but he drank water from a cup handed to him by a woman in the street. Without his helmet on, and caked with sweat and dust as he was, she didn't recognize him and called him "dearie." He drank, gave the cup back to her and thanked her politely.

Before a few hours of uneasy sleep, he talked with Tatullus, Malchus, and Andronicus, with Prince Torismond, who looked grave and sad, suddenly old for his years; and also with Zeno of the Isaurians, and one Portumnus, a plump burgher of fifty years of age who seemed to have appointed himself leader of the citizen militia. He would have to do, even though, as Aëtius reflected, those who appoint themselves leaders are rarely the best at it.

"It's been a good day," declared Malchus, wiping his encrusted sword and grinning. "They sustained a lot of losses. And not a few, I don't mind saying"—he held his sword upright and inspected its freshly shining blade—"by my own heroic hand."

Aëtius wasn't impressed. "They can *take* a lot of losses," he growled. "There are a hundred thousand of them out there. Today we killed, what, two or three hundred at most? We lost maybe a dozen men. That sounds fine, but they could fight for a year like they fought today, and still not worry about losses. Could we? They still teach you arithmetic in the cavalry, Captain Malchus?"

Malchus refused to look chastened, but he had no reply.

"Plus, two of our artillery machines are wrecked, and our walls have taken a bad pounding, and we have neither the men nor the energy to rebuild any more."

"The citizen bands fought like lions, though," said Portumnus.

Aëtius nodded, and even Andronicus grunted.

"But if we win this one—if we survive *at all*—we'll win up here." Aëtius tapped his head. "Today was the first day in Attila's reign of terror when he didn't get exactly the result he wanted. Not a defeat, no, but he must have seen his men streaming back across the plain, with nothing to show for their pains. He will be back again, of course. But tonight, some of his men will have begun to doubt him. He can only regain their faith in him by a crushing triumph over us, so he will come back harder than ever." His voice was thick with emotion, looking out over the small campfires of the Visigoths, Isaurians, Palatine Guard, and citizen bands. A brave but motley crew, and not one straight Roman legion with them. So it had come to this.

"But each day that his forces do not prevail against us, the Huns' confidence wanes and their strength ebbs. It is our one hope. We certainly cannot defeat them directly. We are too few."

The council of war brooded in silence on his words, and then they departed to sleep.

In his tent, Attila ground his teeth and glowered down at his fists. The day had been accursed from the start. He had always known that Constantinople would be no Viminacium, but he saw now that it was ten, a hundred times harder. They said this was the greatest fortified city in the world. Not even the cities of China had anything to compare with the walls of Constantinople. And now came the news that another of his beloved Chosen Men was fallen.

Old Chanat told him. "It was the Lord Juchi, Great Tanjou. He fell upon the battlements, run through by the sword of one of those Gothic princes fighting with them."

"I had him," hissed Attila, "that straw-haired German puppy, I had him before me in my very tent. At Azimuntium I could have destroyed him, destroyed them all. And when they came to our camp to parley, only to assassinate me like polecats in the night. I could have killed them."

"My lord is too merciful!" said Little Bird's singsong voice. "His heart is as tender as a young girl's. And oh, a young girl's heart will be the death of him!"

"Our brother Juchi," said Chanat, "took the prince's arm off as he died, or as good as—sliced it through."

"Would it had been his neck." Attila leaned forward, rested his elbows on his knees and buried his face in his mighty hands. "One by one my Chosen Men fall from me." His voice was low and muffled.

Chanat hesitated a while, then departed so as not to witness this unseemly grief. Little Bird twirled his hair ribbons, like an oblivious toddler beside its weeping mother.

Attila remained motionless on his wooden throne. Only Noyan was left of the four powerful brothers, the sons of Akal. Juchi slain by a pale-haired Visigothic boy. Bela bludgeoned and drowned at Margus Bridge. Then there was eager young Yesukai, bright eyed, loyal, and unquestioning as only the young can be—he had been the first to die. How long ago it seemed. How far to the east, unimaginably far, many months' ride east upon the steppes into the heart of Asia, and long, long years ago. There was the time he set off a covey of partridges, just outside the camp of the Kutrigur Huns, and nearly got them all killed. The fool. Attila smiled though his eyes were sad and swimming with memories. Yesukai died fighting those same Kutrigur Huns, died that the Kutrigur Huns and the people might come together in glorious conquest. Attila could picture him now as he lay dying, young Yesukai, an arrow through his arm and into his chest, Chanat cradling his head.

Let the vultures cry it among the Tien Shan, Let the winds tell it over the Plains of Plenty, Let the rains fall year long on the green grasslands in mourning for Yesukai!

And now let the vultures cry and the skies weep for Juchi, too, and for Bela. For Csaba also, perhaps, so grievously wounded below the walls of Viminacium in his battle madness, and half mad from that day to this. But that accursed traitor and deserter Candac, let there be no weeping for him.

There were left only his ever-faithful Orestes, and old Chanat, and Geukchu, and lonesome Noyan. And Rome still so far away.

Aëtius had enjoyed all of three hours' sleep, on a rough straw pallet in the guard room of Military Gate V, when he was awakened by wild shouts. Still exhausted, he felt he was still dreaming when he stepped out onto the dark battlements to see that another full attack was under way. Attila was using their own tiredness to destroy them. How could they fight another battle, by night, after a day such as they had just endured?

But fight they must.

It was like a dream for the exhausted defenders on the walls. As in a dream they saw the great siege engines rumbling toward them through the night, and the flames of ten thousand torches, and in the torchlight came the flash of arrow and the glint of iron arrowheads in the midnight air, and the cry and fall of men to the ground below. There were distant juddering thumps of onager strikes against stonework, and the slow crack and susurrus of collapsing masonry. In reality, they could not win again. Not now. But perhaps in a dream . . .

The Huns were attacking by escalade again, too, against the Palatine Guard and whatever armed citizens were still stout hearted enough to stay and fight, strung out along three miles of walls. Though the Huns came up in their hundreds, and even their thousands, the slash of soldierly swords and the cruder bludgeon of improvised citizen weapons made their progress over the walls slow and bloody indeed. On the ground below, the bodies of Huns slain in the cruel ascent of that implacable forty-foot cliff piled up like summer flies.

From away to the south came the sound of a more resonant, wooden thump, and the defenders knew another gate was being rammed again.

"Isaurians!" roared a deep voice. There was the steady trot of the mountain men, and Zeno once again led them into the breech.

Everywhere there were burning torches, and out on the plain the Huns had built huge beacon fires, for no military purpose, it seemed, but to illuminate for the dispirited defenders the vast numbers of the enemy. But Master General Aëtius was everywhere at once, striding, roaring, gesticulating, harshly joking, and seeming anything but dispirited.

Knuckles eyed the beacons balefully. "Very kind of them, I'm sure," he growled, then looked prayerfully heavenward. "Come, friendly gods, and piss their fires out."

Nearby, the more orthodox Arapovian crossed himself and slid another arrow onto his bow.

The Huns were at every gate now, stacking up oil-soaked bundles of dry reeds and looted haybales. Soon those gates would be burned to wood ash, and the warriors would come in at every entrance. But the citizen bands were teeming up to the walls in ever greater numbers as panic spread through the city. They poured water onto the brushfire stacks and hurled missiles onto Hunnish heads, a primitive but terrible rain. At gateway after gateway the besiegers were driven back, until finally the defenders at the Rhegium Gate, hammered into an impromptu fighting company by Malchus, leading from the front as always, were actually able to shove their own gates open and make a defensive sortie, driving the Huns away in disorder before their grimly marshalled lines, and dragging free the deadly oil-soaked stacks. They bundled them back over the middle wall onto the lower *peribolos,* and then flung a flaming brand onto the pyre, burning it uselessly far from their own gates. They ran home to mighty cheers from the walls, and the great wooden barriers slammed shut behind them. Not one citizen of that hardy crew was hurt.

On the walls above the Lycus the escalade was densest, and there the best of the fighters stood together through the night. Roaring defiance, Tatullus slashed his billhook across faces and throats as they appeared atop the nets, then jabbed downward, splitting skulls, severing heads from shoulders. Arrows clattered around the defenders in the darkness but it was hard even for Hun archers to shoot the enemy and not their own, fighting in such close combat and at night. Time and again a Hun warrior screamed and fell back from a net or a ladder, a black-feathered arrow of his comrades in his back, until eventually one of the Hun generals gave the order to cease firing. The Gothic wolf lords, meanwhile, continued to return fire into the densely packed besiegers as ruthlessly as ever.

Captain Malchus was soon back from the Rhegium Gate, anxious not to miss out on the fighting, his sword swirling and slashing, his eyes gleaming mad and white out of a mask of blood. He was even heard to yell, "This is the life!" And there was Andronicus slashing and stabbing by his side—the two were like brothers—and repeating low and sonorously as if it were a dark refrain from the Byzantine liturgy. "You shall not take this city, you shall not have it, not one of you shall pass. . . ."

The stars had vanished from the sky; only sparks illuminated the black-clouded vault of heaven. From the heart of the city, even now, there came the voices of priests and deacons chanting psalms, and it was to the sound of this sublime and serene plainsong that the men of war fought on.

Near the Blachernae Walls, the Isaurian auxiliaries identified more underground tunnelling taking place. Attila was trying everything, every trick simultaneously, believing that night and numbers were on his side, and the city
must be won soon.

"You haven't time to countermine," said Aëtius desperately. "Drop the
column drums on 'em!"

The great marble cylinders that he had had stowed along the battlements
at regular intervals were rolled out, craned up onto the walls, and dropped
onto places where the tunnelers' activities had been felt. The huge weights
thumped down into the ground below, sank half buried, and caved in the
tunnels beneath. It was crude, temporary, but effective. A group of Palatine
Guard rolled one of the precious column drums down onto an approaching
ram and its team, resulting in comprehensive obliteration.

Everything needed to be done lightning fast, every new variety of assault
needed to be met with an instant reaction, still more ruthless and violent
than the assault itself. Thanks to Aëtius's foresight, his energy and commanding presence, again and again the Huns were met by just such savage resistance. It was the last thing they had been led to expect, and already a few
were voicing doubts.

Some went further. From beneath a monstrous pile of Kutrigur Huns near
Military Gate IV, a survivor came crawling, slathered red in his own and his
comrades' blood. He knelt below the walls of Constantinople, clutching his
near-severed right arm to his chest, seeming oblivious to the arrows that
hissed around him. Instead he raised his head and looked up to the starless
sky, blinded with blood, and howled with such fury that his words carried far.
"Astur curse you, Great Tanjou Attila! Astur damn you, Attila son of Mundzuk! Lord Widow Maker! World ravisher! Blood worm!" An arrow struck
him in the thigh, yet he barely stirred, continuing to gaze heavenward open
mouthed, panting. Eventually, grim-faced old Chanat strode out from behind
the middle wall and cut his head off. Yet his words had been heard, by attacker and defender alike.

Still the Huns continued to ascend the walls, fast as quicksilver, lassoing
the battlements, swinging themselves up like acrobats in a circus.

"Like Barbary apes up the cliffs of fuckin' Gibraltar," as Knuckles put it,
clubbing another one down.

But the pace of the battle was slowing. For each fresh wave of Hun warriors, the greatest obstacle before the walls was the slippery heaps of their own dead. This was not, as Aëtius observed, good for their morale. Another ram was smashed, the siege engines were either burned or stuck fast amid jagged hillocks of rubble and broken walls, and the onagers, too, had fallen into dismayed silence. Aëtius leaned on the battlements and checked along the ranks. His men stood firm. No arrows came in.

"We've broken them," muttered Tatullus. Centurion and general exchanged glances, both thinking the same: for now; but they will come again. And again. And again.

With their numbers thinning, and the coherence of their command structure going, the Huns resorted to individual heroics, which only caused them greater casualties. Vainglorious adolescents came galloping wildly across the mess of rubble, breaking their horses' legs beneath them, leaping free, yowling and flailing their whips. Most of the nets had been cut free and burned, so these last-ditch attackers tried to cast their lassos high enough to noose the battlements and swing themselves up. One of them dangled half way up the wall, a dagger between his teeth.

Aëtius rapped out an order to the nearby artillery unit. They swiveled their arrow firer at an enfilading angle and punched two heavy bolts into the dangling warrior. One of the bolts cut him through the spine, and he hung there noosed by his own lasso, head back, mouth open, sightless.

Aëtius went over and cut him down himself. The youth, perhaps fifteen or sixteen summers old, slithered back and lay splayed almost shapeless on the stones below, no longer in the shape of man or youth or any thing. Aëtius turned away. How foul was war.

He felt something on his bare arm.

Tatullus said, "It's rain."

Aëtius turned his face up to the cleansing waters of heaven and prayed with closed eyes. The fires of the Huns began to sizzle softly, and then the rain grew heavier and they smoked and began to die, and darkness fell over the crowded plain.

He went to inspect the walls, overseeing hurried rebuilding and blockading here and there.

Gamaliel came to find him.

"The boy?"

Gamaliel nodded and smiled, drawing his long wet locks back from his cheeks. "Both he and his right arm will survive."

Aëtius exhaled, as if he had been holding his breath all this time.

"He will have a fine old scar to prove his manhood, though."

In his tiredness Aëtius forgot formality and grasped the old vagabond's scrawny hand and shook it. "Thank God, thank God," he muttered. Gamaliel laid his other hand over Aëtius's, looked into his eyes, and saw the passion burning beneath the iron control, and the gentleness beneath the soldierly steel. They parted again. There was work to do.

"By the way," Gamaliel called after him, "this rain." Aëtius turned. "It will do the Huns in their camp no good. Standing puddles, mosquitoes, even this late in the year. . . ."

Aëtius frowned. "Mosquitoes? Annoying little buggers, sure, but I don't think they'll bother the Huns too much."

"Well," said Gamaliel, "I do have a theory. . . . In any case, rain and foul air and camp fever go together."

"Damn right. By my reckoning, our besiegers are going to need around nine thousand gallons of drinking water and thirty tons of fodder every day, and their people and livestock between them will produce about a hundred tons of shit a week. You can work it out. Such unsavory and unheroic facts can win whole wars. They're going to poison themselves out there. Meanwhile, I want this city kept as clean as marble. In fact," he added, "when you're done in the hospital, you can check the streets and make sure all's well. Organize the civilians; speak to that Portumnus. Good clean water, no refugees sleeping rough, sewers clear, all bodies burned. Any incidence of plague or dysentery, isolate the victims immediately and report back to me. Yes?"

Gamaliel was already gone.

Not long before dawn the Huns came again in another wave. They didn't trouble with unwieldy siege engines this time, only a vast, two-mile long escalade with nets and light cane ladders, hoping to achieve victory against the exhausted defenders through lightning speed and sheer bravado. But the Palatine Guard and the auxiliaries were as indefatigable as ever, the Gothic wolf lords seemed to be men of iron, and the civilian bands would not even forsake the walls to allow fresh reinforcements to take their place. Already battle bloodied, though trembling with fatigue and showing many a wound, their confidence was higher than before, their self-belief a powerful weapon in itself. When the sun rose, they had saluted it in greeting, as a brother. Heaven and earth were both with them.

The Huns surged up the walls and met a solid blockade of men and blades. Here and there they did break through, but could still not build on it and capture a single tower. In the thickest of the fighting Knuckles found himself surrounded, his club knocked from his hand, and a lean, wiry Hun pulling back his spear to drive it into him. Then the Hun reeled and arched, his back sliced open by Arapovian behind. In the space of three blows, the silent, implacable Armenian had kicked the slain Hun off the parapet, knocking one of his fellow Huns askew as he fell. Arapovian drove his sword into him as he stumbled, a light but effective stab, so as to draw the blade free again in time to parry a mighty swashing blow from a third attacker, an ugly painted Kutrigur, his teeth blood red and filed to carnivorous points. Arapovian spun out of reach of his heavy blade, then ducked back and rose up at his side to behead him where he stood. The rest of the Hun bridgehead was taken apart from behind by six Imperial Guards working in close order, spears held low, and their bodies tossed back over the wall.

Knuckles was down on all fours, shaking his head like a wet dog. He clambered to his feet a little blearily. One side of his face was caked with blood, his thatched hair matted and shiny.

"You need attention," said Arapovian, retrieving the Kutrigur Hun's head from where it lay at his feet, staring up at him with a perplexed expression, and tossing it over the wall.

"Not before I've thanked you profusely for so heroically coming to my rescue, my lissom Parsee playmate," rumbled Knuckles, touching a great paw to the side of his dented skull and staring down at his wet, red fingertips. "I do 'ope you think it's worth it, in the long run. You must have trained as a dancer in the theater, the way you skipped around that lot."

Arapovian looked haughty.

"Very noble of you anyway, I'm sure. Thought I was a goner there. And I've lost me club."

"You'll find it down below," said the Armenian. "On your way to the hospital."

"All right, all right, I'm going to get myself stitched. By the way," he added as a parting shot, "there's some more of 'em coming up behind you. Best turn round."

And the stained eastern sword blade flashed in the air once more.

Knuckles was back with bandaged head and rescued club within ten minutes, fighting alongside Tatullus close to the north side of Military Gate V. They fought in a relentless duet of club and billhook as of old, still fired by the memory of Viminacium and their fallen comrades. Knuckles grunted and roared and swore, raining down colorful curses.

"You barbarous fuckin' horse fucker, eat that! Here, you, come and get a fuckin' headache! I got one off one of your lot like you wouldn't believe! You wriggling little fucker, keep still while I brain you! Now fuck off back over the wall. Gah!"—lurching forward and caving in another skull.

Tatullus fought in silence, jaws grimly clenched, steel helmet lowered, forearms like oak and those deepset eyes even and unblinking as his billhook cut a murderous swathe through unarmored men, a true veteran unperturbed by screams of the dying. When a stray arrow fired from an agile climber pierced the brass-studded leather guard protecting his left shoulder and stuck fast, he neither cried out nor even turned his head. Pausing only to break off the shaft and toss it clear over the wall, he pressed forward to slash and slash again, like some nightmarish iron automaton dreamed up by a Jewish cabbalist in the smoke-filled inventiveness of his hermit cell, created out of the fires of his furnace while chanting of Adonai and Jahweh and the Elohim and all the ten thousand names of God.

Suddenly they were gone.

The attack was over.

Only then were the defenders overcome by their unspeakable weariness. Men sank down behind the battlements, almost too exhausted to pull their helmets from their sweat-drenched heads. Aëtius ordered food and water to the walls.

He saw Knuckles's bandaged head. "You, Rhinelander. You might get a *corona obsidionalis* for breaking a siege, if we all come out of this alive."

"Thank you, sir, but I'd rather rather have a cup of wine right now, if it's all the same to you."

"I thought you didn't drink?"

Knuckles gawped at the master general's astonishing memory for detail. Then he said, "Well, sir, I admit that there was that unfortunate incident with the fishmonger's daughter at Carnuntum, whose sordid details I'd rather not burden you with, sir, begging your pardon, as they might put you off your dinner. Suffice it to say that, although I did then take a pledge to stay off the booze for a good while thereafter, I . . ." Knuckles tailed off.

The general was walking away, not having quite the leisure needed to hear Knuckles out when he was in full flow. But he called back over his shoulder to one of the runners, "Get that man a bucket of wine. A *horse* bucket," he added with a flash of a grin.

He resumed his station on the tower of Military Gate V, and exhaustion hit him like a wall. He could barely stand. But he could not sleep. There was too much to do. He ate only dry bread and drank water. Tatullus and Captain Andronicus of the Guard came to him. Now the fighting was finished and the rush of blood had subsided, they, too, looked beyond exhaustion, and the light was gone from their eyes. He knew how they felt. This did not feel like victory, and there was no cause for wild celebration. Not yet. This felt only like temporary survival. Out there on the plains, Attila still crouched like some beast of prey ready to spring, with his vast army diminished by all of one or two thousand men.

Now it was time for Aëtius to hear their own losses.

Of the two companies of Imperial Guard, one hundred and sixty men in all, over sixty were dead and another forty or so wounded beyond fighting. That ratio alone spoke volumes; and that percentage. Well over half the Palatine Guard was destroyed, and every single one of them had shed blood this last day and night. For Attila, though, those piles of Hun dead at the foot of the walls were only a fraction of his forces. Of the forty-four wolf lords, only three were slain, and three lay in the Emmanuel Hospital. Astonishing figures, and no reflection of the bravery with which they had fought, all day and all night, unrelenting. Even Andronicus was forced to admit that they had taken so few casualties because they were such skilled and ferocious fighters. Flaxen-haired giants, they fought like lions.

As for the eighty Isaurian auxiliaries, again, more than half were dead or else wounded beyond fighting. Their active numbers were down to thirty. Of the citizens who had given their lives for their beloved Holy City—ordinary men, fathers, husbands, brothers, sons, men whose only skill in life was to bake bread, or hammer horseshoes, or even trim beards—the number slain was beyond reckoning.

Down there below them, those slaughtered heaps of feathered and tattooed wild men, who had fought virtually naked, tooth and claw, howling in a language that none but Aëtius himself understood—they, too, were fathers, husbands, brothers, sons. It was too terrible. It was nothing but loss and waste. This was the time, when the battle ebbed and stilled awhile, that grief could overwhelm even the strongest man. What had they fought each other for, these fathers and sons? What had it all been about?

Aëtius, Tatullus, and Andronicus stood silently side by side on the tower, watching unarmed Huns returning under the burning midday sun to retrieve their dead and take them back for decent mourning and burial. It was a foul task which would take hours. Aëtius did not need to give the order not to fire on them. None of the defenders would be so cruel. He bowed his head. His heart was like a stone with sorrow.

Behind them, one of the guards suddenly muttered, "Oh my God, no."

The three exhausted men turned round.

Turning round also to look back across the city they had fought so courageously to defend, their backs to the armies of Attila, all along the walls exhausted men were sinking down to their knees, dropping their weapons, calling on the name of Christ and weeping openly. For the Holy City was lost.

The air was still, distant smoke rising into the autumnal air, the sun bright on the city's rain-washed golden domes, starlings still wheeling about the spires, the monks still chanting the *Kyrie*, sweetly oblivious. Away to the east, near the Imperial Palace itself, tall flames were licking up into the pale September sky like flames going up from a pyre.

22

ST. BARBARA GATE

S ir," cried a runner, appearing up the side steps, his hobnailed sandals ring-ing on the stone. "News from the city, sir."

Aëtius said, "We can see."

The Huns were inside the city after all, and all was lost. They had made it, tunnelling in under the walls, or perhaps by treachery, an unremarked pos-tern gate unlatched for them by some craven Byzantine Judas for thirty pieces of silver. Already the eastern end of the city was burning. Soon they would hear the distant cry and wail of the people. The soldiers and citizens on the walls could not speak, gazing out over the suffering city aghast. All they had fought for was finished. My God, my God, why hast thou forsaken us? It is finished.

Beyond that, all of Asia was finished, too. There was nothing left to op-pose the Huns' murderous progress. Rome did indeed stand alone, her sister city destroyed, and her inevitable destiny, as Aëtius could well judge now, inscribed in stone. They themselves, the last of the few, were effectively sur-rounded, attackers before and behind, and this battered wall a mere promon-tory in a sea of blood. The city they had fought so hard to defend was already taken. Words came back to him from the past: "You are fighting for a cause that is already lost."

He, Tatullus and Andronicus gripped their sword hilts tightly. Captain, centurion, master general of East and West: all three would die like common bloody soldiers today, shoulder to shoulder, and proud of it.

Surely it was the Imperial Pala e itself that was burning? Aëtius's eyes were bright with emotion and despair. The view was increasingly obscured by a thickening pall of funeral smoke, but somewhere in that palace was the woman he loved—had always loved. He saw the scene. Tattooed warriors howling down marble corridors, priceless statues thrown down and broken, mosaics smashed, cloth-of-gold tapestries cut to ribbons and burned, prayer books, gospels, and missals spat on and abused, slaves hung from hooks, or bound to pillars and used for target practice, maidservants raped and murdered, debauched even where they lay groaning in their own blood. The emperor pitifully down on his knees, babbling and pleading. She, the young, brilliant, bright-eyed daughter of Leontes of Athens, so full of youthful innocence and hope when he first saw her, now ravished and slain.

With his very last ounce of strength, Aëtius shouted the summons: "All men standing, to me!"

It was still just possible they might find her . . . a rescue . . . a seaward escape . . .

The three hurried down the steps to inspect the gathering men, a pitiful scraping of less than a hundred, badged with wounds, hollow eyed, sleepwalking into nightmare. Aëtius did not even heed the arrival of a second runner.

"Sir, news from the St. Barbara Gate," he panted.

So that was where they had come in. From the sea, after all. With the aid of their Vandal allies? It could be.

"Company!" he cried out. "Forward!"

The few surged into a fast trot, every sinew crying out against it.

"Sir," gasped the runner, only a youngster, trotting alongside, "the Vandal fleet is destroyed."

Through what felt like smoke inside his head, the words slowly penetrated. Aëtius called the halt, and stared at the runner. The fellow was still panting.

"Repeat," he rasped.

"The Vandal Fleet . . . mouth of the Golden Horn . . . burning."

It was like a slow dawn coming up. A slow, beautiful dawn over a desolate, frozen plain.

"The city is not taken?"

The runner frowned. "Not that I know of, sir."

The men had already broken formation, against all the rules, and were crowding round.

"Speak, man, for God's sake!" roared Tatullus, close to skulling the poor wretch with the butt of his short sword.

The runner spoke rapidly. "The defenders attacked the approaching fleet with everything they had—clay pots of quicklime, serpents, scorpions, chains and flails, spiked sling balls, anything that might cut through the rowers' overhead screens. They also moved operations up to the roof of the Church of St. Demetrius, despite the priests' objections. The Vandal ships tried to pull back, only to find themselves crammed up against the Great Chain with a following wind, and having trouble getting back out. The attack took them by surprise. And then the defenders launched another kind of weapon. There was this great flash, and at the same time, the St. Barbara Gate was . . . sort of . . . *singed*—but also a great sheet of flame shot out across the water and hit the nearest couple of ships. It was as if the flames were actually *clinging* to the timbers. The sails went up like oil paper, sir, and what with the following wind—only a light breeze off the Bosphorus, really, but enough—the rest of the Vandal ships soon caught fire as well. That's them," waving eastward, "still burning."

Aëtius was suddenly racing back up the steps to the platform of Gate V, the runner and the men all hurrying after, still stunned and silent, but a light beginning to shine again in their eyes.

The general waved toward the palace. "So the city's not burning?"

"Only"—the runner coughed, as if slightly embarrassed—"only the St. Barbara Gate, sir, a bit. But . . . but the enemy fleet is all but destroyed, many of their sailors and marines killed in the firestorm, and even when they leaped into the water, it was like a holy miracle, sir, they—"

"Don't tell me," said Aëtius in a low voice. "They continued to burn. So maybe not all Cretans are liars after all."

Then he did a most ungeneral-like thing. He threw his right arm around the lad's shoulders, hugged him, ruffled his hair, and kissed the top of his head like he was his son, and said he'd be getting a gold *solidus* before the day was out. The boy looked pink and pleased, and a huge roar went up from the men, and all along the walls. From the houses people slowly emerged, and from the churches came priests, and from the hospital came the shuffling figure of Gamaliel, suddenly looking old now, but his eyes dancing, and with him several bandaged and faltering figures on crutches. And then everyone was cheering.

"But, sir, I must emphasize," said the lad, determined to transmit his message in its solemn entirety, "that the St. Barbara Gate is very badly compromised."

At that grave news, Aëtius said something about Huns swimming as well as cats, and bugger the St. Barbara Gate, and began to laugh, his eyes watering, slapping his comrades on the back, chest heaving, face running with tears, all decorum gone.

More messages came. The emperor and empress sent greetings, and bade them all give thanks for God's mercy.

"Always nice to be appreciated," growled Knuckles, jabbing the ground with his club.

"The alchemist, the Cretan, what's his name, Nicias," demanded Aëtius. "He's still with us?"

"He is, sir, and drunk with victory."

"Let him stay that way. Meanwhile, we must get news of this to the Huns. Any setback to their allies is a bonus to us."

"Sir," said the runner, "a Hun war party was spotted on the hills above Galata during the sea battle."

"Observing, you mean? You think they saw?"

"They must have done, sir. They'd left by the end of the show."

Aëtius grinned. "Spread the news." He broke into a stride again, his voice rising, his energy renewed. "All church bells to ring twenty-eight full peals! Spread the word throughout the city. A massive naval battle has been fought off the Horn, our Vandal enemies have been driven before the fiery Breath of God, our gallant artillerymen and our ingenious men of science have triumphed over a flotilla of thousands. You're runners and heralds, for God's sake! Run and herald! Publish the news! The Battle of Constantinople is already half won. Scram!"

Among the soldiers, the outburst of joy subsided into tired grins all round.

"That's marvelous, sir!" said Malchus. "The battle half won already!"

Aëtius drawled, still grinning despite his words, "Of course it's not, you dolt—that's absolute bollocks. The Vandal ships were never more than a sideshow. The battle's less than a hundredth won. But morale is everything. Now, back to your posts."

Hobnailed boots rang on stone. "Sir!"

No more Hun attacks came that afternoon, and toward evening the sky clouded and it drizzled again. In the graying light, Aëtius stood on the tower and gazed out. A mosquito hummed nearby. He slapped his neck. Heavy clouds rolled in from the south, the wind got up, and it began to rain harder. He flung an oiled woolen cloak round his aching shoulders. The rain drummed the plains to an indistinct mist. Tonight he might actually get some sleep.

An hour later, and the rain still fell. Out there beyond the moat, its surface stippled like pewter by the rain, the Huns' ten thousand tents were camped amid mud and swamp. Many bodies had been burned, but many of the Hun dead still lay round about. The stench must be awful in that rough camp. Was it wrong to pray to the God of Love to bring pestilence on men? Yet remember the plagues of Egypt, Aëtius prayed.

23

THE SICKNESS

In his tent Attila sat glowering, digesting the news that the Vandal fleet had been destroyed. No, it was no more than a sideshow, but it was damnable news nevertheless. Astur's punishment, perhaps, for his beloved people having allied with Teutons, ancient enemies? But Attila refused to believe that. All the world would be united under his rule one day. Astur still spread his mighty wings over their heads. The sword of Savash still shone brightly. Attila himself liked to forget its spurious provenance, and treated that sword as a holy thing. So faiths grow.

A warrior appeared in the tent door, crouching low. Attila glared at him. All news was bad news these days.

"Speak."

"The Lord Aladar, Great Tanjou. He has the shivering sickness."

This, too.

In a matter of hours, it seemed, the pestilence had swept through the camp. Unaccustomed to living so densely packed together amid so many numberless tents, unaccustomed to stagnation, accustomed only to the rapturous solitude of the clean and windswept plains, the Hun people found living in a foul-smelling city of felt and canvas disgusting. And their bodies sickened from it along with their souls.

Attila had summoned their families from the north before the frozen Scythian winter, to join them here on the plains and witness their victory. Living like the barbarians of old, warriors, ancients, women and children all together; a mighty host of perhaps half a million, stripping the land bare, looting and pillaging for their daily bread, and yet there was never enough. Hunger and pestilence stalked the camp. The rivers were foul with their refuse. Now many, even the strongest of the warriors, lay sick with fever in their tents, vomiting and shaking uncontrollably. Then within hours, unbelievably, though it seemed they had done no more than drink too much kumiss, or eat bad meat, the next thing they were dead. Widows wailed, pyres burned, and the news kept coming to Attila. He turned away. The enemy must not know. Did they not suffer, too, behind their city walls?

The pyres grew larger, the dead were many, and more of the people were falling ill by the hour. How could this be happening, beneath the great protective outspread wings of Astur the All Father? Yet the air was heavy, and the wings of the Eagle God stretched from horizon to horizon were a louring gray. They did not seem wings to give shelter to men. The witch Enkhtuya recited many spells and performed many shadowy rituals. For a while the rain ceased and the sun shone, and the mosquitoes hummed by night, and at dawn under the rising sun the wet earth and the befouled rivers stank the worse; and then the rain came again. How the people longed for the peace of the dry and windy plains.

Now the Lord Aladar was sick, handsome Aladar, with his seven wives too many.

"And, Great Tanjou," said the warrior, still crouched, his voice hesitant and afraid, "Queen Checa."

Attila raised his head, his deep-set eyes unblinking, his thoughts inscrutable.

Queen Checa lay on her back with her eyes barely open, her fine, high-cheekboned face drawn into a tightness painful to behold. Attila ordered the women out and knelt by her side. He was in there all night and all the next day. That was why the Hun attack on the city came to a halt. The siege no longer seemed to concern him. His remaining generals, old Chanat, Geukchu, Noyan, and Orestes, awaited their orders. But none came.

At dusk the king emerged from the queen's tent and stood outside a while, breathing heavily, looking at the ground.

Orestes eventually went to him. He knew what had happened. He was still framing in his mind what he might say—what worthless consolation he might give—for Attila had loved his first wife very much. She had married him when he was no more than an exiled and penniless prince by birth, a bandit chieftain by trade, and she had stayed with him all those bitter years, bearing him sons and daughters, riding with him, salving and tending his many wounds. There had been a deep, unspoken love between them.

Before Orestes could speak, Attila shrugged his powerful shoulders, raised his head and said, "All men must die. And all women, too." Then he strode away.

Checa was buried without great ceremony at the edge of a flattened orchard. Attila showed no emotion, but a light had gone from his eyes.

Aladar, too, lay on his sickbed, his eyes red rimmed, his face streaked with sweat, his fine long raven hair plastered to his cheeks.

Chanat entered his tent.

"Father," he murmured.

Chanat knelt beside him. His rib cage heaved with sobs.

Aladar became agitated. "Father, I see such terrible things." He tried to sit up, but was too weak. His voice rasped hoarse and desperate. "I see this tent on fire. I see the whole world on fire. I see the people crucified all along a barren track across a desert. I see even Astur himself"—his voice shuddered—"a great eagle, with an arrow—"

"Hush, boy, hush," said Chanat, laying his rough hand across his son's forehead. "It is the fever. It is all a fever dream."

Slowly the agitation subsided, and when Aladar spoke again his voice was calm, though he still fought for every breath. "Father," he said, "let me not die in sickbed. Let me not die like a woman in childbed."

Chanat clasped his son's hands in his own and bowed his head and nodded.

Then he called the wives in, and had them bathe their lord one last time, and anoint him with oil, and comb his long hair and his fine black mustache. They dressed him in his finest robe, as he stood clinging to the tent post for support, ashen faced, his vision swimming, his forehead running with sweat, breathing in short, painful gasps. At last he was dressed. He kissed each of his wives chastely on the top of their heads, and commended his sons and daughters to their care, and was helped outside by his aged father.

His mother wept and would not be comforted, trying to cling to him, though if she had he would have fallen like a day-old fawn. In the end she dropped to the earth and buried her face in the dust, her sobs terrible to hear. Two of Aladar's wives came with little bowls of red and black paint, and brushed his hair back and decorated his face with the symbols of war.

A mounting block was brought and he was helped up into his wooden saddle by his peers, Orestes and Noyan. He rode the finest white horse of the eastern steppes. He clasped the reins in his left hand, and they handed him a spear which he clasped in his right. His father mounted another horse and reined in beside him. Aladar's head was bowed and he sagged in the saddle.

"My son," said Chanat softly, his eyes bright with tears.

Aladar stirred himself, and bade his mother and his wives and comrades "*bayartai*," the farewell to those one will see no more. He raised his head and straightened in the saddle, gazed heavenward into the Eternal Blue Sky, and held his spear aloft. "It has been good to ride with the Lord Attila all these years!" he cried. "Bless you, Great Tanjou! In the name of Astur and Savash and the Lady Itugen and all the gods, this is a good day to die."

His spear dropped down again, his arm trembling with the effort. Then father and son rode out of the camp, the wives and concubines kneeling on the ground, wailing and throwing dust over their heads. The Lord Attila himself did not appear from his tent, but the people lined the way in silence, for such reverence do a noble people feel for death.

The rain had ceased again, and the two horses splashed through shallow puddles gilded by the setting sun, their tails swishing. Ahead loomed the high walls of the city, the foreground strewn with the wreckage of broken walls and engines and mounds of the slain yet unburied.

As they neared the walls the two warriors saw men stir and rise behind the battlements. Chanat raised his right arm and Aladar his left, and they clasped hands above their heads, and gave the battle cry. Then they dug their heels into their horses' flanks, and the beasts reared, whinnying, came down and broke into a canter, then a gallop.

Aëtius was watching from the walls.

Arapovian said, "The warrior on the right, I know him. It's the old general who met us on the road, the one we captured at Azimuntium."

Aëtius nodded. "And the one on the left?"

"I do not know him. He is younger. He seems wounded, or sick."

"Ah."

The two Huns were already approaching the flooded moat, slowing to a trot, picking their way across a half-broken pontoon.

Jormunreik and Valamir came near.

"Ready your bows," said Aëtius. "When you can hit him cleanly, kill the one on the left, the sickly one."

The wolf lords looked faintly disgusted.

"Trust me," said Aëtius. "It's what he wants."

The horsemen were across the moat now, and kicking their horses into a gallop across the shattered terrace below the walls, yowling their battle cries, waving their spears, shouting defiance in the very faces of the defenders. Aladar made it as far as the base of the walls, and had his shaking hand outstretched upon a remnant of net which would not even have supported his weight, when three arrows slammed into him from above, two angled into the shoulder and one straight through his heart. His hand fell back from the net, his spear dropped from the other hand, and he sat his horse, bowed forward, still. The horse shifted its hooves uncertainly but did not move.

"No more!" cried Aëtius. "Lower your bows!"

The old warrior rode over to the dead man in his saddle, put his arm round him and pulled him across his own horse, face down. Let him sleep now, face turned away from the sun. For did not his warrior soul already soar with his heavenly father, a great eagle, into the eternal blue sky? High over the measureless green grasslands of his beloved homeland where the flowers would bloom again yellow next spring, soaring forever and ever over the white and gleaming mountains of the Holy Altai? For the earth itself was heaven.

The old warrior took the reins of the riderless horse and turned round and headed back toward the moat with his son across his lap and the riderless horse walking close behind. At the last moment he turned again and gazed up at the walls. His old eyes were very bright, even as he stood there darkly silhouetted against the sinking sun, the sky a blaze of color behind him.

For a moment the old warrior and the defenders on the walls gazed at each other, and Chanat tried to identify the commander who had understood so well and given the order. His eyes were tired, and a little blurred, and he could not see so far. Yet it seemed to him that some of those on the walls raised their hands to him, without weapons. So he raised his hand likewise, then pulled his horse round again, with the second horse following, and walked them back over the broken pontoon bridge and away over the darkening plain.

BLOOD AND GOLD

That night Aëtius and his men slept. At dawn he was summoned to the palace.

Before he went, Captain Andronicus sent word that he should step up onto the platform of the tower. He did so, and looked out.

There was nothing but a low haze of dust. The Huns had vanished, like a people who had never been.

There in council were the emperor and the empress, and inevitably the emperor's sour-faced sister, misnamed Pulcheria; and Themistius, an aged scholar and orator, and also the chief chamberlain, and the bishop of the city, Epiphanius. When Aëtius entered, to his embarrassment several present bowed down to him and touched their foreheads to the ground. The emperor hastily ordered them to their feet again.

"General Aëtius," he said, "we have done well. You have seen the results? The enemy is"—he spread his hands wide and smiled—"gone!"

Aëtius nodded. "But not forgotten."

"Against the stone of sickness they stumbled," intoned Bishop Epiphanius, "the steeds and their riders both. The sinners drew the bow and put their arrows to the string, and then sickness blew through them and hurled the host back into the wilderness. Glory to God in the Highest."

There were murmured affirmations and many crossings of chests.

A little poetic, thought Aëtius, biting his tongue. The horses didn't actually suffer from camp fever. But the people were dying like flies. He thought his men deserved a little praise as well, but that was probably too much to hope for.

"Peace has been made," said the emperor. "See, we have the paper."

Old Themistius passed it to the general. Attila himself had signed it. *Attila, Tashur-Astur. Flagellum Dei,* the Scourge of God.

"His royal sign," added Theodosius eagerly.

Aëtius shook his head. "It is not his royal sign. It is Hunnish."

Theodosius sat back. "And you speak that rough tongue, of course."

Aëtius did not answer.

"Well," said Theodosius impatiently, "what is it that makes you look so solemn, man? This is the paper of peace! This is the signal for the end of bloodshed, and surely a cause for celebration! Or do you want still more war?"

"Not I," murmured Aëtius.

Themistius glanced at him, but the jubilant emperor had not heard.

"Once more," he said, rising to his feet and stepping down from his throne, "as of old in the days of King Uldin, the great Hun nation, those fierce, barbarian yet, I think, noble-hearted steppe warriors, are our allies!"

"Allies!" cried Aëtius. "But he has signed himself Attila, Scourge of God."

Theodosius laughed an uncertain little laugh. "The name given to him by a Gaulish chronicler, apparently, which he has adopted with alacrity. And with good humor! A royal moniker. They have fierce names, those Germanic tribesmen, you know. Godric the Wolf Slayer, Erik Blood Axe and so forth. Like our own emperors. Why," he asked jovially, "do they not call me Theodosius the Calligrapher?"

Aëtius could have wept with frustration. "Majesty, this is not so innocent a name. He believes he is our punishment, sent by the Eternal Blue Sky—by his heavenly father—to be our destruction, and to announce the end of our world to us. He will never be our ally, nor at peace with us. He was mocking you even as he signed this paper. He will always be our enemy."

"Nonsense, nonsense." Theodosius came forward and actually put his sovereign arm around the broad shoulders of his grim and difficult general. He walked him round the vast audience chamber. "Indeed, far from being our enemy, it seems that Attila might even have become one of the imperial family, if a certain plot of the Princess Honoria's had not been uncovered."

"Plot?"

But at a signal from his sister Pulcheria, Theodosius shook his head. "Never mind; all that is discovered and dispensed with. Nevertheless, as things stood, I was quite prepared to trust his word, and to meet his demands in full."

Aëtius stopped abruptly. Even while he and his men had been fighting to the death on the walls, the Imperial Court had been secretly negotiating with Attila himself. Was that possible? He felt sick to his stomach.

"Demands? What demands? We'd beaten him—or stalled him, anyway. He knew he couldn't take this city, these walls, without sustaining terrible losses, even undermanned as we were. Then disease broke out in his camp. He had to fall back, he had no choice." The general was glaring most rudely full in the emperor's face. "*What demands?*"

"My lord," interrupted the chamberlain.

Theodosius raised a pacific hand, and replied to Aëtius, "Demands in response to *our* demands, of course. We demanded that he retire from our territories and molest our people no more. In return for . . . recompense."

Aëtius's grip on the treaty parchment tightened visibly. "You mean gold."

"I mean . . . recompense." Theodosius's arm dropped away from Aëtius's shoulders. He was tiring of this. This coarse soldier should be *grateful* for his Earthly Lord having negotiated such a delicate treaty with the Huns, for having saved so many of his people's lives, and secured a lasting peace. Instead, he was positively *leaking* resentment and bile. Jealousy, really, Theodosius presumed. His own diplomacy had stolen Aëtius's martial thunder.

"You mean gold," repeated Aëtius in his harsh and gravelly voice, like the voice of a waterless desert. "How much gold? What have you given him?"

The man's eyes blazed. He was unstable, so moody. It was very displeasing. The chief chamberlain snapped back, "The finances of the Imperial Court are of no matter to a Western general."

The general would not let go; he was like a mastiff locked on a hind. His gaze was still on the emperor. "You cannot buy off a man like Attila. Look how he has mocked you. The Scourge of God. Can you buy off the Scourge of God? Can you divert his barbaric Almighty God of War with mere gold?"

Now Theodosius was angry. "You talk gibberish, man. His god does not exist, or he is at most some outcast demon."

"He exists in Attila's heart. That is a mighty engine."

Theodosius replied crisply, "Soldiers should stick to soldiering, and leave theology to higher minds."

"How much?"

It was outrageous that he should be addressed like this, but Theodosius would not have his judgment questioned. "Seven thousand pounds," he snapped, walking back to his throne.

Aëtius' ears rang. *"How much?"*

"Attila received the treasure chests gracefully, my ambassadors report, the night before last. He even referred to them, with a pleasing laconic humor, as reimbursement for 'the expenses of war!' A small price to pay for the happiness and well-being of my peace-loving people, Master General, from the Holy City to the Danube border, from the Euxine to the—"

The vast audience chamber echoed to a furious roar: *"You fool!* He has already slaughtered thousands of your innocent people, and now you think you can make peace with him? You have welcomed the enemy within your gates, and you have paid in advance the bill for your own destruction!"

A collective gasp went round. Bishop Epiphanius drew sharp breath, Themistius cried out "My lord!" and the emperor paused on the steps up to the dais, his back still to Aëtius. The empress gazed down on the enraged general, her hands twisting in her lap.

"Have a care, Master General," said the emperor quietly.

Aëtius at that moment looked like a man with many cares. He did a swift mental calculation. Seven thousand pounds of Byzantine gold, much of it ingots stamped for purity by the Imperial Treasury. Enough to buy—his blood ran hot and cold—twenty thousand of the best mercenaries for a year or more. Maybe thirty thousand. Alan lancers, Gepids, Sueves, Teutonic axe men, Sarmatian cavalry, maybe even renegade Persians. Why had Constantinople not bought those mercenaries for its own protection? The reason was simple. The mercenaries would not have fought for Theodosius, nor for Rome. They would only take gold to fight for what they believed was a winning cause.

Attila's finest and most loyal Hun warriors could have numbered no more than thirty thousand. The rest were Kutrigurs, Hephthalites, lesser tribal followers, nameless easterners who would soon melt away. But *seven thousand pounds*: Attila's command of crack troops had just doubled. And the great sacrifice so many had made in the East—at Viminacium, Ratiaria, calamitously on the Utus, and here on the walls of the City—was wretchedly degraded. They had saved the Holy City, and the Asian provinces. But Rome now stood in a danger beyond all reckoning, and perhaps beyond all opposition.

He spoke dazedly. "Not even the treasuries of Byzantium can have held this much. How . . . ?"

Theodosius seated himself again, seeing with relief that the general was growing calmer—though he hoped he would be sailing back west soon.

"The city's loyal senatorial classes responded with alacrity. Some even handed in their wives' jewelry and most precious heirlooms. And we ourself have parted with many of our private possessions, for the sake of our people."

The courtiers murmured sycophantic assent. Themistius added, "Although in consolation an ambassador from the court of an Indian king has recently sent His Majesty a tiger for his menagerie."

There were gentle chuckles, and a smile from the emperor. He inclined his head gracefully.

The frightful general only glowered the more.

Theodosius added, "We have also ceded to our new ally Attila the territory of Pannonia Secunda, for his people to settle."

Settle. A fine euphemism. But damn Pannonia Secunda—he'd have taken it soon enough anyway.

Aëtius was striding about and muttering. The emperor looked pointedly at his Palatine Guards.

"I had him," said the over-wrought and over-tired commander, his fist before his face, "in the palm of my hand. Sickness stalked his camp. He would not have fled before it. I knew there was something else. He was haughty, even as a boy. He never bowed the neck, neither to prince nor to pestilence. His own pride had him trapped there. 'Whether we fall by ambition, blood, or lust, Like diamonds we are cut with our own dust.' He would have been so cut, and his warriors laid out across the plain. Windrows of the dead, scythed down like a wheatfield after a hailstorm."

He turned violently back toward the imperial throne. "And you have paid him off, enriched the gorgon's purse! Oh, merciful heaven!"

Theodosius rose again and declared that the council was ended, adding acerbically, "This Attila, who makes you tremble with such unmanly cowardice, is a man of reason and candor. More so than you, I think, Master General Aëtius. And he has already moved away north."

"With his gold!" cried Aëtius. "Gone to buy more troops! How they will flock to his banner now, the wealthiest robber and ruler in all of Europe! How dazzled they will be by his gold—by your gold, *our gold,* the gold of your hardpressed, hard-taxed people. Sweet Jesus, did they not deserve better than this? For their oppressor to be paid off, like a thug intimidating a market stall? Now he will turn his vast army, twice, three times as strong, against the West. Is this your idea of Christian solidarity?"

Theodosius had had enough. "Get him out! *Now!* He offends my ears!"

But, to the horror of the assembled courtiers, Aëtius began tearing the treaty parchment to shreds before their eyes. The man was mad. Two Palatine Guards moved nervously near him, but neither dared to lay a hand on him.

Theodosius meanwhile had fled through a side door and was gone, though not without the general's last words still offending his ears.

"You pigeon-livered, dung-brained, degenerate excuse for a Roman emperor!" He freed himself roughly from the guards' hesitant grasp. "Unhand me, you dolts. I'm going. I've got work to do."

He glanced back only once, and it was toward the empress. She still sat upon her throne, and she had not spoken nor stirred, but her luminous eyes were upon him, and he saw in those eyes something like pride at his rage.

Then he was gone.

Aëtius returned hurriedly to the east of the city and summoned all the men who had fought on the walls, all the women who had hauled heavy supplies, ammunition, food, and water up to the battlements, even the children who had helped. He had them all assemble outside the Church of St. George, and he climbed atop the Charisius Gate.

"People of Constantinople," he declared, "Isaurians, Imperial Guard, Gothic wolf lords, you have won a great victory. I, Aëtius, master general of the West, regard each and every one of you as a hero, and were such things possible I would have you all in my army!"

There were great cheers.

"Your spirit has been indomitable, your faith unwavering, your victory richly deserved. The pagans are gone, their hearts heavy with defeat, and I do not think that they will return. They know under whose Protection this Holy City stands. Now go, with my heartfelt blessings, and live in peace."

There were more cheers, and weeping among the cheers.

He descended the steps, mounted his horse, and looked over them all one last time. *"Weep not, weep not. It is we in the West who must weep. Your city will stand for many centuries yet."*

Then he spurred his horse, and made for the Harbor of Eleutherius.

The wolf lords rode with him. They would take ship back to Massilia, since Valentinian still would not permit Visigoths on Italian soil. At the docks he clasped the princes in farewell—Theodoric carefully, since his arm was still splinted and bandaged, though his healing had been remarkable.

"We will see you again," said Torismond.

"You will."

Theodoric said, "Our father has a deep love for you."

Aëtius coughed, somewhat embarrassed.

They led their horses on up the gangway.

"No vomiting over the side, you landlubbers!"

They grinned. Yes, he would see them again. He knew it with foreboding.

There was Gamaliel, looking old and stooped and tired.

"Old man," Aëtius said. "You know your stuff."

"I know other stuff, too," said Gamaliel. "We also shall meet again. One last time, I think. But it will be enough." With those riddling words he was gone into the crowd.

There was Captain Andronicus, fantastically colorful with cuts and wounds. He grinned.

"The city's in your hands now, Captain. But you will be at peace."

"I know it," said Andronicus. "Damn it."

And Zeno.

"We owe your people all thanks. Back to Cilicia?"

The chieftain's eyes glimmered. "Back to banditry."

Aëtius grunted. "Mind you don't get caught."

There were also the four: last remnant of the VIIth legion. He eyed them.

"You put us in your close guard," said Knuckles, reading his thoughts. "Besides, I'm no easterner, anyhow. Dodgy, slitty-eyed lot, they are, sell their own grannies for a bunch of grapes."

Arapovian snorted.

Aëtius regarded the other two, Tatullus and Malchus. They looked resolute.

"Very well," he said, "jump aboard. But don't expect any peace and quiet back West."

PART III

THE LAST BATTLE

1

DEATH OF AN EMPRESS

Aëtius and his few companions arrived in an autumnal Ravenna to find the city in the throes of terminal panic. Riding up from the port of Classis along the causeway over the marshes, past stagnant pools and stands of bog willow, they emerged into the streets of the sprawling suburb of Caesarea to hear rumors of distant, calamitous wars, omens of apocalypse, and everywhere intimations of things coming to an end. People said that statues had been seen weeping real tears, oysters opened welling with blood, and from empty churches at night came the sound of many voices lamenting. They had heard the steely clash of weapons from the clouds, there had been numerous earthquakes, and the ghosts of ancient emperors were haunting the sacred palaces. In Rome itself, Bishop Sebatius had gone to pray at the tomb of St. Peter and been granted a terrible revelation. . . .

Aëtius listened, unimpressed. Nearby, another bearded and wild-eyed millennial doomsayer ranted from the steps of a church, claiming that only days ago, while Valentinian was out hunting, two wolves had started up from nowhere under the emperor's horse, and he almost fell to the ground. The wolves were speared and killed, and when they were cut open, their bellies were found to be full of severed human hands.

Aëtius snorted. "This emperor doesn't *go* hunting." He glared around at his men, walking behind his horse. "Anyway, we have problems enough without wolves full of severed hands. You're under orders to silence any idiot prophet you come across."

Knuckles hefted his club and went over to talk to the wild-eyed doomsayer, shouldering his way through the crowd, which parted promptly before him. The prophet argued a little, until Knuckles dropped his club on the fellow's bare toes, at which he howled and limped away, talking of demon wolves no more.

They made for the palace, asking for news as they went.

Yes, Ravenna had heard of the Huns' retreat from Constantinople, but didn't that simply mean that the barbarian hordes would now be on their way *here?* Aëtius didn't reply. Instead he tried to ascertain what was left of the Western Field Army, but the only replies he got were of lightning bolts from a cloudless sky, and a wolf cub found in the heart of the Imperial Palace, and tales of the long-foretold awakening of the Seven Sleepers of Ephesus.

He kicked his horse onward. "I need to find my General Germanus," he muttered.

The news from the imperial court was no better. A chamberlain said that the emperor was . . . indisposed. Imperial finances were in disarray, and the last revenue had been scant. Ever since the loss of the African grain fields, taxation had been less than—

"The legions?" demanded Aëtius.

"The Field Army remains encamped inland of the city," said the chamberlain. "But its mood, alas, without pay for these few months, is sadly . . . restive. Winter is approaching, and I fear numbers are less than they were."

"And Her Majesty Galla Placidia?"

The chamberlain lowered his eyes. "I regret to say that Her Majesty is dying."

He found her in a darkened chamber, seated upright on a high-backed wooden chair beside an iron brazier, swathed in white woolen blankets. She was clearly very weak, yet she knew him immediately. He sank to his knees before her.

"On your feet, General," she said, her voice no more than a dry whisper. "The rest of the empire is on its knees. At least you should stand upright."

He promptly stood again. How he loved this old battle-axe. She might be dying but her mind and her tongue were as sharp as ever.

"And I'll try not to die in your company," she added. "There might be talk."

"The emperor?" he dared to ask.

She waved her hand, saying not a word, but the meaning was clear. The emperor was mad.

"So," she whispered, "Attila has gone north."

"For now."

"The Western world stands on the brink." She fixed him with her watery green eyes. "And the Empress Athenaïs—Eudoxia?"

He was startled. How her mind flitted. Perhaps she was losing her sharpness after all.

"You loved her," said Galla.

No. She was not losing her sharpness.

"Yes," he said quietly, after a struggle. "But I was needed elsewhere."

She gave the slightest nod. "You still are. Stop him, Aëtius. With all your might. With all our prayers. You must stop him. Christendom depends on it." She held out a skeletal hand, and he understood and passed her the cup of water by her side. She drank and he set it down again for her.

"This is a time of waiting," she said, "to see where he will strike next. But we know, do we not? We know he will come."

She gestured to him to sit down.

"It is twelve centuries from the founding of Rome. You know it. And it has been held, since before Cicero and Varro, that the twelve vultures who appeared to Romulus when he founded the city signified the twelve centuries Rome would endure. This is borrowed time."

She breathed slowly. "Has the fratricidal death of Remus at last come back to destroy Rome? The shedding of his brother's blood was the price Romulus paid for Rome's twelve centuries of glory. They say Attila slew his brother, too—for all of a dozen years of glory. Perhaps now both debts are being called in. The first city was called Enoch and it was built by Cain. The murderer. Perhaps all cities and empires are founded in blood; and in the end that blood must be paid for." She closed her eyes, the lids leaf thin, fluttering. "I cannot see the future, Aëtius, but it must be . . . remade. Rome may not be the future. But Attila and his pure spirit of destruction must not be, either."

She opened her eyes again. "Some of the wise say that it is only the old world that is dying. A new world is being born. Well, ask a woman how painful childbirth can be. As one of Euripides' women says: 'I'd rather stand in the line of battle than lie again in childbed.'" She smiled weakly.

"I have heard," said Aëtius, "that the harvests were poor, and weather watchers say we have an exceptionally hard winter ahead."

"Which will hurt Attila more than us."

He grunted. "You should have been a general. That's good insight." He stood again. "With your leave, Your Majesty, I must check troop numbers, find my general, Germanus."

"I can tell you," she said.

He laughed aloud. "You really *would* have been a good general."

"Hm. Wrong gender."

She drew painful breath and then told him. The Rhine and Danube frontiers had been pretty much stripped bare. She herself had given the order, via her son. The East had no army left to speak of, and every last decent soldier in the West was with the Field Army, not six miles east of Ravenna. She reeled them off. The expeditionary force Aëtius himself had assembled in Sicily for the reconquest of Africa: six crack legions, including the Batavian, the Herculian, the Cornuti Seniores, the Moorish Cavalry, numbering some eighteen thousand in all.

"Twenty thousand," he interrupted.

"There have been desertions, even there."

He looked down.

From the frontiers, a few sad remnants. The only legions worth the name, at around a thousand men each: the Legio I Italica pulled back from Brigetio, the II from Aquincum. The fierce IV Scythica at Singidunum had absconded entirely, quite possibly to the Hunnish side. But Aëtius also had the XII Fulminata, the Lightning Boys, good artillerymen; the XIV from Carnuntum; a useful troop of Augustan Horse, around five hundred men; and, finest of them all, the two thousand crack troops of the Palatine Guard. That was it.

The frontiers were, for the first time in centuries, undefended. He saw in his mind's eye those once mighty legionary fortresses, now desolate and forlorn beside the cold, bleak waters of the Rhine and Danube, an eerie wind blowing through their narrow windows and around their squat U-shaped bastions, starlings nesting in their proud, deserted towers.

He had around twenty-five thousand men. Attila had more than double that in first-rank warriors alone. In total, with mercenaries, lesser tribes, opportunists, nameless eastern peoples, the wild rumors that he rode at the head of half a million were edging toward the uncomfortable truth.

Galla's old face was bleak indeed. "I do not doubt," she said at last, very slowly, "that if Attila defeats us this last time—if his greatly superior numbers defeat yours—then, with nothing more to oppose him, he will not simply colonize our empire for his kingdom. He will destroy it. He will make a sacrifice to his gods upon an altar called Europe."

Aëtius did not disagree. He said without expression, "We gave the order for him to be killed, when he was no more than a boy. Now we are paying the price."

"*I* gave the order," said Galla, unflinching, "that he be slain. That the Huns not turn against us. Even that they fight *with* us, against Alaric and his Goths. His uncle Ruga was not our enemy." She shook her head. "So long ago. It seems another world. And we failed: we did not kill the boy, though we tried hard. Yet I am not the first ruler who has given the order to take innocent lives in order to save more. And I shall not be the last. I still do not repent it. But God be my judge."

There was a long silence, and then she said, "I feel—forgive an old, dying woman's hackneyed prophesying—but I feel that he will never see Rome again." She seized his hand. "I *feel* that, Aëtius. He saw Rome as a boy, a savage boy, and he rejected it and all it stands for. He will not be offered that vision of the city again. I tell you . . . he will never . . . see . . . Rome again." Each pause was an agonized intake of breath, her face implacable and unpitying throughout.

"One day, one day . . . and in another world," she whispered, so quietly that he had to lean down to hear her. He told her she must rest, but her thin lips curled with scorn. She had not rested once in sixty years. She whispered, "I have always . . . held you in the highest esteem . . . and the deepest affection . . . Gaius . . . Flavius . . . Aëtius."

Her hand went lifeless in his.

She was expertly embalmed and robed in purple cerecloths in the Triclinium of the Nineteen Couches, the diadem of Roman royalty on her head. In the center of the hall, the great golden catafalque held her slight body. Forests of candles burned on golden pricket stands amid clouds of incense. Friends and mourners passed where she lay and kissed her: then bishops and priests, senators, patricians, prefects, magistrates, wives, ladies-in-waiting, all coming to kiss her cold cheeks and lament.

Valentinian came, too, to kiss her good-bye, with tears running uncontrollably down his cheeks. Aëtius was shocked to see his appearance. He looked an old man, his hair thin and gray, his legs strangely bowed, his gait an exhausted shuffle, clutching a little white cloth to mop both his tears and his constantly dribbling mouth. He brought his mother a present: a lavish set of jewels for her to wear in the tomb. They would have been better used to buy mercenaries, thought Aëtius. Galla's head was gently raised by an attendant, and the sobbing emperor placed the jewels round her neck with trembling hands, and then held her for a long time. He had to be led away.

The funeral cortege processed down to the magnificent Basilica of the Resurrection, accompanied by chanting priests and wailing women mourners. All the way, riding his white horse, Aëtius could only think, In the lost boyhood of Judas, Christ was crucified. It was as if, he began to realize, Galla herself had killed the one thing she loved: Rome. She had maltreated the boy Attila so harshly, unwittingly instilled in him such hatred, that now he came back to destroy the city and the empire she stood for. Truly the drama of the world had been written not by that warm-hearted praise singer, blind Homer, but by the lonely tragedian Galla had quoted on her deathbed: Euripides, gazing out to sea from his hermit's cave.

In the basilica, Galla's diadem was at last removed and replaced with a band of purple silk.

The Patriarch called out in a sonorous chant, "O Princess, the King of Kings and Lord of Lords calleth thee!"

She was entombed in her own sarcophagus in the mausoleum nearby, between the two men who had gone before her: her second husband, Constantius, and her brother, the Emperor Honorius. Her own sarcophagus was the largest of the three. She was seated upright within it, as if still reigning over the domain of which she had been ruler in all but name.

The door was drawn closed and there was silence.

2

THE END OF TIMES

It was well that Galla died when she did. Only three days later, a message came to the court of Ravenna. It was from Attila's amanuensis, Orestes. He wrote that Attila was betrothed to the Emperor Valentinian's sister, Galla Placidia's daughter, the Princess Honoria, and that he would take as his dowry half the Roman Empire. Specifically, the Western half.

Valentinian laughed hysterically. Even Aëtius nearly smiled. That demonic sense of humor was still intact. Then he recalled something Theodosius had said, something about a plot of Honoria's being discovered. . . .

It was no joke of Attila's, as rapid communication with the embarrassed court of Theodosius proved. It was all true.

In this winter of AD 450, Princess Honoria, still living an enclosed life with the emperor's sister Pulcheria and her pious ladies' maids in the palace in Constantinople, was still only in her late twenties. Amid the chaos of these days, she had at last seen her chance for escape, and for revenge upon the family who had humiliated her and stolen her girlhood from her.

She managed to bribe one of the guards who was escorting the seven thousand pounds of gold to Attila—what manner of bribe it is perhaps best not to inquire but, given her character, it is not difficult to imagine. She persuaded the guard to smuggle out to Attila a gold betrothal ring, and a brief message from her. An offer of marriage, if he came to her rescue and liberation. Quite what sort of freedom Honoria thought she would enjoy as one of the junior wives of the Great Tanjou in the Hun camp, one can only speculate. But Attila accepted the offer, adding that for dowry he'd expect half the empire. She said that he was welcome to it.

Hence the message sent by Attila to Ravenna. In deadly earnest.

Thank Christ, thought Aëtius, that Galla Placidia had not lived to see her daughter conspire with Attila himself. Constantinople was all ready to have Honoria strangled for treason on the spot, but further hurried communication dissuaded them. Personally, Aëtius thought the poor girl had suffered long enough. One youthful indiscretion as a girl—and a clumsy attempt to have her brother assassinated. . . . Well, that was certainly understandable. Why couldn't she be married off now to some unfussy old dotard, for God's sake? Pen her up there in the Imperial Palace like a nun, with that old harridan Pulcheria, and it wasn't surprising she dreamed of marrying what she must have pictured to herself as an exotic Scythian warlord.

Theodosius gave the command, and at the age of twenty-nine, Honoria was married instead to the fifty-nine-year-old Fabius Cassius Herculeanus. By all accounts it was a very happy marriage—not least, court rumor had it, because the husband turned a blind eye to his wife's numerous and entirely characteristic indiscretions, his own interests being primarily boys.

It was a ludicrous and squalid affair. Even more farcically, it gave Attila the paper-thin pretext he needed for an attack on the West, as the punitive expedition had for his attack on the East.

"Helen was the destruction of Troy," murmured Aëtius, "and Honoria of Rome."

He read the message again.

The last line read, *"Attila, my Master and yours, bids you prepare a palace for his reception."*

Aëtius found General Germanus in a makeshift hot bath at the field army's camp outside Ravenna. Germanus looked red faced, lightly poached, and embarrassed.

Aëtius flung him a towel. "Saddle up," he said. "Attila's coming."

They rode northwest up the Flaminian Way, the field army visibly delighted to be on the move again, away from that vast, wretched, stagnant campsite—even if they were riding to meet the greatest army Rome had ever faced. Despite rumors of the vast difference in numerical strength, it always felt good to be one man among a solid twenty-five thousand.

The two thousand men of the Palatine Guard, grudgingly released by Valentinian after much persuasion, marched at the front, black armor gleaming. Then came the central legions: the Herculians, numbering nearly six thousand men, the ancient complement, with their gold-rimmed shields decorated with black eagles; then the Cornuti Seniores, their shields a red icon on white; the Batavians, their shields a solid red with an evil-eye boss, and among them a single century of intensely trained *superventores* or special forces, their typically Batavian speciality being to swim fully armored across rivers of any depth, even in full flood, and slip in among the enemy by night, cutting throats by the dozen, loosing horses, setting fires. Used well, they could be massively destructive.

Then came the Mauri, the light Moorish cavalry, horses' white manes and riders' white woolen cloaks of finest camel hair flowing together in the wind beautiful to watch. The horses were skittish and high stepping, manageable only by the very best horsemen, possessing astonishing speed and stamina beneath their pretty white manes and high-tossed tails. You mistook those Berber horses for useless, girlish mounts at your peril, and the Moorish javelin shower at full gallop, javelins tipped with cruel barbed angons, was famous. Next came the equally elite Augustan Horse, positively prancing to be on the road and heading for battle at last. Finally there came the four doggedly surviving frontier legions: the I, II, XII Artillery, and the XIV. Aëtius rode at the front with General Germanus and with his own motley, hand-picked close guard. He glanced back over the huge column of men. They looked good, on this bright winter morning. Outnumbered, depleted, certainly; but they still looked good.

"Where will we draw up our line?" Germanus asked.

"Beyond the Padus."

"You think—with respect, sir—but you think he will lead his men across the Julian Alps in winter?"

Aëtius nodded. "He crossed the Julian Alps in winter once before, when a boy of no more than eleven. He was fleeing from us, with only two companions, another boy and his sister. It will appeal to him: coming back that way again."

They skirted the marshlands of the Adriatic shore, and then, traversing the rivers Padus, Athesis, and Plavis, in five days they came to the broad, flat plain of the Venetia. A good place to fight. Here, history would be decided. Aëtius sent scouts out as far as Aemona and the headwaters of the Savus, but from the east there was no sign. The Huns would not be here for at least another three weeks, then. That was to be expected. Attila would be in no hurry, preferring to make them fret, wait, and stagnate. He had not conquered this far without being a master tactician.

Aëtius would not let his men stagnate or fret for one moment. Their camp having been built, he had them dig trenches, cut down woods and copses, even engage in competitive games, one regiment against another. And there were more solemn rituals, such as the *tubilustrium,* the purification of the war trumpets for the campaign ahead, one of the numberless centuries-old traditions of the legions. It crossed Aëtius's mind that this might be the last such ceremony ever performed.

Then, leaving his men under the capable command of Germanus, he rode into Aquileia.

He went to find an obscenely wealthy senator, one Nemesianus, a man whom he despised but who had influence. A man close to the emperor, it was said. Perhaps some good would come of it, some change of heart. . . . So far the senatorial classes had been singularly lacking in martial or patriotic spirit.

From Nemesianus's vast villa—one of his villas—he was directed to Aquileia's amphitheater. Yes, even with the Hunnish hordes riding down upon them, a few tired games were still being held.

Nemesianus was elderly, but he had the golden glow of the very rich, promising great longevity. Aëtius found him seated in the higher stalls, wearing a beautiful cloak of what looked like pure ermine, and flanked by two of his *spintriae,* his young boys, one of them working away with his hand beneath Nemesianus's furs. Nemesianus greeted the general with no interest, only mild irritation.

The crowds stamped their feet and clapped and hooted as a chain gang of criminals was whipped into the arena, to be crucified and disembowelled for public edification. The Church might have put a stop to gladiatorial combat decades ago, but the torture and execution of law breakers was still regarded as a necessary lesson in civility. All round the expensive upper tiers, there were many spectators whose skilled *spintriae* or whores would bring them climax at the very moment of death in the arena; sex slaves with names like "Desire," "Happy," and "Beloved."

Aëtius hated the games. The cruel faces of the spectators, brutalized by their own entertainment; the rotten fish sold at the stalls, deep fried to disguise the stink; the scrawny prostitutes underneath the arches, their lines of customers waiting. That these games today were so shabby and meager did not help. Two burglars were forced to fight to the death with nets and rusty swords. An aged horse which had trodden on a senator's foot was roped down and clubbed to death. There was the inevitable reenactment of the story of Pasiphaë, Queen of Crete, always a crowd pleaser. An aroused bull in a huge harness was lowered from a crane onto a tethered and shaven-headed female slave, guilty, so they said, of attacking her mistress and clawing the skin from her face. The girl died. The crowd was delighted.

Later, slaves would come and gather up the various organs and body parts that littered the ground, strew fresh sand, scrub down the seats. A cocktail of blood, semen, urine, and feces—for none liked to leave their seats during the entertainment, and the plebs always urinated or defecated where they sat— would flow away down to the city's sewers and out to sea.

Aëtius heard a voice saying, "Your empire is tottering. Rome's all done. You have already lost whatever it was that you fought for. Join us."

It was the voice of Attila, the voice of temptation. With it, Aëtius had a vision of a wide and endless steppe land, a clean wind blowing over the emerald spring grass; vast herds of beautiful horses running, or drinking at crystal streams; a peaceful encampment of free and simple-hearted people, men idly chatting, women busily cooking, children playing and laughing, plumes of wood smoke rising into the still, clear air. Perhaps a girl there, an ordinary girl with a shy smile and kindly eyes, one hand on her pregnant belly, the other in the hand of a scarred, battered, fugitive man who had once called himself a Roman. And beyond them, great snow-capped mountains, and a golden eagle soaring into that eternal sky. . . .

The crowd roared.

He shook himself free of that impossible dream, closed his eyes, and drew breath, then laid out his plan to the bored-looking senator.

"Rebuild the navy, you say?" drawled Nemesianus. "Here at Aquileia?" He shooed the slave boys away for a moment.

Aëtius nodded. "And turn the lagoon of the Veneto into a huge harbor. Defense would be easy. From there we could oversee the Adriatic, sail against the Vandals of Africa, recapture the grain fields. . . ."

"Bold plans!" Nemesianus was looking at him with amusement—*amusement*! At this late stage. "And all this will cost a great deal of money? *My* money?"

"Inaction will cost more. If Attila defeats us, what will be left? He will destroy everything. But if we defeat him, we, too, will be exhausted. We must plan for the future."

"I'm sorry," said Nemesianus, "but at times such as these, each man must shift for himself. In the harbor of Aquileia a nice galley awaits me, ready to sail east. I have always fancied one of the Ionian islands. My wealth is secure, much of it now in a Levantine bank in Constantinople. My dear man"—he made to touch Aëtius's knee, but thought better of it—"my dear, old-fashioned, stern, public-spirited, republican-hearted, patriotic Master General Aëtius, you were born out of your time." He clapped politely at the scene being enacted below, then resumed. "Veritably, the Scipio Africanus of our age."

The fear of sincerity, the faithlessness, the catch-all ironic twang, the enervated drawl, the emptiness beneath the cleverness, the baseness of vision: Aëtius could have wrung his neck.

Instead he steeled himself and arose and wished the senator well in his future life, with his private villa on an Ionian island, and his obedient slave boys. A noble dream.

As he left the amphitheater, brushing the clawing prostitutes away, the lines that the exiled Euripides wrote during the ruinous Peloponnesian War returned to him.

In the theaters, the People laugh at phalluses. On a fair Aegean island, beardless boys are butchered in their name. This is the world from which I take my leave. How far and fast we fell.

The games had left a foul taste in his mouth. He strode through the narrow streets of the old city, leading his horse, glaring down. For this was not the whole story of Rome. There had been courage and sacrifice and human dignity. There had been Regulus and Horatius, Trajan and Augustus, rulers of decency and vision. But was the good all in the past now, and the glory departed?

Despite himself he thought again of the bare steppes, and the copper-skinned warriors, their honor and unflinching bravery, their lean self-denials, their magnificent scorn for death   their love of their king.

On the one hand, cruelty and magnificence. On the other, cruelty and squalor. What a richness of choice.

Hardly aware of his actions, he tethered his horse and went into a lowly church, a small, chilly, whitewashed building with an arched apse, narrow windows, half a dozen smoking candles. He was greeted by an old deacon, gray beard streaked with lampblack, his cassock faded to a powdery stale-bread green, a cheap wooden cross on a string of olive-wood beads around his neck. On the west wall was a clumsy, deeply sincere painting of Christ with the loaves and fishes, and the faces of the hungering people crowding round. He sacrificed himself; the people ate. They lived.

Even here could be heard the intermittent roar of the crowd in the arena. The old deacon crossed himself as he watched the powerfully built old officer on his knees before the cross. Then he went over and began to speak without preamble, as is the way with holy men who live much alone; they lose their taste for small talk.

"We live in the end of times," he said, his voice croaky with disuse. "But the choice before each human soul is clear. The broad path or the strait? The arena"—he jerked his head—"or the House of God. *Quo vadis?*"

"Neither," said the general. "My place is on the battlefield."

The old deacon looked grim.

"But I fight for this," said the general, gesturing around the church. "Not for that," and gestured toward the arena, where another massed roar went up.

The deacon's dark eyes bored into the general's. At last he said, "St. Michael and all angels ride with you."

When Aëtius arrived back at camp, he was told he had a visitor.

"No time," he said brusquely.

"He has come a long way, sir. From Britain."

"Britain?"

3

LUCIUS THE BRITON

He was an old man now, perhaps sixty-five, or even seventy, his garments travel-stained, and not as tall as Aëtius remembered him. But then when Aëtius had last set eyes on him, he himself had been only a boy. He remembered the gray eyes, the broad shoulders, the determined look. The old Briton had close-cropped white hair now, and sported a long white barbarian beard. Underneath the beard, Aëtius remembered, he had a scar on his chin.

"You're Lucius," he said.

The old man nodded but didn't salute. He was no longer a soldier of Rome, after all. "I always knew you were a smart lad. Now you rule the Western Empire, I hear."

"The emperor rules the Western Empire."

"Is that so?"

They regarded each other. Not equals in power, but maybe equals in spirit.

"And your friend, the old Jew, Gamaliel," said Aëtius. "I have met him since."

"Old Jew?" Lucius frowned. "I have not seen him for years, but he is a true Celt." The two stared at each other a moment, then Lucius sighed. "In truth, I don't think we will ever know what he is."

"He's old now, and he no longer pretends he used to know Aristotle. But at

Constantinople he was a good physician." Aëtius grinned, despite himself. "Come on in."

They sat on stools and Aëtius poured his visitor wine with his own hand. They clunked cups. Once, decades ago, Lucius had come to the Hun camp and taken Aëtius back to Rome, along with his own freed son, the boy Cadoc. And Attila had ridden into the wilderness of exile.

On the long journey back to the Danube, Lucius, a Roman lieutenant in those days, and the haughty Roman boy Aëtius, solemn beyond his years, had developed a friendship of sorts.

"I remember now," said Aëtius. "The scar on your chin. You got it from tripping over a dog, when you were drunk, and hitting a stone water trough, in Isca Dumnoniorum."

Lucius raised his cup. "I salute your memory, Master General. You're out of date, though. The city, what's left of it, is called Esca now."

"Esca?"

"I shouldn't worry. As I say, there isn't much of it left. A couple of broken walls, the remains of a marketplace, a ruined church, a few sad kale yards. The old basilica's a furnace and marl pit." There was bitterness in his low voice. "And I am Ciddwmtarth. Lucius was a Roman name. But the Romans abandoned us. I know Britain never contributed much to the empire: in four long centuries, we produced only a heretic, a rotten poet and three traitors. So it's said."

Aëtius smiled faintly and then looked grave again. "Is there peace with the Saxons?"

Lucius snorted. "There will never be peace with the Saxons. They already call us the *Wealha,* foreigners and slaves. In our own country! They crucify one in ten captives to their heathen gods. They are the worst: their drunken barbarism knows no limits, they shall never count among the civilized peoples of the world. My people are few and hard pressed. I lead them in the fight, but the fight is continual, and they are very weary. They dream only of fleeing into the mountains westward, always westward. Already the Saxons have pressed as far as Corinium, and Viroconium of the White Walls. To think that we invited them in to work for us, and now they want the whole island of Britain for themselves, under their laws and customs. We have destroyed our own world."

Aëtius set down his cup. "My old friend and guide, I know why it is that you have sailed here all these weeks—and in winter, too. I know how bitter it must be for you. But we cannot send men to help you."

Lucius seized his arm, suddenly impassioned. "Just a thousand of your men, I implore you! For the sake of old friendship, for the sake of Christ! Master General of the West, whom I knew and traveled with as a boy, do not deny me. One thousand of your best, and I tell you we will meet the Saxons in open field, even ten thousand of them, and defeat them once and for all. They are many, but they fight wild, all solo howls and heroics. One good legion could take them. *Then* the kingdom of Christian Celtic Britain will be at peace. But my own people, they're no warriors, only simple farmers. They cannot do it."

"Nor can I do it." Aëtius's tone was unbending. "I cannot give you a hundred, not fifty. There are twenty-five thousand men under my command, and every one counts. The barbarian army coming west numbers at least a hundred thousand mounted warriors, with twice as many followers. I cannot do it."

"And Rome matters more than Britain."

"It does," said Aëtius evenly.

Lucius glowered at the ground. "And to think," he muttered, "that three times I saved his life—the Hun boy."

Neither of them could speak the name of the barbarian warlord. Ironies were many, but none of them amused. At last, Lucius tried for a joke.

"Even if he does destroy you," he said, glaring at Aëtius, "and comes with his one hundred thousand tattooed horsemen to the shores of northern Gaul, above the white cliffs of Gesoriacum, and gazes across to the answering white cliffs of Britain, not even"—he gritted his teeth—"not even *Attila* would invade us. Not even that all-devouring world conqueror would want our miserable, fog-bound little islands."

Aëtius's eyes glimmered with humor. He touched the older man on his strong right arm. "Believe me, old friend and guide, in these latter days you and all your people are better off on your own, in your gentle, sweet green island."

Lucius would never have imagined hearing Aëtius talk like this, as if already defeated.

"How is your family?" added the general.

Small talk was absurd. It was time to leave, empty handed, and sail back

for war-tormented Britain. But Lucius, rising to his feet, said that his wife
still lived and his children were all grown and well.

"Your son? The dreamer?"

"Cadoc. Still dreaming, but he fights beside me well enough."

Outside, Aëtius was waiting for Lucius to remount when a horseman came
galloping up the road from Aquileia. Aëtius's eyes narrowed. The fellow's
face was taut and his clothes were both sodden and dusty, as though he had
been traveling heedless of weather. He almost fell from his horse and stood
gasping.

Lucius pulled his own horse round as if business were concluded, but Aëtius's blood was like ice. "Speak, man."

The fellow saluted rapidly. "Sir, the Huns have crossed the Rhine. All of
Gaul is ablaze."

Lucius stilled his horse again.

Aëtius stared at the messenger in a daze. "Gaul?" he repeated dumbly.

"News from the Rhine stations. He crossed—"

"There are no bloody Rhine stations left!" roared Aëtius, finding brief solace in blaming the messenger. "All remaining frontier troops are with me! All
four bloody thousand of them or less!"

"Nevertheless, news came through from some last scouts, sir. He crossed
the Rhine near Argentoratum, then turned back and fell on the city and destroyed it."

There was a moment's stunned silence.

"And?"

"Then the cities of Vangiones, Moguntiacum, and Colonia Agrippina, sir."

The greatest of all the Rhine frontier cities. Even Aëtius's strong voice faltered. "Colonia . . . destroyed?"

"So the reports say, sir." The fellow's face was agonized. "Laid waste, all
citizens put to the sword. The ice on the Rhine is dyed red, they say."

Thousands more slain—tens of thousands. He had outwitted them. He
had not turned on Rome, but had gone north and west. He would destroy
everything else first, and leave Rome, the sweetest dish, till last. How could
Aëtius not have foreseen? He could have damned himself for his folly. All of
Gaul lay undefended before the Hun holocaust. If they ever did defeat Attila
now, there would still be nothing left afterward, anyway. The empire had already been destroyed. The East had been devastated. Africa was in the hands

of Attila's allies, the Vandals. And now the rich fields of Gaul, wealthiest and most beautiful of all the Western provinces, would be turned into another land of ash. Italy would be left until last; and then only Rome.

His fists were clenched, white knuckled. "You have not told me all yet."

The fellow shook his head. "Then it seems his army split into two. One rode due west from the ruins of Colonia and laid waste to Tornacum and Cameracum, and then south and fell upon Lutetia. The second army rode south up the valley of the Moselle, and destroyed Augusta Treverorum, Mediomaurici, and Rhemi."

"Treverorum, too." Its great black gate tower, the Porta Nigra, with its massive portcullis, one of the wonders of Belgia.

"It is believed that the first army—perhaps both—is aiming to fall upon Aureliana next. And then . . . come south."

Leaving nothing but corpses behind them. All down the roads of Gaul, all down the Via Poenina and the valley of the Rhône, nothing but corpses.

He had crossed Germania in winter. Not only his army, but his entire people, old men and wives and children in their high-wheeled wagons laden with loot. That could not be done, not through those trackless and silent forests. An impossible task; but for Attila, *Flagellum Dei,* what was impossible? Did he not have God on his side? He had ridden through those dark and snowbound pine forests, never weakening but only augmenting his strength. Perhaps he had chosen a colder climate for his people to destroy the sickness and fever among them. And it had worked.

With his Byzantine gold, he would have bought more and more support along the away. Among his latest allies would be Gepids and Alans and lean Sarmatian lancers. As he traversed Germania, more and more forest tribesmen would have flocked to his banner, seeing this as the greatest raiding party in history—easy loot. Among those Germanic tribes, surely there still burned an ancient hatred of Rome in the race memory. Those distant sons of old Arminius, still singing their lays of the Battle of the Teutoberg Forest, four long centuries before.

Aëtius stood stunned. Then out of the corner of his eye he saw Lucius moving to dismount. He turned on him angrily.

"No! You go!" He mastered himself again, spoke more quietly. "Old friend and guide, for God's sake, go. Ride back to the coast, take ship for Britain once more, even in winter seas." Lucius hesitated. "As I said before, you are

better off there in your green and gentle island. The rest of Europe is burning. Only you are left. Only in your far west, it may be, will anything of the
old world survive. Let that put strength in your swords when you fight the
Saxons."

Lucius regarded him gravely from under his bushy white eyebrows. Then
he heeled his horse, slowly pulled round and, without another word, headed
down the road to Aquileia.

"There is more news, sir—not of Attila."

Aëtius was gazing after the horseman riding south, longing in his eyes.
"Go on."

"From Constantinople, sir."

Aëtius turned to him again.

"The Emperor Theodosius is dead. He fell from his horse while out riding,
and injured his spine badly. He bore his agony with great fortitude and piety,
it is said, and died three days later, the name of the Savior on his lips."

Aëtius crossed himself. That scholarly, kind-hearted fool . . .

"The new emperor is one Marcian, sir. He has already married the old
emperor's sister."

Aëtius blinked with disbelief. "Pulcheria? That prune-like perpetual virgin?"

"The same, sir."

"And what of Theodosius's widow? The Empress Eudoxia?"

"She has retired to Jerusalem. It is said that relations between her and
Empress Pulcheria were always difficult. Emperor Marcian has meanwhile
already communicated with Emperor Valentinian, wishing him every success
against the Hunnish hordes, expressing only regret that the East cannot be of
any more assistance. But they have too little manpower, and besides, they are
busy with the great new Church Council of Chalcedon."

Aëtius smiled a faint, sour smile, nodding, his mind racing, for a moment
forgetting even Gaul. So she was back in her beloved Jerusalem: further
away from him than ever. Long, long ago there, a young army officer had once
kissed a beautiful empress, adulterously, on a moonlit balcony. Now she was a
widow, and free. Yet the times were against it. It was impossible. He was needed
elsewhere.

He pressed his finger and thumb into his eyes. At times he could come
close to cursing God. He felt as if he was about to be torn apart. Everything

was in ruins, the world was sick, and yet above he could hear the sound of heaven laughing. He felt on the brink of hysterical laughter himself for a moment. The messenger moved uneasily. But when Aëtius opened his eyes again, there was that stolid Germanus before him, and Tatullus just behind. They saluted. He could have clung to them like a drowning man. The sense of illimitable horror faded a little.

Time to take command again. He told them the news from Gaul. They looked grim.

"Men ready to move out at dawn tomorrow, sir," said Tatullus.

"But nowhere near enough ships at Aquileia," said Germanus.

"Nor at Ravenna," growled Aëtius, "quite apart from the fact that the military harbor there was condemned to neglect decades ago, and has since been planted with fruit trees."

Germanus shook his big bullet head. "Bloody disgrace. How's Rome supposed to fight her enemies these days? Throw figs at them?"

"Quite. So we march. We have a prior appointment overland, anyway. Six hundred miles away, so it will take us a month."

"In winter?"

"In winter."

Germanus and Tatullus both looked puzzled.

"At Tolosa," said Aëtius. "At the court of the Visigoths."

4

THE TRAIL OF DESTRUCTION

Attila crossed the frozen Rhine six miles south of Argentoratum, the bitter winter suddenly his ally, the great river as solid as a marble pavement. It took his titanic army over a week to ride from east bank to west over the sparkling ice. He rode with his remaining Chosen Men and his best warriors, and then the rest of the Hun people behind. There rode with him the Kutrigur Huns under their leader, Sky-in-Tatters, and the people of the Oronchan Valley under Bayan-Kasgar; Hepthalite Huns, White Huns, Black Huns, Huns from the shores of the Aral Sea and the very northern limits of the Scythian steppes, clad in furs, with their wicked curved bows and their quivers bristling with arrows.

Now there also rode with him Gepids from the Transylvanian hills, under their King Ardaric; Sarmatian horse warriors, and blue-eyed Alan lancers, an Iranian people, cunning and untrustworthy. The ancient Persians, it was said, had been taught three things as boys: to ride a horse, to shoot an arrow, and tell the truth. The Alans still excelled at the first two.

There were stocky, bearded Rugians from the far northern shores of the Baltic Sea, Scirians in leather body armor, carrying long javelins and battle axes, and flaxen-haired Langobards with great two-handed swords. As the horde passed through Germania they were joined, as Aëtius had guessed, by Thuringians, Moravians, Herulians, Burgundians, and even the sons and grandsons of those nationless freebooters who had once ridden under the banner of Rhadaghastus, and been so savagely defeated by the Huns themselves upon the Tuscan plain.

The losses that Attila had sustained at Viminacium and the other cities of the East, at the battle of the River Utus, and finally beneath the walls of Constantinople—a few thousand in all—had been made up forty- or fiftyfold. The chilly dust cloud and the steam from their horses could be seen a day's march away. His army shook the earth as it rode west.

In the cities along the Rhine they slew every living thing they found. They would have driven off the sheep and cattle as their own, but already they were overburdened, and it was late winter still, and not enough forage. So they took only what they could carry from those wealthy cities, loading it onto their groaning wagons: armor damascened with gold and silver, silken stuffs, rugs, and furs all heaped together with sacred objects looted from burned churches, reliquaries studded with precious stones and housing the bones of forgotten martyrs, chalices, pattens, jewel-encrusted gospels they could not even read.

Among those they captured at Colonia Agrippina was a nobly born Cornish maiden called Ursula, who was to be betrothed to a son of a patrician in the city, and her eleven maidens. After amusing themselves for a while trying to make the girls fall to their knees and worship their god Astur, the Huns ravished them and slew them and hung their bodies from the walls of the city, along with many others. The Cornish maid was soon declared a saint, and a legend rapidly grew up about St. Ursula and her Eleven Thousand Virgins. In this way, history was already reverting to myth, and in place of sober chronicles a new age was being ushered in which would prefer extravagant tales and foolish superstitions to hard-headed facts. It was as if Attila was drawing in, in the very wake of his horse as he rode, a new dark age which would cover all of Europe.

The invaders laid waste the lovely valley of the Moselle, which Ausonius had once so rapturously praised, with its handsome villas amid lush meadows, its valley sides thickly planted with green vines, its bargemen transporting bales of cloth and casks of wine, shouting out to the laughing girls dressing the vines as they passed. At Augusta Treverorum the citizens showed spirit merely by shutting the gates, but Attila had his men drive forward at spear point women and children captured from the surrounding farms and villages, and threatened to slaughter them all unless the citizens of the town opened the gates and treated with him. The gates were duly opened to save innocent lives, at which the Huns slaughtered them all anyway, captives and citizens alike. At Mediomaurici there remained not a building standing except the solitary little chapel of St. Stephen.

Often they came to towns and cities already deserted, and then the Kutrigur Huns galloped forward with particular alacrity, like hounds on the traces, putting their hunting and tracking skills to use. Almost always they found the absconded citizens, huddled in terror in a nearby stretch of forest, and put an end to them there.

After two or three weeks of wreaking havoc all down the Moselle, Attila and his horde left behind them a two-hundred-mile-long valley of the dead.

In all this destruction they met not a breath of opposition, yet all the time Attila himself grew more and more silent, solitary, and withdrawn. He also became increasingly superstitious, never tiring of consulting Enkhtuya for signs and portents, and demanding to know when the Western Roman Army under Aëtius would be marching north to meet them. Every night there were strange ceremonies in his tent, with fur-clad shamans beating deerskin drums to summon the ancestral dead, and antlered sorcerers dancing with rattles, flagellating themselves, wailing nasal incantations. The future was descried in the foam of boiling water, the entrails of chickens, sticks flung at random; by scapulimancy from signs read in the heat-cracked shoulder blades of cattle, and from the gyrations of smoke from burning incense. The portents were always good, but the Great Tanjou looked more and more like a man haunted by some vast and nameless sorrow.

Someone sang,

Turn back, turn back, my mad master,
For things are not as they seem,
My dreams are awakened to nightmare,
And all the world is a dream.

Such are the wages of vengeance,
Such is anger's yield,
My master with all his sad captains
Lying silent in the field.

Kites and crows his companions,
His banner a banner of blood,
All treasures, all holy things
Lost in the flood.

Attila did not silence the singer. He only bowed his head. So let it be.

From the Moselle, Attila's army swung west through the dark and dense Carbonarian Forest: the country of the Batavians, of ghoul-haunted birchwoods and fens, stagnant ponds, thick mosses, dripping ferns, and foul-smelling bogs which could suck down a horse entire and close over its last pitiful struggles in silence as though it had never been.

One night as they lay encamped in that haunted country, Orestes heard his master crying out in terror. He ran into his tent with his sword drawn, and saw to his horror that Attila was rolling on his pallet, eyes wide and mouth foaming, yet apparently still asleep, unable to see. Orestes thought the king had gone mad. He dropped his sword and, seizing his shoulders, tried to shake him back to sense. The next thing he knew was an agonizing pain in his side. Attila had stabbed him.

Orestes sat back, clutching his ribs. The wound was not deep but it bled badly. Gradually the king regained consciousness, staring wild eyed. Orestes drew his hand up from his side, his fingertips wet and red. He held them before Attila. Attila stared at him, the wild light going from his eyes, reason returning, and with it that depthless sorrow. How haunted he looked. He drew his arm across his spittle-flecked mouth and stared up at Orestes, panting.

"I dreamed," he whispered, almost inaudibly, his voice a dry and exhausted croak between gasps, "I dreamed that you had turned against me, that you came into my tent to kill me, saying that I was mad, for I had vowed in my madness to slaughter my way into heaven."

Orestes said nothing, pressing his side to stop the bleeding. Attila seemed oblivious of his hurt. At last, the Greek said that his lord should sleep now, and went to find a comrade to bandage him up.

As he left the tent, he glanced back. Attila sat up on his furs, staring around, lips working, seeing nothing.

The next city the Huns came to was Rhemi, all but abandoned like the rest. Bishop Nicias had refused to desert his post, however, seeing the threat of death as any true Christian should: nothing but a portal to eternity. With him there remained a handful of Gallo-Roman knights, too young to have wives or children and so perfectly contented to die likewise, but adamant that they would not flee before the heathen invaders.

The weather turned bitter, and there were flurries of snow. The great host of Attila remained outside the city, but Attila himself, having heard of this holy man's stubbornness, rode on through the narrow streets with a small company of his favored warriors and Chosen Men. They were wary of ambush, but none came. They emerged into the main square of the city, with the fine façade of the cathedral on the eastern side, facing the Basilica, and the splendid baths and the portico of the marketplace along the other two sides. Attila sat his horse and stared around. A cold spring wind blew through the square, and the horses stamped their hooves. The ghostliness of the depopulated town was eerie and unreal. Even more so the little group across the square from them, on the steps of the cathedral, a Christian priest and eight youthful knights, gazing back at them, silent and unafraid.

"What is this?" roared Attila with sudden anger.

"Welcome to our city," Bishop Nicias called back. "I believe you have traveled far."

Such mocking insouciance enraged Attila all the more. The eunuch priests of that pale, etiolated, defeated Christian god were not supposed to face death as fearlessly as his finest warriors. They were supposed to kneel and plead and whimper, before having their heads snatched back and their pallid, lamblike throats briskly cut. Attila drove his heels into the flanks of his skewbald pony and cantered across to them. His warriors instantly fanned out and nocked arrows to their bows, training them on the little group on the cathedral steps. It could still be a trap. A hundred soldiers might lie in wait inside that stern gray cathedral.

Attila reined in fiercely before the nine, his sword hanging loosely from his right hand.

"Do you not fear me, eunuch priest? I will shortly slay you where you stand."

Bishop Nicias looked mildly puzzled. "Well, first, I am no eunuch, having all my parts intact, as the Good Lord made me." At this wretched jest, his accompanying knights actually smiled. Attila shot them furious looks. "Second, why on earth should I fear you, just because you are about to part my spirit from my mortal flesh? It will only free my soul to fly heavenward and be with my Christ. Death is the fate of all men. It is your fate, too, great Lord Attila."

Attila gazed at him intently. "Do you truly not fear death, old man?"

"Truly not. But I know you do. Which is why I have remained behind here, on the steps of my cathedral: to invite you to throw down your sword, and enter in, and be baptized in the name of Christ. I am here in the hope of saving your immortal soul."

Attila's fury erupted, and he raised his sword and brought it down. The holy man died where he stood, unflinching, slumping almost gently to the ground before Attila's horse. A moment later, arrows slammed into the eight knights, killing some and mortally wounding the others. Even then, not one of them reached to draw his weapon and fight, as if the example of their bishop had been his last word to them. Attila himself loomed over them and finished them with thrusts of his sword.

His men gathered round him, but crying, "Leave me be!" he drove his heels into his horse's flanks and surged forward, up the steps, over the bodies of the slain and in through the great west doors of the cathedral. The moment he had passed through, they slammed shut.

His men waited, perturbed. Orestes had visions of Attila's horse leaving bloody hoofprints all down the white marble paving of the aisle.

He appeared a short while later, still mounted, dragging the doors open again awkwardly from the saddle. He stared up at the sky. "Strange," he muttered.

Orestes said, "My lord?"

He still gazed upward, as if searching heaven. "That there should be thunder out of so clear a sky."

His men exchanged anxious glances.

"Great Tanjou," said Chanat, "we heard no thunder."

Attila's reaction was shocking. He rounded on the venerable old warrior and gripped him about the throat with his mighty left hand. With his right he held his sword point to his throat. Chanat's horse whinnied and backed away, but Attila held on with a vicelike grip, his own horse moving in tandem.

"You lie!" he cried, and the stately buildings around the square echoed back, *lie, lie, lie.* "You heard thunder! You lie, to make me think I am hearing phantoms, that I am haunted by the Christian god there in his charnel house church! You would have me think myself mad, ride out into the wilderness, fall on my sword, that you may plant the first of your own seed on the throne of the Huns!"

But Chanat was no man to be bullied, even with a sword point at his throat. "No, my lord," he said quietly. "The first of my seed, the Lord Aladar, died serving you under the walls of Constantinople. And we do not lie. We heard no thunder."

Attila's eyes bulged, his mouth worked. Then he released Chanat, and sank back in his saddle. There was a long silence. In a nearby street, the cold wind slammed a wooden shutter back and forth in a desolate rhythm. Finally he pulled his horse around, his expression once more blank and hollow, tossed his sword away to clatter on the worn cobblestones, and rode back out of the square.

Geukchu glanced inquiringly at the old warrior, almost with sympathy.

"I still endure," growled the old warrior. And he said it as if he were under a curse.

They rode after Attila, only Orestes dropping down from his horse— clutching his side still bandaged and sore from the stab wound—to retrieve the sword. For was it not the sword of Savash?

The northern battle group under the command of Geukchu had swept through the valleys of the Mosa and the Scaldis, destroying the cities of Tornacum and Cameracum along with many others, and then descended on the city of Lutetia, on the island in the River Sequana in the country of the Parisii. Attila's horde was approaching likewise from the east.

Here again, history has already become legend; and yet it is an established fact that the Huns did not, after all, ever capture or destroy Lutetia, but passed it by and rode on south. Some say that the men of the city were preparing to flee, horrified by the sight of not one but two approaching dust clouds: on both northern and eastern horizon. But the women of the city, made of sterner stuff, insisted that a holy maid called Genevieve had promised them the city would never fall to Attila.

"A holy maid!" scoffed the men. What did holy maids know of war and warriors?

The women said she was praying to God even now, quite calm and resolute, in the circular Baptistery of St. Jean-le-Rond. Some of the men went to look, peeking in on her, and saw that it was as the women said.

Across the river, the Hun horsemen were already massing. The modest walls of the city and the narrow stretch of river seemed little protection. Even less did the prayers of an unworldly young girl called Genevieve. But a large group of the women took refuge in the baptistery with her, singing hymns and psalms, and then men joined them, crowding around outside. The spring air resounded with many voices lifted in praise of the Lord God of Hosts, the God of Abraham, Isaac, and Jacob. And when they looked again, they saw that the Hun horsemen had miraculously disappeared.

It is impossible to distinguish the truth from the legend of St. Genevieve. But, for whatever reason, the Huns never laid a violent hand upon Lutetia. Maybe it was entirely pragmatic of Attila to wish to push on south as rapidly as possible. He wanted to destroy another enemy, before that enemy could join up with the Roman Army. He wanted to make it to Tolosa.

5

THE RIDDLE OF THE WOLF

Aëtius's legions marched the six hundred miles from Aquileia to Gallia Narbonensis in twenty-six days, each legionary carrying his full forty- or fifty-pound pack on his back. It rained much of the way, and snowed heavily at times. Reviewing their achievement, Aëtius felt they had performed satisfactorily.

As they neared Tolosa, he ordered his men to stand down while he and his commanders rode on in alone. It would not do for a force of twenty-five thousand to appear suddenly below the walls of the city unannounced. The irascible King Theodoric might get the wrong idea.

It seemed only moments after they had announced themselves at the East Gate, that there came a frenetic clattering of horses' hooves down the steep cobbled street within, and there were the princes Theodoric and Torismond on their white chargers, faces shining.

"You have come to destroy Attila at last!" they cried.

"I must speak to your father first," said Aëtius gravely.

Old Theodoric received him in a small chamber heated by a burning brazier, and wearing a great white fur cloak across his back. He grasped Aëtius's hand in his bearlike paw and squeezed it tight, smiling beneath his beard.

"By God you gave my boys a good time of it, so you did, out there in the East. My eldest damn near lost his arm, and if he had I'd have come after yours! But he's well now: young flesh and bone knit well. Sit. Drink. You, boy, bring us wine—well cooked."

Cooked wine? In the name of Light . . .

There was no time for small talk. "So," said the old King, "you will face Attila on Gaulish soil."

"It seems so."

"You know his numbers?"

"A hundred thousand."

Theodoric shook his great shaggy white head. "More. I think two hundred thousand. They are ill provisioned, and far from home, living only on what they can loot. Can you calculate how much fodder two hundred thousand horses traveling in winter need?"

"A lot—more than the Huns have prepared for. The country will be stripped bare."

"You could just leave them to starve. The asses. Your own lines of supply are well ordered, I presume?"

"Of course. Are we not Romans?"

Theodoric guffawed. "So you are. Well organized as always, I'll stake my beard on it."

"And our numbers: twenty-five thousand. They are the finest: well trained, fighting fit, and full of confidence. But they are only twenty-five thousand."

Theodoric shook his head again, his eyes gleaming in the light of the brazier. "It is not enough."

"If the wolf lords of the Visigothic nation rode with us—"

"*No!*" Theodoric roared. "Do not ask us. This is not our war. We are not Attila's enemies. He comes for revenge against Rome."

The cooked wine arrived. Aëtius tasted it. It was heated, spiced, honeyed, and quite revolting. He drank it down manfully.

"And after, when Rome is destroyed and Gaul laid waste?" he resumed.

"Then we will see. Maybe our own kingdom will . . . extend. But I will not sacrifice my beloved people for Rome."

There was a long silence.

Then Aëtius said, "Give me your hand."

Theodoric frowned but held out his huge bear paw of a right hand, a fat gold ring on every finger.

"What danger is a wolf with only one jaw?" murmured Aëtius.

Now Theodoric listened. He liked riddles.

Aëtius began to press his thumbtip into Theodoric's palm. Theodoric stared down. What game was this?

"Does this hurt?"

"Of course not, you dolt," growled the king.

Keeping his thumbtip in Theodoric's palm, Aëtius circled his strong fore-finger round the back of his hand. Finger and thumb came together in a cruel pincer movement, biting in deep between the narrow bones, setting the nerves tingling.

Theodoric snatched his hand away. "Son of a . . . Now, that hurt!" He tucked it into his left armpit and glared at Aëtius. "And this illustrates what, pray? Except that a wolf with one jaw is harmless, but one with two less so, which I knew already."

Aëtius waggled his thumb before Theodoric's eyes. "Attila." And his fore-finger. "Genseric"

Theodoric shrugged. "It may be so. I still do not believe there is an alli-ance between the Vandals and the Huns against you, but it may be so."

"Not against us," said Aëtius quietly. "Against you."

Theodoric got to his feet and strode about the little chamber, the walls feeling as if they were about to burst asunder, too small to contain his huge presence. When he had calmed down a little, Aëtius resumed.

"Of course, Genseric is already at war with us, fighting with Attila. His ships were at Constantinople and got a nasty surprise."

"My boys told me. What was that flaming weapon exactly?"

"Information reserved only for our allies."

"Damn your balls!"

Aëtius smiled. Then he said, "Amalasuntha, your daughter."

Theodoric's expression softened instantly.

"She is married now to Genseric's son?"

"That she is. And not a day goes by when I do not miss her sweet smile, her laughter like a running stream." He looked stern again. "You see, my old Roman friend, we are kin, the Goths and the Vandals. Our tongues are the same, our religion, our very names."

"Your religion? But Genseric fights with the heathen Huns. He is a creature of treachery."

"He is my kinsman now. Have a care, Roman."

"Forgive me. But I do not trust him."

"Well. Each man to his own. Let us eat."

They dined in the great hall of the palace, and it was like a scene out of Homer, a barbaric magnificence, tempered by the Visigoths' only recently acquired and civilizing *romanitas*. A huge fire blazed in the center of the hall, and they ate sitting upright at long wooden tables, while bards sang old lays of battles in near-legendary eastern forests and open plains, against long-forgotten enemies. There was no mention of ancient battles against the Hunnu.

Aëtius tried to tell himself this was not wasting time, and forced himself to eat well, avoiding staring into the great hearth fire and thinking of all of northern Gaul ablaze. The Visigoths took it as a personal affront if their guests did not stuff their stomachs almost to vomiting. The princes sat nearby, grinning from ear to ear and devouring plateful after plateful of roasted venison and boar. On the adjacent table, those valiant wolf lords Jormunreik and Valamir drank beer from huge auroch horns decorated with silver filigree, draft after draft until they both fell drunkenly asleep where they sat. Nobody took the slightest notice. Probably they would be up at dawn tomorrow and out hunting, with headaches that would have kept any lesser man groaning in a darkened room for a week.

These were the allies the Romans desperately needed. . . .

Looking distinctly uncomfortable amid these scenes was a fresh-faced, rather purse-mouthed young deacon of the Church of Gaul.

Aëtius made polite and tedious conversation with him awhile, and then asked, "And what of this Council of Chalcedon? While Attila and his hordes are on the brink of engulfing the entire civilized world in flames, what keeps Emperor Marcian and the pious Empress Pulcheria so busy, exactly? What are the Eastern bishops debating?"

His sarcasm was lost on the fellow, who loved nothing more than discussing theology, and explained with animation, "Well, firstly, the barbarous enormities of the Irish."

"The barbarous . . . ?"

The deacon nodded vigorously. "Enormities. Of the Irish. And then, following the Second Council of Ephesus, and the considerable progress made there on the issue of *homoousion* and *homoiousion*, they will be discussing the heretical teachings of Nestorius—the *Christotokos* rather than the *Theotokos*, of course. Harsh was his own treatment of the Arians and the Novatianists, as you know, but against Nestorius himself, that great thinker Theophilus of Alexandria will be urging the strictest anathemas."

"Indeed." Aëtius broke a bread roll. "Well, that's good to know."

"But there will be other, more heterodox voices present," said the young churchman darkly, "including both Philoxenus of Maboug and Zenobius of Mopsuestia."

"And we do not approve of Zenobius of . . . ?"

"Zenobius of Mopsuestia!" he cried, flecks of spittle flying from his mouth in his sudden fury. "That . . . that . . ." But he could not find the appropriate words to describe Zenobius of Mopsuestia.

Truly, thought Aëtius, there is no hatred like the hatred between fellow believers. After Arius's death, didn't his great theological enemy Athanasius spread the news that he had died in a public lavatory?

The young deacon drank a little wine, then resumed more calmly, "It is to be hoped that the final *Ekthesis* of the Council will find that the difference of the Divine Natures is in no way altered by Union, but rather that the properties of each Nature are preserved in one single—one *Prosopon* and one *Hypostasis*—with various monoenergist and monothelite qualifications, naturally."

"Naturally." Aëtius munched his roll. "And isn't that precisely what Christ himself spent so much time teaching? Rather than preaching about the poor, and brotherly love and so forth?"

At last Aëtius' sarcasm dawned on the deacon and he glared at him. Aëtius smiled politely, rising from the bench. "Excuse me. I must go and talk to someone more interesting."

He went and squeezed in between the princes. "Truly," he murmured, "the Church must be under the protection of God. It would never have survived this long otherwise."

The next day, Aëtius and his retinue saddled up and rode soberly out of the east gate back to their encampment. They would have to face the Huns alone, outnumbered by as much as ten to one. He reined in and looked at his twenty-five thousand men. "It is not enough," had said Theodoric himself.

"Then why in hell's name does he not join us?" growled Aëtius. He yanked his reins savagely and rode on down into the camp.

"We ride out today?" asked Germanus.

Aëtius shook his head.

"But why should we delay? All of northern Gaul is burning."

Aëtius said nothing for a long time. Then he gazed back toward Tolosa. "I cannot tell you why, but we must wait. Just one more day."

The men grumbled and ate little that evening and slept badly. Waiting was the worst. Every campfire made them think of another burning building, another blazing town, and in the ruins of each blood orange fire they saw shapes of the Devil's horsemen, trailing catastrophe in their wake.

Aëtius, too, had a feeling of impending horror, but he knew he must await it. Evasion was impossible. And as sure as the sun rising, the following morning brought horror, and the horror brought with it a sort of salvation. When he understood, he wished salvation had come otherwise.

6

AMALASUNTHA

A messenger turned off the road into the camp, stiff and cold from his night ride.

He had come at the gallop from Narbo. Princess Amalasuntha . . .

Aëtius raced back to Tolosa, and straight to the royal quarters of the palace. Even as he approached, he could hear a terrible, bull-like roaring.

A ship had come in from Carthage. It bore a small party of Gothic maids, and the princess. She had been expelled by Genseric, who had become suspicious that she was a witch trying to put his son Euric under a spell, and then eventually convinced that she was planning to kill both her husband and her father-in-law. She, an innocent girl of no more than sixteen summers.

But there was worse. . . .

The expelled and humiliated party was on its way. A column of wolf lords rode out to escort them home.

Never would Aëtius forget the glimpse he had of the girl as he looked down from an upper window of the palace. He saw her being helped down from the carriage, and remembered how he had seen her only two years before, a flash and a blur of long fair hair and laughing smile, as she threw her slim arms round her father's great hoary head and covered him in kisses. And now . . .

There was wailing and grieving as in a Greek tragedy. The elderly Queen

Amalfrida looked near to collapse as she leaned on one of her six sons, speechless with sorrow. Another son turned away, unable to look, at once broken hearted for his sister and burning with a rage for vengeance. And old King Theodoric himself took his daughter in his arms and wept, and held her to his great chest, but very gently. For her head was wrapped in bandages stained with blood: her ears and nose had been cut off by Genseric in punishment for her imagined sorcery.

As in Greek tragedy, sorrow followed on the heels of sorrow, like hounds in a slavering pack. The sweet princess, hardly understanding what had befallen her or why, a pawn in a great game played between cruel god-kings or gods, developed a fever as she lay in her bed, and within hours they were saying that her blood had become poisoned by infection. She died the following day, her mother holding one hand and her father the other, begging her parents not to sorrow, and giving her blessings to them and to her brothers and to all her father's people.

None was cruel enough to whisper that perhaps it was a blessing. The queen was speechless with grief, but the king's voice was heard throughout the palace, his agony all the greater because he felt he himself was to blame. His revenge would be terrible.

He cried out in the old Gothic as he took his daughter's body in his huge arms and clutched her to his chest, and all those who heard closed their eyes and turned away.

"*Me jarta, O me jarta,*" he lamented. "My heart, oh, my heart," his own great heart almost cracking in remorse. "May God forgive me. She was my all, my heart, my soul, she was my dawn, my evening sun, my lamp, my earth, my staff, her mother's daughter, my only comfort. How I loved her. My tongue is too weak to tell."

At last he laid her down, and the girl's mother and father clung to each other by her silent bedside and wept until they could weep no more.

Soon the whole of Tolosa was in uproar, with everywhere the sound of horses' hooves and tramping men. Aëtius asked for one last audience with the king. He was denied: "The king is busy with preparations for war."

Aëtius pushed the guard aside, burly as he was, and strode into Theodoric's council of war. With him round the table stood his two eldest sons, Theodoric and Torismond, and his two wolf lord commanders, Jormunreik and Valamir. The rest looked up at Aëtius's entrance, silent and grim faced, but Theodoric did not. The fact that Aëtius's darkest warnings about Genseric had turned out to be true did not endear him to the king, far from it. They only compounded the warring guilt and anger in Theodoric's breast.

He growled, "My heart is set, Roman. We sail for Carthage tomorrow."

"You cannot."

Theodoric exploded into fury, a fury all the more terrible because it was half grief. The table shuddered under his great thumping fist, and then he strode round to Aëtius and roared in his face, "Do not come between me and my wrath, Roman! Do not involve me and my wolf lords in your puny squabbles with your enemies! We have a nobler cause by far. Which is to lay Vandal Africa waste from Tingis to Leptis Magna, and leave nothing behind but a desert of the dead. None shall reckon our vengeance for what that accursed Genseric did to our daughter, but it shall be a vengeance visited on him and his seed and his people a thousandfold—ten thousandfold. The very name of Vandal shall be wiped from the earth, and I will slay all his sons and daughters before him, and I will gut that accursed cur of a king with my own sword and hang his still-breathing body from the towers of his burning capital, to watch over his kingdom's final cataclysm."

Aëtius did not flinch and his voice was low. "My heart breaks for you and your sweet daughter, friend Theodoric. Do not doubt it. Nor would I come between you and your wrath or your righteous vengeance."

"That is good, or I would strike you out of my way with my own fist."

"But if you ride against the Vandals, and we ride against the Huns, our forces are divided. Remember the wolf with one jaw."

Theodoric glowered at him, but the passionate old man was thoughtful for a moment, his chest still heaving.

"They were Vandal ships at Constantinople," continued Aëtius, still quietly. "The Huns and the Vandals are in alliance. They mean to divide the world between them, and this is only the start. I give you my word, when we ride north against the Huns we will find Vandal horsemen fighting alongside them. And I also give you my word that, when we have defeated the Huns and wiped out the name and seed of Attila, Rome will be your ally until death, and we will ride against Vandal Africa together." He dared to seize Theodoric's thick, gold-banded wrist. "Brothers-in-arms, riding together till ruin and world's end."

An ancient Teutonic phrasing, this last. It worked on Theodoric's very soul. At last he turned back to his council.

"It sickens my stomach and wrings my heart not to ride out in vengeance this very day. But there may be wisdom in what our Roman friend says. Vandals may already be fighting with the Huns. What say you?"

The four at the table looked at one another.

She was buried in a coffin of solid gold, in the most beautiful mausoleum in the Cathedral of St. Mary the Virgin in Tolosa. Aëtius thought he had never seen such deep and sincere mourning among the ordinary people for the death of a princess. It was as if the sweet girl had been the daughter of all the Visigoths, and they remembered the sunlight she spread wherever she went.

Her mausoleum was inscribed with a verse in both Gothic and Latin. It read,

Hic Formosa iacet.
Veneris sortita figuram
Egregiumque decus
Invidiam meruit.

Here lies Loveliness.
Hers was the beauty of Venus,
And hers the envy of heaven
For a gift so rare.

7

AURELIANA

They rode out north the next day, banners fluttering, spear points gleaming. There was not a moment to be lost. They had delayed too long already. All of Gaul would soon be overrun.

Aëtius could not help glancing back. It was a proud army. But did a sweet and innocent young girl have to be tortured half to death so that the Romans and the Visigoths could come together? Did God truly fulfill his purposes that way?

Now the resolution of the wolf lords and their aged king was grim indeed. Theodoric had given orders that three thousand of his finest should be stationed down at Narbo, ready to repel any Vandal attack by sea, and another two thousand remain upon the strong walls of Tolosa. The rest rode north: fully fifteen thousand of the finest barbarian warriors in Western Europe. Together with the legions they numbered forty thousand. They rode at the fastest trot they could without tiring their horses beyond fighting speed.

The land rose to the central mountains of Gaul between Aëtius's horse's nodding ears. He had always known in his heart that one day the Visigoths would ride with Rome. Those noble horsemen from the distant steppes, with their mighty ashwood spears, their *Spangenhelm*s with nodding flaxen plumes, and their finely combed hair which shone like the burning sun. These things were written from the first dawn.

In order that they should not be outflanked or harried from behind, there was one more city Attila's forces must take before they could ride on south: Marcus Aurelius's city, fair Aureliana on the Loire, below the hills. For here was stationed Sangiban, the wiliest of Alan warlords, supposed Roman ally, and his force of several thousand horsemen.

The wanderings of the Alans, a people of Iranian origin, were almost as epic in nature as the wanderings of the Huns; and many times the two peoples had fought each other, as many times they had allied together, their friendship like the shifting sands of Khorasan. How an Iranian war band came to be guarding the city of Aureliana for Rome is a story too complicated to be told here. But it is written in the chronicles.

Attila had expected the city to surrender promptly to his vastly superior numbers. The Alans were known for their taste for survival rather than for heroic death in battle. But, to his surprise, as the vanguard of the numberless Hunnish horde approached the city there came reports that the citizens of Aureliana and their Alan protectors had closed the gates of the city and were preparing for siege.

Attila cursed violently, and sent a blunt message to Sangiban and the people. *"Since you have decided to oppose me, I will lay the city to waste and destroy you all."*

To his surprise, the reply from Sangiban received only a few minutes later read, *"Your reputation rides ahead of you, Great Tanjou. You would have destroyed us anyway."*

For a moment, the old sardonic smile flitted across Attila's face at Sangiban's show of insolent spirit. It soon vanished. He smiled rarely these days.

"Prepare the siege," he ordered.

The Bishop of Aureliana was one Ananias, an ecclesiastic of the type who was as willing to carry a sword as a crozier if the battle was on the side of right. Unknown to Attila, it was he who had pressured Sangiban into replying so impertinently.

Now he began to organize the citizens into armed bands and to fortify the city walls wherever possible. Beyond the eastern side of the city, the Hun horde, or that part of it which they could see—for it stretched for many miles, and the majority of those under Attila were in fact riding far and wide to pillage the countryside for leagues around, and would not even be required for the siege—already the Hun horde to the east of the city was busy constructing new siege engines.

Ananias went up the tower of one of the churches with a younger priest, and they stared out.

The younger priest squinted hard, then said quietly, "Those building the engines, they are not easterners."

Bishop Ananias nodded grimly. "I see them. They are Vandals."

The people of Aureliana worked all night to prepare for the onslaught, but the next day broke gray and desolate indeed. Ananias came to address them. His message was short.

"Our Alan friends," he said in his sonorous voice, "have deserted us. They crept out of the city last night."

A low groan went up.

"Whether they have gone to join Attila and his heathen horde, I do not know. But let us rejoice. They did not betray us into Attila's hands, either. The gates remain barred, the city still stands. God is with us. And so: to work."

The Huns did not trouble very long with the attack by the siege engines and the onagers. Before an hour of the onslaught was up, the city's east gates were smashed off their hinges and lying flat. In the exposed gateway, men of the city scrabbled to build new barriers, but Hun horsemen galloped in as close as fifty yards and shot them down. The open gateway was piled with the slain. It was a mockery of a battle. Other Huns simply sat their horses and waited, grinning and sharpening their knives. They would ride into this stiff-necked, barely defended city in an orderly column. What were the fools thinking of? Yet still they could see them rushing about on their simple walls: middle-aged men, young men and old, armed with fire irons, butcher's knives, and pitchforks. They could even hear a deep, sonorous voice, a leader of sorts, shouting continual encouragement.

In the church tower, the young priest with the good eyesight kept continual watch on the road south.

Aëtius was riding at the front of his column, having just stopped for grain. He summoned Knuckles and Arapovian alongside him. As his close guard, they, too, were mounted. Arapovian rode with elegance. Knuckles slumped like a sack of turnips, the fast trot jolting him terribly. He disliked horses in general, and the one beneath him in particular. The horse didn't look too happy either.

"Give me a donkey over a horse any day," he used to say. "Donkeys have brains. Horses just have nerves."

Aëtius wanted to know what else they had learned of the Huns in the disaster at Viminacium. Speaking as survivors.

"They are the finest warriors in the world, man for man," said Arapovian bluntly.

Aëtius inclined his head noncommitally.

"They are hunters," explained the Armenian, "pure hunters. They have spent their lives hunting over the Scythian plains, creeping up unseen and unheard, even unsmelt, on creatures far more sensitive than us—wild horses, saiga antelope, deer. The children begin hunting fieldmice and marmot this way. Beware of any people who are great hunters, you city dwellers, you townsfolk. You will be hunted next."

Knuckles added his own more light-hearted observation, somewhat coarse in nature, expressive of his suspicion that they were also far too intimate with their horses—an observation which had Tatullus threatening to clock him for impertinence before his commanding officer.

Aëtius reined in sharply and gazed along the road north, his eyes narrowing. "Do you see dust?"

"I've been watching it grow for the last half league or so," said Arapovian calmly.

Aëtius rounded on him. "Well, why didn't you say, you damn fool?"

Arapovian arched his fine black eyebrows at the master general. "You didn't ask."

These two . . . as good a pair of soldiers as he'd ever had under his command, but they drove him to distraction.

"Get back in line," he growled.

The dust cloud rose above the horizon. Aëtius sent out his fastest scouts to ride north along the hills on their right and report back with all speed. They returned within minutes.

"Lancers, you say?"

The scouts nodded, their horses foaming with sweat.

"Easterners?"

The scouts looked hesitant.

"You're scouts, damn you!" roared Tatullus in their startled faces. "Didn't you use your eyes?"

"I think they were easterners," said a scout nervously. "They had black mustaches, a lot of them."

"Mustaches," growled Aëtius. "We're planning our campaign around bloody mustaches. You,"—he glared at the scouts—"into line. And bring me better intelligence next time."

"Sir!"

Aëtius regarded his colleagues.

"It can only be one thing," said Germanus.

"I agree." Aëtius looked grim. "That moustachioed, yellow-bellied runaway Sangiban fleeing from Aureliana. Which means we know precisely where the enemy is now."

"And Aureliana is entirely undefended."

"The last milestone said sixteen miles. We'll be there in two hours. Meanwhile, we must first persuade Sangiban of the error of his ways. Bring up the Moorish Horse!"

In moments the five hundred splendid African cavalrymen had appeared under their commander Victorius, a prince of Mauretania.

"Take those hills," said Aëtius, indicating the ridge to the northeast. "Don't trouble about concealment—in fact, make sure you're seen. There's a column of Alan lancers coming down the road, and I don't want them thinking they can turn tail and run. I want them to think they're surrounded. Yes?"

"Yes, *sir.*"

The Moors on their white chargers went coursing away across the meadows and up the low green hills, their white camel-hair cloaks flowing in the wind.

Sangiban cursed in the name of Ahura Mazda the moment he realized there was a column ahead on the road, and cursed again when he gave the order to turn round and one of his commanders pointed out to him that there were more horsemen occupying the ridge all along their left flank and behind.

Sangiban adopted a fixed smile, and rode forward to greet the new arrivals.

The Roman commander cantered out alone to meet him. It was Master General Aëtius. Sangiban had met him before. He cursed a third time, silently, and his fixed smile broadened. They reined in their horses. Aëtius's glance took in the Alan warlord's eyebrows curved like black scimitars, his flashing, unstable eyes, startlingly blue in his swarthy face, his thin lips, and aquiline nose. Behind him, a good proportion of his easterners even had freckled faces and fair hair, which they wore scooped back in gold bands. Some said they were descendants of the army of Alexander the Great. They were handsome devils, right enough. But they were riding the wrong way.

"Lord Sangiban."

"Master General."

"I am glad we met you. You were coming to warn us of the approach of the Huns?"

Sangiban let his smile go at last and nodded gravely. "They are besieging Aureliana. We managed to evade destruction by the skin of our teeth, and raced southward to inform you."

Aëtius's eyes roved over the elegant Alan horses: no sweat.

It was his turn to smile. "Do not fear, our gallant ally Sangiban. You shall yet have your chance to be avenged on your ancient foemen."

Sangiban looked puzzled. "General?"

"We will put you and your lancers in the thick of the fight." The smile vanished. "Fall in."

As he watched the Alan lancers ride past and join the column, Germanus joined him.

"Three thousand in all?"

"More or less. Useful." Aëtius looked after them. "Fine fighters when committed. Otherwise, totally untrustworthy." He pushed himself up in his saddle and bellowed back to the column. "To Aureliana, riding trot!"

"The Huns will be inside the city by the time we arrive, sir," said Germanus as they moved forward. "This will be no cavalry fight."

Aëtius knew what he meant. What did it matter if their horses did arrive tired? This would be hand-to-hand fighting in the streets—if there was any fighting at all left to be done. But Germanus didn't know the terrain.

"The Huns will be ranged north and east of the city," he said, "between the Loire and a low line of hills. Well-wooded hills."

"You mean . . . ?"

"Not enough room for them. Not for an army of two hundred thousand. They've got themselves trapped. We want our horses fresh enough to fight, believe me. The people of Aureliana must hold out just a little longer."

Bishop Ananias turned to his citizen leaders. "They're coming in now. Prepare yourselves."

He sent word once more to the lookout in the church tower. One last desperate hope. No, the answer came back: still no sign of a relief column.

The Huns came galloping in through the east gate tightly packed, swords and spears at the ready, and found themselves in long, narrow East Street. They surged on, only to find the side streets blockaded by overturned carts, crates, stacked wine barrels, blocks of building stone. Immediately they began to feel trapped and claustrophobic. The houses and churches hemmed them in. This was no terrain for horse warriors. This was like fighting in a cavern.

The people of the city had vanished into their houses, or maybe underground. The sky overhead had turned a bruised gray, threatening heavy rain. Some Huns rode forward in their fury and began to hack at the wooden carts with their swords, howling. Others punctured the wine barrels with their spears and lay on the ground with their mouths open beneath the crimson spouts. Then missiles started raining down on them—stones, bits of twisted iron, horseshoes, anything. Barely armored as they were, and few wearing helmets, since they were riding in to slaughter unarmed civilians, several horsemen reeled in their saddles, skulls cracked, blood coursing down into their eyes. Others leaped off their horses and kicked in doors, dragging out the occupants and butchering them in the streets. It was to be a foul fight.

Behind them, more Huns were still trying to get into the city, packing ever closer and closer. Bishop Ananias directed operations as best he could from the bell tower of the cathedral. The Huns had thus far made so little progress through the city's narrow streets that his runners were able to transmit messages freely. Once more he sent for word from the lookout priest, and once more the reply was "Nothing." Inside the cathedral, women lit candles, pale imitations of the devouring Hun fires already roaring in the city's suburbs, and the air was filled with the sounds of prayer and lamentation.

The fight was becoming desperate. The sturdiest citizens had appeared on the streets with their fire irons and pitchforks, more frightened of huddling in their cellars and waiting to be slaughtered than of fighting out in the open streets. But this was a mistake, for as soon as the Huns saw moving living targets they unslung their bows and punched them full of arrows.

With every street blocked and every house barricaded, the barbarian horsemen's progress was slow and painful, and their longing to be free to gallop and shoot and cut down was frustrated at every turn. They yelled brutal taunts and savage war songs, dragged people from their houses by the hair and slit their throats, lassoed the wagon blockades and tried to haul them free. But it was slow and dispiriting work.

Then there came a new sound over the roar of the flames and the cries of the people. The church bells were ringing: a moving dust cloud had been seen on the far horizon.

Attila ground his teeth. "They cannot have ridden this far so soon. This cannot be the Romans."

"It is, Great Tanjou. And with them . . ." Even Orestes hesitated.

"*Speak.*"

"And with them ride the Visigoths."

Attila's roar filled the tent. A wooden stool flew and smashed into the main post. He strode outside and surveyed the view. His men were crowded round the pent-up gates of Aureliana. Behind lay a low ridge of thickly wooded hills. The silver river gleamed. There was no room to breathe. No room anywhere.

"That city"—he pointed with his spear—"that city . . . I will return . . . that city . . ." He was jabbing the air now, his mouth working, his face livid, beaded with sweat. Orestes was already untethering their horses. "That city, I will not only lay it waste, I will torture its every citizen, every man, woman, and child, I will have daughters murder their fathers, mothers their sons. Their bodies will hang crucified all along the road from here to . . ." With a mighty heave he hurled the spear into the air where it arced and sank to the ground and stuck fast. "To *Tolosa*!"

Orestes mounted.

Attila wiped the spittle from his beard. "Pull them back," he said. "We cannot fight here." His barrel chest heaved, he clutched his side. "I cannot breathe!"

The moment the Roman and Gothic banners were perceived in the wind, the mood in the city changed. The bells rang from church to church, spreading like birdsong through a wood in springtime, and the great cathedral bell rang out over all of them. The Huns in the streets stalled and looked around, bewildered, as word gradually spread that they were to retreat. Some ignored the order and pushed on into the city. None of them survived. The citizens, newly fired with confidence and anger, struck them down and slew them wherever they found them.

Then came the sound of Roman trumpets and bugles giving their sharp, precise commands, and the Huns were suddenly fleeing in a drunken panic with the citizens at their heels. When the tattooed warriors emerged again from the East Gate, which they had entered not an hour or two previously, it was to see their vast host already disappearing over the low hills to the north under the threatening sky. They remounted and galloped after, but a great serpent of gleaming armor cut between them and their comrades, and the would-be sackers of Aureliana were put to the sword, one and all.

The Romans reassembled their column on the outskirts of the city, and rested and watered their horses. The citizens brought them provisions, and Bishop Ananias spoke with Aëtius, and also with Theodoric.

" 'And lo, I shall smite them with the sword,' " roared the old king, " 'and the heathen shall flee before me into the hills!' "

Ananias nodded. "Thus spake the Lord of Hosts."

"You fought well, my lord Bishop," said Aëtius. "But turn your attention from the Scriptures just for a moment. Your Majesty, did you see the banners of the enemy riders on their left flank as they fled?"

"The banners of the heathen," rumbled Theodoric, "barbaric ensigns, covered with the runes of savagery and unbelief."

"Among them, the Black Boar."

Theodoric gasped and clutched his beard.

"Genseric's sons are here." Aëtius nodded coolly. "Frideric, Euric, and Godric."

Theodoric was already turning his horse and digging his heels in, but the princes rode in either side of him and calmed him.

A scout rode up.

"Have your skills improved?" snapped Aëtius.

"Sir, they ride northeast. At least some of the horses look lean and sickly."

"Hm. Another job for the Moorish Horse."

Victorius appeared.

"Centurion, spread out the map."

Tatullus knelt on the dry ground and spread out a huge campaign map, made of the thickest rolled vellum and taller and wider than the height of a man.

"Listen closely, Moor. Ride east and then north with fifty of your best men. Ride as fast as you ever have ridden. Overtake the Huns, but be on your guard for their outriders—they range far. Here, at Melodunum"—he pointed with his staff—"and also here, at Augustabona, there are vast *horrea,* granaries. The locals will direct you to them. The Huns must not get to them. You understand? Burn them to the ground, then circle back and find us again. The Huns won't catch you, not with them on their half-starved ponies and you on your fine Berber horses."

"And what of fodder for our fine Berber horses?" said Victorius.

"They'll be well fed from our supply lines south. It's not a problem; we've got it covered. You know that a full marching legion of five thousand men needs eight thousand pounds of grain a day, plus six hundred pounds of fodder for its auxiliary cavalry. A full cavalry division needs a whole lot more. And you think nomads like the Huns will have planned ahead for provisions? They'll never find pasture enough, not in cultivated Gaul." The cool gray eyes scanned the horizon. "Sometimes military victory lies in details, not in heroics. Attila and his horde in Gaul are going to starve."

The Mauretanian grinned, and without another word stretched out his arm and galloped forward. Fifty men surged after him, swinging east, wide of the retreating horde.

Aëtius looked at the map again. "The nearest flatlands northeast," he said. "The valley of the Marne?"

Tatullus nodded. "Catalaunia."

"The battle of the Catalaunian Fields," murmured Aëtius. "Sounds good."

8

THE CATALAUNIAN FIELDS

The Huns retreated from Aureliana, barely able to believe that they had fled before the long-awaited Roman Army. The skies darkened further and it began to rain. Their horses would not move fast enough. They hung their heads low, their flanks were tightly drawn in and their haunches jutting and bony. There was never enough grass, not even now in early summer. The winter had been bitter, and spring had been wet and overcast. At the head of the vast horde, Attila rode out in front, his head bowed, hatless, his coarse gray locks sodden and dripping, his face deep graven and grim, speaking to no one. Orestes and Chanat rode a little way behind him.

As for the nomad horsemen themselves, the Kutrigur Huns under Sky-in-Tatters, the Hepthalite Huns under Kouridach, the Oronchans under Bayan-Kasgar, and many others, their leaders were no longer admitted to the Great Tanjou's councils. Somewhere along the way, the Tanjou had become sole commander, and they his wordless slaves. Already they had begun to fade away from his ragtag army. Riding cold and hungry through these rainy western lands, they had begun to feel homesick.

Here, in these prosperous, well-farmed provinces of the Western Empire, there were roads and towns and farmsteads everywhere, and no room to gallop or breathe. The fields were hedged around and enclosed, the forests fenced and owned, and an alien, man made world it seemed to them. How their hearts ached for the wind on the treeless steppes and the white glittering mountains beyond. All the vastness of Asia was theirs for the taking. What were they doing here?

Too far we have come from our homeland, they said. In the Pastures of Heaven there is such peace and space that it is sacrilege even to shout in those high meadows, so near the home of the gods. Here men say that the world is fallen and darkened with sin and wickedness, but they have not seen the Pastures of Heaven. The world has not fallen there, on the very thresh-hold of heaven. There peace comes on every soft breath of the wind, whisper-ing over the emerald grass, and how fat the horses are there. Their sad horses now could do with the green grass of those Pastures, but they were months and years away. So distant, it was pain for the heart to think of them, and the snowdrops and alpine asters and edelweiss in the passes of the mountains surrounding the plains in a giant ring, the nodding oxeye daisies and cycla-men and wild garlic and the cranes crossing the sky beneath the eye of heaven.

But still they must fight, it seemed. The Great Tanjou had decreed it. And had heaven itself not appointed him?

Aëtius gave orders for his army to rest, feed the horses, do their hooves, give 'em a good brush down, all that horse stuff. Also to feed themselves, get some sleep. No booze. "We'll be on the road and fighting again tonight."

His men groaned. He grinned. He himself appeared to need no sleep.

Toward dusk, fresh war parties came in to join them. Not large, but good for morale. Stocky Bretons from Armorica, Burgundians from the north, noblemen from Aquitania, moustachioed Frankish fighters with their lethal *franciscae* or thowing axes.

"Rome's a bit like your health," Aëtius commented dryly at this sudden show of alliance.

"Sir?" said Tatullus.

"You never appreciate it till it's on the wane."

Tatullus laughed. True enough. Suddenly every citizen of the empire, from the most indolent patrician to the near barbarian on the fringes, with the Hun war machine on their doorstep, seemed to have become intensely appreciative of the benefits of Roman civilization.

They rode out at dusk under a rising summer moon and the golden globe of the planet Jupiter. The great column, lit by torchlight, was a magnificent sight, like something out of the ancient world.

By the strong moonlight they could see the devastation the Huns had wreaked: vineyards and orchards ravaged and burned; entire villages razed to mere circles of charcoal and ash; slaughtered cattle all along the road, like boulders haloed by moonlight in the darkness. If the Huns could not take them, no one else would have them, either. Already there was a bitterness in the Huns' savageries which looked like the last retribution of a defeated army.

Aëtius and his men might even have taken comfort from that thought had the atrocities they encountered not been so foul, nor the glimpses of un-housed and starving people been so frequent. Filthy, snot-nosed children scur-ried away from them like frightened animals, to find what shelter they could in the remnants and ruins. They were the lucky ones—luckier, at any rate, than those who had been roped and torn apart by horses, or crushed under wagon wheels, their split limbs left at the roadside for the dogs.

This was the nightmare landscape that the Huns had carved out of the most civilized and affluent of all the Western provinces. A land of vineyards and orchards, fine towns and elegant villas, rendered down to a primeval country of well-fed wolf packs howling under the moon, dark smoke drifting across the extinguished land. Some ancient sorceress with sloughed snake-skins knotted into her hair, stirring a foul-smelling pot by a dung fire. Naked horsemen taking scalps with hand axes. History itself erased.

Lastly they came to a village where a group of naked children hung from the lower branch of a chestnut tree. They had been tied back to back and a heavy rope wound round their necks, bunched together like dried flowers. The rope had been lashed over the lower branch and they had been hauled up to hang there, turning slightly in the night breeze on that creaking rope, ghostly in the dappled moonlight through the lanceolate leaves above their heads, their naked bodies white and innocent still, but above the rope their heads black like old and withered seed heads on young flowers.

Men of war as hardened as Tatullus and Germanus and Knuckles were frozen in horror for a moment, staring up in disbelief.

"Cut them down!" said Aëtius savagely.

To think that only lately he had entertained thoughts of noble, copper-skinned warriors on the free and windy steppes. He yanked his horse away. He was a dreaming fool. Nobility and evil mixed in the Huns, as in all men.

The battle-hardened legionaries lowered the bodies down. There was no time to bury them decently: atrocity would follow atrocity along the road ahead. But of course they did bury them decently, and set a wooden cross in the fresh-dug earth for each and every one of them. Afterward, Knuckles was seen taking his club to the trunk of the tree itself in maddened but silent anguish.

Aëtius called him over. The hulking Rhinelander stopped and wiped his brow and then came slowly over.

"We were never going to give Attila quarter," said Aëtius. "Now you see why." He looked away down the dark road. "Back on your horse now, man. It's Huns we're here to fight, not trees." Then he addressed all the men within range. "We catch up with them and harry them tonight. They are going slowly because their horses are starving, and because they have . . . amusements to practice along the way, which slow them still further. They're defeated and out of fuel. Now it's their turn to suffer."

There was a terrible shout, and the column moved out at a grimly determined pace. The miles raced by beneath their horses' hooves.

At the front of his army, Attila heard the distant hubbub. It was the Romans falling on his Gepid rearguard and taking it apart piecemeal. Others of his followers were harried bloodily away into the night, losing formation and quickly being destroyed. The vast horde was being eaten up from behind, driven east in bewilderment and terror along the dark roads.

Attila rode on regardless.

Only toward dawn did the Romans fall back and give them respite.

The day was unseasonally cold for summer, and there was a thick mist, an unseen sky. It was a country of tall poplars and slow-moving streams, tributaries of the River Matrona. The Catalaunian plain: a flat, sodden land which filled the steppe horsemen with heaviness and dread.

For three nights Aëtius's forces harried the invaders, and then let them camp, exhausted and deeply demoralized. There was a river running roughly east–west, wych elm and alder, heavy plowland, stretches of forest, and a thick mist again. No moon.

The Romans camped, too. They would do battle in the morning.

In the night there was the sound of approaching horsemen, but it was only the returning Moorish cavalry. Mission to destroy the granaries fully accomplished.

At last the two great opposing armies faced each other in the Catalaunian Fields. Dawn broke slowly on that mist-shrouded day, and as soon it broke a shape was seen looming up on the Huns' right, the Romans' left. In the moonless, misty night, neither army had seen it as they drew up their lines and committed themselves to battle. Yet this could change everything. It was a hill. A solitary round-headed hill, maybe a couple of hundred feet above the plain, lightly scattered with beeches. It commanded the entire field. And it was nearer to the Hun lines than the Roman.

No sooner did the dark green bulk of the hill loom out of the thinning mist, the sun itself not visible yet, than horsemen from each side were galloping for it. From the Hunnish lines came a stream of warriors on shaggy ponies, bristling with spears and without formation. On the Roman side, Prince Torismond vaulted onto his horse bareback, seized his spear from where it stuck butt-first in the soft ground, and led his wolf lords racing across the wet grass for the slopes.

Aëtius circled his bare sword in the air and ordered his Augustan Horse round the side of the hill to hit the oncoming Huns in the flank. They rode off at all speed, their horses stretched out, ears flat and nostrils flared in a furious gallop, but it was clear that they wouldn't make it. The Huns were already streaming up their side of the hill toward the tree-crowned summit. As the Roman cavalrymen neared the enemy lines, not one of them having had time to don helmet or cuirass, the Hun arrow storm hit them and took a terrible toll. Aëtius instantly called them back.

Both sides tensed and waited. Somewhere away to his right, Aëtius heard old Theodoric bellowing at his armorer, but it would all be decided by the time he was done.

Mist still shrouded the summit of the hill. There came the sound of horses' hooves galloping in soft turf and beech leaves, and the muffled cries of men.

Prince Torismond did not hesitate for a moment, though he had neither saddle nor armor, not even a sword, only that long ashwood spear. Grief for his
sister still drove him. His forty or fifty wolf lords were similarly light on armaments. So were their enemies, but the Huns had gained the summit and
were aiming their first volley of arrows at the hated Visigothic horsemen galloping arduously uphill over wet ground toward them. Yet the timing was
wrong. Some of the Huns managed to let fly, and inevitably found targets at
such close range, but so ferocious and unflinching was the charge of the big
horsemen that in the next instant they crashed into the Huns and sent them
reeling.

Beside Torismond rode the huge Jormunreik, showing his true mettle
by revealing at this late stage that he had had no time to bring any weapon at
all—his burning loyalty to his prince had been everything. There was no
time for consideration, and so he had galloped uphill against the Huns
entirely unarmed. As his big gray mare erupted between two startled Hun
archers, the best he could offer was huge back-handed swipe of his fist which
sent one spinning off his pony to the ground. The next instant he had
snatched the bow from the other's hands, and lashed him across the face with
it, blinding him. Then he wrapped his forearm round the Hun's neck and
broke it. He pulled the dead Hun from his pony like a thing stuffed with
straw and tossed him to the leaf-strewn ground, snatching the Hun's ten-inch
yataghan from his leather belt as he did so. With this as his only weapon, he
fought on.

Near Jormunreik, similarly disadvantaged by his own haste, Valamir was
wielding a huge fallen tree branch for a weapon, swiping startled Huns from
their ponies to the ground and then leaning over and stoving in their skulls.

The violence and unexpectedness of the wolf lords' onslaught was such that
the Huns were already being pushed back in disarray from the hilltop.

There came the stir of a breeze and a sliver of sunlight across the fields,
and then out of the wind-thinned mist on the hill, figures came tumbling
back down the slopes on the Hunnish side. Ponies rolled over and over, warriors staggered with their own arrows plucked from their quivers and driven
through their torc-decorated throats. The mist thinned further, and it was a
rout. The Visigoths' white horses reared up against the eastern sunlight,

snorting, magnificent, triumphant, swords circling overhead and flashing silver in the morning air, and the Hunnish archers broke and fled.

"Palatine Guard, second cohort!" roared Aëtius. "Consolidate the position on that hill! Improvise brakes, trenches, whatever it takes. That hill is ours and it stays ours. Move it! You've got about five minutes before the shooting starts."

The black-armored Palatine Guard ran as swiftly as four hundred Achilleses over the wet fields to the hill and up, while the wolf lords drove the dispossessed Huns all the way back to their own jeering lines.

"Call them back, Sire!" Aëtius galloped over to King Theodoric, who was by now firmly seated on what looked like an eighteen-hand plowhorse, in a huge and elaborate carved and painted wooden saddle with solid gold finials, thoroughly enjoying the grandstand view of his wolf lords' heroics.

"Your Majesty, call them back! The Hun archers will kill them all when they come in range."

"Nonsense," bawled Theodoric. "Let them have their glory. My son Torismond is a fine lad, is he not?"

Aëtius could hardly bear to look. Yet even though they rode as near as eighty or seventy yards to the Hun lines, the wolf lords took not a single hit, veering away well after the last moment and galloping back round the hill toward their own lines. They returned to festive cheering as if they were all at an afternoon of the games and their chariot team had just won. King Theodoric's voice sounded most loudly of all, as he cuffed his boy jovially round the head.

Now the dispositions of the two opposing armies were clear.

Attila had concentrated his own warriors in the center, with the Kutrigur Huns to his right, their flank protected by a lesser river, and other peoples to the left and behind. At least a mile back or more were his baggage wagons and the noncombatants; for the women and children had followed even here to spectate at this great day in the people's history.

Aëtius's dispositions were more complex. He had placed Sangiban and his three thousand Alans at the center—as promised. They were dismounted, their long lances set in the ground like pikes. Behind them were ranged his best field-army legions, the Herculians, Batavians, and Cornuti Seniores, and held in deep reserve were the remaining cohorts of the Palatine Guard. On the left wing he had his Augustan Horse, themselves saved from outflanking by the presence of the hill, along with the last few centuries of the frontier legions, excepting only the XII Fulminata, the Lightning Boys. These Aëtius had despatched up to the hill to dig in their sling machines and arrow firers behind the fierce ranks of staves and trenches that the Palatine Guard would already have established. Only lightweight field artillery, but very effective from that commanding height.

On the far right of the Roman field was the great, fifteen-thousand-strong wing of the Visigothic nation. Among the many brightly colored pennants decorated with Christian symbols could still glimpsed the occasional likeness of a raven: Odin's bird. Before them lay all the space of the desolate plain in which to arc out wide and scythe into the vast war machine opposite. They had already identified the banners of the Black Boar: the Vandals.

Theodoric nodded gravely, gazing across at those fated ensigns from under his bushy white brows. "So let it be, for weal or woe," he rumbled. "Let us have one afternoon of righteous happiness, before our long evening time of sorrow."

He summoned his sons alongside him, and laid his hand on his armored breast; the princes did likewise. Beneath their bronze cuirasses, father and sons each wore a silver locket containing a single lock of a young girl's fair, fair hair. They clasped their right hands together. For them, this battle was not about the future of the world.

The sun was rising fast in the eastern sky, flashing on shields and swords. Aëtius rode ceaselessly among his lines on his white horse. He gave many curt orders but no great oration. There were multiple motives and loyalties here today—all nations from the Volga to the Atlantic were present. But he spoke to each legion and body of men in turn, and saw resolution in every face.

Across from them, a mile off at most, was the army of Attila. It was impossible to count, but the Romans were probably outnumbered five to one. Yet it was only the second time that Attila had faced a professional army on an open battlefield—and the first time he had faced a commander who knew how to win. Already the Huns, and their less committed followers even more so, were haunted by a deep fear that the might of Rome remained intact, despite all assurances of decadence and decline.

The sun rode higher, the plain burning clear of mist. It was the perfect terrain for the lightning attack of the Hun horsemen with their lethal arrow storm. But Attila did nothing. He sat his muddy skewbald pony like a stone horseman, staring across at his adversary, the great Master General Aëtius, as he tirelessly worked his lines.

"Great Tanjou," said Chanat, coming alongside him.

Attila did not react for a long time. Then he said something about how even an ancient and ivy-grown castle can still resist attack if its walls are strong.

"My lord?"

"But no matter." He turned to Chanat and showed his teeth. "My guide Enkhtuya has examined the entrails. 'Today, the leader of your enemies will die in battle': there is a simple and straightforward prophecy for you, old Chanat." He gazed out over the field again. "Aëtius's day is almost ended," and he struck his fist upon his saddle so that his horse harrumphed and shifted.

"Then let us fight, Great Tanjou. It is time."

Attila nodded. "My order is coming."

"General Aëtius, sir. War band approaching from the north."

Aëtius sighed. Another little volunteer force to mess up his lines. He could do without them, frankly. He rode around the back of his lines and skirted the hill.

Across the sunlit farmland came a neat column of, at most, two hundred men, spears to the sky. Aëtius's heart stirred, despite his more rational reservations. Two hundred, coming to fight two hundred thousand. Here was valor.

As they drew nearer he saw the leader of the column, a broad-shouldered fellow with a white beard. He gasped.

The leader reined in and nodded. "Master General Aëtius of the Romans. Ciddwmtarth of the western Celts and his knights, at your service."

Aëtius tried to speak but could find no words, could only seize Lucius's arm in its studded leather forearm guard.

The old soldier's eyes twinkled in his lined face to see this famously stern Roman general so moved. He had a heart after all.

"Gallant little Britain comes riding to rescue all of Europe from the hand of tyranny and the Hun." Lucius's voice was deep and dry indeed.

Aëtius spoke with deep sincerity. "You are welcome, friend, welcome. You asked for our aid and got none. Now you come riding to our aid unbidden." He shook his head.

Lucius said nothing.

"Are your people safe while you are gone?"

"There will be more fighting to be done upon our return," said Lucius laconically.

Aëtius recovered himself. "This will not be forgotten." He looked at the man riding behind Lucius: perhaps fifty or so but his hair still dark, his face unlined, his brown eyes observing this exchange with quiet attentiveness. "And you. You are . . . ?"

The man nodded. "My name is Cadoc, son of Ciddwmtarth." And he smiled. Yes, fate was strange.

"To think," Aëtius murmured, shaking his head again, "to think, there were once four boys who played together on a Scythian plain. A Roman and a Hun, and Greek and Celtic slaves."

"*Taken* for a slave," growled Lucius. "Not slave born."

"Not slave born, no. Nobly born," said Aëtius quickly.

Lucius harrumphed. Cadoc still smiled. Then he said, "The sisters who weave the web weave in many tricks and turnarounds. The Greek boy . . ."

"Orestes. He still rides with Attila, too. The Four Boys. Today we are all together again."

"To play together on a wide and windy plain, as of old."

Aëtius could feel his eyes begin to swim. How desperately sad was life. Not boyhood: boyhood was sweetly ignorant. But how sad to grow to manhood. He steadied himself by telling them once more that they were most welcome.

Lucius's only response was to ask where he and his knights should fight. Aëtius said that they might choose. He had no jurisdiction over men of such valor.

"Very well," said Lucius, heeling his horse forward. "But first we must speak with Attila."

"You . . . ?"

Between the astonished lines of the opposing armies, two men rode out from the Roman lines across the divide between them, walking their horses slowly and unhurriedly. One was a fine old fellow with long white hair, wearing a gold fillet, and a middle-aged, mild-looking fellow followed just behind.

Ready to greet them, the Huns drew back their bows.

The old fellow scanned the Hun lines until he saw who he wanted, and rode straight over to him. Hun bowstrings creaked. The Great Tanjou came forward a little on his pony. The pair stopped. Eyes met fearless eyes.

"I know you," said the King of the Huns.

"Since you were a boy you have known me," said the old man, and his voice was strong and bitter and unafraid.

The Great Tanjou glanced at the other man, then back at the leader.

"Once I saved your life in the backstreets of Rome," said Lucius. "Once I saved your life in a vineyard. Once I saved your life on a lonely plateau in the mountains of Italy. My men died rather than hand you over to your enemies."

"Who turned out to be Romans, too."

"Who turned out to be Romans, too," the Celt agreed, almost with impatience. "Did I save a boy's life, only to bring all this"—he waved his arm wide—"this destruction down upon the world?"

"Eternity's work!" snarled Attila. "Every man has his burden to bear. You have yours. I have mine."

Lucius's voice shook with anger. "If ever you owed a man anything, you owed your life to me in those days, Attila. No more than a friendless runaway, you were then."

The king flinched, storm clouds moving over his ravaged face.

Another man approached: the bald-headed Greek. He regarded the two closely, and then a smile flitted over his habitually expressionless features. "Well, well," he said softly.

"This battle," demanded Lucius roughly. "How many men will die? How many widows will you make?"

"Many tens of thousands!" cried Attila. "Yet still far fewer than the Romans have made in their twelve hundred years of tyranny. You are a fool to be here, old Lucius. This day will be cruel beyond imagining. But I remember you. Stay here and when the battle is concluded, I may reward you with gold—though doubtless you are too noble of soul to be interested in mere gold."

Lucius did not honor this with a reply.

Attila's eyes flashed dangerously. "Then drop your spears and depart, you and your Celts. No one is interested in you any more, neither I nor Rome. Go back to your miserable, fog-bound island, if you have any sense. You are worthless here. What has your little island kingdom to do with Rome, or Rome with you?"

"Much," said Lucius. "Britain may be an island, a sweet green island. But no man is an island."

Attila leaned forward and spat. "For myself, and my people, and this great battle before us," he said, "the die is cast." His lips curled at the bitter allusion, and he added in a low voice:

By a King of Kings from Palestine
Two empires were sown,
By a King of Terror from the east,
Two empires were o'erthrown . . .

The second Celt instantly responded, his voice still quiet but his every word clear:

When the wise man keeps his counsel,
The conqueror keeps his crown;
One empire's birth was Italy,
The other was his own.

Attila glared at him, jerking his reins up to his chest as if for protection. "What is that?" he rasped. "What is that you say?"

Cadoc only smiled politely and said no more.

Instead, Lucius said, "He is a remarkable one for poetry, my son. I taught him much—old rhymes, verses, even snatches of ancient prophecy, supposedly!" He gave a curt laugh, skeptical or ironic, it was impossible to say. "And do you know, he remembers every word. It is a gift of my people." He looked Attila in the eye, and then Orestes. *"Every word."*

Attila's horse was restless beneath him, side stepping, champing at its bit, sensing his agitation. "Speak that verse once more. Repeat it to me," he rasped. "Speak!" There were storm clouds over his face again, and beside him

Orestes, too, seemed strangely perturbed. But father and son had already pulled their horses round and were walking back to the Roman lines.

"Speak!" Attila roared after them. "Damn you, brown-eyed poet!"

All along the Hun lines, his warriors levelled arrows at the backs of the departing riders, but Attila swept down an angry arm, and their bows were lowered.

Ahead of them, the distant Roman lines began to shimmer in the rising summer heat. Attila's yellow, wolfish eyes seemed to shimmer, too, those ancient, glittering eyes which had seen all and known all and found no rest or contentment in all the world. Those eyes shimmered as if even he were deeply moved. The gallant Celtic war band would soon meet its death here on these lonely Gallic plains, loyal unto death to an empire whose days were done, trampled beneath the hooves of two hundred thousand of his warriors. Had not Astur willed it long ago? *"Yet hard is the gods' will, My sorrows but increase, And I must weep, beloved, That wars will never cease":* an ancient song that someone he once knew used to sing to himself. And then it came to him, who it was who used to sing that ancient song to himself, softly, by firelight, in Italy long ago.

Then let it begin.

Or let it all fall.

Twenty or thirty yards off, Lucius reined in, turned sideways in his saddle, and spoke to Attila one last time.

"By the way," he said, "your baggage wagons are burning."

Attila glanced back, and instantly began lashing his horse into motion, sorrow transformed into howling rage. From a mile or two behind the Hunnish horde, thick black smoke was roiling up high into the morning air.

9

THE HARVEST FIELD

Aëtius had used his Batavian special forces, his *superventores,* exactly as they were supposed to be used, skilfully and in secrecy.

The single century of lightly armored men had skirted the hill as soon as its possession was consolidated by the Palatine Guard, well dug in around the summit. They had crawled along a drainage ditch, well wide of the Hun lines, running down to the river that formed Attila's supposedly safe right flank. Safe enough from major attack or cavalry, true. But the Huns wrongly supposed their own fear of deep, strong rivers to be universal, and their focus was elsewhere.

The Batavians came across the river as swiftly as crocodiles across the serpent Nile, breathing through hollow reeds, swimming strongly. They slithered up through the sedge of the far bank, dripping like watery ghouls, duckweed stuck to their lightweight leather cuirasses. Their backpacks dripped, too, but the contents were still as dry as desert sand, triple wrapped in oilcloth. They crept along the riverbank until they reached the baggage wagons.

The great high-wheeled Hunnish wagons were entirely unprotected by warriors, although crowded on top of them were old men, women and children, gazing southward, munching strips of smoked meat, eagerly waiting for the battle to begin. On the nearest wagon, the *superventores* noted, chuckling to themselves, one old woman was even making the best use of this tedious time before the fight by doing sewing repairs to a leather jerkin.

Shock and terror would clear them off quickly enough. And then speed of retreat would be everything.

The eighty men came screaming and yelling up through the reed beds, muddy and plastered with weed, swords whirling. The women took one horrified look at these river demons, snatched their infants down from the wagons and fled. The *superventores* were at the wagons in an instant, kneeling down behind the solid wooden wheels emptying their backpacks, plastering the dry old wooden wheels with a special mix of naphtha, sulfur and highly refined oil on wads of fresh lambs' wool, sticky and murderously flammable. Right across the rear of the Hun lines the wagons stretched away, piled high with the loot of half the civilized world. There might have been a hundred, no, three or four hundred—they couldn't possibly damage them all. But by the time word got to the nearest Hun warriors, sitting their horses in the rear battle lines, the Batavians had fixed up over thirty wagons.

A couple of hundred horse warriors came galloping furiously back across the grass toward them.

The commander of the *superventores* knelt, flipped open his tinderbox, and flicked the wheel.

"Sir, we're in range!"

The first arrows hit the ground nearby. A junior lieutenant held out a wooden staff topped with a blob of pitch and the commander lit it.

"Now run!" he roared. "The rest of you—to the river!"

The main body sprinted for the water, crouching low, while the lieutenant dashed along the line of wagons with the flaming torch extended. Every time it brushed against a treated wheel, the wagon exploded into flames like a bone-dry hayrick.

The Huns were bewildered and indecisive, some making toward the burning wagons intending to extinguish them and save the loot, though God only knew how. That moment of confusion was the lieutenant's chance of escape, and he took it, sprinting toward the river, dashing beneath a low-hanging alder for cover even as arrows sliced through the leaves around him, and diving headlong into the river. Horsemen arrived on the bank above, howling with fury, their horses champing, tossing their brutish heads, fighting against entering such a fast-moving current when unable to see the bottom. The riders drew back their bows and arrows slapped into the water but instantly lost trajectory, flattening out across the surface like skimmed pebbles or spinning round to face the powerful current. In any case, the Batavians were already down in the murky depths, lungs forcibly emptied, navigating only by the feel of the current dragging them back to safety, swimming like tritons with grins across their water-stretched faces.

As Aëtius well knew, such flamboyant tactics had absolutely no effect on the material progress of the battle, but they could do wonders for morale. His lines cheered wildly as the black smoke billowed up into the air behind the Hun army, and they saw the Hunnish leader himself, fearsome Attila, galloping furiously back to view the damage.

"An ostentatious little jape," muttered Aëtus, "but a useful one."

Tatullus grinned. "What's he wasting his time for? He needs to get on with it." He jerked his head right.

Aëtius nodded. The sun was indeed, as usual, coming round. With every delay, the Huns would have to fight facing more and more directly into it.

The commander of the *superventores* reappeared, still at the run. Well, special forces were expected to be able to cover forty miles in a day with sixty-pound packs on their backs. This was a nice day out for them.

He saluted. "Job done, sir."

"Casualties?"

"None, sir, apart from one novice who slipped coming out of the river and bloodied his pug. Getting bandaged up right now."

Aëtius grinned. "Good man. To the rearguard now. There'll be more work for you later."

"Sir."

It was late morning, and still nothing. Attila's delaying tactics were wearisome to the Romans, but they would test his own, undisciplined warriors' patience to the limit. Sooner or later they were going to have to charge. That mile between them would tire them, especially with their horses, poorly fed for these past weeks and months. And then they would hit the earthed-up pikes of the Alans and, behind them, the Roman legionaries. That was what

Aëtius wanted. As for the coming arrow storm, he had two ways to deal with that.

Meanwhile the two armies stood motionless, and the sun kept coming round. Tube-like *dracones,* wind socks, droned in the wind. The Hun horses stamped restively. Occasionally there were sorties from their lines, jeered at and sharply rebuffed, the horsemen retreating in disorder. Then as the air warmed a light southerly breeze blew up.

Aëtius looked sharply at his centurion.

Tatullus produced a small white feather, raised it above his head and let go. It twirled briefly, then drifted steadily toward the Hun lines.

The centurion looked around, scanned the horizon. "A calm summer's day. June. Gaul. A few clouds low in the west." He grinned at Aëtius. "Yep. I reckon."

Aëtius nodded, and Tatullus roared over the front rank, "Fire the smoke screen!"

Immediately a great sheet of flame coursed along before the Roman line, and then quickly burned down to thick smoke. The auxiliaries ran between the files and poured on oil and dead branches, sacks of leaves, commandeered hay bales and, best of all, thick green summer grass. The pall of smoke thick-ened, rose into the air forty, fifty feet, and drifted always north toward the Hun lines. In a few minutes they'd be blinded by it. And, when they came through it, by the sun.

Sweaty hands tightened around butted pikes, men crouched low. Some used corners of grimy neckerchiefs to wipe the sweat trickling down their fore-heads and stinging their eyes, then quickly returned their hands to their pikes. The sweat would have to drip, because they all felt it now. The earth was rum-bling. Beyond the smoke, the Huns were charging.

The next noise was the distant, muffled strum of the torsion springs of the Lightning Boys' arrow firers and sling machines. Of course. From their posi-tion they could see the Huns charging below them. Thank God they held that hill. Then there were the screams of men and horses erupting soprano above the deep rumble of the charge. First blood. Those steel-head bolts were hit-ting home, horses rolling forward and tripping, the charge running in be-hind, getting tangled.

The smokescreen had worked. The Huns weren't firing, not through that thick curtain. They were coming through it.

"Steady, lads!" shouted Aëtius. "Lean all your weight on those pikes, now. Hold the line. Here they come."

Many of them saw it in slow and dreamlike motion. Out of that drifting, cloudy wall of smoke only thirty or forty yards in front of their pikes, first emerged those big, brutish horses' heads, and their hooves, and legs, then the whole animals, and riding them the naked savages, spiraling their swords, hatchets and lassos above their shaven, tattooed heads, howling like demons loosed from hell.

They hit the Alans hardest, but not before the Roman legionaries had stood up behind and hurled their javelins from their jointed javelin throwers in a ferocious volley, so perfectly aimed and timed that perhaps every other front-rank Hunnish horseman was brought down, slowing his comrades behind and tangling them up just where they didn't want to be. Many flew to the ground and lay uninjured but stunned. Then the Alan lancers broke rank and ran out to butcher them where they lay.

"Back into line you fools! Hold formation! Pull back *now*!"

But the Alans lacked the discipline. Seeing what they thought was the impotent chaos of the Huns before them, they acted as headstrong individuals, dropping their pikes and pushing forward, drawing their swords. It was madness. Though a hundred or more Huns had fallen in that first javelin volley, many more were coming on behind, and those who had lost their horses and been stunned in falls were instantly on their feet again, daggers and sharpened *chekans* in hand. The Alans were surrounded and cut to pieces.

Sangiban, watching from his horse, bellowed with anger. "Shoot them!" he screamed. "Where are you, archers?"

But Aëtius's men could not shoot without hitting the disordered Alan foot-soldiers, who were slaughtered before their eyes. Cornered, the Alans fought like lions, it was true, but without formation they were lost.

"Herculians, move up. Take pike positions."

It was a relief to know that those old hands would hold the line: hold it until they were cut down where they stood.

The milling Hun horsemen, their charge broken by the enemy javelins and by their own bloodlust as they paused to stab and scalp the bewildered and fallen Alans, came on again but without discipline, single vainglorious warriors hurling themselves on the line of pikes yelling, "Astur is Great and will prevail!" only to be skewered and dashed to the ground. Time and again horses reared, screaming, their riders flung back, hooves scrabbling in the air, a pike head buried deep in their mighty chests. The legionaries knew better than to admire their handiwork, promptly dragging their pikes free and butting them in the ground again. The next attack would soon come round.

"Arrow storm coming in!" went up a cry from the wing. Instantly the rear-rank troops raised their shields above their heads and locked together. Arrows skidded off the bronze, thocked down into the leather and wood, and stuck there, quivering. Legionaries dropped their shields down in front of them and lopped off the arrow shafts with their swords. Here and there a cry went up as a man was hit, too slow with his shield or just unlucky. But Aëtius could judge immediately from the thinness of the cries that little damage had been done. Now came his new tactic, for he knew how the Huns would fight.

The front line had come in charging and was stuck on the Roman pikes. Meanwhile, lightly armed horse archers were galloping back and forth behind them, intending to loose off their arrow storm over the heads of their front-rank comrades and down onto the Romans' rear ranks. That was their plan. But the moment they began, Aëtius gave the nod and the heavy Visigothic cavalry rode out, visors lowered, shields hefted, mighty ashwood lances couched.

They galloped round the rear of the fighting lines in a gigantic sweep, through the smokescreen, and scythed into the Hun horse archers from behind. Many of the archers barely had time to turn before that great gleaming metallic serpent, head diamond shaped like a pit viper, cut through them and bowled them apart, wreaking havoc. Nor did they stop for one moment, cutting across in front of the main Hunnish army, round the hill, and back to their station on the Romans' right wing. In their wake were the strewn and broken bodies of many hundreds.

While the triumphant Visigothic cavalry drew breath, the artillerymen on the hill piled in, loosing their arrows sidelong into any Huns crossing the field to engage the line of pikes. Attila must be cursing. That hill was proving pivotal, a permanent outflanking fixture. Once battle was messily engaged, no one could shoot close to their own. But from that accursed hill . . .

Each individual tactic of Aëtius's was paying off. The arrow storm was weakened if not neutered by countercharge and good, old-fashioned shield discipline. The Hun cavalry charge, their horses tired before they started, was locked up against the legionaries and their implacable line of pikes. With the Visigothic cavalry and also the superb Augustan Horse and the Moors always ready to ride wide and sweep in from both left and right across the advancing enemy, it seemed that everything was going Aëtius's way. And so they fought on. Past noon, past mid-afternoon. *Pedites* ran with water. The Herculians dropped back, exhausted, and the Batavians took their place in the center. The bodies of the enemy were piled high across the plain. The artillery from the hill worked on implacably. Yet the Huns kept coming.

Now it was a terrible battle of attrition. The Huns fought with ferocity but without imagination, without fresh tactics. Given that, Aëtius knew grimly, it was just a matter of whether the Huns' sheer weight of numbers would eventually triumph over the Romans' exhaustion.

He rode behind the lines to see the wounded being bandaged and salved, the dead laid out for later burial. Already there were many there. He asked for numbers from only one legion, finding the *primus pilus* of the Herculians.

"Over half my men, sir."

"Wounded?"

"No, sir. Slain."

He held the back of his hand to his mouth. All war was foul, but this was war at its foulest. A whole generation was being swept away in one day by the madness of one king.

An *optio* came running. "Sir, the Batavians are near exhaustion, sir."

He nodded. "Pull 'em back. Send forward the frontier legions."

"And the Huns are launching fresh attacks on the hill, sir."

Hell. That must not fall. "Send in the rest of the Palatine Guard to secure it."

"Sir."

The twelfth hour from dawn? He reckoned so. Another four hours of daylight this long summer day. By nightfall it would be decided. And already they were stretched to breaking point.

On the front line the battle was bloody, fierce, and unrelenting. An ugly, stagnant stand-off, a process of the grimmest and goriest wastage. There was no room for the flamboyance of the wide-arcing cavalry charge now, no brilliant outflanking maneuvers, nothing but the old moves of stab and slash, slogging it out knee deep in the reddening mud. In the melee, Knuckles, Arapovian, and Malchus fought side by side as of old, protecting one another as well as holding back the Huns.

The Huns hated this hand-to-hand fighting. Their lassos were useless in the crush, their bows and arrows dead weight, and their swordsmanship poor and without order. Their small ponies, so rapid and sure-footed on the vast steppes of Asia, here only stumbled wearily over the heaps of the slain. The Romans gave no quarter. A few crossbowmen on the flanks picked off any Hun unhorsed and sent him reeling to hell.

King Theodoric came riding over to Aëtius when two runners arrived at once.

"Sir, the Palatine Guard are pinned down and surrounded on the hill."

"They must hold it—to the last man."

"The artillery boys are done for, sir. The Guard couldn't save them."

Yes, the arrow firers had indeed fallen silent; the sling machines worked no more.

"And you? What happy news?"

The second runner, still gasping, said, "Sir, large numbers of the enemy seen drifting off north and west beyond the baggage wagons."

"Which people?"

"Too far off to say, sir. But many, many deserting."

King Thedoric punched his mighty fist into his palm. "This is going to be a close day of it, Roman."

So it was. But there were no more tactical choices to be made. There weren't enough men left for Aëtius to make any new dispositions. They must just hold out.

King Theodoric shook his shaggy head, already pulling his horse round and moving back to the right wing. "It is time for the Visigoths to charge the enemy."

"You will leave our flank open!" called Aëtius. "You must hold it!"

Theodoric looked back. "With respect, old Roman friend, I am not, and never will be, under your command. But have no fear. My wolf lords will finish the Hun with our charge. Your flank is safe."

The sunlight was now behind them when the wolf lords rode in, a single vast column of thousands of heavy-armored horsemen. Ahead of them, a horde of many more, but already looking hesitant, indistinct, squinting into the sun. The Visigoths needed to ride wide indeed to avoid the piles of the slain. At their head rode their white-haired king, carrying no shield but only a two-headed battle axe. Some in the Roman lines who saw him ride said he must have wanted to die.

Hun arrows came down onto the column as soon as their charge was spotted. But with shields raised and *Spangenhelms* lowered, they sustained little damage. And their huge chargers, despite having galloped all day, still had the power to gallop once more, thundering over the churned and deep-scored field, divots gouged out, manes flying, lances massed and lowered.

The Huns started to buckle and fall back as the thunderous column approached, but they could only fall back on their own rear ranks. They were packed too tightly to move, pushing and panicking and crying out when the wolf lords slammed into them. And the Visigoths drove through with such ferocity that they were soon lost to Roman view, only the occasional banner showing above their heads.

For some minutes it was impossible to say what had happened. Meanwhile the last of the frontier legions had fought themselves to an exhausted standstill. Here and there, Hun horsemen came close enough to whip the pikes out of the ground and ride in over them. The center, the very breastplate of the Roman force, was coming apart.

"Send in every last man!" roared Aëtius. "Hold that line! Keep formation at all costs! Not a man to break or we are lost!"

The last few remnants, the Batavian special forces, the Breton volunteers, and the two hundred Celts with Lucius at their head, pushed forward through the ranks and gave their last-ditch support to the exhausted and ravaged legions. A pocket of Hun horsemen had broken through, wheeled, and were charging at the Roman front line from behind, curved swords whirling. The men looked over their shoulders and cried out, knowing they were about to be surrounded and cut down, whatever they did. It was at this moment in a battle, always always, when men broke and ran to save their skins and formation crumbled, that the day was lost.

But now the Huns themselves cried out and turned again to defend themselves. Two Roman horsemen rode into them at full tilt. One actually wielded a huge billhook from the saddle, whirling the long handle over his head and slicing through men's chests and throats, roaring and spattered with blood.

The Hun horsemen fell apart. One tried to leap over the Roman line and flee, but a huge fellow with a weighted club knocked him clean out of his saddle, then drove his face in with a single stomp of his left boot. As the Roman turned back to regain the safety of his line, he reeled. The curved spike of a *chekan* sliced across his skull and he fell forward, his face a thick mask of blood. The Hun warrior, an old but muscular fellow with flying long gray hair and fine mustaches, galloped in again, swinging low off the side off his horse, thighs clamped tight, and was about to swing a second time with his *chekan* when a lean eastern swordsman leaped to stand over the fallen club-wielder, poised askance, sword level as the desert horizon. At the last second he ducked, stood again, whirled round and sliced his sword blade though a wide arc in a single sinuous movement. The old warrior flung his head back and howled, the *chekan* flying out of his hand as he clutched his thigh, cut through leather and flesh to the bone. His exhausted horse slowed to an absent-minded trot as it felt its rider's grip loosen. The easterner sprinted after him, his sword still whirling. Then he stopped abruptly, and let the old warrior ride slowly back to the Hun lines, slumped in his wooden saddle.

The easterner looked down at the fellow with the club. He was kneeling, stunned, with a second wound in his big shoulder, where an arrowhead was buried deep.

Arapovian called to him.

He looked up and grinned slowly. "Fuckin' top of the world, my lissom Parsee comrade!" Then he was back on his feet once more, laying his club on his shoulder, turning to face the onslaught yet again.

The Roman line curved and billowed, split apart and came togther again. Men fell forward and backward, screaming, clutching throats and chests. Many lay in the mud, dying, and many of those, even the most battle hardened of the legions, ended their lives as they had begun: crying for their mothers. No medics came; they were all slain. None of their comrades came, either; they were all slain or fighting. The sun was sliding down the sky, and the field was mown flat like a harvest field.

Aëtius crawled out from under his third fallen horse, helmet and sword both gone, and hauled himself up onto another sagging beast standing haggard, nuzzling bloody grass, desperate to eat but sickened. He stared around. His army was almost gone.

But across the field . . . the enemy army was thinning out. The flanks were receding. There was a huge concave bow near the center, and the limitless depth that the horde had shown this morning, stretching back and back into the blue distance, had shrunk away. They were stretched thin and to breaking. Away in the east there was a dust cloud burnished gold in the setting sun, so many were retreating.

Nearer, before that haze of dust, there was a gleaming serpent of armored horsemen: the wolf lords curving into the scattered flank of the Hun line yet again. They rolled it up. Before Aëtius's dust-blurred eyes, the Hun line folded in on itself, collapsed. The wolf lords drove on, too tired to gallop now, only trotting, but with lances still lowered, implacable. The Huns broke and fled.

Night seemed to fall fast on that day. The sun had seen enough.

Aëtius, too, had seen enough, but it was not over. His work was not done yet. Runners were too few. He must find more. He called for a wagon to be drawn up and piled with saddles and he climbed onto it. A filthy fellow passed beneath him, knelt, cleaned his sword in a rare patch of unsullied grass.

"You, man," Aëtius called to him. "Up here. Lend me your eyes."

The fellow came up and stared north.

"You," muttered Aëtius.

"I," said Arapovian. After a moment he said, "Here is an irony. Attila is piling up a wagonload of saddles like ours." He glanced at Aëtius. "How emulous he is of you in all he does."

"What else?"

"They're drawing their remaining wagons into a circle, the oldest Hun tactic. But so many have fled that the circle is small. Why does he not retreat?"

"Because he thinks we will fall on him by night and destroy him."

"We would if we had any men left."

Arapovian was immediately sorry for his cruel joke. Aëtius bowed his head and raised his hand to his eyes. Arapovian said softly, "But the battle is over."

Aëtius looked up again and out over the carnage field. "The battle is indeed over," he said. The note in his voice wrung the Armenian's heart. "And both sides have lost."

10

LORDS AMONG MEN

Attila knelt in the dust beside the dying man.

Orestes, standing behind him, said, "The body of the Lord Geukchu cannot be found, but he was seen fighting to the last before the Roman line. Noyan fell before the Visigothic horses."

Attila barely reacted. His face was ashen gray and deep furrowed, his cheeks sunken, his eyes flat. He reached his strong hand under the fallen warrior and raised his head a little.

Chanat's eyes fluttered. Blood continued to flow from the deep sword cut in his thigh, tight bandaged though it was. He managed to lay his hand upon Attila's arm. "Great Tanjou," he whispered.

Attila lowered his head and his straggling gray locks brushed the back of Chanat's hand. "How far we have ridden together, old friend, first of my Chosen Men. That you were the first to meet me upon the plain of my homeland when I rode out of exile. That we rode against the Kutrigur Huns together, and forged our people into a mighty brotherhood. That Chanat the Chivalrous, the Merciful, made us turn back and fight for that forsaken village in the desert, for his great heart was greatly moved. None of this will be forgotten in the songs of the people, my brother Chanat, son of Lord Subotai, proud father of the warrior Aladar, who chose his death before the walls of Constantinople."

Chanat's hand tightened a little on Attila's arm. Then he was gone.

After a few moments Attila rose, stripped to the waist and dropped his bone jerkin to the ground like a thing of trash. He poured a handful of dust over his gray locks, unsheathed his sword, unbuckled his scabbard belt, slashed the scabbard away from the leather belt, and let it drop into the dust. He buckled the belt back round his waist and thrust the naked sword through it. Then he looked around the crude wagon laager.

"We die here," he said. "Beside our brother Chanat."

King Theodoric's bloodied and trampled body lay on a pyre of splintered timbers. His two sons kept vigil and wept. Some said that the king had been ridden down by the Huns, others that in the furious thick of the fight his own wolf lords had trampled him. But that was all one now. Amalasuntha had been truly avenged. The Visigothic column, driving into the enemy again and again, had finally broken through to where the three sons of Genseric sat their white horses beneath the banner of the Black Boar, horrified to find that thousands of their own, finest Vandal horsemen had been unable to protect them. The three sons, Frideric, Euric, and the idiot Godric, he who had been so briefly married to the Princess Alamasuntha, were roped up, dragged back to the Gothic lines, and beheaded. Their heads would be salted and despatched to Genseric in a sack.

As he lay dying, Theodoric had whispered, "That is justice. That is Gothic justice for that tyrant among men. Now the spirit of my beloved fair-haired girl will sleep easy in the Courts of Heaven." Tears and blood mingled in his white beard. He closed his eyes, and his breathing slowed. Then he laid a great bloodstained hand on young Theodoric's head. "This life is a sigh between two secrets, the sparrow's flight through the mead hall beset by night. But *Gaeð a Wyrd swa hio scel*—Fate goes ever as fate must. You, my son, will be a great king of my people. Rule wisely and well, as befits a Visigoth. Torismond"—he touched his head—"you will be a great servant of your brother, and a great man among men. The Lord bless you and keep you. Love your mother and care for her in her last years. As I have loved you, with all my heart." His hand slipped down, his head sank back, and his breathing stilled.

Long after sunset the wolf lords' torches blazed for their dead king, and Aëtius came and held a torch, too. They lamented Theodoric and lauded him.

Lord and lavisher of rings,
From his golden hoard, on the funeral road.
Bravely he bought them, hardily hoarded them,
Grimly he guarded them, against the eastern kings.
A lord among men, high his renown,
Let pyre take him, fire enfold him,
Furled in the flames, our king of men!
Heavy our hearts with the mighty memory of him,
Silenced our laughter but fluent our tears,
No torcs will they wear now, our loveliest maidens,
Silver not shine on them, brooch not bedizen them,
Oft and repeatedly, in sad paths of exile,
Deeply will mourn for him, the people's defender,
Bereft they will walk, soft they will talk,
Bowed under woe, high spirits quenched,
Many a spear, dawn cold to the touch,
Laid down at morning, harp swept in mourning,
Warriors shall not wake to that sorrowful dawning,
The raven wings dark over doomed hills,
Tidings of the eagle, how he rode and made war,
Numberless his enemies, countless the slain,
Lord of the wolf lords, he harrowed the dead!

"A great pyre is burning," said Orestes.

Attila turned away from the distant orange glow, not wanting to see. "It is as the sorceries said. The enemy's commander is slain. Aëtius is dead."

But word soon came that it was Theodoric. Aëtius still lived.

Attila gripped the messenger's arm fit to break it. "You are sure of this?"

"He was seen at Theodoric's pyre."

Attila's expression was fathomless. Thus were sorcerers' prophecies fulfilled.

Nearby, a little-regarded person sat cross-legged in the corral as if at a Hun feast, rather than the worst killing field in his people's history.

"Here is another prophecy for you, my master," he said. "No man will ever understand a prophecy aright, until it comes to pass. You understand a prophecy only as you understand your own life: looking backward."

Attila said not a word, but walked away from that singsong, tormenting voice. He climbed up on a wagon, drew his bare sword, and stood for a long time staring south through the night: toward the burning pyre of that much-loved, noble-hearted king, laid out on his hide shield amid the prayers of his Christian priests, surrounded by a forest of lances.

It was like the pyre of an ancient hero of legend. Flames wrought havoc in the hot bonehouse, the bone lappings burst, ribs fell like timbers into the fire. The sons watched their father's body consumed without flinching. Their sister and father were together again.

As the pyre cracked and fell in a huge blaze of sparks, Torismond looked around for Aëtius. Now that his father was gone, he wanted to be near the master general. But Aëtius had slipped away.

He had walked out alone onto the darkened battlefield, nothing but a knife in his hand. Everywhere there came to his ears the groans of the dying. Small groups of surviving Romans soldiers worked tirelessly among them, trying to stretcher them in. But there were many, many more wounded than unscathed. They would be working all night. He would come back soon and work with them. In final exhaustion he might find solace. For the groans burned into him like hot daggers, each one an accusation. Some of the dying called for God, some for their mothers, some for death. Of the three, only death the ever faithful came to them.

And for what? It had taken the united forces of all of Rome and the Visigothic nation to stop him, the Scourge of God. And that is all they had done. They had not defeated him. They would never defeat him. You might as well try and defeat the wind. As for what men remained to Rome, Aëtius had silenced an *optio* who tried to give him the numbers. He knew them already. Half the Gothic wolf lords lay dead upon the field. Seven or eight thousand had laid down their lives for Rome. Of the twenty-five thousand in his own army, who had borne the brunt of the Huns' attack, he doubted if five thousand were left standing. The Herculian and Batavian legions were effectively no more. The Palatine Guard had indeed fought to the last man, guarding the army's left flank on that hill, the Huns pulling back only when all the guard were dead and they saw their own horde in full retreat. The *superventores* were wiped out. The Augustan Horse, barely eighty left . . . Was it any consolation to know that, however many they had lost, the Huns had lost three times, four times as many?

He stopped beside one of his dead. No, it was no consolation. Captain Malchus had one arm completely severed; his face was a staring mask of blood. Aëtius covered that face with a corner of his cloak. The Visigothic wolf lord Jormunreik lay prone, his right hand still gripping his axe. Aëtius reached out and touched his head, just once, wordlessly. He had seen cows touch a dead calf thus, just a gentle nuzzle, and he understood why. And here lay that great hulking brute of a Rhinelander, Knuckles. Aëtius remembered the first time they had met, on the road to Azimuntium. Knuckles, son of the Rhenish whore Volumella. Aëtius knelt by him and ran his hand down over his face, closing his eyes. "No son of a whore," he murmured. "Bravest of the brave."

11

THE MAD KING

Another man moved across the battlefield, too, carrying a bare sword. He cared not. He muttered to himself, of Rome, and of China, moving among the dead. They were all gone into a world of light. Was it not so? Angelic work, then. He did not smile. Eternity's work.

The moon was reflected in pools of horse blood. As if it had fallen to earth.

There was a looter rifling through the wallets of the dead, stealing enameled brooches, fibulae, rings from broken fingers. Maybe a villager or even one of his own, but he killed him anyway. Stepped up silently behind him and drove his sword down into the back of his neck. But immediately in the darkness, there was another. He felt weary. You cannot kill them all.

There was a warrior dying one-legged. There was a still-kicking horse. He was tired of killing. Tired among the heaps of the dead and dying, among the pools of blood and the broken weapons of war, among the dead rainbows and the fallen moon lying reflected in the pools of blood. He knelt abruptly and planted his sword in the earth. Let it remain there among the cold and dead.

At dawn, Attila realized that the Romans could attack him no more. They, too, were exhausted, what remained of them. He gave the order to break camp and the bedraggled remnant of his horde rode away east.

Once they were gone, the Romans and the Visigoths did likewise. Two thirds of the men were wounded and dying, and the column moved very slowly. A vast silence settled over the Catalaunian Fields, and over the heaps of the innumerable dead.

That winter, there were many wolf packs in that country.

Broken in spirit, the ragtag army of Attila and his embittered mercenaries wreaked horrible, fitful revenge on the native populations through which they passed on their sullen retreat to their homelands. Some Burgundian captives were roped and dangled from trees and and used for target practice. They made the Burgundian children watch, thinking it amusing they should see their fathers stuck to death with arrows.

Their amusements left splayed bodies by the roadside, women with child torn open, the unborn whelps harrowed from their wombs and set on pikes. Molten gold was poured into the mouths of captured Jews, whom the mercenaries derided as Christless unbelievers. The last encampments and cave dwellings of the quiet forest people of the Bohemian Forest, who hunted dormice and foraged for roots and berries, brown eyed and dreamy and silent, a tribe of children, who even in that age lived on as they had lived in Europe for centuries, perhaps for millennia, speaking a language that no one else understood, as if from Eden before the Fall: they, too, were extinguished by the Harrowing of Attila, a nameless, unknown, preterite people, innocent as air. They were rounded up and put to the sword, going to their deaths mildly as they had lived, their small villages of straw huts left smoking in their sunlit glades. All suffered from the hordes of Attila.

Europe groaned and bled, and the king himself rode on in silence at the head of his defeated murderous horde, eyes fixed ahead, indifferent to the devastation left in his black and smoking wake. All the world burning and nothing left to save. If he could not be the Master of the World, he would be its Destroyer.

Only one thing is more terrible than an approaching army, they said in those days: a retreating army. With all hope and all order gone, left to derive only a bleak satisfaction from wreaking on the weak and defenseless the wholesale destruction that they had failed to wreak on their armed enemies, in sour reprisal for their fate. Even dumb nature suffered, punished by their sullen wrath. Whole late-summer forests were put to the torch, laid waste like tinder sticks, entire landscapes left ashen and silent and denuded of life.

Down the roads into Italy and the East, the people came fleeing. See them fleeing, harried by the wind, blown like chaff before the empty wind, puppets dancing to its ancient tragic roar, through the desolate fields. Through the long ages.

Aëtius was right to believe that Attila had failed yet would not stop. Destruction had become the very air he breathed. Death had become his life.

Aëtius eventually arrived back in Ravenna to face Valentinian's harshest accusations and demands to know what had become of his army. Aëtius told him with exaggerated calmness that there was no Roman army left to speak of. Perhaps they should negotiate with the Visigoths, the only remaining armed force of any significance in Western Europe. Valentinian howled and rent his robes, and bit his tongue till he spat out blood on the white marble floors of the palace.

Then the unbelievable news came to them that Attila was on the march again. He had looped back across Noricum and was riding down toward Aquileia. That he still had the men to fight and, more unbelievably still, the *will* . . .

It had all been for nothing. There was none left to oppose him. He would ride into Ravenna, and then Rome, and burn them flat. How many men had he still? All of ten thousand: the tattered remnant of his once mighty army, the rest having either been destroyed upon the Catalaunian Fields, or else deserted and vanished back into the vastness of Scythia. But still, ten thousand of the most loyal rode with him—and the Romans had none to oppose him. None. The Visigoths could not be expected to fight for Italy as they had fought for Gaul.

Outside the palace, Aëtius told the last of his close guard, "You should go now. Take ship for the east. There is no more for you here."

Arapovian stared hard at him with his coal-black eyes, and at last nodded. "I would feel like a deserter," he said, "except that, as at Viminacium, there is nothing left to desert."

"You have served Rome well, easterner. As well as any."

Arapovian pulled himself up onto his horse.

"Where will you go now?"

"East, as you say. Not to my country—it no longer exists. But east somewhere. Perhaps a long way east. The farther the better." He kicked his horse into a walk.

"God go with you, easterner."

Arapovian raised his right hand and called back, "And with you, Master General Aëtius."

"And you, Centurion?"

Tatullus grimaced. "I stay. As ever."

Lastly he went to a simple lodging house and asked to speak to two of the lodgers. Moments later, they appeared at the door. Lucius and Cadoc.

Aëtius told them of Attila's approach. "You should sail home now, for good. Forget about Rome, as Rome forgot about you."

Lucius shook his head. "Britain will wait for us. Even I cannot exactly explain why, but we, my son and I, are still needed here, with you. We stay until the end."

Every night now, Attila suffered visions and broken sleep. He saw his horsemen riding up the steps of the Roman Capitol, gouging out the eyes of emperors' statues with their spear points. In his dreams he ceaselessly called the name of Rome, and of Aëtius.

Aquileia offered him no resistance. Rounding up its notables, he demanded to have one Nemesianus brought to him. That venerable senator was old and too weak to move, he was told. But his villa was—

He galloped away, Orestes barely able to keep pace with him.

He dragged the white-haired old senator out of his bed and out onto the fine terrace looking down upon the great city of Aquileia, and the autumn Adriatic beyond. He waved his drawn dagger over the city.

"All this," he rasped, "all this will be destroyed first. Because of you."

Nemesianus was on all fours, weeping. Orestes halted his horse and dismounted with half a dozen warriors. The senator stared at them—their tattoos, shaven heads, weals, garlands of teeth and jawbones—with sick disbelief. Then he turned back to Attila, almost sobbing, "But why me? *Why me?*"

Attila squatted down on his haunches and sighed, stropping his dagger on a fine sandstone paving slab.

"D-d-don't, don't do that," stammered Nemesianus. "D-d-dalmatian stone, the finest . . ."

Attila looked at him with arched eyebrows, and laughed. He continued stropping. "*Why me?*" he repeated. "A question the gods find tiresome."

The old man had bitten his lower lip till it bled. The spots of blood stood out against his ashen face like berries in old snow.

"Forty years ago," said Attila, "on the road to Aquileia, there were three children. They were small, weak, hungry. There was no one to care for them. And then you came along the road."

Nemesianus looked hopeful. "Forty years ago is a long time. Perhaps it is difficult for you to—"

"There was a boy, a rude barbarian boy, his cheeks scarred with the blue tattoos of his people. A frightful creature." Attila drew his hair back over his gold-hooped ears and the man saw and groaned. "There was another boy, a blond Greek slave boy." He pointed his dagger at Orestes. Nemesianus stared to and fro. Blood spotted his embroidered robe.

"And there was a little girl. Her name was Pelagia. She was the sister of the Greek slave boy. He loved her dearly. She was six years old."

There was silence but for Nemesianus's sobs. Then he began to say "Please" over and over again.

Attila eyed him. "Shsh," he said softly.

Nemesianus fell silent.

"The tattooed barbarian boy loved her, too, for she was as innocent as the spring. Perhaps because she was everything he was not."

The old man began shaking his head very slowly. "No, no, no," he murmured under his breath, almost inaudibly.

"You took them in, you cared for them." Attila shook his head likewise, as if in sympathetic sorrow. "Oh, how you cared for them."

He stood up and went over to the old man. "So this is the answer to your bleating question, 'Why me? O cruel gods, why me?'" He locked the old man's head in the crook of his left arm. "The gods are not cruel, after all. They are but just, and their punishments are hounds of heaven on the traces of our sins. In time, over long years, sometimes as much as forty years after the sin has been committed and enjoyed and forgotten, those tireless hounds of heaven will find you out. They run all night through the midnight forests, their path ahead lit by the fire in their burning eyes. They will neither slow nor cease, noses to the ground, following to its source and origin the stinking scent of your sins which cry to heaven for vengeance." He held the dagger motionless in front of the old man's left eye. "Do you see now? Do you see, *why me?*"

With a jab and sideways flick of the dagger point, he impaled and dug out Nemesianus's eye. The aqueous blob flew from the dagger's end and splatted onto the ground, quivering there slightly like some primeval sea creature dragged untimely from the deep. The old man howled and struggled and tears flowed from the socket where the roots of his eyeball hung out over his lower lid, like the gory roots of some unearthed plant of flesh and blood. Tears and blood flowed down his furrowed old cheeks, and his liver-spotted hands tightened round Attila's thick forearm in feeble opposition.

"Do you see now?" said Attila again. "No. I fear you still only half see."

Another jab and flick, and there were two sightless eyeballs losing their luster in the dust. The old man's twin eye sockets welled with watery blood.

"Now you see," said Attila. He released Nemesianus's head from its lock and wiped his dagger blade clean on the old man's robe. "Now you see."

Nemesianus collapsed and lay groaning.

"You will not, I fear, be able to see the imminent burning of your beloved city." He stowed his dagger inside his leather jerkin. "But you will smell it well enough."

He looked at Orestes. The Greek nodded. And they rode back into Aquileia.

It was a great city, a great port, one of the greatest in all of Italy. And now? Now the site of Aquileia can barely be found. No more than a heap of stones over which the south wind sighs. Sighs and moves on.

After Aquileia, Attila rode on across Italy and burned Patavium, Vicentia, Verona, Placentia. . . . At Mantua a local poet called Marullus addressed florid verses of praise to the conqueror. Attila had him burned on a pyre of his own books.

Not until he came to Mediolanum did he learn that Galla Placidia had died a year before. He ground his teeth and flogged the man who told him. That night he dreamed of staggering through a gallery of statues, sending them crashing to the ground, crushing them underfoot. Galla in a green *stola* stepped between them and vanished before he could break her. At the end of the hall sat a horned king on a wooden throne, his hands no more than claws, divested of kingly robes, nothing but a filthy loincloth on him, his old dugs sagging low, his hair matted with fur and feathers. The king raised his head slowly, eyes bloodshot, haggard, horror struck and then the terrible smile. . . .

Attila awoke, screaming.

Orestes calmed him. "We are getting near Rome."

"And Rome is coming to meet us," said Attila.

Ravenna itself was no more than a court of chattering apes in togas. They still talked of buying Attila off.

Valentinian demanded to know, "Why? Why? What does he *want*?"

"Do not inquire too deeply into that black heart, Majesty," Aëtius said quietly "You might lose your way as in a midnight labyrinth, and never find the light again."

"He was a friend of yours, wasn't he?" The emperor was clutching himself now, staring at Aëtius fixedly. "A great friend. You knew him well."

"A long time ago."

Aëtius set about marshaling the last band of soldiers he could.

In Mediolanum, Attila had himself installed in the Imperial Palace, where he ceaselessly walked its endless marble corridors, muttering to himself. He seemed in no hurry to advance on Rome. Some whispered that he was filled with superstitious dread, remembering the fate of Alaric, who had marched into Rome triumphant and died only six days later.

Despair and fury competed in his breast. One day in a deserted vestibule he found a vast mural depicting the kings of Scythia kneeling in tribute to a succession of Roman emperors. Roaring through the deserted corridors of the palace, he demanded that the mural be repainted depicting himself on the throne and the emperors of Rome kneeling to him. Afterward, for no obvious reason, he had the terrified mural painters executed.

At other times he ranted his grandiose plans, while his little force beyond the city walls ebbed by the day. He would soon take Rome, and then Constantinople—that would become his base. Then he would turn on the tottering Sassanid Empire of Persia, and then India, and finally the Great Wall. They would destroy China itself, the greatest and most ancient enemy of all. . . .

· He would be king of the world.

His men felt aimless and abandoned as they looted the country round about. Orestes stayed with him, as did the witch Enkhtuya and, on the farthest fringes, appearing and disappearing again daily like dew, the shaman Little Bird.

"A king had a mighty empire once," said Little Bird, "but what did he give it away for? For a bigger empire."

Attila frowned.

The shaman laughed. "The boundless and infinite Empire of Nothing." He dared to lay his hand on Attila's hoar head. "O Little Father of Everything and Nothing."

"Silence, fool, or I shall take away your tongue."

"Take it freely, master. You have already taken everything else from your people."

A savage blow, a stamp on his ankle, an agonized cry, and the little shaman limped from the palace.

A strange, feathered creature sat on a stone lion in the forum of Mediolanum and sang to the frightened people.

In our loneliness wandering
Storm cloud and empty steppe
We thought these things would never cease.

We saw the white man bowed to earth
With his swords and his spears and his gold,
His cities, his streets, his cloud-capped palaces,

And with the people's land,
And with the vanished lion's hide
He hunted to nothing, the fierce Libyan lion,
And we thought, this cannot last. This will cease.

Twice now, O my people, we have been wrong.

He raised his arms up and laughed. The people of Mediolanum scurried away.

One day Little Bird tiptoed into the palace and found his master seated alone on one of the old imperial thrones in a vast audience chamber. He was talking with himself, his eyes roving over the frescoed walls and ceiling, seeing nothing. Little Bird could have wept, but instead he sat down before the Great Tanjou and waited. Attila stared at him. At the heart of his madness was despair, as perhaps at the heart of sanity there is hope.

The king suddenly stood and swept his arm wide. "Be still and hear me, O people!"

Little Bird sat looking up at him, cross-legged and wide eyed, a child in his seventh decade.

There was a long silence, Attila standing with his head hung low on his breast. Then he said, so softly that Little Bird strained to hear, "He is very wroth with us, he has utterly cast us off, we are rejected and despised. It is in the book of the Christians—I knew it as a boy. Long Roman winter afternoons with the pedagogue, a hostage, the cold sun sinking low beyond the bars. We are the people of Gog and Magog. I despised the bones and rags and worshipped fragments of the saints in their charnel-house churches, and the prophecies of their holy books, but now they come back to haunt me in my age. Now I go to the house of death myself with faltering steps, and I leave my people abandoned by their god."

"Oh, my mad master, do not say so."

"We will be blown away as the old song says, 'like the wind, like the wind.' And of the great Hun people in after years there will be neither sight nor sign in all the wide world, as if we had never been. And is it I . . . ? A King of Kings from Palestine, a King of Terror from the East. Oh, my dreams are relentless now, they come to me nightly without cease, those seers and tellers beside the haunted stream beneath the trees in that misty morning in my boyhood long ago, when I had none but my beloved Orestes to comfort me. We laid his sister in the earth. . . ."

Little Bird went to him.

Attila did not see. His eyes roved. "Comfort is not, consolation is not, in the midnight my heart murmurs that even the gods are not! You have taken the east from me, you have taken the west from me, you have taken my hate from me and my love from me; sad is my song now, my head is heavy, my heart hums a song of ash. And you who have taken all from me are nothing but a formless Void without voice or sense or feeling, the Beginning and the End of all things, forever and ever.

"Their prophecies hum about my ears like angry flies. Two empires were o'erthrown. . . . One empire's birth was Italy, the other was his own. And is it I . . . ? It is a thought that I can hardly bear, oh, help me bear it, little shaman, as you would help an old man staggering under a burden. Fortune's fool, history's halfwit." He leaned forward and put his hands on Little Bird's skinny shoulders.

Little Bird winced as if the touch was as cold as Scythian frost. "You might as well ask a mouse to bear a boulder on his back, my master."

Attila's arms fell by his sides again, and he sat back again.

"In my hoar old age I thought I had had reverence, piety, glory, empery, and now it is gone from me, everything is taken from me, my empire stutters and fails like a pauper's tallow candle. A seer once said my beloved son Ellak would inherit my empire. I know now what empire he spoke of: the great, the infinite empire of nothing."

"Do not say so, master."

"My sons quarrel with one another and soon enough they will war with each other, once their father is gone and nothing remains of him but fading footprints and bones. My Checa is gone the way of all flesh, motes of dust in the sun, the ribs of long-dead cattle bleached white, no birdsong, no sweet waters, an empty desert place, a tattered village beside a dying lake.

"I am as broken as the earth riven by ice. There is none to help me bear it; a king must die alone. My heart sings with grief, a lonely, mountain-top grief which only a dying king can know. The Madness of King Goll. I heard the Celtic slave boy singing, long ago, who knew the ancient prophecies of the Sibyl. The gray wolf knows me. . . . The hare runs by me, growing bold. . . . 'They will not hush, the leaves a-flutter round me, the beech leaves old.' King

Goll, old friend, I know you, and I see your face in the water. Is it I who has brought them to this pass and this predestinate end?" He stirred and trembled, his eyes wild, his hands gripping the finials of the alien throne. "Oh, I shall go mad! Oh, let me not be mad!"

"O Father," said Little Bird, laying his head in his lord's lap, "my heart will keep company with yours as both break."

12

THE GOD WHO THUNDERED

At last word came that Attila was marching on Rome.

Aëtius rode down the Flaminian Way from Ravenna to cut him off, with a force of little more than one thousand men. A ludicrous number. He had hoped that the citizens of Ravenna, Fiorentia, Rome itself, might have joined him in this last, wretched battle in Roman history, little more than a skirmish. But the people had already fled.

As Aëtius and his column neared the half-abandoned city on the seven hills, however, they met an extraordinary sight: a cortege headed by the Bishop of Rome, Leo, proceeding north, unarmed, to meet Attila. Priests in their chasubles carried crosses, banners, censers, and chanted hymns; the gold of the monstrances and dalmatics gleamed in the Italian sunlight; Bishop Leo himself, stocky and round faced and cheerful like the Campanian country-man he was, riding a plump white horse slightly too small for him, was flanked by long lines of choirboys and deacons.

"What the hell is this?"

The bishop reined in. "Master General Aëtius? Join us. Ride with us. And allow us to talk with Attila first, before—"

"Talk with Attila! Your Holiness, with all due respect, *talking* with him, pleading with him, paying him off—at this late stage—is like a hind pleading with a lion, when the lion has already got its teeth in her arse!"

The bishop smiled indulgently. Such vigorous similes reminded him of his country boyhood. *"Talk* with Attila," he resumed composedly, "before you and your brave soldiers line up to face him for battle."

Aëtius stared. Then he gave the order to fall in behind.

It was near the Mincius river that Attila and the Bishop of Rome had their talk. The gentle farmland of Virgil and Catullus, now trampled by barbarian cavalry.

In Leo's small party of priests and chaplains was also a burly old fellow with a white beard, and a younger man with brown eyes. Some said they were all the way from Britain, but others doubted that as a tall tale. Many tall tales grew up about that meeting. That Attila and the Britons and the papal party exchanged ancient Sibylline verses, and that after he had heard them in full the dread King of the Huns, the Scourge of God, hung his head, and began to pull his men back and turn them round. Some even claimed that Rome was saved by Attila's superstitious dread of the Christian Church, and a few old, garbled rhymes. Others commented that Attila's force was spent anyway; he had been defeated on the Catalaunian Fields.

The meeting did confirm one thing. The legions of Rome truly belonged to the past. Attila did not fear armies, but he feared the God of the Christians: the God who had thundered at him from the dark depths of Rhemi cathedral. The old military power of Rome was extinguished, but the new power of the Catholic Church had replaced it.

"It was not the priest of the Christians who made me depart," said Attila, "but that other, in the white robe, standing behind him."

Orestes frowned. "There was none such."

"He bore a flaming sword."

Orestes fell silent and then stepped out of the king's tent. He heard a sing-song voice away in the darkness.

The Great Spirit wills it.
Dry your eyes.
The white man comes.
A people dies.

13

THE DEATH BED

In the west of Britain, an old man and his son at last came home to their simple longhouse. The old man eased himself off his horse and a woman only a few years younger came out and wept and embraced him. They clung to each other, then went inside. The younger man went to stable the horses.

The woman said, "The Christians prevailed?"

Lucius nodded. "This time." She helped him off with his heavy British cloak. "What news?"

She shook her head.

"From the fortress of war?"

"It has been silent. A messenger rode out, traveling by water. But . . ."

"He has not returned?"

Seirian shook her head again, pleading, "But the fortress of war cannot have fallen?"

Lucius turned to see Cadoc stepping over the threshold, unbuckling his sword belt. He reached out a hand to his son.

"Keep it on."

Cadoc looked up, his hand still on his buckle, eyes bright and prophetic.

———————

Attila's sons were already squabbling over his inheritance while the aged king sat upon his wooden throne in his tent upon the Hungvar, bow clutched in hand, staring ahead, his face ; gray as old lead, his thoughts devouring him.

"For of this generation of men they shall not say we were the mightiest. The great Eagle of the Skies turns his head away, his golden eyes no longer mark us, his gaze is upon far other kings and empires now. We are little creatures to him, we are chirruping crickets in the grass, we are tedious to him, and all our vaunts and wars are ridiculous to him. He has left us here, our All Father has abandoned us, and we are but orphans of the steppe, orphans of the world. The gold and the precious stones and all the treasury of his divine blessing is passed on to another people, and we are utterly forgotten.

"I read it all in the book of the Jews and the Christians. He has cut us off in the day of his fierce anger. He has led us into darkness and not into light. Surely he has turned against us. He has made our chains heavy, and our ways desolate. The joy in our hearts has ceased, for he has set his bow against us and made us a mark for the arrow. Our dance is turned into mourning, and the crown of the world is fallen from our heads.

"The ghosts of my people came to me, skeletal, barely fleshed, clawing at me, ancient hags with wrinkled dugs, saying I killed my father; and now my Father kills me. The Lord Astur is against me, the wind of the world is turned upon me, my sons fight before my eyes, the battle is lost and the dream is done. We are all orphans in the end, O my soul.

"How all things fall and perish! And how all things come about again. Our crimes and iniquities, which we fancied we left on the road behind us, long ago, as we went forth to our glory, in truth ran ahead of us in the night while we were sleeping, and wait for us on the road ahead to greet us, their smiles grim and their hands outstretched."

But his pride was very great and, rather than ask forgiveness, he would go down stiff necked and unrepentant to Hell. A great city which looked much like Rome.

Only the wind plays the shepherd's pipe,
Only the north wind sings your song,
O my people . . .

At a banquet he apportioned out his imaginary empire among his favorite sons. China to Dengizek, Gaul to Emnedzar, Italy to Uzindar, the Homeland of the Hungvar to his beloved Ellak, Persia to Ernak, and Africa to Geisen. Even as he was talking, his sons were laughing among themselves. The old fool!

They were sly and small of spirit, Attila's sons. They had no strength in them. It had all been crushed out of them by the great rock that was their father. In his shadow they were blanched little weeds, sunless and sly. Little Bird turned away, weeping, unable to look. They mocked him before his face, those unworthy sons.

Attila announced that this was also a wedding banquet, for he had taken a new wife, a Burgundian girl. Her name was Idilco, and she was but nineteen or twenty years old. The women brought her into the tent. She was very beautiful, and the sons of Attila made lewd comments and catcalls. They joked among themselves that old boars had no business with young sows, and they shouted out that, though the knife gelds quickly and age gelds slowly, they both make geldings in the end.

Orestes' hand was on his sword. But Attila only stared ahead, his once-mighty fist clutched round his wooden goblet, not hearing them.

Idilco smiled.

That night, Emperor Marcian in Constantinople dreamed of a great broken bow in the sky, like a strange new constellation. The dream puzzled him deeply.

Among the tents of the Huns, the chill dawn revealed the revelers asleep amid the empty flagons on heaps of animal furs. The fires burned low. But there was no sign of Attila. After some time, his faithful servant Orestes batted on the leather door of his inner tent. There was no answer. Orestes called again and again, but there was only silence. At last he cut the ties and went in.

At his anguished cry, warriors came running.

Idilco was crouched in a corner, shivering like a frightened animal. Attila lay on his back on the couch, naked. Blood had gushed in torrents from his mouth, drenching half his body. His eyes stared skyward.

Orestes moved over to the girl, knife ready.

She stood and held out her hand, an accusing, shaking finger.

"I will not allow you the time for a dying curse," he said, grabbing for her long fair hair.

She stepped back. "Not a curse, a truth. You will hear it."

Orestes paused. The atmosphere in the tent was heavy with horror and thick with the metallic odor of blood.

"The Huns fought the Burgundians twenty years ago. I am twenty. Under their King Ruga, that foul drunkard, that hireling, the Huns were paid by the Romans to fight the Burgundians, my people." The girl grew in strength as she spoke. "My mother was very beautiful. She was raped. My father was slain. Perhaps I am half Hun, I neither know nor care. So all things come around. The Huns destroyed my family." She tossed back her hair and smiled. "Now I have destroyed their king." She looked at the horrible mockery of a marriage bed. "Cut his thoat like a hog. I have his blood and his seed on me still. But perhaps it is as the ancient prophecies say. His own shall destroy him. It is right. The Hun people have devoured themselves. Now kill me." She seized Orestes' forearm. *"Kill me!"*

He looked into her blazing, triumphant eyes. Then he killed her.

Attila's body was burned on a flaming pyre, laid out beneath a silk pavilion. Horsemen galloped round it, slashing themselves to bloody ribbons. Many horses were sacrificed, their bodies hefted and impaled on long pikes around the pyre. There were mourning pipes, angry drums, and wailing women. Dust obscured the sun as thousands of horsemen galloped wildly over the plain, firing arrows into the reddening sky.

His calcified bones were laid in a triple coffin of gold, silver, and iron, with many ornaments and jeweled weapons, goblets of gold and sacks of jewels. The River Tisza was diverted into a neighboring channel, the huge coffin buried in the riverbed, and the river's course restored, to flow over the place of burial again for all time. The captive slaves who buried him were slain and hurled into the river. To this day his burial place remains unknown.

All night the drums continued to beat, weary warriors shaking their heads, their hair loosed from their topknots and hanging low like the manes of horses in rain, shuffling and dancing round the fire. Their eyes were closed, their scarred cheeks caught the firelight and gleamed. In their deep throats a collective murmur, a low humming song like one voice, old as the earth, tired but implacable, willing to surrender to none but the earth itself.

Without anything being discussed, with no word from the eldest son, Dengizek, now supposedly king, the people took down their tents the next day and set out for the eastern wilderness from which they had so suddenly erupted to shake the pillars of the earth. The great wagons rolling through a haze of orange dust, their songs fading on the air as they vanished into the darkening steppes. A people in their proud strong noonday more feared than any other on earth, never to be heard of more. Children of witches and demons of the wind, now melting away. *"Like the wind, like the wind."*

After the great horde of the people had gone, a single man remained. He had feathers and ribbons in his hair, and wore a goatskin shirt decorated with little black stick men. He sat high on a golden limestone bluff looking away over the great river toward the south and the west, looking out over Europe. A soft evening breeze stirred the grass and the yellow rockroses, and the sunset was beautiful on the water. How beautiful the world was in all its mystery. He understood nothing of it, after all. The world was as it was, unimaginably beautiful, and it broke his heart to leave it.

Weep not, Little Bird,
Tribe lonely, restless,
Unheeded, nestless,
Words on your lips that hold
The people's history,
More rare than gold.

And I salute you, earth breaker,
Bridge builder, fortress maker,
Danube tamer, Roman brother!
You called us the storm from the east,
Storm that shall not cease,
But you are the storm from the west,
Storm that shall know no rest.

14

DEATH OF A TRAITOR

It was some weeks before the news arrived at Ravenna and Constantinople that Attila, King of the Huns, was dead—at the hands of a girl of twenty.

Marcian understood his dream.

Valentinian got drunk.

Aëtius hung his head.

Valentinian observed Aëtius, and what looked like his sorrow. Only a few days later he summoned him to the palace.

The emperor had more guards around him than usual, and also several of his closest courtiers and advisers, including that old orator Quintilianus, the library expert on Huns.

The general bowed curtly. There was a prolonged and unsettling silence, but Aëtius was not unsettled. He had experienced many things worse than the ritual intimidation of an imperial audience.

Standing there in all his sad majesty, alone and silent and unafraid in that vast and echoing hall, its walls covered in gleaming mosaics showing the emperor as Lord of All, its great porphyry pillars disappearing up into the vaulted darkness overhead, the emperor high upon his dais gazed down in divinely appointed judgment. Everything was designed to dwarf any mortal man who stood before the resplendent gilded throne. But Aëtius was not dwarfed.

The emperor's eyes were watery and unfocused, and his voice was soft and sinuous. "So," he said, "he is slain by a cruel fair maid. Your . . . *alter ego*."

Aëtius said nothing.

Valentinian's mouth began to work. "Your boyhood friend, the Scourge of God, is no more. You must feel that a light has gone out of your life, that your sense of purpose, of *mission,* is over. That your whole career is over, in fact."

Still Aëtius said nothing.

Valentinian leaped to his feet and stood shaking. "Answer me, damn you! Standing there in dumb insolence like Christ before Pilate! Who do you think you are?"

"My apologies, Majesty. I was not aware that you had asked a question."

The emperor gave a strangulated cry and rushed down the steps toward him. He fought for self-control, grew quieter again, and began to pace around Aëtius, examining him as he might a strange animal in his menagerie. Aëtius remained quite still.

"You make me anxious, Master General. You are not like other men."

Aëtius could almost have smiled at this. *Coming from you, Your Majesty . . .*

"And, you see, this leaves us with a problem. Indeed, my dreams point to many problems, and the word of God which comes to me in the night tells me of only one solution."

"Majesty, my most ardent wish is to be quit of the court, to relinquish my command, and to go on a pilgrimage. To Jerusalem."

"To Jerusalem, you say!" His mouth began to work again, and his words became garbled. "And what will you do and say and plot out there in the mysterious shining east, I wonder? Is not the old empress, there, too? Old Eudoxia, a great and cunning enemy of the Empress Pulcheria, eh?"

"Majesty, I do not believe—"

"And I do not believe, either!" cried Valentinian furiously. "I do not believe that it is your 'most ardent wish' at all to go to Jerusalem, to dirty your knees in prayer all the way up the Via Dolorosa to the Holy Sepulcher, along with all the other low-born pilgrims! You would not so humble yourself, Master General, great victor of the Catalaunian Fields! No, we must not let you get away, we must *monitor* you. There is no need for you to visit Jerusalem, to see Calvary with your own eyes. I will show you Calvary right here!"

The emperor began fumbling beneath his robes. Aëtius's gray eyes were very still, looking straight ahead. He did not stir to protect himself.

"I will show you Calvary, you, you . . ." Imperial spittle flew in Aëtius's face. "You brazen *traitor!* Hold his arms out!"

Four guards seized him, two on each arm. He could not resist, and he did not try. He only glanced left and right to see their faces. Lads of eighteen or nineteen, new appointments, obedient slaves. Even though they hardly knew him, they lowered their faces before his searching gaze. He wanted to say something to them at this last moment, knowing that they were not to blame, but suddenly his body was ablaze with agony and his throat was taut and wordless. For Valentinian had produced a long blade and thrust it up beneath his ribs. Aëtius gasped and his eyelids fluttered and lowered. Through the haze he saw the emperor's grinning face, his spittle-flecked chin almost touching his own as he twisted the knife.

The four guards let go of his arms and stepped back, and he staggered. Only then did the other courtiers and counselors crowd around with their own daggers in hand, and join in killing the man who had saved them from ruin a dozen times. Old Quintilianus alone stood back.

His eyes filmy with death, glazed and misted, his body twisting and falling, his last breath exhaling, what did he see as he fell? Did he see the Triumphal Way, the City on the Seven Hills, the great Basilica of St. Peter, the Capitoline? Did he see his beloved legions, scarlet plumes and pennants fluttering in the breeze? Did he see the grim face of his enemy, the Scourge of God? Or did he see a vision of Jerusalem?

As they stood staring down at the savaged body, Quintilianus spoke from behind them.

"Your Majesty," he said quietly. "You have cut off your right hand with your left."

For Aëtius there were no songs of praise or lamentation. Reader, it is not I who concoct the ironies of history. I can but tell the truth. Only a handful mourned Aëtius's passing, a handful in all of Italy. Most of his friends had died on the Catalaunian plain. If the news ever reached the island of Britain, there would have been mourning. In the Court of the Visigoths at Tolosa, there was deep, deep mourning. But in his homeland . . .

Attila the Destroyer went to his death praised and beloved and glorified by lavish funeral rites, much loved among his fierce people.

Aëtius the Savior, the last and noblest Roman of them all, to whom all of Christendom and the West owes an incalculable debt—his savaged body was wrapped in sacking and quietly dropped in a marsh. This much he has in common with his great enemy: none knows where he is buried.

But surely the believers must be right, and the history of this world is not everything; but there is another story, in which justice will be done. Oh, let it be so. Or else this world is not worth a handful of dung.

The widow of Emperor Theodosius, Eudoxia, was still in Jerusalem when she heard news of the death of Aëtius. She immediately went to the Church of the Holy Sepulcher to pray. She prayed for a long time. And for many evenings after, she loved to sit on a moonlit balcony and look out over the Golden City of Zion.

She never returned to Constantinople.

Only a few weeks later, the Emperor Valentinian was watching soldiers drilling on the Campus Martius when he was set upon by two of them and slain. The soldiers observed, "He dies easily for a god!" None of the other soldiers fought in his defense. Some say that the emperor's killers had served with Aëtius himself, and had even fought at the battle of the Catalaunian Fields. Some say that one of them was a centurion with an iron countenance and hard, unblinking eyes.

Two years later, the Vandals sailed up the Tiber and sacked Rome. They had sailed from Carthage. The sack was savage and merciless, for there was barely a defense force to speak of, and King Genseric had grown no less cruel since his three sons were slain in Gaul. Bishop Leo pleaded with him to spare lives. When the Vandals withdrew, they left behind them crumbling theaters and circuses, dazed and wandering remnants of the populace lost in the immense space and emptiness of their ruined public baths, once-stately libraries and halls of justice. All were ransacked and stripped bare. Yet from the Church of St. Peter, hymns of praise still sounded. What were treasures and statuary compared with human lives? The Lord giveth and the Lord taketh away, preached Bishop Leo. Blessed be the name of the Lord.

The Vandals did not grow rich from their raid. A huge summer storm blew up, and much of Genseric's fleet was wrecked and sunk. All the treasures of Rome lie on the Mediterranean seabed somewhere between Rome and Carthage. They lie forever in those silent depths among the weeds, half the treasures of the ancient world: diadems of Indian pearls, Egyptian emeralds, silver chalices, that priceless chandelier of solid gold, hung with fifty dolphins, that once hung in the Lateran Palace. Perhaps even the Ark of the Covenant, which Titus had looted from Jerusalem four long centuries before. . . .

After Valentinian there was a succession of emperors enthroned and then soon murdered, each one feeble and less memorable than the last. In the year 476 the last enervated act was played out.

The penultimate Emperor of Rome, Julius Nepos, was deposed by an old and treacherous soldier, and the soldier's son, Romulus Augustulus, installed in his stead. Many said that the boy was in truth the old soldier's grandson, but he lied to prove his potency. The old soldier must have been in his seventies. He was a Greek by birth, and his name was Orestes, and his son inherited his fair hair. In his younger years he had been Attila's right-hand man. It was incredible, but it was so. The last emperor was Orestes' son.

"Four will fight for the end of the world, One with an Empire, One with a Sword; Two will be saved and one will be heard, One with a Son and One with a Word." Aëtius, Attila, Orestes, and Cadoc, four boys who had played together on the Scythian plain, long ago. It was as the ancient rhyme had said.

But the reign of Romulus Augustulus was no more permanent than his predecessors." Only two months later, Orestes' own standard-bearer, Odoacer, an Ostrogoth, rose up in his turn and murdered Orestes. Romulus Augustulus was officially deposed on 4 September 476. It was precisely twelve centuries and six lustra since the first Romulus founded the city.

The Muse of Irony was not done yet.

Odoacer had previously visited Severinus, the most celebrated saint in Noricum. The huge Gothic warlord, clad in a black bearskin, had to bow low to enter the saint's cell.

The saint said, "I give you two pieces of advice. First, go to Rome and you will become King of Italy. And second, mind your head on the way out."

I write this in the Monastery of St. Severinus, where the saint lies buried.

Odoacer slew the last emperor's aged father, Orestes, who died as he had lived, speaking never a word in protest or explanation; but Odoacer could not bring himself to kill the boy. He was so small, aged all of six or seven, with blond curls, blue eyes, and looking quite absurdly like a cherub.

"What would you like, boy?"

The boy stared up at the towering warrior and then whispered, "I'd like to grow vegetables in a garden."

Odoacer despatched him to a monastery near Neapolis, to be cared for by the lay brothers. For himself, meanwhile, he disdained the imperial purple and diadem. He bluntly pronounced the Empire of Rome at an end, severed all ties and allegiances with Constantinople, set his borders at the boundaries of Gaul, Rhaetia, and Noricum, and declared himself King Odoacer of Italy.

EPILOGUE

The World That Was Lost and Won

And I, the meanest of them all,
Am left to weep, and sing their fall. . . .

Thus I, Priscus of Panium, in my ninetieth year, with crabbed and arthritic hand lay down my pen, in my simple cell in the Monastery of St. Severinus.

I have a small gold coin on my desk before me. It is the only gold I own. It is beaded round the rim, crudely stamped with a stylized eagle, wings outspread, and it was given to me by the man they once called the Scourge of God. He now lies buried and silent along with the rest of the dead. When I go under the earth in my turn, perhaps the monks will find it and wonder at it, and keep it safe in the sacristy as a treasure. Or perhaps they will melt it down for cloison work or foil for an illuminated Bible. Perhaps this gold from the hand of a pagan king will become leaf in a page of the Gospels. Ironies are many and nothing remains unchanged, not even gold.

At evening I can close my eyes peacefully in this Italian monastery amid the delicate tracery of stone carvings, silent but for the soft slap of sandals and the whisper of brown woolen habits over worn flagstones. Here the seven offices of the day are kept with a serene regularity for which I am thankful in a world given over to darkness and chaos. In a kingdom much tattered and torn, much threatened by the darkness beyond, but under the rule of a Christian king, Odoacer, I can give thanks with the rest of them for the triumph of Christendom.

Neither Attila's insatiable appetite for ruin, nor Rome's own great, monolithic sternness, but a gentler way than either survived those evil days. Here where the quiet, sandaled brothers tend their vines and their olive trees, and bend to cut the wheat with their wooden-handled sickles, and the goat bells tinkle from the surrounding hillsides. Here indeed is another way, which I for one think might be true civilization. . . .

But who is to say that those who thought differently, and fought for a different way, were not heroes, too? Mine is only one version. God when he walked on earth provoked many versions.

And so in memory of these things, and of that man whom I think the noblest as well as the last of the Romans—at one time my recalcitrant pupil—I leave these scraps of history to posterity. I know that posterity seems to me now, in this year of Our Lord 488, a dark and uncaring place, where the scrolls and books of the histories of past ages will be regarded as so much tinder for kindling a fire. The light of learning is going out across Europe.

Yet, although it seems to me likely that posterity will not care what I write, and that the name of Aëtius, the noblest Roman, will be lost in the scattered leaves of the coming years, which name should be as widely known as Alexander, or Hannibal, or Caesar—yet it is for him that I have written.

There is a shy and rather simple lad of eighteen or so who lives with us here in the monastery. A lay brother with a shock of golden curls called Romulus, who loves nothing better than to help the monks in the vegetable garden, and to feed the chickens and the goats. He has a little herbarium all his own, filled with coriander and parsley and chives. He loves to grow beans and lentils, radishes, lettuces, and is very fond of the humble turnip. Once, he sat on the imperial throne of Rome, and wore the purple—but that was long ago, and in another world.

Never again will an emperor sit in purple upon the throne, nor stand beneath his yellow parasol on the steps of the Capitoline to greet another Roman army returning south in triumph amid the sound of brazen trumpets and thumping drums, down the Flaminian Way, past the Mausoleum of Augustus, the Column of Marcus Aurelius, winding up the Capitoline Hill to the Temple of Jupiter. Never again will the sunlight dance upon the bronze helmets of the cavalry as their horses champ upon the Field of Mars, nor senators gossip and plot in the vast Baths of Caracalla, lounging over the *latrunculi* board or strolling among the shops and gardens, libraries and sculpture gardens of that thirty-three acre Palace of Water. What use have barbarians for libraries and baths?

Nor will fathers take their sons up the pine-clad Palatine, past Domitian's Domus Augusta, to see the cave where the monster Cacus once dwelt, nor the fig tree beneath which Romulus and Remus were suckled. Never again will a quarter of a million Romans roar in the Circus Maximus as the chariots race and swerve round the *spina,* nor in the Colosseum at the feats of the gladiators and wild beasts. Rome's far-famed Insula of Felicula, sixteen stories high, is vanished into rubble, and how long will it be before another such wonder is built, tier on tier?

Europe is a land of log cabins and mud huts now, of grass-grown roads, crumbling aqueducts, passing war bands playing crude games with handfuls of colored mosaic in the ruins of fallen villas. Whatever is done can always be undone. Already the Forum itself, where Cicero and Caesar once spoke, is the abode of wildcats. The Rostra is ruined which was once decorated with the beaks of captured ships; and, yes, with the severed head and hands of Cicero, too. Rome was never perfect, but we loved her.

All these things will soon be forgotten in this new world. Never again will the great grain ships ply their way through the salt furrows from Libya and Egypt, never again will the harbor at Ostia resound with the cries of merchants and traders from halfway round the world, bringing copper and tin and Silurian gold from Britain, glass and leather from the Levant, gems and spices from far Ceylon. Never again these things, for they are all done now. Yet as we can begin to discern, most strangely, Rome was a world both lost and won. Her soul was not destroyed, but miraculously lives on, in other bodies, other forms. She was the mother who died in childbirth—a long, agonizing century of labor, her offspring the stern but gentle faith of Europe's new, barbarian kingdoms. Any other triumph would have been much worse; and it was for this that so many fought and died to defeat the pagan darkness of the Hun.

Everything in the human world must vanish and nothing shall remain, though some there are who cannot change but are caught in time like insects in amber, trapped and killed there in its bright, clear, mindless gum, forever loyal to a world they do not realize has gone. Such was the last and noblest Roman of them all. . . .

The people are moving on, over the endless plains, stumbling in the cracked earth, about their covered ears the ancient songs of penitence and ash. Songs of grief and the graveside, the young buried before the old, children buried by their parents, and sorrow immeasurable at the right way of nature overturned by war and famine and pestilence. Broken temples, falling towers, clouds of brick dust, bricks colored like dried blood, hard-baked in the ancient ovens of Babylon, Nineveh, and Tire. . . .

They will come at last to a green valley, those pestilence-stricken multitudes, the Angel of History always at their back, harrying them, her sword blazing cruel and bright as the sword of the cherubim at the gates of Eden. They will look out on that pleasant valley of quiet streams and pastures, and they will begin to build again. Oh, the pity of it, and the grandeur.

The very stone of their building destined to fall again, their house never safe, their building never done, they will never know rest from heaven's weathering. Their buildings will always fall, they will always build again, they will never surrender. They will never stop wandering, searching, over the endless plains, a storm that will not cease. It is mankind itself that is the storm, god-driven, god-haunted mankind, most pitiful, most magnificent of all creation.

They will never despair, though their proudest towers are burned to ashes, though their cities are inundated by the waters of the deep, though plague and famine encompass them round, though the sun burn them by day and the frost chill them by night, though the day holds its labors and the night its terrors, though they are but so many small, weak, naked, biped creatures, so many little parcels of mortal flesh, and death walks beside them daily. They will never lose hope, walking on resolute into the coming storm which is their own reflection, unbowed, undismayed, undefeated. They were made to suffer and to endure, to fall and to triumph, and never to surrender.

Among all the wonders of the earth, most wonderful is man. So I salute him, recognizing him as made by the very hand of the Living God, in the tragedy of his fate and in the greatness of his heart.

Hic finis Historiae Prisci Panii, Anno Domini 488

AUTHOR'S NOTE

Readers may want to know how much of this trilogy is fact. The short answer is, a lot. Obviously it's a work of historical imagination rather than straight history, but many of the details are authentic, from the scandalous character of the Princess Honoria and her premarital pregnancy, to the Emperor Honorius's obsession with his pet chickens, to Attila's magnificently scornful treatment of the clumsy Byzantine assassination attempt and the fifty pounds of gold.

Where I have invented, I have at least tried to stay within the bounds of possibility in the story's most important details. For instance, although there's no evidence for Attila having spent time in Rome as a hostage, we do know that Aëtius was a hostage in the camp of the Huns, where it seems almost certain he must have met and known Attila. Furthermore, it was very common for barbarian client kings to send their sons to Rome for a year or two, partly as a promise of peaceful intentions, and partly for them to be "civilized." The Vandal princes Genseric and Beric were both hostages in Rome, so it seems perfectly feasible for Attila to have been, too.

To list the sources for every fact in this trilogy would be impracticable, and pretty dull reading, too; but if you want to know more about this tempestuous, apocalyptic period in the history of the West, here are the books I enjoyed most when researching: Peter Heather's recent *The Fall of the Roman*

Empire is a lively and readable survey of the 5th century as a whole; John Julius Norwich's *Byzantium: The Early Centuries* is informative and a lot of fun, packing in plenty of sly gossip along the way. (My favorite Byzantine Emperor is Constantine Copronymus, literally "Constantine Shit Name," on account of his having shat in the font at his own infant baptism, poor little chap. Unfortunately this was a good three centuries after Attila, so there was no way I could justifiably squeeze it in.)

If you can get hold of a copy, try Edward Creasy's *The Fifteen Decisive Battles of the World, from Marathon to Waterloo,* first published in 1851 and still a cracking read. It's where I first read in detail about the Battle of the Catalaunian Fields. And beyond that, there's the daddy of them all: Edward Gibbon's huge and magisterial *Decline and Fall of the Roman Empire,* completed in 1788, and surely still the greatest single work of history. It looks intimidating, and the style is classical eighteenth century, but I still recommend it. It's fantastically erudite and often very funny, too, with all Gibbon's malicious, feline ironies. There are good abridged versions around nowadays as well.

There are two fascinating and haunting footnotes to the tale, which Priscus himself cannot have known. It was exactly a thousand years after the death of Attila, almost to the day, on 29th May 1453, that the great city of Constantinople finally fell to a foreign invader: the Islamic army of the Ottoman Turks. But although the religion of Mohammed was of course unheard of in Attila's time, most historians are now agreed that the Huns themselves were of Turkic-Mongolian stock. And so it was their direct descendants who finally stormed the mighty walls of Theodosius, where their fearsome ancestor had failed a millennium before.

The last poignant footnote to the story comes as late as 1577. For eleven long centuries, Galla Placidia's mummified body sat enthroned in robes of state within her mausoleum in Ravenna, as rigid and implacable in death as she was in life. You can still see her sarcophagus today, much the largest, between the smaller ones of Valentinian on the left and Honorius on the right. And then in 1577, some children stuck a lighted taper through the peephole, and the tinder-dry robes and body caught fire and burned away in seconds. Ashes to ashes, as they say, and dust to dust.

TIMELINE

DATE	EVENT
378	The Battle of Adrianople. The Eastern Roman Empire defeated by the Goths
395	First rumors of the Huns, in attacks on Persia and Armenia. Honorius becomes emperor in the West
398	Birth of Attila and Aëtius
406	Birth of Athenaïs
410	Invasion of Italy by Alaric the Goth. The Sack of Rome. The boy Attila, held hostage in Rome, begins his long flight back to Scythia
419	Birth of Valentinian
422	Birth of Honoria
425	Death of Honorius. Valentinian III, son of Galla Placidia, becomes emperor in the West

429 North Africa falls to the Vandals under King Genseric

437 Honoria exiled to the East in disgrace

441 Attila returns to his people. The Gathering of the Tribes

449 The Huns cross the Danube and attack Margus fair. The Invasion of the East

450 Death of Galla Placidia, and of Theodosius II. Marcian becomes emperor in the East

451 Attila invades the West, laying the cities of the Rhine and Northern Gaul to waste. The Battle of the Catalaunian Fields

452 Attila invades Italy

453 Death of Attila and Aëtius

454 Death of Valentinian

455 The Vandals sack Rome

476 Odoacer the Goth forces Romulus Augustulus to abdicate. Declares himself King of Italy. The Roman Empire is at an end

LIST OF THE PRINCIPAL PLACE NAMES MENTIONED IN THE TEXT, WITH THEIR MODERN EQUIVALENTS

Modern equivalents marked with an *asterisk are approximations only

Adrianople—Edirne, Thrace, European Turkey

Aemona—Ljubljana, Slovenia

Altai Mountains—mountain range in western Mongolia, sacred to the Huns and to many other peoples

Aquileia—present-day city dates only from Middle Ages

Aquincum—Budapest

Argentoratum—Strasbourg

Augusta Treverorum—Trier

Aureliana—Orléans

Azimuntium—in Thrace, precise location unknown

Bononia—Bologna

Britain—England and Wales

Burdigala—Bordeaux

Cameracum—Cambrai

Carbonarian Forest—the Ardennes*

Carnuntum—Petronell, Austria*

Carthago Nova—Cartagena, Spain

Catalaunian Fields—near Châlons in Champagne, France, precise location unknown

Cisalpine Gaul—Lombardy

Colonia Agrippina—Cologne

Constantinople (also Byzantium)—Istanbul

Corduba—Cordova

Dacia—Romania

Dumnonia—Devon

Dyrrachium—Durrës, Albania

Euxine Sea—the Black Sea

Fiorentia—Florence

Gades—Cadiz

Gallia Narbonensis—Southern France*

Gaul—France

Gessoriacum—Boulogne

Hungvar—the Hungarian plain

Illyricum—Croatia/Bosnia/Serbia/Albania*

Isca Dumnoniorum, also **Esca**—Exeter

Lauriacum—Enns, Austria

Leptis Magna—Labda, Libya

Londinium—London

Lutetia—Paris

Maeotis Palus—the Sea of Azov

Marcianoplis—Devnya, Bulgaria

Margus—Pozarevac, Serbia

Massilia—Marseilles

Mauretania—Morocco*

Mediolanum—Milan

Mediomatrice—Metz

Mincius—River Mincio, Northern Italy

Moesia—northern Bulgaria/Macedonia*

Moguntiacum—Mainz

Mosa—River Meuse

Naissus—Nis

Narbo—Narbonne

Neapolis—Naples

Noricum—Austria*
Padus—River Po
Panium—a humble and unremarked little town in Thrace
Pannonia—Hungary*
Parthia—Persia, Iran*
Philippopolis—Plovdiv, Bulgaria
Ratiaria—Archar, Bulgaria*
Rhaetia—Switzerland
Rhemi—Rheims
Sardica—Sofia, Bulgaria
Scythia—Russia, Ukraine*, Kazakhstan*, and all points east
Sequana—River Seine
Singidunum—Belgrade
Sirmium—Sremska Mitrovica, Serbia
Tanais—River Don
Tingis—Tangier
Tolosa—Toulouse
Tornacum—Tournai
Trajanopolis—Maroneia, Greece*
Utus—River Vit, Bulgaria
Vangiones—Worms
Viminacium—Kostolac, Serbia

EMPERORS OF THE EASTERN & WESTERN ROMAN EMPIRE

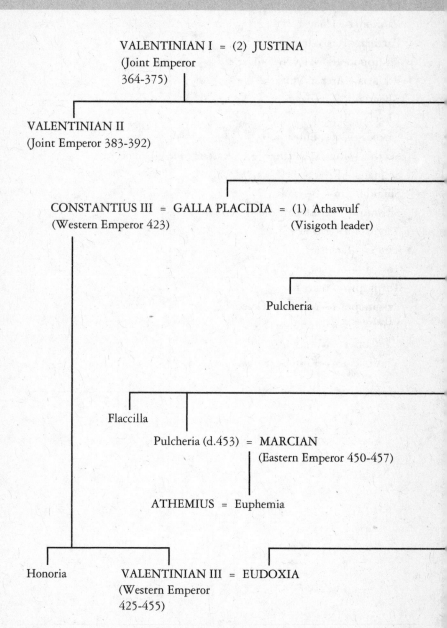

VALENTINIAN I = (2) JUSTINA
(Joint Emperor
364-375)

VALENTINIAN II
(Joint Emperor 383-392)

CONSTANTIUS III = GALLA PLACIDIA = (1) Athawulf
(Western Emperor 423)   (Visigoth leader)

Pulcheria

Flaccilla

Pulcheria (d.453) = MARCIAN
(Eastern Emperor 450-457)

ATHEMIUS = Euphemia

Honoria   VALENTINIAN III = EUDOXIA
(Western Emperor
425-455)

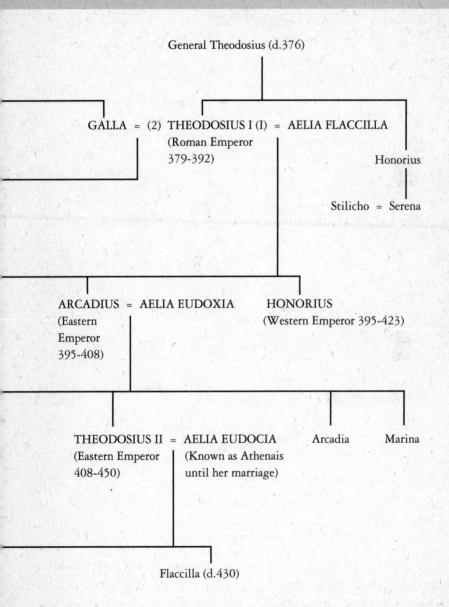

General Theodosius (d.376)

GALLA = (2) THEODOSIUS I (I) = AELIA FLACCILLA
(Roman Emperor
379-392)

Honorius

Stilicho = Serena

ARCADIUS = AELIA EUDOXIA   HONORIUS
(Eastern   (Western Emperor 395-423)
Emperor
395-408)

THEODOSIUS II = AELIA EUDOCIA   Arcadia   Marina
(Eastern Emperor   (Known as Athenais
408-450)   until her marriage)

Flaccilla (d.430)